# Praise for Twyla Ellis's debut novel, *The House on Camp Ruby Road*

*"I read the copy of The House on Camp Ruby Road you sent the Big Thicket Association, and found it delightful. Such a warm picture you painted, rich in detail, peopled with unforgettable characters, your love of place so evident on every page. And speaking of pages, what a page-turner!"*

—Phoebe Dishman, BTA

*"... Set in 1963 just outside the Big Thicket (where law seems just a rumor), this beautifully written, unique page-turner is unexpectedly wonderful. There are strong, consistent characters to love or hate, a star-crossed romance, a Buster-Billie romance, period racism, domestic abuse with perpetrators that would have been at home in Deliverance, and cameo appearances by a helpful ghost. I liked everything about this book. I could see this as a movie or tv series."*

—Jackie M., NetGalley

*"... We read about hatred between poor and rich, black and white, town-dwellers and country. All in all the book has a message for us all kindness to our fellow man, and making assumptions based on first impressions, a message for us all."*

—Helena M., Educator, NetGalley

*"Fun, fast moving read with the predictable character to dislike and main characters you want to see more of. Looking forward to the second and successive books in the series."*

—Nikki B., Librarian, NetGalley

*"This sprawling novel had characters I fell in love with, a Texas town that felt inviting and a house that felt like home. Long buried secrets were revealed, a mystery solved & a perfect ending achieved ..."*

—Brandy H., NetGalley

*"An old house, secrets, and ghosts. Throw in a little romance and you have a great read! ... This story takes place in 1963 and has so many elements that make it a page turner. I thoroughly enjoyed reading this and look forward to book #2."*

—Lisa G., NetGalley

# The House on Camp Ruby Road

## Twyla Ellis

# Twyla Ellis

## The House on Camp Ruby Road

Book One of Ghosts of The Big Thicket

# The House on Camp Ruby Road

## Book One of Ghosts of the Big Thicket

# Twyla Ellis

ZIMBELL HOUSE
PUBLISHING
UNION LAKE, MICHIGAN

For permission requests, write to the publisher
"Attention: Permissions Coordinator"
Zimbell House Publishing
PO Box 1172
Union Lake, Michigan 48387
email to: info@zimbellhousepublishing.com

© 2019 Twyla Ellis

Published in the United States by Zimbell House Publishing
http://www.ZimbellHousePublishing.com
All Rights Reserved


Hardcover ISBN: 978-1-64390-028-5
Trade Paper ISBN: 978-1-64390-029-2
.mobi ISBN: 978-1-64390-030-8
ePub ISBN: 978-1-64390-031-5
Large Print ISBN: 978-1-64390-032-2
Library of Congress Control Number: 2019935464


First Edition: August 2019
10 9 8 7 6 5 4 3 2 1

ZIMBELL HOUSE PUBLISHING
UNION LAKE

# Dedication

This book is lovingly dedicated to my grandmother, Iris Lee Nettles Lunsford, who was born on Beech Creek in the Big Thicket in 1906, and who, in 1999, was interred where she had been born ninety-four years earlier. She couldn't wait to escape her primitive life there but was constantly drawn back to it because of family. She maintained a love-hate relationship with the Thicket her entire life, but in the end, she became a part of it, body and soul.

# Prologue

*Heart of the Big Thicket*

*1947*

The woman behind the wheel was furious, her car weaving wildly along the county line road in the sweltering heat of the Texas afternoon sun. Her face, contorted in anger, was made even more garish by the smeared lipstick and the tracks of mascara-stained tears running down her heavily powdered cheeks.

"How dare he!" she seethed. "Doesn't he know who we are? Doesn't he know what my daddy will do when he finds out?"

An animal-like growl came from her throat and released some of her anger into the newly mown, hay-scented air. It was a smell that would always bring this day back to her, no matter how hard she would try to forget.

"A *bottom* lander! From the slime of that old, big muddy! I swear I'll ... I'll ..."

In that moment, as if the coastal shell roadway accepted her challenge, she saw the woman who had caused this anger. There she was, walking along the side of the road, her body swaying beneath the cheap red dress, drawing the driver's ire as surely as the red cape of the matador draws the bull to ruin. Behind the wheel, the driver choked on her own, angry bile.

Whether it was a conscious thought or not, she would never remember. But as the anger in her exploded, she turned the wheel of her car and stomped the gas pedal.

What she would remember was the woman in red turning toward her, the fear in her eyes, the gaping mouth, and at the last moment before impact, the wide eyes of the little girl who walked beside her.

The woman in red screamed and jumped aside as the car's breath propelled her into the ditch, breaking an ankle.

*But the child!*

The impact caught her square on, hurled her up into the windshield that shattered beneath her small body and sent shards of glass across the driver's face.

*Whose woods these are,*

*I think I know ...*

# One

Summer was exceptionally hot, even for central West Texas. The land dried up and cracked open. The native grasses turned brown, and the trees struggled to maintain life. Wildlife was driven from the hills into the populated areas by their hunger and thirst, and backyards became less safe for children to play. Wells dried up, and still the skies refused to yield to rain clouds. Crops shriveled in the fields, and men's hearts failed for fear of losing family farms.

Eden had been restless all that summer. She roamed the rooms of her mother's house seeking any cool place. Fans whirled everywhere, moving the steaming air from one hot spot to another. The porch offered an occasional respite, but only when there was a flat-land breeze blowing. Breezes were rare, as even the wind collapsed under the weight of the superheated air.

At night, glistening and exhausted from the heat, Eden moved in and out of a strange dreamscape that always took her to a different world, a different time, a different place.

*In her dream, Eden is a little girl walking through heavy fog. She is wearing a warm coat and little gloves to match. She is holding someone's hand, and when she looks up, their face and shoulders seem to disappear into a strange fog. She knows it's late and she feels sleepy, but she is riveted by the sound of her little Mary Jane shoes clicking on the concrete beneath her, the only sound in the fog.*

*A huge, hulking car materializes through the fog directly in front of her. The hand pulls her toward the car and opens a rear door. As she is lifted into the car, she hears sobbing somewhere far off. For a moment, she clings to the hand. It is familiar to her, long red nails, and a huge ring with a large, black onyx circled by smaller, clear stones. In the center of the onyx is the initial "R." Her eyes move from the ring to the hand, and up along the arm until they adjust to the dark outline of a hat. Beneath the hat is only darkness, and she seems relieved not to see the face there. A deep, unfamiliar voice says okay, and there is louder sobbing from behind them. The engine grinds to life, and it makes her jump. She hears another sob and suspects it came from herself. She doesn't understand what is happening to her. The motionless hand is outside the window now, and as the car moves away, she focuses on it until it is licked up in the fog.*

*She sees someone else then, rushing toward the car, just an impression of movement that sends the fog dancing in swirls. But the car is too fast, and they are quickly overcome by the milky haze and the darkness. She turns and looks at the back of the driver's head, a mass of matted, graying hair beneath a black fedora. She seems to understand that she is not to speak, and she does not. Instead, she molds herself into her little coat and slumps down into the back seat and into a deep sleep.*

❦

Eden hadn't had the dream in a long time. There was a time when the dream had dominated her sleep more nights than not. However, with the passing of time and her childhood, came the distancing of the dream as well.

As a child, Eden wanted to be the winter wind when she grew up. The winter wind left people breathless, and she liked the idea of that. "What a remarkable young lady!" she wanted them to say breathlessly.

"Isn't she exceptionally smart?" Breathless.

"How wonderfully clever the girl is!" Breathless.

"I want to marry that girl someday!" Breathless.

But she was not the winter wind, and with the possible exception of her mother, she left few people breathless. She was more akin to the soft summer breeze, well thought of, and strong, but gentle. People loved how she could warm them with her crooked smile. Warmed, but not left breathless.

She had always longed for dark hair and Elizabeth Taylor eyes. Perhaps her nose could be straighter? Although, she did like the way it tipped up on the end because she liked to think that somewhere, hidden in her mysterious genealogy, there had certainly been a fairy or two.

Fairy, winter wind, and, oh yes, Wonder Woman— all things she aspired to be but never was. She was, and would always be, Bett Devereaux's little girl and Wynn Beckett's sweetheart.

Wynn Beckett was a remarkable fellow, and Eden often wondered how they came to pair up. His black hair always stayed perfectly still where the comb had placed it. His eyes were a deep blue, much darker than Eden's. He carried himself well for an honor student and a football captain, never showing Eden anything but an intense and calculated demeanor. Sometimes she wished for something more—more silliness, more spontaneity, just more fun. But that was not Wynn.

"Why can't we go? No one will ever know."

Eden was hoping she and Wynn could join up with their friends, all seniors, who were determined to make their mark on the high school by painting in bold blue and gold letters SENIORS '61 FOREVER–GO BEARCATS in the middle of the football field. It was a bold move and would put them in the Rising Star underground Hall of Fame.

"We'll be those rebels they talk about in the locker rooms for years to come."

"Those guys are only going to get into trouble. You know they could get arrested. Vandalism is a criminal offense."

Eden laughed at that, thinking of Wynn behind bars.

"You'd be a really cute criminal. I like you in stripes."

He wasn't amused.

"Come on, Eden. Just forget about it. Let's go get burgers at Jax."

Eden pouted, but not for long. It was easy for her to forgive Wynn anything, and of course, he had been right. The kids did get taken in by the police. Though they didn't get arrested, the police did call their parents to come pick them up. That was worse than a night in jail.

Yes, Wynn had been right. He was always right.

It wasn't that she was remarkable. She felt she was not. But still, she carried herself as if she were exceptional. Thus, people believed that she was, and she was treated accordingly—a little blonde, blue-eyed girl, walking through life as if she was something splendid.

Bett Devereaux, Eden's mother, was a big woman, six feet tall and large boned, yet her movements were tender and graceful. Her hair was a shockingly red color, almost surreal, wiry, full, and in need of constant attention. Rather than trying to manage it, she often hid it beneath hats and scarves.

Bett loved her makeup, caking her eyes with heavy layers of it, at an age when it was expected of proper ladies to become natural in appearance. That, and the heavy amount of rouge she applied to her cheeks made her seem tacky to some folks. But to Eden, she was perfection.

The two had always been just that, just the two, no need for anyone else. Nonetheless, there was an odd sullenness to Bett that left Eden confused and uncomfortable at times. When Eden was seven, she had asked about her father. She was sitting at the kitchen table eating a bowl of Bett's Cabbage Patch soup when the words spilled out of her mouth almost involuntarily.

"Why don't I have a daddy?"

The words bounced off the walls and echoed through the house. Immediately, Eden knew they were not welcomed and cringed slightly, waiting for Bett to answer. Her back was turned to Eden as she stood at the stove and stirred her soup, the metal ladle tinging against the sides of the pot.

"Mama?"

She waited in silence for a few minutes, then added, "Everyone has a daddy. Why don't I?"

"Hush and eat your soup, baby girl."

"But I need to know about him. Was he handsome? I bet he was a soldier, a commanding officer away in the service of his country. Or maybe an FBI man on some secret assignment overseas. Or a filthy rich Texas oil man. Or ... well, I've just imagined him to be all kinds of things, Mama. Please tell me, Mama, was he tall and brave and wonderful?"

Bett continued to stir her soup, though she no longer looked at it. Instead, she stared at the steaming mess blindly, lost in some netherworld that was calling a darkness down on herself that even Eden could feel.

Eden became frustrated and raised her voice, "If you don't tell me now, I'll … I'll …"

"You'll what?" Bette asked softly, sounding weary.

"I'll run away. I'll find him myself."

"You foolish girl!" Bett exploded. "If you only knew the truth of it, you'd never ask again!" Eden shrank from the threatening tone.

"Go!" Bett spat out. "I'll help you pack, drive you to the bus station, buy your ticket. Only leave me in peace about it all. It's unthinkable, and I've tried all these years to forget."

Suddenly, Eden realized her mother was crying. Her tears cut ridges through the powder caking her cheeks. She couldn't remember her mother ever talking to her that way before, and it scared her. Bett gritted her teeth to stay the misery as she rushed from the kitchen, and Eden heard her bedroom door slam. She didn't see her mother again until the next morning.

She never asked about her father again.

It was the end of August, in the wee morning hours. Even though she was hot, she shivered. The dream was back, stalking her like a cat whose hot breath was puffing in her face, and she wretched.

*Blast it all! Why did it always have to come back to the dream?*

She sat up on the side of her bed next to the window and let the moonlight envelop her. From there she could see the swing where Wynn had first kissed her, and she realized again how much she had missed him these last couple of years.

Eden had completed two years of college and was home for the summer when her mother became ill. She didn't want to return to school, but her mother seemed to be improving and had insisted on it. Their parting had been brief, with sweet promises of a special Thanksgiving dinner upon her return, when the summer heat would be gone and Bett would be feeling better.

"I love you, Mama," Eden had said, waving a kiss from the front seat of her little, red sports car.

"And I love you even more than is humanly possible, baby girl!" Her mother had waved back. "Come back to me soon."

It was a bittersweet goodbye that Eden would always remember.

❧❀❧

Bett died three weeks into the semester, and Eden knew her life would never look the same again. How could it? Eden had been called home by Dr. Terry, but it was too late. Bett was already gone by the time she arrived, and Eden was lost in her heart-rending pain.

"Why wasn't I called?"

"It was how your mother wanted it," Dr. Terry told her matter-of-factly. "She wouldn't let me call you, kept thinking to herself that it wasn't that bad. She wouldn't listen to anyone. You know how she was, stubborn to the end. And none of us knew her heart would give out like it did. There were no warning signs."

"I should have been here with her."

"That was not what she wanted, Eden. She thought she could hang on until summer. Said she was making plans for a nice vacation. Just the two of you."

"Why didn't she want me with her? I could have helped. Been a comfort."

"I suspect seeing your pain would have been worse for her than death itself. Be grateful that you didn't have to watch her linger. I think she would have preferred it this way if she'd been given a choice. You know Eden, you made her so proud. You were all she ever talked about."

That silenced Eden. *What could I possibly say about a woman who had been my whole life? Who would be there for me now? Who would make me laugh and dry my tears? Who would tell me it would be okay when other people wounded my heart? Who will be Bett to me now?* The pain came like a flood.

The time of bone-jarring grief floated by, moving one agonizing day after another. Friends and neighbors brought food. Well-wishers stopped by briefly. Her mother's old friends took her to the funeral home to help her make arrangements. Her own friends helped her find a black dress and cleaned her house from top to bottom. They all hovered over her during the funeral service and the burial, followed her home, and made small talk late into the night. Until one by one, they abandoned her for their own homes, where there was still the promise of life.

She was alone then, at midnight, listening to the tick-tock of the grandfather clock in the foyer. The house had become haunted. Not in the typical sense. Bett had not returned, although, just then, Eden would have welcomed it. But it was haunted by a cacophony of memories, like the photos on the mantle, a waxy flower arrangement on the table, crocheted arm covers on the sofa. Things Bett created, things she had touched.

She remained in Bett's overstuffed chair all night. Just before dawn, she fell into a troubled sleep, and the old dream came to haunt her once again.

><del>&#8226;</del>><

Four days after the funeral, Wynn came home from Princeton unaware of Bett's death. His mother had kept it a secret from him, knowing he'd rush home to be with 'that woman's' daughter.

Wynn's father was a prominent attorney, and they were of a certain social standing in town. His father was known for his dapper suits and polished shoes, and his mother by her diamond rings and red Mercedes. People bowed to them when passing on the street, but the Becketts bowed to no one.

By virtue of being Bett's daughter, Eden was not welcomed into the Beckett's social circle either. Wynn's mother hoped attending separate universities would put an end to her son's long-standing, high-school relationship with 'that woman's daughter,' and it had.

It had been a friend of Wynn's who told him about Bett's death, and much to his mother's ire, he rushed to Bett's house immediately.

Eden hadn't left the house since the funeral. She hadn't gotten her equilibrium back yet when Wynn climbed the familiar stone steps. He remembered Bett bringing them lemonade on this exact porch on hot summer evenings, and sometimes she stayed while they talked long into the night. Wynn Beckett had come to love Eden's mother too.

He was nervous when he rang the doorbell, not knowing what he should say exactly. What could he say? He knew nothing would help. When the door opened, and their eyes met, he could tell she was fighting hard to keep from collapsing under the weight of it all. He wanted to hold her, she wanted to be held, yet neither moved.

"Wynn," she said softly, "you're home."

"Yes," was all that came out.

Eden's hair was loosely pulled back into a ponytail, but sprigs of it fought the restraint and fell lightly around her face. She tried to smooth it back with her hand, but it would not hear of it, and at last, she let it have its own way. She tugged the collar of her terry robe up under her chin, feeling exposed and unworthy of the concern in Wynn Beckett's eyes. She had to remind herself that they were no longer a couple.

"Please, come in," she managed, struggling to get the words out.

Inside, he encountered the familiar scent of the house, and he followed her into the parlor where he took a seat on the familiar, rose-splashed sofa.

"I only found out today. I'm so sorry, Eden. I should have been here for you."

"You're here now, Wynn," she said softly.

The house felt uncomfortable in deep shades of quiet.

"What can I do to help?" he asked as he touched her arm.

For a moment, there was only the stillness and the ticking of the clock.

"She's still here," Eden said at last, looking around the room. "No matter what, she will always be here. We're all tied together you know. Over the years there will be other people in our lives, but they won't know her like you and I do, how wonderful she was. Don't you think that's sad?"

She didn't know that what lay waste to him was the thought of Eden, *his* Eden, suffering so profoundly. Wynn wondered what had happened to them. Why had they been apart these last two years? His hand wrapped around hers and held it against his cheek as he answered her.

"We have lots of fantastic memories, Eden. Bett is a wonderful one. But there are others too, some special things that only we share."

"I know," she said, as they sat silently for another heartbeat. "I think of you often, especially on nights like this. When darkness comes, it brings sweet memories of our high school days. Do you ever think of all those good times we had back then?"

"Of course, I do," he said as he put his arm around her. She laid her head back, and they sat there quietly, late into the hot Texas night.

# Two

The following morning Eden awoke, still on the sofa and wrapped in Bett's quilt. Wynn was gone, and she longed for the comfort he had given her. *He loved Bett too*, she thought, and she waited for the tears to come, but this time they didn't. She realized that Wynn's being home had helped cleanse her of the roughest edges of the grief.

Wynn phoned at noon.

"How are you doing today, sweetheart?"

"Better, much better."

"Would you like to go to Italiano's tonight and get some spaghetti?" He could hear Johnny Mathis singing *Chances Are* in the background, and it flamed memories.

"I'd love that."

Italiano's was where they had their first date, and she knew this would feel like a first date too.

She spent the afternoon soaking in lilac-scented water, listening to more Johnny Mathis and some Elvis. The records were still playing when Wynn picked her up.

As they were eating and reflecting on their lives, she felt them falling back into the old relationship.

"You're so young to have to deal with all of this. But you're coping well. Are you sure there isn't something more I can do for you? Did Bett take care of the financial end of everything? My dad said he would help you if you need legal counsel to settle her estate."

She smiled at him and remembered when she had been the most precious thing in his life.

"I'm alright. I wasn't sure before you came home. But it feels like it'll be okay now. She took care of everything. She knew this was coming and had her lawyer deal with all of that." She looked away. "Thanks for staying with me last night until I was able to sleep. It meant a lot."

"Hey, I loved her too. You have to know that. I'd have done anything for the lady, and I'll do anything for you too."

"I know."

"Remember when we first came here?" he asked.

"Our first date, and afterward we went to the Junior Class Back-To-School dance. You were so handsome," she said as she winked playfully.

"I was shaking in my boots. You were so pretty in that lavender dress, remember?"

"Yes, the one with the matching sweater. I saved my lunch money for weeks to buy that dress just for that dance."

"All I could think about was how in the world did I get this beautiful girl to go out with me?"

"I thought, how could a boy as cute as you ever have asked me out on a date? I just knew I'd mess up and spill spaghetti all over my dress before we even made it to the dance."

"And if I remember correctly, I was the one who went home with spaghetti stains on the front of my shirt."

"That's right," she laughed. "I'd forgotten that."

They laughed, and the laughing felt good.

"I remember how much I wanted to kiss you when I took you home," Wynn said, leaning in with a mischievous smile.

"I was scared to death that you'd try. I wasn't so sure about the kissing thing, and I felt really shy. So, why didn't you?"

"It was just our first date. And besides, that German shepherd of Bett's came out of nowhere and chased me back to my car. Don't you remember that? I still think Bett let her out just to run me off the place."

"That was so funny, you running from sweet, old Dolly. She'd never hurt anyone."

"She wanted to kill me that night."

"Yes, she kind of did," Eden said with a laugh.

"Oh, I remember a few times she almost did."

"She was always protective of me. Mama taught her to be."

Her thoughts turned pensive again as she sipped her soda, suddenly uncomfortable under his intense scrutiny.

"I've missed you," he said, laying his hand atop hers.

"I've missed you too."

When at last he walked her to the door that night, he did kiss her again. A soft, caring kiss that made her feel loved.

But as she lay in bed that night, her thoughts grew dark again, and she couldn't sleep. Her tossing and turning finally drove her outside to the porch swing and the cool breezes of the night that made her cotton gown melt against her. The breeze rattled the screen door and sent leaves scurrying across the cement floor beneath her, so she lifted her feet and tucked them under her gown. A trumpet-shaped flower from a hanging basket floated down, and as it softly landed beside her, Eden thought she heard Bett's voice.

"Eden," half-whispered, half-dreamt, and then again, "Eden?"

Eden heard it clearly then, and she stood and pushed herself against the house, her eyes scanning the yard. The darkness was broken by random rays of moon streaks that the oaks let pass through their weighty branches. Eden strained her eyes. Bushes bent in the wind, and their motion drew her attention, but there was only the flicker of moonlight in the swaying branches.

She was telling herself that she had imagined it, that the wind was only playing tricks when she heard the voice again.

"Eden, Eden, come ... find me."

She had not imagined it. She heard the words clearly this time. She called out, "Where are you?"

"Come ... look for me," the voice repeated. "Find me ... you'll find ..."

"Find what?"

"Yourself."

The word was low, whispered in her ear, not at all like Bette's booming voice.

Eden's skin turned to gooseflesh as her hair beat against her face. The louder crackle from the scattering of dry leaves that attacked her bare feet in the wind sent her fleeing into the house. She slammed the door shut, turned the deadbolt, and sat down on the stairs. Her mother's voice rang in her ears.

*"Find me, and you'll find ... yourself."*

"I want to find you, but I don't know how," she said aloud.

Just then, the grandfather clock struck twelve. The vibrating gongs sent Eden running up the stairs to her bed, to the protective sheets that hid all but her huge eyes.

Somewhere, along a red clay road, Camp Ruby Road, drenched in southern moonlight, deep in the heart of the

Big Thicket, an old house was watching, and waiting for her as it had her entire life.

〜〜〜

Bett's attorney, Mr. Cantrell, called the next day and requested a meeting with Eden. Wynn drove her there. Mr. Cantrell's office smelled of musty, old books and tobacco. His secretary was reed-thin, ancient and statue-like, with a pointed nose on which horn-rimmed glasses were perched. She made Eden nervous as she escorted her into the lawyer's inner sanctum and seated them.

Mr. Cantrell shuffled papers and seemed uncomfortable as if wishing to be somewhere else.

"Miss Devereaux," the lawyer began, as if he was about to discipline a child, "Your mother had a sizable amount of money in savings, as well as stocks and insurance. You, young lady, are quite well off."

He peeked out at her from above the top of his glasses. He knew that Bett Devereaux had worked part-time as the county librarian all her days in Rising Star. That job certainly didn't justify the amount of money she had squirreled away.

"Ahem!" he cleared his throat and returned to his papers. He knew exactly what the estate was worth. Also, how much his percentage would be as its representative. Mr. Cantrell forgot himself and briefly grinned.

"These assets were assigned to your accounts at the bank after all of Mrs. Devereaux's debts were settled. Of course, the house and all the personal property are yours as well, since there are no other heirs. She took care of all the legalities before ... well, just before." He cleared his throat again. "I'm sure you are aware of all of this."

"Not until now, sir."

He sounded uncomfortable as he continued, "There is one other thing though." He handed her an envelope. "A piece of property in Two Rivers that consists of sixty-five acres with a house, a barn, and other outbuildings. The property was put in your name years ago, but the previous owner requested that you not be given the deed legally until the death of your mother."

"The death of my mother? How strange."

"I thought so too," the barrister said.

"Who was the previous owner?"

"I don't know. The transaction was done under a judge's name, who had power of attorney over the property. The previous owner requested total anonymity, and all the records have been permanently sealed by the courts."

"Did my mother know about this property?"

"Yes, she did."

"But she never told me about it."

"Yes, she told me that, too, but nothing else."

Eden was perplexed. "Where is Two Rivers?"

"East Texas somewhere, over past Liberty, Big Thicket country, I believe. Perhaps the judge can answer any questions you have. His name is Josiah Abrams, Third District court in Liberty. Here is the number that was with the papers. Why don't you give him a call and see if he can help you?" Clearly finished, he stood and dismissed them.

Eden could hardly wait to get home to call Judge Abrams. There were so many questions running through her mind. *Why had Bett never mentioned the property? Who could have given it to me? Could it be the father I've never known?* There was no other guess beyond that one. She kept fumbling the phone number until Wynn took the phone and calmly dialed it for her.

"I'm calling for Miss Eden Devereaux of Rising Star. She would like to speak with Judge Abrams, please." Wynn frowned as he looked down at Eden.

"Oh, alright … yes, certainly. I understand. Thank you anyway."

"What?" she asked.

"Judge Abrams died seven years ago."

"Died? He can't have died. We'll have to go to Liberty and look up the court records ourselves then."

"Mr. Cantrell said the records were permanently sealed. That judge was the only one who could tell us who your benefactor is. It seems we've come to a dead end."

Wynn felt useless, unable to help her solve her mystery. But Eden was never one to let others solve her problems for her anyway. She knew she didn't need his help. It was something only she was meant to do. Her resolve solidified, even as her dread over what she might find in her mother's past began to grow. In the back of her mind, she kept hearing her mother's words, 'Come find me. Find me, and you'll find …'

*"Who, Mama, who will I find?"*

Three days later Eden saw Wynn off to Princeton, but he promised to return and spend Christmas with her. The day after that, without telling anyone, Eden Devereaux packed up her car and headed east to Two Rivers.

# *Three*

*Two Rivers, Deep East Texas*
*1963*

If there was ever a place in the U.S. that should have its own passport, it is Big Thicket in Deep East Texas. The Big Thicket at one time covered three and a half million acres. But by a decade or so into the twentieth century, it had been cut back to about a half million acres and has become a national preserve. Its tropical rainforest atmosphere, poised against West Texas' deserts and hills, the plains of North Texas, and the southern coastal counties, create what has been called the Biological Crossroads of North America. It contains four of the five carnivorous plants found in the U.S., a myriad of orchids, wild magnolias and dogwoods, stands of wild peach and wild plum trees, palmetto groves, and moss-covered oaks. But the main attractions are those towering pine thickets that gave it its name.

It was so dense and deep that, over the years, it was a natural calling card for outlaws of all sorts, because few in law enforcement dared to enter the Big Thicket. Civil War deserters found safety there from the hands of fellow soldiers who would have otherwise left them hanging from some grand, old oak. It is still a dark and brooding place where a man can get lost on purpose if he so desired.

There are places in the Big Thicket that are remarkably beautiful, just as nature intended. The area where Old River and Lost River merge is such a place. The town, Two Rivers, was once the gathering spot for the river bottom people—a group of backwoodsmen, fugitives, and ne'er-do-wells, who shunned modern progress, along with the law and order codes that were part of that progress. These people were a rough lot. They seldom bathed so the game they hunted wouldn't pick up the scent of civilization on them. The men mostly wore old boots and coveralls, some without shirts, and their women and children were almost always barefooted. Although they were too poor to buy shoes, the truth is that they simply didn't like wearing them. They liked that their dirty, bare feet set them apart from 'them stiff in the heels, sweet smellin' townies in their spit-shined boots.'

But as the town began to grow and spread away from the river, the bottom land people began to lose their hold on it. Finally, sometime back in the twenties, with the election of a sheriff, they retreated entirely into the shadowy deep woods of the Big Thicket.

To enter the Big Thicket was to enter a world as different from the townie's world as heaven is from hell. Both intriguing and dangerous, one could lose their reputation and even their life if they lingered too long in its cypress-swamped shadows. Townies who went into the Big Thicket usually came out bloody, if they came out at all. Many a brave high school boy gained respect from his buddies by surviving a night in the deepest parts of the dense piney woods.

Most of the townies pretended the river bottom people didn't exist and the bottom landers seldom came out of their shadow world to testify of their existence. But the town abounded with rumors of their unholy rituals and dark secrets.

Nub Henry was a bottom lander and a dark secret. His beard was long and gray, almost meeting the dull, crackled belt that held up his frayed, khaki pants. His teeth were yellowed and gaped where one had broken its mooring. His once white skin was browned and wrinkled by the sun, with a yellowed tint, which made folks wonder if he was jaundiced or just filthy. That long, gray hair was pulled to the back of his neck and kept in place with some sort of twisted wire. He was a local legend who moved in and out among the bottom landers, but had only been seen in town a handful of times, in his seventy plus years. He was a creature of legends and young and old were afraid of him.

J. D. Callahan had heard the stories about Nub Henry all his life. J. D. grew up in Two Rivers and as a child, had believed the stories about Nub's supernatural powers. Why, all the children knew that if they ever encountered Nub on a cold, dark night, not to look the old man in the eyes, "'cause one of 'em is glass, and he could hypnotize you good, and maybe even turn you into a bullfrog or somethin."

J. D. was one of the few who had actually seen Nub.

It was while he was still in high school, as the family gathered around the Thanksgiving table, that his Uncle Jimbo told everyone that he had seen Ol' Twelve Point the night before, and they knew he had come out of the deepest parts of the Thicket.

J. D. had been in his deer stand on the edge of the great meadow by five that morning and had waited quietly for the early morning sunrise. It was cold, and his breath hung in the air like an opaque veil.

Just as the sun began to top the tallest of the pine saplings, J. D. witnessed Ol' Twelve Point for himself. The huge buck slowly moved from the tree line into the meadow's edge, and J. D. took quick aim. The buck snorted in the air; his head held at an alert angle. Had he caught J. D.'s scent? But it wasn't J. D.'s scent that the buck had picked up. Whatever it was that threatened the animal was somewhere off to J. D.'s left. The majestic animal lowered his magnificent rack and stomped the ground.

Ever so slowly, J. D. turned his eyes, trying to keep his head and his .30-6 from moving, until he saw the apparition that had captured the buck's attention. The breath that J. D. had held since the buck stepped out of the woods escaped his lungs in a swoosh. J. D. instantly knew who it was. Who else could this strange creature-man be, who was more like an old, gray bear than a human? Nub Henry looked across the meadow directly into J. D.'s eyes, and the boy felt his body stiffen.

"Jefferson Dixon Callahan! It is not for you to kill this buck!"

J. D. felt the words push him down into the stand. Nub knew his name! When the weakness finally left his legs, and he was able to stand again, the man and the buck were both gone.

J. D. 's eyes darted all around the high meadow. A gray rabbit sprinted across a deep furrow and disappeared into his earthen home. A dead leaf fell close to him, and he jumped, sure it was Nub coming up from behind. Flies were buzzing nearby, and their whirring and the swish of the wind were the only sounds to be heard.

He never told anyone about that morning, or how it had taken him half the afternoon to get up the courage to climb off that stand and walk into the woods to where he'd left his daddy's pickup. But for years thereafter, on cold, dark nights, he would encounter Nub again in his dreams.

It had been years since J. D. had thought about Nub. He'd left Two Rivers the following fall to attend Texas A&M. Returning home for good now, he was already set up as a junior executive officer at the Lone Pine State Bank in Two Rivers. He planned to look for a good plot of land to raise cattle on the side.

J. D. 's car was loaded with packing boxes from college as he returned to Two Rivers. Each carried moments in time that had shaped him the last six years. His freshman beanie seemed foolish now, but he couldn't bring himself to throw it out. Nor the letters from a special girl who was two years married to someone else now. There were newspaper clippings of his football prowess and debate team wins. Things that made no sense to keep. Things that should be discarded, but still he held on to them.

As he left the highway and headed into town, he had to smile. This town was a step back in time. It had a voice all its own, and it spoke to him. Strong and demanding, it called home all its sons and daughters who had begun life in the Big Thicket of East Texas. Not all heard it, just a few, and J. D. had always been one of the few to do everything Thicket-born.

He drove casually down Main Street and his eyes locked with the old men who lined the benches along the storefronts. These ancients smiled at him, thinking of his daddy or granddaddy, while their arthritically gnarled hands waved tired welcomes to their native son. Young men of his breeding usually didn't come back to Two Rivers once they went off to school or left town for better-paying jobs. Many of the debs had waited for his return with hopeful hearts and dreams. Only time would tell for them.

He was waving back at the old men when blurred motion drew his eyes, and his old friend, Ryder Lee, slid across the hood of his car. J. D. hit his brakes and almost threw Ryder to the ground. Ryder's grin was huge when he landed on the opposite side, flung open the passenger door and took a seat next to J. D.

"Where we headed, buddy?"

"My stars, Ryder! I could have run over you!"

"But you didn't. Where're we goin'?"

"I'm going to Mom's bookshop. I don't know where you're off to."

"That'd be your mom's shop then. Look, I've waited for six years for you to get that MFA so you could come back, and the three *desperados* could ride again. You are home for good, ain't you? I mean, you didn't flunk out at that fancy college, did you? You're here to stay, right?"

"I am. You don't know how much you miss this old place until you leave it. 'Course once you get back, you have to put up with the likes of you, Ryder Lee!"

"Hey, my friend, you know you love me," Ryder laughed. "Look, the siege has begun."

"What siege?"

"Everyone knew you were coming home today. Been a flock of girls camped out at your mom's shop ever since the word got out. There they are. And here you are. Looks like a siege to me."

"Ryder, you need to grow up!" J. D. said as he pulled in front of his mom's bookstore.

"Watch for it ... watch for it ..." Ryder pointed. "There! They spotted you. Now they'll giggle and pretend not to notice us."

Ryder was right. A group of five girls circled outside the bookstore. When one spotted J. D., they quickly turned their circle inward, and the group tightened their perimeters. A couple did giggle, but the others kept their eyes lowered and smiled.

As J. D. and Ryder left their car and passed the girls, there was an uncomfortable silence that only made Ryder grin more obnoxiously. J. D. just frowned.

"They ain't here to see me," Ryder said, under his breath.

J. D. opened the door, and Ryder stepped through it, as one of the girls dropped her purse, spilling its contents all over the sidewalk.

"Oh dear," she said dramatically.

"Here, let me help you," J. D. said, without even looking at the girl. The shop door closed, and Ryder stood inside the glass watching his friend being reeled in like a fish.

J. D. scooped the things back into the purse, clipped it shut, and stood to hand it to the girl who was smiling down at him.

"Paige Gresham, as I live and breathe," J. D. said.

"Why, Jeff Callahan. I didn't know you were back in town."

*Oh sure*, Ryder thought from inside the door.

"Look at you!" J. D. said, "When I left here, you were just a skinny little thing in braces. You've grown up rather nicely, Paige."

"Thank you, Jeff."

"How's your daddy getting on?"

"He's doing fine," she said, the color of her cheeks darkening.

J. D. liked what he saw. Paige's black hair, held back by a pink plastic band, had a deep sheen that matched the bright sparkles in her deep navy, almond-shaped eyes.

Her lips were plump and pale white from her *Touch-of-Frost* lipstick.

"I'd better get inside. Haven't seen Mom yet."

"Good to see you, Jeff," Paige said as she rejoined the circle of girls, who were all grinning from ear to ear.

"Hope to see you again soon, gorgeous," called one of the other girls, as the door closed behind J. D. The whole group giggled as they hurried away.

Clarice Callahan loved her cozy bookstore. It was a social hub, where people gathered to sip coffee and gossip. Rarely were there no groups sitting on the overstuffed sofas in the center of the shop, or around the claw-footed table in the back, sampling Clarice's legendary pastries. As the door of her shop opened, it hit a tiny bell that signaled Clarice.

"J. D.!" she called out as he permanently came into her world again. As she hugged him, she had to chide herself for fighting back happy tears that she knew J. D. would hate.

"Where did you come across that mangy vermin?" Clarice asked, acknowledging Ryder.

"He jumped on my car, and I almost killed him."

"Hey! Just hurt my feelin's, why don't you two?" Ryder mocked, grabbing his chest.

Before the coffee was brewed, the shop began to fill up with starry-eyed hopefuls, and each one competed for J. D. 's attention until he finally excused himself and told his mother they would talk later that evening. He sprinted out the rear of the shop where Ryder picked him up, and the two disappeared down a side road and into anonymity again.

Clarice's oldest son was tall, as his father had been. His light sienna hair always seemed a little wind-blown, and his expression always made his mother think he was up to something he shouldn't be. He towered over his mother at six-feet-four, and she adored his soft, brown eyes that reminded her of his father, Robert E., who had recently passed away.

Besides being handsome and well mannered, J. D. had been respected by everyone in town before he went off to school. If anyone ever needed a hand, they knew they could always call on the Callahans, first Robert E. and now J. D. He was responsible, level-headed, and even after he left for school, men were known to say, "Just wait until summer or spring break. We can ask Jeff Callahan. He'll know what to do."

Clarice had another son, Johnny, but he looked more like her side of the family. Johnny was much younger, yet his dark hair and boyish ways made him the center of the Callahan family. However, Clarice had always depended on J. D., who was so much like her late husband. She was glad he was home for good.

The town welcomed J. D. home. Especially since, when they sent their best young men off to school, they never seemed to return. Ladies, recognizing his marriageable age, sent their eligible daughters to the Callahans with pies and cakes, fried chicken and casseroles. The First Baptist Church honored him with a 'Welcome Home Fellowship' on his first Sunday night back. He grew embarrassed by all the attention.

Since J. D. 's return to Two Rivers, the ladies, from thirteen-year-old debs to fifty-year-old fading magnolias, seemed to be dressing up more and spending more time in public places. Clarice couldn't help but smile from the porch swing of her veranda when she counted the fourth young lady casually strolling along the brick walk that ran in front of her house.

"Mornin' Miz Callahan. My, your roses are lookin' pretty this year."

"Thank you, Emily."

"Enjoying your morning coffee, ma'am?"

"Yes, dear. Would you like a cup?"

The girl's eyes searched the veranda, and disappointed to find Clarice alone, said, "No ma'am. But thank you. My mama's waiting for me."

On and on it went. Each one waiting. Each one hoping. It was indeed a spectacular sight to see all those ladies when Jefferson Dixon Callahan was in town. They opened up like flower buds, trying to out bloom the others, hoping to be the one he picked. Even Clarice had kept score. Did he look at this one longer? Did he smile more sincerely at that one when he tipped his baseball cap?

But as each remained close to her phone, no one received that coveted call until late one evening on the first day of July.

"Hello?"

"Paige?"

Paige Gresham recognized the voice, and the pulse in her neck began to throb, "Yes?"

"This is Jeff Callahan."

"Oh Jeff," her voice as smooth as wet satin, "How nice to hear from you."

Their conversation followed the same script as millions had before—teasing, wondering, asking, holding back, and ending with the plans for the first date.

"Are you going to the Fourth of July picnic at the fairgrounds?"

"I hadn't thought much about it, Jeff." Smooth, even though she had been hoping for weeks that he'd ask her.

"I'd sure be pleased if you'd go with me, Paige."

"I think that would be lovely, Jeff."

"I believe the parade kicks off at four on the square," he said, "I'll pick you up at three-thirty so we can get a good spot by the courthouse."

&gt;—&bull;—&lt;

J. D. pulled his car up a side street until he found a shaded spot where the parade would pass. He lifted Paige onto the hood where they could have a better view and jumped up beside her, her shoulder pressed against his chest. He smelled clean and lemony, and her eyes scanned the crowd to see who was watching her triumph.

Ordinarily, there would have been little notice, but J. D. Callahan and Paige Gresham were not ordinary. Paige saw the older girls whom she had envied in her younger years, staring at her with envy, and it tasted sweet. Across the street were the football boys that had been her dating pool in high school, but they had been entirely eclipsed.

Brightly colored floats passed, covered with tissue paper flowers and crinkled streamers, in red, white, and blue. Bands marched by playing loud Sousa marches, and J. D. had to press in close to Paige's ear to make himself heard. Her eyes stared ahead, but the parade had become smeared blurs of colors and sounds, and all she knew was the beat of her own heart, as his warm breath caressed her cheek.

"J. D.! Hey, J. D.!" someone called.

Paige was only aware that J. D. was no longer paying attention to her. He had moved away and was waving wildly at his kid brother, Johnny, who was hanging onto a rather large goat on the FFA float. The animal was panicking, and its barnyard smell filled the air. As the old goat butted at the fluttering tissue flowers, sending them wafting in the air, it also kicked two of the FFA boys, knocking one off the float and causing the watchers to hoot in laughter.

The band behind the float began to play *Stars and Stripes Forever*, and the goat went wild, landing Johnny on the seat of his pants, as the other boys on the float tried to stop the rampage. The goat leapt off the float, and took off down the cross street, sending parade watchers scattering. The FFA boys emptied from the float and gave chase, as the crowd hooted and clapped. J. D. jumped down and followed to make sure no one got injured, leaving Paige alone, and she didn't like it.

The boys were able to corral the goat but were too late to get it back onto the float. Those further down the street could only scratch their heads and wonder at the empty FFA float as it glided by. All the while, Paige sulked watching J. D. taking care of everyone but her.

J. D. thought Paige's pouting was cute—after all; he shouldn't have gone off and left her like that. But by the time they were sitting down to a bar-b-que supper at the fairgrounds, she had regained a more pleasant demeanor.

"It's getting dark. They'll start the fireworks soon. Let's get my mom's quilt and stake out a place over by the gazebo," J. D. said.

As he spread the quilt on the rise that overlooked the Victorian-style pavilion, the community orchestra began to play *America the Beautiful*. The loveliness of the music in the pastoral setting was emotional. J. D. wrapped an arm around Paige, and he liked the way she leaned back against him.

Paige liked it too. But not because of the music or the setting. She savored the warm rise and fall of his chest. Jefferson Dixon Callahan made her happy.

J. D. said something amusing and Paige threw her head back and laughed, as her eyes swept the hill above them. It was dotted with townies on patchwork quilts, and she knew they were watching her, wondering if there was still a chance for their own daughters, or sisters, or themselves. This was as good a time as any to put an end to the speculation.

"Jeff?" Paige said, lifting her face up toward his.

"Yes?"

Paige wrapped her hand around J. D. 's neck and pulled his head down until his lips were on hers. J. D. allowed the kiss. To pull away would have been impolite, but he was embarrassed by the public display. Somewhere in the crowd, his mother was watching. He could feel it. He could also feel her disapproval.

Two little girls who were watching them, ran by and giggled behind chubby, pink hands. J. D. caught the motion of their wide eyes as they curved away and stumbled down the hill toward the music, and he pulled back from the kiss.

Paige smiled contentedly and burrowed herself back against him. He was glad when the concert ended, and the fireworks began. No one would be watching them then. The lights at the pavilion dimmed, as skyward bangs and crackles perforated the colorful bursts that streaked the black night. He was able to relax again and enjoy Paige as she leaned against him.

Paige felt like the fireworks were being flung at the sky just for her. She was the town's favored one, and she knew it. Paige was born for this role. It was her destiny, and for her, the night was magical. When she crawled into bed that night, it was with a still constant flutter of happiness, mixed with a substantial resolve. J. D. Callahan would be hers. From that night on, Paige Gresham made it clear to everyone in the county that Jefferson Dixon Callahan was off the carpet for good.

J. D. was not blind to Paige's family history, one he felt she transcended. The Greshams were the *nouveau riche* of Two Rivers. Their bloodlines were not from centuries of high-born pedigrees but of a brief few decades of questionably amassed wealth. Like Shylock, if you cut them, they would bleed, but not the red blood of the good ol' Texas boys, or even the southern royalty. But their blood was dark and somewhat unholy.

But Paige was not like the others. She was warm, and her smile was pleasing to J. D. He thought of himself as the shining knight who would rescue her from the ivory tower of her father's evil castle. In the end, they would live happily ever after, just like the fairy tales say.

Paige Gresham did come from tainted money, but it was still a thing she loved. She was a Junior Leaguer and a Texas deb. Her coming out debutant ball had been the most lavish celebration of them all. The whole town of Two Rivers turned out, as well as all the upstate Greshams, and they were many—handsome, successful men with beautiful wives who knew their places as Gresham women. There were three generals, a senator, five doctors, and too many lawyers and bankers to count. Jeff Callahan would be a welcome addition to the elitism of this good ol' boys' family.

Jake Gresham saw to it that his daughter, Paige, had always had the best of everything, and Jeff Callahan was the best. It was divinely ordained that they would make a match. She'd waited, knowing it was inevitable. But that was before her father had his ugly affair with Nora Dancy, a waitress at the Feedlot Café. It wasn't as much the fling itself, as it was that Jake flaunted it in public, that caused Paige's mother to bid this world goodbye via sleeping pills, four short years ago. Through it all, Jake Gresham continued to see Nora Dancy and everyone in Two Rivers, including Paige, looked the other way.

Nora knew Jake loved her. They had been together longer than anyone really knew. After his wife's death, no one saw Nora for several months. Jake didn't want her brought into it. But eventually, her isolation and loneliness drove her back to waitressing at the Feed Lot Cafe. Jake hated it, but she only wanted to be around people again. She needed to earn her own money and not feel like a kept woman, but she didn't fool anyone. They all knew.

⊰⊱

It was autumn, several dates and several weeks later that J. D. and Paige walked casually from the Majestic Theater, her arm through his, her full skirt matted to her legs in the wind.

"The night feels funny," he mused.

Paige only sighed. She certainly wasn't an impressive conversationalist, but few girls in this antiquated town were. Most of these belles were raised to display beauty, charm, and manners.

Still, he persisted, "Can you feel it?"

"What?" she asked, bemused.

"Just a feeling. Like something's coming. Like something's fixing to break loose that will turn all our lives upside down."

"I don't know what you mean."

"I know," he said condescendingly. It seemed sad that she didn't know, that she didn't feel it too. He stared down the empty, darkened main street toward the interstate. A gale of wind hit his face, and he shivered, because the wind seemed a precursor of something else entirely, something moving ever closer in the dark Texas night.

# Four

Noon heat swallowed up the fresh morning air as the red Mustang convertible whipped up whirlwinds of dust, racing toward town on the farm-to-market that connected Two Rivers to the interstate. The driver wore dark cats-eye sunglasses and a leopard print scarf to keep her hair back, a picture of sixties sophistication. She gripped the wheel with a fiercely taut nervousness, overwhelmed as she passed the first few scattered farmhouses.

*My stars! I've been here before. I think I've lived here before. Could this be the place in my dreams?* Eden wondered. Something deep inside her wanted to bubble up and overpower her with what? Tears? Or laughter?

She slowed to a crawl. A pickup full of teenage boys rushed up behind her and honked, but she couldn't seem to move any faster. They finally raced around her and yelled something harsh at her, but she was unaware that they were even there. She removed her sunglasses as she approached the first houses that circled the outskirts of the town. It was eerily familiar, but seemed like a caricature of old memories.

She knew she had been here before. There was the great live oak that split the road, but it was larger, more sweeping. There was the post mistress's home, *a Mrs. ... oh, what was her name?* But her pristine cottage looked faded, and one shutter was slightly askew. The entire town was a duller hue than what she could remember in her snippets of memories, older and exceedingly tired.

She must have lived here when she was younger. She had walked on these sidewalks, enjoyed a cherry phosphate at the soda fountain in Miller's Pharmacy, purchased Necco Wafers at that Piggly Wiggly. *How has the Dairy Queen not changed at all?*

The town was slowly waking up in her memory. But here and there, new businesses cracked open the past, looming between the Woolworths Five and Dime and the Li'l Ol' Tobacco Shop, between Etta Mae's Bar-B-Que and the Lucky 7. She was jarred by the new places and resented their distraction from her remembered town.

*I did live here when I was little,* she thought, *and in the years I've been gone, I've held onto this town in my mind. But it's true. I was here.*

No one seemed to notice the little red car creeping from street to street as many of the physical features of the town had come back to her. But the mystery of what had happened to her here remained. By two o'clock she was hungry, but too excited to eat.

Eden stopped at a Humble Gas Station and asked directions to Camp Ruby Road, the street name on the legal deed giving her the title to the property.

"Well, miss, go on down about a mile, and you'll see Bohannon's Emporium. That's Bick Bohannon you know, his people been in Two Rivers since forever. Anyway, turn right. That's Highway 6, cuts straight through town to Lufkin. Old Bick's granddaddy surveyed that road off, back before the turn of the century. You go down another three miles, and you'll come across Oz Delany's place. He's our sheriff. Kinda' gruff, but handy to have around if you've got trouble. His place is the one with the big ol' log barn to the right of the house. Turn next by the barn, and that's Camp Ruby Road. Used to be an old sawmill camp up there. You can still find some of the old buildings if you look through the brush hard enough."

She smiled as the old gentleman sized her up.

"You got friends up there?" he asked.

"Actually, I don't know."

The man looked puzzled.

"I've inherited some property up there."

"Ain't that nice for you. I'm Jiggs Macky. Welcome to Two Rivers. I'm sure you'll like it 'round these parts. That's sure beautiful country up there at Camp Ruby."

"I'm Eden Devereaux, and I'm sure I'll like it too. Thanks for the directions and the local history lesson," she said, smiling.

Jiggs tipped his straw hat and nodded her on her way.

The land along Camp Ruby Road was beautiful. Thick pine forests split open by large green pastures full of black and red Angus. She crossed a wooden planked bridge where there was a sign that said, 'Copperhead Creek.' She passed several mailboxes as she wound slowly up the hill. Some were marked, some not.

She finally spotted 810 Camp Ruby Road on the shabbiest of the mailboxes, sporting rust and bullet holes, barely clinging to the tipped, weathered post. Beside the mailbox was a narrow, dirt road, and the remnants of an old wooden gate and fence line long ago forgotten. She was disappointed she couldn't see the house from the road. The climb up the dirt drive took her deeper and deeper into a dense pine thicket.

Eden sensed the house before she saw it. The forest cleared a bit, then opened, exposing two Bluetick hounds lying in a patch of sunlight. They sprang to attention and growled when she came into their view. Her first sight was of a small cemetery off in the distance. Only the tops of the circular cut stones were visible above the knee-high grass. Then her car was pulled into deep, red clay ruts that turned her to the left, and there was the house. It was large and imposing. Peeling paint revealed greying weathered boards and rust ate holes through the center of the window screens. There was a second floor that held court over the front yard, and she had to lift her head back to see all the way to the housetop. Decorative wood-work incased the windows and posts, but bits and pieces had rotted away or stood askew. Vines crept up around the house, but as for the yard, there was none. Absolutely, no grass or vegetation of any kind. Just the dust of dried up East Texas red clay, overlaid by a carpet of pine needles and a splattering of loblolly pinecones and acorns.

Eden sat in the car for a while. As rundown as the old house was, it still looked lived in. She expected that at any moment, someone would come out onto the porch, rifle in hand, and threaten her away. But no one did.

Summoning her courage, she stepped from the car into a patch of afternoon sunlight. The front door, standing open behind the screened one, seemed to sway just a little, so she called out from the bottom of the porch steps.

"Hello? Is anyone home?"

Out of the corner of her eye, she saw the most incredible creature, old, gray, and menacing. He came around the corner of the house and stopped some twenty feet from her. His clothes were ragged, and he seemed filthy. His expression was not one of welcome.

"What you want here? You one of them social workers?"

"No. I'm not a social worker. Do you live here?"

"No. I just help out Miss Alma."

"So, a Miss Alma lives here?"

He didn't answer for a moment. As he tried to reign in his temper, he said, "What business you got here?"

"My business is with the person who lives here. I assume that is a Miss Alma. Is she home?"

Again, he didn't answer her, but Miss Alma did, with a chuckle, "I'm home, little girl. You come on up here and never mind that old bear. He ain't nothin' at all," she laughed.

Miss Alma was a portly, black woman, with beefy legs and arms, and a smile so wide and bright, that she reminded Eden a little of Bett.

"Come on little girl. Ain't nobody goin' to mess with you here."

Eden started up the steps and noticed that the old man had disappeared to where ever he had come from as if he'd been spirited away.

"Already October and the heat's still on us," Miss Alma said, matter-of-factly.

"Let's sit out here on my porch where we can catch a breeze."

Eden sat down on an old chair placed next to Miss Alma's rocker. She knew that the old woman had to be curious about why she was there. It didn't look like she'd had visitors for quite a long while. But to her surprise, Miss Alma seemed to know who she was and exactly why she had come.

"You came to see your property, right?"

"You were expecting me?"

"I've always expected you, little girl. I'm just surprised it took so long."

"Miss Alma, who do you think I am?"

"You the little girl who gets this here place. But I got a piece of paper that says I get to stay here 'til I die. Did you know 'bout that?"

"I don't know anything. And of course, I'd never expect you to leave your home."

"That's good for this ol' soul to hear."

The old woman studied Eden's face as she chuckled again, "Well hush my mouth, little girl, if you didn't turn out to be a purty little thing!"

"Miss Alma, can you tell me what this is all about? I've been told nothin' other than that I own this house. What is this place and why was it deeded to me? Why did I only find out about it after my mother died?"

"Oh, now that's a sad thing. I hate to hear that." She turned directly toward Eden and said, "You tell me what your name be."

"Eden. My name is Eden Devereaux."

"Uhm hmm. I reckon that's a purty enough name. I don't really give a hill of beans what you call yourself, but I am callin' bull on that one. Just imagine! Deveraux! Still, we do need to call you somethin'. So, Eden Devereaux will have to do."

"Miss Alma, why is my name on the deed to this place? It's obviously an old home place. Why was it given to me?"

The old woman grinned, "You's a curious little thing. Now I don' know that much. And what I do know, I's sworn to keep to myself. So, you just stop frettin' me 'bout it all."

"But Miss Alma—"

"Don't but me, missy. You just get your things, and I'll show you to your room."

"My room? I have a room?"

"It's the Ol 'Missus' room. But we kept it nice for you. Now scoot and get your things."

"But I thought I would stay in town at a motel."

"Nonsense. You own all this now. You need to be here and take care of this sad, old place. Now don't make me get my broom out after you, little girl. I'm too ol' to help you bring your things in. It's all I can do to get up the stairs. But I'll show you good and proper. It's how the Ol' Missus would want it."

Eden yielded and collected her suitcases from the car and followed Miss Alma into the house. Stepping inside, there was the scent of old, musty things and slight decay. It reminded her a little of Bett's house, and she was sure she would find Bett here. Somewhere in this house, in this dark thicket, there were answers waiting for her to find. But she had to find the right questions to ask first.

There was a staircase just inside, and the old woman was already huffing and puffing her way up the stairs. The screen door slammed behind Eden, creating a loud report that made her jump but didn't affect Miss Alma at all. Eden hadn't taken more than a step or two on the stairs when there was a soft swish. As she felt something move past her on the stairs, something unseen and gentle, Eden lost her breath, and her skin prickled. She started to speak, but Miss Alma had already made it to the top of the stairs without noticing, so she said nothing and just followed. At the top of the stairs, Eden looked down on the silent entryway, and her skin prickled again. She was still holding her breath, and it came out in a sudden, soft gasp as a curtain in the entry window moved slightly. Miss Alma didn't notice that either, or the shadow that fell across the doorway and quickly disappeared.

At the top of the stairs, there was a hallway with two doors on each side. At the end, Eden could see a bathroom through the open door. Miss Alma took her into the first room on the right, a large room, with a large window that overlooked the front yard of the house. The room was spotless. But what was even more surprising, was the quality of the furniture. It was all old and refined, ornately carved in rosewood, and the wood gleamed. The bed was enormous, probably nine feet tall, and it matched the marble-topped dresser and washstand. The linens looked old and elegant. They were hand stitched, and without stains or blemish.

"This is so lovely, Miss Alma."

The old woman grinned from ear to ear. It seemed important to her to please Eden.

"Afton Donner, she comes in each mornin' by boat down on the river, same as that ol' man, Nub, does. She come to take care of the Ol' Missus' things. She belongs to Carl T. and Jewel Donner down on the river bottom. The Ol' Missus left money to pay her each month. She's a sweet, little thing, mighty good to me, and she'll be takin' good care of you now, too. She'll be back in the morning. You'll meet her then."

"I don't really need anyone to take care of me. But it's nice that she does so well with the house."

"Come on then, little girl. Let me show you around."

Eden was shown the other bedrooms, all nice and as clean as the first. But none of them were as elegant as Eden's room.

Downstairs was more of the massive furniture. The parlor was full of overstuffed chairs, heavily carved marble-topped tables, and lamps that were ringed with crystal prisms. There was a study that held a large desk that had lions carved into the legs.

But it was the dining room that left her amazed. It held a huge, triple pedestal table, with twelve tall, ornate chairs, and a massive sideboard that towered over the two women. The sideboard seemed to be holding court over the entire house, and Eden wondered what dramas it had seen and what secrets it knew, if only it could speak. It must have stood there for many generations of families who had gathered around its vast table. It knew everything, even who she was and why she was there. But it wouldn't tell her any more than Miss Alma had.

The kitchen was primitive. Miss Alma told her it was part of the original cabin that had been built of logs, back in the eighteen-hundreds. The house grew up around the original stone hearth. A well-worn table was in the center of the room, and a wood-burning stove stood by the back door. There was a rocking chair by the potbelly stove, and to its left was a wooden crate that held a tiny sleeping piglet. Eden couldn't keep herself from picking the little thing up, and it squealed, angry at having been awakened. Its small hoofs kicked in the air and its soft, pink belly pushed out squeaks and grunts that brought out Eden's own squeals. She thought it was perhaps the cutest thing she'd ever seen.

"That's Zandy. She was the runt of her litter. All her brothers and sisters was gettin' all their mama's milk. She'd have died if Nub hadn't brung her to me to feed. See, we use that toy doll bottle there. When she reaches her proper weight, Nub'll take her back to her family."

"Nub?"

"That old gorilla you ran into out front. I know he seems like something from the dark side, but he's really soft-hearted. He helps me when Afton ain't around. Stays down by the barn in the old smokehouse some. Don't you be feared of him, you hear."

"I'll try not to be."

"That room there," Miss Alma said, pointing to a side door, "is my room. It's comfortable and close to this warm, old stove. Yes, ma'am, me and little Zandy, we do right well back here. Yes, ma'am," and she chuckled to herself.

# Five

Eden spent an uneasy first night in the dark, imposing house. *What was I thinking, staying out here all alone, with people I don't even know?* Eerie night sounds were heightened, and she strained to see from one dark corner where the wind made a door groan, to another dark corner where a curtain fluttered.

As she listened, she felt she could hear the house breathing, a breath going in and a breath coming out. A clock ticking somewhere far off pinged eleven times and still she couldn't sleep.

Something hit the roof. *An acorn? Squirrels?* A low grating sound seemed to come up the stairs. *Do I hear a whisper?* That made her sit up and listen carefully. Her mind could have transformed the sounds into whispers, but she was too sensible for that.

"I am Bett Devereaux's daughter, and I will not be afraid," she said to the house.

She crept from her bed and slowly opened the bedroom door. It was dark and quiet as she stepped into the hall and stood tall with her hands on her hips. She was vulnerable, but she was fierce. She felt Bett would be proud of her at that moment.

Then the door at the end of the hall slammed shut with a loud bang. As she turned, suddenly her bravado disappeared, and a chill ran throughout her body. Something fell in one of the bedrooms and seemed to shatter, but when she flipped on the room's light, there was nothing on the floor or out of place. She rushed back to her own room and flipped on the light switch as she slammed the door. But the light didn't come on. She flung herself against the washstand and shoved hard until it slid in front of the door to block it, and she listened. She slowly stepped back toward the bed, but there was no other sound other than her own footsteps. When she stopped at the foot of her bed, she turned and yelled, "Stop it!" as loud as she could.

That was met with total silence, and she began to breathe again.

"Truce," she spoke sternly, "You don't scare me, and I won't scare you. Okay?" No answer, but the hem of her nightgown fluttered against her ankles. Eden fancied the house knew it was being challenged by this girl that it wrapped itself around. She was the intruder, nervously fidgeting inside the beast's belly. Her only thought was to jump into the bed and save herself under the protection of her sheets. For her, on this night, they would become magic sheets and would not let any harm come to her.

Once in bed, and safe under the magic sheets, she wondered if she hadn't dreamt her mother's directive to come here in the first place. The tapping of a branch on the window-pane turned her thoughts back to the adversary at hand. This house, this living, breathing thing, would not send her running away. She would stay and do battle for what she needed to know. She would not allow herself the luxury of fear. She would not lay cowering under the covers. Indeed, she kicked them off, closed her eyes, and spoke aloud, "I am not afraid of you!"

By morning, the air had cooled, and Eden's fears had vanished as the morning sunlight cascaded in. It was different now, in the light of day. The house was sleeping, and the eeriness was gone. She sat up and stretched. *How many people slept in this bed? Was it the 'Old Misses' marriage bed? Did she have her children in this bed?* She felt a part of something bigger than herself in this old house. For the first time, it suddenly occurred to her that all of this belonged to her.

Eden washed up quickly, put on her green capri pants, along with a white sweater, and took the stairs two at a time. She could smell bacon frying in the kitchen and knew Miss Alma was up. She hoped she was in time to feed Zandy. But when Eden entered the kitchen, Miss Alma was finishing with Zandy's bottle. It was amusing to see Miss Alma holding Zandy as she would a human baby. She placed the piglet over her shoulder and patted its back as if expecting it to burp. To her surprise, Zandy did!

"You sleep good, little girl?" Miss Alma asked.

"Yes, ma'am, after a while. This house has a strange effect on a body, doesn't it?"

"'spect so, if you ain't used to it. It's a good place to be though, a safe place."

But it hadn't felt safe last night with only the moonlight for company.

Eden went over to Miss Alma and rubbed the piglet's forehead. Only then did she notice the young girl at the cook stove. She was a wisp of a girl in a dress that had seen better days. Her hair fell about her shoulders as if the girl gave it little consideration. But her face was sweet, and Eden thought she had an angelic, otherworldly look about her.

"Miss Eden Devereaux," Miss Alma said, "this here is Afton Donner."

Afton Donner had the greenest eyes Eden had ever seen. Eden noted that she wasn't outstanding in any other way, except for those doe-like, emerald eyes. But they hid behind the brown hair that hung across her face and halfway down her back.

The girl actually curtseyed to Eden.

"I'm honored to meet you, Miss Devereaux."

"I'm Eden, just Eden. I'm glad to meet you, too. You've done such a fine job of taking care of this place and Miss Alma, I'm told."

"See there," Miss Alma chuckled, "I done told you she liked things here."

"So, you'll be stayin' on then?" the girl asked.

"I have a home already, but I would like to stay for a while. I need to find out some things about this place." She turned to Miss Alma, "And all the secrets you people have."

Miss Alma only grinned at her, so she turned back to the young girl.

"So, tell me, Afton, do you know why this place was deeded to me?"

Afton and Miss Alma exchanged glances. "No, ma'am. I don't know any of it. Not a thing."

Eden felt she had been coached, so she asked, "Would you tell me if you did?"

Afton looked confused and turned back to her bacon.

"Now, little girl, don't you start pesterin' Afton. Just accept your blessin's and thank the good Lord who give 'em to you. How many folks get handed a piece of land like this?"

Afton placed a plate of bacon and eggs on the table and pulled the chair out for Eden to sit down.

"That bacon smells delicious, Afton."

"Oh, we don't say bacon in front of Zandy here," Miss Alma laughed.

"Sorry." Eden showed appropriate horror but ended up giggling. "Aren't the two of you eating?" she asked.

"I had my grits and honey at daylight," Miss Alma said.

"And you, Afton? Won't you have some breakfast with me?"

"Oh, no ma'am. I couldn't do that. My mama would thrash me."

"Thrash?"

"Whup her," Miss Alma said, giggling at Eden's faux pas. "She's paid to serve you. She could never sit down to a meal with you. Ain't our ways."

"But that's silly. Here, Afton, this is more than I can possibly eat. Give me another plate, and I'll put some on it for you."

Afton looked confused and excused herself to sweep the upstairs.

"You ain't going to be changin' things that easy, little girl," Miss Alma said as she put Zandy into her box, walked to the sink, and began to rinse some collard greens. "Our ways may be old-fashioned, but we're pretty set in 'em. Least we ain't as uncivilized as them bottom landers."

"Bottom landers?"

"The people from the river bottom. They got the mark of Cain on 'em. Angry and mean, the whole lot of 'em. Afton's from the river bottom. But she ain't like the others. Ever' once in a while, a little flower will bloom down yonder. But mostly, we just stay clear of them heathen devils. You just leave that baby girl alone and let ol' Alma give you a tour."

After Eden finished her breakfast, Miss Alma showed her the outbuildings: the barn, the old crumbling carriage house, the laundry house, the chicken coops, and pointed out the hay meadow and the pastures on the north side. The more Eden saw of her property, the more she began to fall in love with it. She was a city girl, but Bett had always talked about one day living in the country. The only ache in her heart was that it wasn't *their* home, and Bett wasn't with her.

This journey had taken Eden into a strange world, built on two, separate social strata. But she didn't know that yet, or that she would become a conduit between the two. In the end, painfully, she would have one foot in both. The trick would be not to be torn in two.

≻━═╫═━≺

On the following morning, Eden woke slowly. She wasn't asleep, and yet, she wasn't fully awake either. She hadn't fully emerged from the world of dreams and shadows, and in that dark mid-place, she distinctly heard her mother's voice.

"Eden, get up sweetheart. Your breakfast is getting cold."

She smiled, her eyes still closed, and inhaled the scent of bacon frying.

"Yes, Mama. I'm coming."

She stretched her arms out, pointed her toes under the sheet and willed her eyes to open.

Shocked, she bolted upright as Bett's voice still lingered. This wasn't her room in Rising Star, and that couldn't have been Bett who called her. This voice was a dream, and she knew it.

"Mama?" she called softly, knowing there would be no answer. Tears formed, and she wondered if she would ever be able to remember Bett without this gut-wrenching pain.

That morning, Eden found herself exploring Two Rivers. The streets and buildings were just beyond her recall. Her car weaved in and out of thoroughfares and back alleys, searching for one elusive memory that would tell her everything.

At noon, she pulled into the Dairy Delight and ordered a burger. A girl on roller-skates delivered it to her car. An old Chevy, full of grinning, flat-topped boys in lettermen jackets, pulled in beside her. From the laughing, hushing, and slapping, she felt it best not to look in their direction.

"Aw, come on doll, give us a smile," one of the boys yelled.

The others slugged him and guffawed as they tried to slink out of sight in the old car. But to their surprise, Eden turned directly toward them and flashed them her most dazzling smile. The boys grew silent and sat up straight, a little ashamed of themselves. They hadn't expected her to respond, and they weren't sure what to do.

Finally, the one behind the wheel spoke, "Sorry, ma'am. Slats here is a jerk. We didn't mean to bother you."

Eden nodded and went back to her burger, successfully having put an end to their shenanigans. She was glad when their burgers and sodas were delivered, and they rushed off down the farm-to-market.

Once she was finished, she headed down the same road, and it wasn't long before she came upon the boys, stranded on the side of the road, with smoke billowing from beneath their hood. As she passed them, the one called Slats jumped to the side of the road and stuck his thumb out for a ride. She passed them with only a smile and a wave.

Eden watched the steaming car in her rearview mirror and began to feel sorry for the boys. They were stranded. There were no other cars on the road. They could be there an extremely long time, so, she turned the car around and headed back.

The driver, the polite one, had continued to watch the car as it cruised past, and he noticed when it slowed and turned around.

"Guys! Guys, heads up!" he yelled. "Be cool!"

Eden pulled onto the grassy shoulder directly in front of their car. "Need some help?"

Slats sauntered to her door, leered at her and said, "What did you have in mind?"

"Good grief, Slats!" the driver said, grabbing his friend's arm and pulling him back. "Sorry about him. He doesn't mean any harm."

"Don't worry about it," Eden smiled. "Every group has one of those. Can I give you a lift?"

All four boys moved forward.

"I meant you," Eden said, nodding toward the driver. "You've been a gentleman. I'd be glad to take you to get some help."

The young man slid into the seat beside her and introduced himself, "I'm Johnny Callahan."

"I'm Eden Devereaux, glad to meet you, Johnny Callahan," she said, pulling onto the road.

"You're new in town. Just visiting?"

"Just visiting for now. I'm not sure how long I'll be here."

"I hope you enjoy our little town, ma'am. And thanks a lot for helping us out after how we acted earlier."

"Where am I taking you?"

"My mom has a little bookstore on Main Street. It's right next to the museum. Do you know where that is?"

"I'm afraid not."

"Just turn left at the third light. I'll show you."

"Will she be able to help you with your car?"

"I can get her car and take the guys back to school. My brother can tow my car later."

"Turn here?"

"Yep and go down two blocks."

Eden followed his directions and ended up parked in front of a quaint little bookshop with a wood shingled awning and white colonial posts.

"Cute store, I think I'd like to come in and look around."

"That would be great. I know Mom would love to meet the lady who rescued us guys."

"And I'd like to get to know some of the people around here."

"You'll like my mom. She's great."

Eden thought that was sweet.

Clarice's shop smelled of rose potpourri and lemon verbena. Two ladies milled around in the cookbook section, and they raised their eyebrows at the young woman who came in with Johnny Callahan. A slightly gray-haired lady, with a pencil behind one ear, sat behind a desk in the back. When she looked up and saw her son, she looked worried.

"Johnny, what are you doing here?"

"Had car trouble. This nice lady gave me a ride."

The older woman smiled at Eden. Johnny kissed his mom's cheek, an endearing gesture, Eden thought, and turned to her.

"Mom, this is Eden, uh, uh …"

"Devereaux," Eden said.

"Eden Devereaux. Eden, this is my mom, Clarice Callahan." Eden shook the woman's hand and noticed her gentle touch.

"Mom, can I have your car to take the guys back to practice? They're stranded out on 146 with my car."

Clarice tossed him her keys, "Call Jeff and see if he can get a wrecker to tow your car home. Pick me up here at five."

"Okay, Mom. Thanks."

Johnny thanked Eden again and headed toward the door where he turned for one final appraisal. His mother was saying something to Eden, and he could barely see the curve of Eden's cheek, as she smiled at Clarice. Feeling a little breathless, he thought she was a lovely girl.

Clarice Callahan was charming, from her sophisticated French-twist to the pearlized, pink sandals that exposed toes polished in the same pink hew. She looked younger than her fifty-something years, and her kind facial expressions made people want to be her best friend. Everyone loved Clarice Callahan, and there were few that Clarice didn't love back, even if they didn't deserve it. Eden enjoyed sharing a cup of coffee.

"Just look," one lady said as Clarice checked her out. She was holding open a gardening book and said, "My roses look exactly like these."

"You should enter them in the competition at the fair this year."

"Do you think I'd have a chance?"

"Of course, you do, dear," Clarice answered, as the woman glanced at Eden, who nodded her encouragement too.

Eden had no idea how the time had passed when she noticed the clock over the door. "Four o'clock! Oh, Clarice, I'm so sorry. I didn't mean to take up your entire afternoon."

Clarice smiled over her coffee, "No, no, no. It was a slow day. I enjoyed the company. People come here just to sit and chat all the time. We're kind of the social hub around here."

"I can't tell you how helpful you've been about the house and its history."

"It was one of the first houses built in Two Rivers," Clarice had told her. "The original cabin was built before there was a town here, somewhere back in the mid to late eighteen-hundreds, part of the huge Gentry estate. The Gentry family has owned all the land up and down your part of the river since old Camden Gentry received it as a land grant, and brought his young bride, Annaliese, to the river bottom. Your house was the second home Cam built for Annaliese after their first cabin burned to the ground. He built it around the stone fireplace of the first cabin. Their daughter still owns their original land, and their old cane plantation, their third house. They don't produce cane sugar anymore though. Years ago, Annaliese Gentry restored the plantation house, and it's about the most magnificent plantation home ever built in these parts. A huge Greek revival, you know."

It was a treasure trove of information. Clarice was shocked that Eden now owned any part of the Gentry estate.

"They've never let an inch of that land go before. And what a strange way to come by it."

"I agree," Eden had said.

# Six

The next morning, Eden slept late before soaking in a tub of rose-scented bath water before putting on her pink sun-dress. The spaghetti straps tugged at her bare shoulders, and one kept slipping down her arm. It was mid-morning when she came downstairs, and there were waffles waiting for her in the kitchen. Miss Alma poured her a cup of hot coffee.

"Where's Afton?"

"Said yesterday, her mama needed her today for gatherin' the elderberries and canning 'em. Where you off to today, little girl?" Miss Alma asked.

"I thought I'd like to poke around the Thicket. Maybe explore the river."

"What for?"

"When I went for a walk back home, it was on a sidewalk past rows of houses. I thought a walk through the woods would be interesting. I can smell the river from the back porch, and I thought I might dip my toes in it."

"Banks too steep for that."

"Well, there is a pier I could sit on, right?"

"Yes, but I don't think you should go down there without Afton. Wait 'til tomorrow, and she can go too."

"Don't be silly. Afton has better things to do than babysit me. I'll be fine."

"I tell you here and now, I'm against it. That ol' muddy ain't safe, even for us folks, what been raised alongside it."

"Duly noted. Now how do I find the river?"

Miss Alma remained silent for a moment, then recognizing it as a losing battle, she said, "Down yonder, past the hay meadow, you'll see a post. It'll point you to the pier. If you're gonna walk upriver, you'll find yourself on Gentry land and that ain't good. The other way is too growed up to walk. So, you just stay there at the pier, you hear me?"

"Yes, ma'am, I do, and thank you."

Eden breached the hay meadow in no time. Miss Alma watched her go and immediately began to worry. A wind swept through the open front door and out the back door as if chasing after Eden. Miss Alma felt as if the old house had just taken a deep breath and was watching too. She wondered if the house was as concerned as she was.

Eden hadn't told Miss Alma what Clarice Callahan had told her about the Gentrys. There was no need. Miss Alma already knew all that, yet hadn't shared any of it with Eden and she wondered why. She decided if Miss Alma could keep secrets, so could she.

It was just a short walk through the trees when Eden found herself at the river's edge, a lovely place with gentle waves lapping at the steep bank. Cypress trees walked in the river. Here and there a cypress knee split the current. The pier forged its way over the water, and Eden took a chance that it wouldn't be rotten. She cautiously made her way to the end. She was right. The pier was sturdy.

A small rowboat was tied to a large, rusty nail and the waves lapped against it, causing it to thump against the pier. A giant sycamore tree grew right up to the bank and covered the old dock with shade, allowing lances of sunlight to harpoon the glistening water. Eden removed her sandals and sat down on the end of the pier, dangling her legs in the current. The water was almost cold. She laid her body back onto the weathered boards and used her arms as a pillow beneath her head. For a while, time stood still, and all was well in her world. When she grew sleepy though, she sat up and shook her head. She would not allow *that* dream to destroy the peace she felt here.

There was a slight pathway that followed alongside the river, and it kept tugging at her. She had told Miss Alma she would only sit on the pier, but what possible harm could it do to take a walk?

Eventually, she left her sandals behind and walked a long way beside the river's edge. The earth felt damp, and she tried to remember the last time she had walked barefoot, but she could not. The path was firm and felt cool beneath her feet as she listened to the birds and the slosh of the water until she came upon a magnificent, old oak. She ran her fingers over the wrinkled bark and leaned into it to breathe in its woodsy scent.

A movement to her left caught her attention, and she saw a heavyset, mud-colored snake in a striking position. She saw the eerie cats-eyes, the undulating movement, the sickening gray pigmentation that had carefully hidden it in the mud. She screamed and jerked her body away from the muddy river, but the water had made the bank slippery where her foot landed. As she began to tumble, she was thrown violently backward, crashing her head against the tree. The force of the hardwood against her head stunned her, and she couldn't focus her eyes. As her vision returned, she found herself lying face to face with the snake, and a sickening feeling caused her stomach to wretch. A strange darkness began to engulf her. Just before she lost consciousness, she saw the silhouette of a little girl step between her and the snake. As she tried to warn the child away, the child raised a small branch and brought it down hard on the snake's head, just as Eden's world turned to darkness.

⚜

By late afternoon, Miss Alma was agitated. She kept telling herself all was well, but her instincts told her differently. She had hoped Nub would appear in the meadow so she could send him to look for the girl, but he had not. Miss Alma placed her rocker in the back doorway where she could see Eden when she came up from the river. She held Zandy protectively, resting her little piglet head on her shoulder, more for her own comfort than for Zandy's. The ticking of the kitchen clock grew louder as time passed.

Around six o'clock, Miss Alma heard knocking on the front door. Placing Zandy in her box, she hurried along the center hall, hopeful that she would find Eden standing there. Instead, there were the setting sun silhouettes of two men, both quite tall, in the doorway.

"Miss Alma, it's just us, J. D. and Johnny Callahan."

The old woman flung the screen door open and frantically looked all around them.

"Are you alone?" she asked, too loudly.

"Yes, ma'am."

"Have you seen Eden?"

Johnny replied, instantly alert, "No ma'am."

"Mom sent y'all this pecan pie to thank the young lady for helping Johnny out yesterday," J. D. said, holding it out. They could tell something was wrong. The distress showed clearly on her face.

"Are you okay, Miss Alma?"

"It's Eden. She left here this mornin' and I ain't seen her since."

"Maybe she went into town," Johnny ventured.

"No, no, no!" she growled. "She went walkin' down yonder by the river much too long ago!"

J. D. handed Johnny the pie and instructed him to put it inside. He took Miss Alma's arm and led her to her rocker on the front porch. He knew she wouldn't be comfortable alone in the house with two men from the town.

"Now Miss Alma, I'm sure it's nothin'. But if you'd feel better, we'll go look for her. Would you like that?"

"Yes, oh yes, Mr. J. D."

Johnny had reappeared, and J. D. motioned for him to follow. They jumped from the porch, headed around to the back of the house and toward the river. Johnny, slightly shorter than his brother, was having trouble keeping up with J. D. 's long strides.

"I'm telling you J. D.; this girl is remarkable. Prettiest girl I've ever seen."

"You say that about every girl you meet, but that's not what's important here."

"Maybe not to you," Johnny smiled.

They reached the river and the pier, but they were not encouraged by the sight of the pink sandals on the weathered planks. Their eyes skimmed the river's surface, wondering if the girl had fallen in.

J. D. cupped his hands around his mouth and yelled out, "MISS DEVEREAUX? EDEN!"

No answer, but they heard the bay of an old hound off in the distance. Probably one of Miss Alma's Blueticks.

"Wonder which way she went?" Johnny mused.

"Let's split up. We'll cover more ground. You go that way, and I'll head north."

For a while Johnny could hear J. D. call Eden's name, his voice getting further and further away. He could tell that J. D. was moving quickly and he hurried too. Night was almost upon them.

J. D. heard a voice, a child's whispered voice, "Come."

"Eden, is that you?" he called. But he knew it was not the voice of a grown woman.

J. D. sensed Eden before he saw her, the minute he rounded a slight bend and saw the tree's crackled trunk. There she was—her pink skirt and blonde hair spread out around her. He was reminded of *Sleeping Beauty*, who had simply fallen asleep. Her face showed no emotion, but Johnny had been right. It was a lovely face. He had to remind himself that this wasn't a fairy tale. If she was unconscious, she was hurt and in trouble.

"Eden!" he called out as he fell to one knee beside her. She felt warm to his touch. Her pulse was strong against his fingertips.

"Eden?" he said, tapping her cheek, and her eyelids fluttered. His face hovered close over hers, and when she finally opened her eyes, she looked confused. She was staring up into the dark brown eyes of a total stranger, and she recoiled. J. D. sensed her discomfort and slowly pulled back.

"It's all right, Eden. I'm J. D., Clarice's son. Miss Alma sent Johnny and me to find you. Are you okay?"

Still confused, Eden glanced around. There was the river, the path, the tree, the ... "Snake!" she gasped. "There was a snake!" Eden sat up and shivered, "It was huge. It was ... I fell ... It—"

"Okay Eden," J. D. said. "It's gone now."

He turned his head and looked at her legs and bare feet—no sign of a snake bite.

"I hit ... head. Dizzy." She spoke softly, closing her eyes.

"Stay awake, Eden. Don't go to sleep on me. I need to get you home. Miss Alma's worried about you, and I think you should see a doctor."

But she didn't move.

"Eden!" He raised his voice. "Stay awake, honey! You have to stay awake!"

But she only sighed as J. D. leaned over her and placed one hand behind her head. His other hand slid around her waist to the small of her back. He lifted her with him as he stood. She felt remarkably light. Eden leaned against him, eyes mostly closed, wrapping her arms around his waist. J. D. began to move, and Eden willed herself to move with him. She knew it was important to get back to the house, to the safety of familiar things. J. D. half carried, half guided her along the way. As they approached the pier, they met up with Johnny who had doubled back as the night began to swallow up the path.

"Eden!" Johnny called.

Her face was buried in J. D. 's chest.

"Is she alright? What happened to her?"

"I'm not sure. Run ahead and call Doc Tobias. Have him come out here as soon as possible."

Johnny fairly flew back to the house where he called Doctor Tobias and waited with Miss Alma on the back steps. A short time later, they caught sight of the pair emerging from the trees. Miss Alma thought Eden looked like a rag doll she had as a child.

When they reached the house, J. D. put his arm under Eden's knees and lifted her up the porch steps. Inside, he placed her on the velveteen sofa in the front parlor. Miss Alma threw a light coverlet over her and tucked it around her bare shoulders. She looked small and childlike lying there. J. D. knelt beside her and gently brushed her hair away from her face, a tender gesture that didn't go unnoticed by Miss Alma or Johnny.

"Eden! Eden, can you hear me?" J. D. said.

She didn't answer.

"She okay, Mr. J. D.?" Miss Alma asked.

"She was talking to me out at the river. I think she stumbled upon a snake, lost her footing and hit her head on an oak tree. I just wish Doc Tobias would hurry," he said, glancing at the front door.

It was after seven and dark outside when Doc Tobias finally arrived. He immediately shooed Johnny and J. D. out onto the porch. Johnny plopped into Miss Alma's rocker while J. D. leaned against one of the porch posts and stared at the fireflies that played chase across the dark yard.

"You like her," Johnny stated, matter-of-factly.

"What?"

"You like Eden. The look of her, I mean."

J. D. looked sternly at his little brother, "I don't even know that girl."

"Doesn't matter. You like her. I mean, what's not to like? Right?"

"I'm seeing Paige, and we've kind of got an agreement."

"Ooooh, an *agreement*." Johnny exaggerated, smiling. "But you're a little intrigued with this girl, aren't you?"

"NO! Paige has my full attention, little brother. I don't even know this girl."

Johnny shrugged at his words.

J. D. 's eyes turned back to the screen door. "I sure hope she's alright though," he said absentmindedly.

<hr/>

Dr. Tobias drove Eden to the hospital so he could run some tests since it was obvious that she had a concussion.

Miss Alma stayed the night with her in the hospital. She heard Eden call out Wynn's name. Puzzled, Miss Alma searched through Eden's address book in her purse until she found Wynn's number at Princeton and had called him. She told him about the accident, and he came early the next day.

Miss Alma liked Wynn well enough, but she didn't see this city boy living out in their pine thicket. She wanted Eden to stay. So maybe, just maybe, this Mr. Wynn would not be a welcomed fellow to Miss Alma's way of thinking.

Two days later, Eden was being released from the hospital. J. D. hadn't seen her since he carried her up from the river. After all, he didn't really know the girl. There was no reason for him to see her further. Of course, his mother really liked this girl and had visited with her in the hospital. Johnny was totally smitten, but he at least had the sense to know that he was too young for her. J. D. 's thoughts turned to Paige. She mattered to him deeply.

He thought it wouldn't hurt to check on the girl though and see how she was doing. He called Paige to ask her to come along, but was told she had gone shopping and would be out all day. J. D. was disappointed—he was sure the two ladies were destined to become friends.

Arriving at the hospital, he went into the gift shop and bought a lovely bouquet of flowers. He found himself alone in the lobby just as the elevator doors opened and out stepped Eden on the arm of a young man J. D. had never seen. J. D. instinctively stepped back to one side of a sizeable potted palm to avoid the couple. But at the same moment, the young man pulled Eden to the seclusion of the other side of the potted palm. J. D. couldn't see the pair, but he could hear their every word.

"Why do you have to go back so soon?" Eden pouted.

Even her voice sounded pretty, J. D. noticed from his vantage point.

"Sorry kid, but you know how tight my schedule is, school starting up and all."

There was a silence, and J. D. wondered what he was doing, hiding behind this plant like a little kid.

"I've missed you so much, Eden. I want to take you home with me. I don't ask you for much. But this is important. This place just doesn't seem safe. Please reconsider."

"Even if I went back to Rising Star, you'd still be at Princeton. And I've got to get some answers to my questions. I can't just walk away from this."

"Alright then, but I want you home by Christmas. Do you hear me?"

"Yes, and I'll try. I really will."

There was another long pause. The young man growled deep in his throat, "I can hardly stand this. We've been apart so long. And I was beginning to make plans for our future together."

There was no doubt at that moment that they were kissing.

J. D. heard Eden laugh and say, "Be gone, you wicked man!"

Wynn laughed too.

"No, really Wynn. You'll miss your deadline if you don't go now."

"You're much too eager to be rid of me. I hope you aren't hiding someone else in this here potted plant."

But the truth was that she was hurrying him on his way because she had seen the shoes planted on the other side of the palm and knew they were being heard. One quick kiss and Wynn hurried from the lobby.

Eden didn't move.

J. D., feeling foolish, stepped forward a few feet, figuring she was aware he was there. As he stepped into her view, she gave him a sidelong glance, her head slightly down, as a magenta blush began to rise in her cheeks. But there was no recognition.

"Please excuse us," she said, as she quickly moved back to the elevator. Only then did it dawn on him that she might not remember him. She had clung to him, but she had not really seen him. He had been her support, but not a living, breathing person. The thought that she didn't know him was disappointing.

"Good grief," he chided himself, "what did it matter to me? That young lady was deeply attached to the young man who just left." The man said they were planning a future together and that was alright with J. D.

He watched as she stepped into the elevator and turned to face him. Their eyes met for a long moment, and then she looked away just as the elevator doors closed. As he left, he dumped the flowers he held in the trash can.

# Seven

After a few days of rest under Miss Alma's care, Eden began to spend her days at the courthouse or the library going over property records, searching for the name of any Gentry who would have the ability to deed her the sixty-five acres. She absorbed the ins and outs of this mysterious little village and its sister village down on the river.

In the evenings, she and Miss Alma sat on the front porch and learned about each other. It was in those quiet evening hours that Miss Alma's life began to unfurl in bits and pieces. After eighty years, it was a remarkable story.

Miss Alma Mayhew, who had been born in 1880, was only fourteen when she married her Thaddeus Mayhew. They produced seven children together—Aubrey, River Lee, Emily, Maddie, Charli Mae and the twins, Laurel and Lily.

"It's an awful, heartwrenchin' thing when a mama outlives all her little 'uns. But that's what happened to me. They're all gone now, all of 'em up there with my sweet Thaddeus, bless all those li'l hearts. All gone before me. Long lives can be cruel things to bear."

"Tell me about your Thaddeus, Miss Alma."

Miss Alma laid her head back on the smooth curve of her rocker, closed her eyes, and smiled. In the distance, a barn owl hooted while Miss Alma's two hounds, Lizzie and Luther, lifted their heads from the porch.

"My Thad, he was so handsome little girl, dark-skinned and tall as a pine saplin'. He come to my papa's church one night in early spring."

"Your papa was a minister?"

"Yes, 'um. A good man of God. But Thad, he was bold as a lion. He set his eye on me, and there was nothin' nobody could 'a done then. My papa, he married us not quite three months later. I thought we'd be together from nigh on. But that wasn't to be. If only we could see the end from the beginnin'. But I guess that's just for the good Lord to do. Be too hard on us, the knowin' of it."

"What happened to your Thaddeus?" Eden asked.

"Little girl, little girl, them was such bad days. Dark-hearted people ever'where. Ever' body hatin' each other."

Miss Alma could only shake her head. She didn't go on, and Eden didn't push.

"I'm so tired, little girl," Miss Alma finally said, lifting her bulk from the rocker. "Can't do much of nothin', and I still get so tired these days. My bed'll be a welcome to this here ol' body tonight." Her voice trailed off as she entered the house.

"Good night, Miss Alma," Eden called after her. "Sleep well."

Eden heard Miss Alma shuffle slowly to the back of the house, turning off the lights as she went. Crickets screeched their rhythmed chorus, and far off she heard the owl hoot again. Then there was a sudden stillness that brought an uneasy quiet. One of Miss Alma's hounds raised its head again, but this time it growled low in its throat.

A twig snapped. Both hounds leapt to their feet but remained quiet. Eden searched the tree line but could make out nothing more than the swaying of the branches and the drifting down of dancing leaves.

Still, an uneasiness brought Eden to her feet, and she moved to the door. She stepped inside, bolted the lock, and pushed the lace away from the sidelight, looking out. She thought a shadow moved across the tree line, but its source was hidden from her. She watched as the two old hounds retreated under the house. Then the shadow was gone, and Eden could breathe again. As she hurried up the stairs, she decided that in the morning, she would ask Miss Alma if there were any guns in the house.

It was late October, and the forests around Two Rivers were splattered with golds, magentas, and reds as the foliage began changing its seasonal color pallet. The morning air left the skin prickly with its chill, but soon after sun up, a comforting warmth settled over the Thicket.

Eden had received a summons from Clarice Callahan to meet with her for a cup of coffee and some information that Clarice had unearthed. Eden was eager to be there. She dressed quickly, grabbed a piece of toast and was out the door.

The bookshop hadn't been open fifteen minutes when Clarice looked up and saw Eden smiling at her.

"My, you're out and about early," Clarice said.

"I couldn't wait."

"You'll just have to while I make us some coffee. Have a cinnamon roll, dear."

Eden admired how gracefully Clarice Callahan moved while making their morning coffee. She had all the grace and style that had been lacking in Bett, and Eden wondered about how each woman had been shaped and molded by the places where they were raised. Bett's lack of grace had at one time been inconsequential. But now, was it a clue? *Just who had Bett been before she had me and our Rising Star lives,* she wondered.

The freshly brewed coffee was Texas strong, and Eden had to add a lot of sugar and cream. Soon, she could no longer contain herself.

"Alright, please, what have you learned?"

"I know who the sole owner of your parcel of the Gentry estate was."

"Who?"

"Annaliese."

"You mean Annaliese Gentry?"

"That's right."

"But she'd have to be …"

"Ninety-two."

"Is she still alive?"

"Barely, I hear. She's bed bound and must have twenty-four-hour care. I heard she was in an elite home for the elderly over in Coldspring. A place called Rose Haven. Your land, dear, was never deeded to Annaliese's daughter as was the rest of the Gentry estate. She kept it, obviously, for you."

"But that just makes things more bizarre. Why would Annaliese Gentry leave it to a perfect stranger, the first land that she and Camden Gentry ever owned, when she has a daughter and grandchildren?"

"I wonder if you *are* a perfect stranger," Clarice mused. "It is intriguing. That place was where she and old Cam were young together. Her children were born in that house."

"But that's even more reason to keep it in the family!"

"I know, dear."

"Maybe her mind is feeble, and she simply made a mistake."

"If that were true, the rest of the Gentrys would have already hauled you into court over it. The greater mystery is why none of them have legally gone after you and your land. They're a forceful lot, used to getting what they want, legally or illegally. I wonder why they have remained so quiet about it, and just let you move in."

"How did you find all this out?"

"I got it from my friend, Eulalea Eubanks. Her housekeeper is the daughter of Ada Mae, the Gentry's old housekeeper, who's been with the Gentrys for over forty years. Housekeepers hear things, and they know things."

"But it's just talk then," Eden mused.

"More than that, I'd say. Ada Mae was there when Annaliese was still running the place. Early on, Ada Mae was Annaliese's personal maid and they were close. Ada Mae said that your parcel of land was the only section of land not put in Annaliese's daughter's name as the land was handed down to the younger generation. Said it held a spell over her, and that she needed redemption. But Ada Mae didn't know why."

"Redemption? That's a strange word to use. She actually said redemption?"

"Yes."

Eden tried to process this when Clarice said, "Did you know that Miss Alma was one of the Gentry's house-keepers for many years?"

"She told me she worked for Annaliese."

"Ada Mae said that Annaliese moved back into your house after Camden Gentry died, and she took Miss Alma with her. She lived there for about ten more years before she was taken home and then put in Rose Haven by the family. I guess Miss Alma just sort of stayed on then. Hon, I think your Miss Alma holds the answers to all of this."

"She won't even discuss it. I know she could clear this up. But she refused to tell me anything."

"I'm thinking she's probably been told not to tell you anything."

"I know she has. By the way, do you know Miss Alma's story? Where she came from?"

"Miss Alma's always been a mystery around here. I heard she came here a little after the turn of the century. Had a bundle of children in tow, but no husband. She was starving and living off the land and Miss Annaliese, I think, felt sorry for her when they found her and her children sleeping on the ground by the river. She took her in and fixed up an old out-building to put the children in. Paid her good wages for that day and age. Miss Alma has worked for the family ever since."

"I wonder what brought her to Two Rivers. I know she had a husband at one time, she told me so."

"She never talked about where she came from, or more importantly, what she was running away from."

Eden sighed, "A mystery within a mystery. Where is Nancy Drew when you need her?"

"I believe she's over there in aisle three, section B, under Adolescent Mysteries," Clarice teased. "Just give it time, Eden. Keep looking. Remember that verse in Corinthians that says, 'He will bring to light what is hidden in the darkness and will expose the motives of the heart.'"

"Motives of the heart, huh? *That* will be interesting to find out."

The ladies were interrupted when the shop door opened, clanging the little bell that hung over it. Two hulking fellows moved through the room like the proverbial bulls in a china shop, their heavy boots cracking along the old, oak floors.

"Miss Clarice, ain't you lookin' fine today."

"What are you boys up to? I'm sure whatever it is, it's *not good.*"

"Why, Miss Clarice, you wound us greatly. Me and Boone here, we're never up to anything, let alone anything 'not good.'"

"Now that's true," Clarice laughed. "Eden, I'd like you to meet the two most corrupting influences in my J. D. 's life. This is Ryder Lee and Boone Bohannon. Boys, this is Miss Eden Devereaux from Rising Star, over in West Texas."

"Miss Eden Devereaux," Boone repeated, "We've heard all about you. You're livin' out at the old Gentry place."

"And Johnny and his crowd have the biggest crush on you," Ryder laughed.

"Now that I've met the lady, that's understandable," Boone smiled.

"Thank you, I think," Eden said.

"Back off, Boone. You know you're taken, old friend," Ryder shot back.

Clarice raised an eyebrow. "Taken? By whom?"

"Oh, nobody," Boone said, "Ryder never knows what he's talkin' about. You know that."

"Actually Boone, I'm right on the mark on this one," he said, sitting down next to Eden and facing her square on. "I've been seein' you all over town, Miss Eden, drivin' around in that cute little red car of yours. I've just been waiting for an introduction."

"So, you two came in because you saw Eden's car outside?" Clarice asked, amused.

"Yes, ma'am, that's about the jist of it," Ryder said, noticing Eden's slight blush.

"I thought it was me you had designs on, Ryder Lee," Clarice laughed.

Ryder laughed back, "Now Miss Clarice, you've always had my heart, from elementary on. But I've just been biding my time until I could ask this here young lady out."

He turned back to Eden, "The Harvest Ball is coming up a week from Saturday. I'd sure be pleased as punch if you'd let me escort you."

All eyes were on Eden as an uncomfortable silence filled the bookstore. Eden could feel the color flood her cheeks. Ryder was handsome and charming in a boyish way. His eyes wrinkled at the corners, and his laugh lines were deep. This young man was used to laughing a lot. But he was a stranger, a touch overwhelming, and his forwardness was a little scary.

"I have a young man that I am seeing, Ryder."

"You engaged?"

"Well, no, not exactly."

"We'll just go as friends and see what happens. Okay?"

"I don't know about that," she finally said. "You Two Rivers fellows sure move fast, don't you?"

"Now, Miss Eden," Ryder said in mock forlornness, "you wouldn't shame me in front of my best friend and my best old girl, would you?"

"Old girl! Really, Ryder!" Miss Clarice huffed.

Eden could only laugh. "No, I guess I can't. Clarice, is this gentleman safe to be around? I mean as a friend."

"As safe as any, I expect," Clarice smiled, winking at Ryder.

"You'd recommend his company?"

"I'm not sure about that. But if I had a daughter, I wouldn't have a problem sending her off with Ryder."

"Well then, I'll go," Eden said, briefly wondering if she had lost her mind.

"Hot dang," Ryder hooted.

When Eden crawled into her bed that night, it occurred to her that things seemed different. Her bed was softer than the one in Rising Star, and the old feather mattress smelled of sunshine and fresh air. She was aware that Afton was changing her sheets daily and she needed to tell the girl that wasn't necessary, but their fresh smell comforted her each night.

Her room glowed for her. The hazy moonlight filtered in through the windows, and the sight of the slightly moving, breeze-brushed branches outside made her aware that the place was beginning to feel like home. She told herself that she had imagined the shadow that had crossed the yard in the dead of night and that she had nothing to fear. Now her eyes scanned the room, and she felt a pleasure she had not known since the comforting presence of Bett. The river house creaked, but even that was now endearing, not at all frightening as it had been on her first nights inside it. She was becoming accustom-ed to its fits and tantrums and was lowering her guard. Eden felt as if the house had, at last, accepted her into its bowels and had decided, perhaps, that she was not a threat to it at all. Indeed, it no longer seemed like a menace to her.

She no longer felt the desire to push furniture in front of the bedroom door to feel safe. In fact, she didn't even feel she had to lock the house at night to be safe. But all the same, Miss Alma locked the outside doors every night without fail. Eden wondered if Miss Alma knew some-thing that she didn't.

# Eight

The Harvest Ball fell three days before Halloween. It was a costume ball, a way for the adults to continue dressing up for Halloween without appearing foolish, Eden supposed. She was afraid she'd regret accepting Ryder's invitation, but she had not. She and Miss Alma had conferred, and finally, she decided to go as Shirley Temple with Miss Alma's approval.

*Why has Miss Alma's approval become so important?* She wondered.

One rainy afternoon, Afton got her mother to come up from the river bottom to sew Eden's costume. It was blue with a white sailor collar, a high empire waistline, and it stopped mid-thigh, exposing her slender legs. She had white roll-down socks and Mary Jane shoes with a thin strap.

On the day of the ball, Miss Alma pulled her hair up high on her head and let it fall around her face in tight banana curls. On the side of her head, she placed a huge blue bow that matched her dress. To complete the picture, she carried an enormous lollipop.

Ryder, who had pestered Miss Alma, discovered that Eden was coming as Shirley Temple, so he decided to be *Spanky* from the *Our Gang* comedies. He parted his hair down the middle, faux freckled his nose and wore a beanie with a whirligig. His pants stopped just below mid-calf, and his clunky boots were old and oversized. Eden and Miss Alma laughed out loud when he showed up on their porch, a bouquet of scavenged wildflowers in one hand, and peppermint sticks in the other.

The banquet room on the second floor of the Town Hall building had been decorated with all sorts of fruits and vegetables in bright autumn colors. Ropes of fall leaves draped from the light fixtures, and corn stalk teepees stood in the corners and beside the doors. People brought delicious foods of all kinds—the only gimmick was that it had to be something they'd grown themselves or something they'd shot and dressed, or fished out of the rivers. Nothing could be store bought except for staples such as cornmeal, sugar, flour, salt, and spices. People who didn't plant gardens put in a tiny patch of tomatoes in their backyard or stuck an okra plant in their flower bed, just so they could come to the Harvest Ball. It was also acceptable for a group of decidedly un-green thumbed folks to share produce from one communal garden. However it was grown, the bounty was a cornucopia of the way their ancestors had feasted not too many years before. The savory scents of pumpkin pie and apple cider drifted around them with the cinnamon candle smoke from the tables.

Everyone was there. George and Martha Washington, Romeo and Juliet, Rhett and Scarlet, Roy and Dale, Marilyn Monroe, Gene Autry, Annie Oakley, Geronimo. Even Clarice looked amusing as Betsy Ross, sitting in the corner of the banquet hall, carefully hand sewing an American flag, that would later be auctioned off for the orphanage in Lufkin. Johnny and his date came as Raggedy Ann and Andy with yarn hair and red dotted cheeks, while Slats and his partner were a predictable *Ken* and *Barbie* in swimwear that showed too much skin for the comfort of this crowd.

The dance had begun an hour before J. D. and Paige made their entrance. True to her royal upbringing, Paige garnered *oohs* and *aahs* as she entered, dressed as *Cleopatra*, the Queen of the Nile, in a spectacular outfit that had been specially ordered from a French designer. At that moment, all the time and expense were paying off, as she swept through the room and people parted in her royal wake.

The costume was gold lamé and form-fitting in two pieces. Around her neck was a huge, gold medallion that was covered with faux sapphires, emeralds, and rubies. The skirt sat dangerously balanced on her hips, the gold lamé falling in a draped fashion to the floor. She wore a cobra tiara that matched the little cobra heads on her golden sandals. Around her eyes, she wore the exaggerated black liner of Egyptian royalty. Paige wanted J. D. 's eyes lined too, as was the custom, but J. D. had refused, and Paige had pouted all afternoon.

None of that was important now. Only the adoration Paige was drawing from the crowd watered her insatiable heart and made her even forget the man who escorted her. J. D. graciously followed behind her, allowing her a solo entrance to enjoy the revelers' high praise. It's what she wanted. It's what she craved.

J. D. was, of course, *Mark Anthony*, shirtless except for the large gold eagle wings that crisscrossed his chest. He wore a short, pleated, leather skirting that exposed the muscular build of his legs. Under his arm, he carried a Roman helmet. Paige had tried her best to get him to wear the helmet, but he had said he felt silly enough in the rest of the get-up. But they clearly were the most spectacular couple there, and that was Paige's goal. She wanted this night to be all about her.

Eden and Ryder were talking with Johnny when his brother arrived, and they grew silent as their eyes followed the royal couple's entrance. Johnny looked back at Eden.

"You don't remember a thing about J. D. bringing you up from the river?" Johnny asked.

"Oh, is that your brother?" Eden asked.

"Yes, that's J. D. He doesn't look familiar to you at all?"

"Sorry. I don't remember anything about that day."

She didn't tell him that what she did remember was the embarrassing moment in the hospital lobby when she and Wynn had spoken quietly behind the palms and J. D. had heard.

Eden felt Ryder take her hand, pulling her onto the crowded dance floor and they began dancing to *The Tennessee Waltz*. The evening moved forward in the glow of the candles, their luminescence casting shadows that moved and swayed with the revelers. One by one, Ryder introduced Eden to Two River's elite, the landed gentry, and the businessmen, as well as their sweethearts, wives, and daughters. Eden couldn't begin to remember all their names, not even the young men who asked for dances while Ryder pouted in the background.

The Harvest Queen's table had been opened, and everyone was asked to vote for the lady of their choice during the next hour. As people began to mill around the table, the master of ceremonies announced a Round Robin.

"What's a Round Robin?" Eden asked.

"The girls form a circle in the middle, and the men form an outer circle. You walk in different directions until the music stops. Then you dance with whoever is standing opposite of you."

"I don't know …"

"Come on, it'll be fun," Ryder said, pulling her to the inner circle and taking his place opposite her.

The music started and Eden, feeling uncomfortable, found herself marching away from Ryder's familiar grin. A sea of faces passed her. Some, like Johnny's and Boone's she knew, but most she did not. She finally stopped looking altogether and stared down at the floor. When the music abruptly ended, Eden turned to face her partner and slowly lifted her eyes. Her first recognition was the golden eagle wings crisscrossing the muscular chest. Her eyes snapped up like elastic, and she stared into the face of her phantom deliverer.

"Well, well, who do we have here? Could it really be Shirley …" his voice trailed off as he recognized her.

"Eden Devereaux?"

She had already begun to blush.

"You're J. D. Callahan." It wasn't a question, just a recognition. "You're the one who found me by the river."

J. D. smiled a tender smile and nodded.

"But I saw you at the hospital. You were by the palms."

"I had come to see how you were doing. I guess I saw more than I was meant to," he winked. "I was afraid I'd embarrassed you, so I just left."

The music began, and J. D. took her hand. He remembered the smell of her hair as he pulled her to him and swayed to the music. She hadn't danced this closely with any others that night, not even Ryder, but she didn't feel uncomfortable. He had been her deliverer, and on this one magical night, he looked the part. The smell of his cologne was familiar. She closed her eyes and listened to the music as a young man sang Dion and the Belmont's romantic *Where or When*.

The music ended, but J. D. and Eden continued to sway for just a brief, lingering moment until the crackle of a feminine voice split the air.

"Gads O' Mighty, Jeff! I had to dance with that awful Jiggs Mackey. I can't even believe they let him come to this ball. He should be downriver with the bottom landers!" Paige was fanning herself and feigning distress. "Can you believe it, Jeff? The one old man in the circle, and I get stuck with him! Me! Paige Gresham! He actually smelled of motor oil!"

"Paige, have you met Eden?"

Paige stopped her agitated fanning, and Eden felt self-conscious under her arrogant scrutiny.

"No, I haven't," she finally said, flashing a wicked smile.

"Then allow me. Paige, this is Eden Devereaux. Eden, this is Paige Gresham."

"Eden, is it?" Paige slowly said, "I heard you have *my Jeff* to thank for saving your life."

"It would appear so," Eden smiled back.

From that moment on, Paige always referred to J. D. as 'my Jeff.'

After an awkward moment, Ryder appeared, taking Eden's hand and pulling her back onto the dance floor. Johnny walked up, nudged J. D. and said, "I saw you dancing with Eden. So, you finally met for the second time?"

Johnny knew his words would rile Paige and he was right.

"You danced with her, with *that* girl?"

"Eden is who I ended up with for the Round Robin."

Paige frowned, "That was pretty convenient. Wonder how she arranged it?"

"Come on, Paige," J. D. said. "If you could arrange anything like that, would you have ended up with Jiggs Mackey?"

It was a tactical victory. Paige wasn't able to return fire.

Eden didn't get another chance to dance with J. D. In fact, he only danced with Paige for the rest of the evening. At midnight, they were ready to announce the Harvest Queen, and the honor fell to Sheriff Delaney, who spit and sputtered when he had to announce that there had been a tie.

"Uh hum," he coughed, "The two winners are Miss Eden Devereaux and Miss Paige Gresham."

"Not a clear win for ol' Paige?" Slats chuckled.

"She rubs a lot of people the wrong way," Johnny replied.

Thunderous applause exploded across the hall as Paige moved to the platform and grabbed the Queen's trophy. Eden was embarrassed though and had to be moved forward. Ryder and Boone lifted her onto the platform before she had a chance to bolt and run. The two young ladies stood side by side, but in stark contrast to each other. Eden's *Shirley Temple* seemed entirely innocent next to Paige's exotic *Cleopatra*. Eden wished she was anywhere else, but on that stage.

"Let's see. What do we do now?" Sheriff Delaney stammered. "There's only one trophy, but we'll have another one made for you, Miss Devereaux."

"That really isn't necessary, Sheriff," Eden assured him.

"And the crown?" He continued to stammer and look worried.

"Please," Eden said, "Let Paige have it. She's the home-town girl."

"Give it to Eden," someone yelled, "Paige has the trophy!"

"That's right," Sheriff Delaney agreed, and with that, he placed the crown on Eden's head.

The crowd applauded again, and both girls stood together, smiling out at all the cheering faces. But what the entire crowd couldn't see, was the bad blood that was germinating inside Paige Gresham. Standing close to her, however, Eden felt it, white-hot and threatening. It wasn't until Paige was in J. D.'s car and speeding away from the ball that she unleashed her fury.

"Can you believe that? Those were my friends, my people! How could they have done that to me?"

"They didn't exactly do anything to you, Paige," J. D. soothed.

"What are you talking about? Half of them betrayed my family and me by voting for that girl. Doesn't the Gresham name mean anything around here anymore?"

"But you won," J. D. reminded her.

"No, *weee* won! And Delaney had the gall to call her name first! I just can't believe it! I was supposed to wear that crown home!"

"Hon, you *are* wearing a crown. You're the *Queen of the Nile* and a beautiful queen at that. How about just being my queen tonight?"

J. D.'s trying to right the ship only made her seethe more. From that moment on, Paige began to look for an opportunity to destroy Eden.

# The Woods Are Lovely, Dark and Deep ...

# Nine

The Big Thicket has always been one of the most remarkable areas in America, though it is mostly un-known except in Texas. Sandwiched by the Trinity River on the west and the Sabine River on the east, the moisture from the rivers, combined with mild temperatures all year round, imitate the humid rainforests of South America. Deep in that unique atmosphere, lush, tropical plants and hostile, brooding people, blanket the forests.

The bottom landers found living off the land in such a primal terrain, peacefully simple. Wild game was drawn to the Thicket, and the land was crisscrossed by streams from which they pulled catfish, bass, and perch. Deer were plentiful, and the wild squirrels grew fat off the acorns and hickory nuts. Hunters could easily find white-tail deer, wild turkey, even possum, and raccoon if you had a taste for it. Wild hogs, wolves, and even the occasional black bear menaced the thick underbrush. There are rumors of black panthers that roam the area, though that has been hard to verify.

Eden wanted to explore these forests, but Miss Alma had forbidden it.

"Much too dangerous for a little snip of a thing like you. If the bottom landers don't get you, a black bear or a gator surely will. You just stay home, safe and sound, with ol' Alma here."

For the time being, she had obeyed.

Eden loved to make a cup of coffee early in the morning, sit on the porch and bathe her face in the morning sun. Rising Star had been beautiful, but in a different way, all desert and scrub brush, post oak savannahs, brown and dead looking for much of the year for want of water. But this! This was a paradise, shocked with color and the scents of primitive life and strange unclassified fauna.

She almost resented Miss Alma calling her to breakfast, pulling her back from where her senses had taken her. But this morning especially, she felt weary from the Harvest Ball the night before. She was still eating her breakfast when she was called away by a knock on the front door. Eden found a ruggedly handsome older gentleman in an expensive, white-linen business suit, standing on her porch. She thought she recognized him from the ball the night before, but she couldn't be sure.

"May I help you?" she asked.

"Eden Devereaux?"

"Yes, sir."

"I'm Jake Gresham, Paige's father."

Miss Alma appeared in the kitchen door behind Eden as if to let the man know that Eden was not alone.

"I've come to ask a favor," he said, as Eden asked if he'd like to come in.

"No, ma'am. I've come to ask you to sell me that crown you won last night. Paige has her heart set on it."

Eden was shocked. *How could such a thing be so important to Paige, that she'd send her father to purchase it on her behalf?* What Eden didn't understand was that it wasn't so much the crown that Paige wanted, but rather, the burning desire that Eden not have the thing.

"Mr. Gresham," Eden began.

But before she could continue, he said, "I'll give you a hundred dollars for the darn thing."

"But Mr. Gresham."

"Alright, two hundred!"

"Mr. Gresham, please stop. I have the crown right here." She stepped into the dining room and picked it up off the sideboard where she'd dropped it the night before. Eden held the crown out to Jake Gresham, but he only looked at it, then at her.

"How much then?"

"You don't understand, sir. I don't want anything for it."

"It's not for sale?" Jake looked confused. "But surely—"

"It's okay. It doesn't mean as much to me as it obviously does to Paige. Here, take it. Really, sir, I'd like her to have it."

This made no sense to him. But he didn't let Eden see how her generosity cut him to the quick and caused him to feel that uncomfortable shame that had defined so much of his adult life. All he could do was grab it and say, "Thank you," before hurrying away. Lizzie and Luther loped along after him and barked him on his way. He felt like a little boy being run off the place. "Blast Paige for her insatiable selfishness," he mumbled.

$$\vdash\!\!\!\prec\!\!\!\Vdash\!\!\!\succ\!\!\!\dashv$$

On the following morning, Afton did not appear at their back door as she did each morning. She sent no note, no message, and Eden fretted about it all day. Afton was such a responsible girl. But on the second day, when she was still absent, Eden decided to find out why.

"Afton's family has no phone?" Eden asked.

Miss Alma laughed, "You sure are ignorant of the bottom landers. No one down there calls anyone. Who'd they be callin'?"

"Where does Afton live?" Eden asked.

"Little girl, you know she's from the river bottom, deep in the Thicket."

"I know, but where? I'm going to drive down and check on her."

"Oh, no you ain't!"

"Why not?"

"There are reasons people don't go messin' 'round the river bottom. Too dangerous. Them bottom landers don't cotton much to townies. Even ol' Oz Delaney got more sense than to go down yonder."

"Okay. I'll give her one more day, but then I'm going."

"And I say no," Miss Alma declared, placing her hands on her considerable hips.

Eden was getting tired of everyone treating her like a southern belle simpleton who couldn't take care of herself. They seemed to block her at every turn, but not this time. Tomorrow she would go see about Afton, and she wouldn't let anyone stop her.

But as it turned out, she didn't have to because on the third day, Eden awoke to the smell of bacon filling the house and she knew the girl was back.

"I'm so sorry, Miss Eden. My mama was powerful sick. I just couldn't get away," Afton said.

"It's alright, Afton. Miss Alma and I did just fine."

"Yes 'um, little girl here's a mighty fine cook," Miss Alma chuckled, remembering Eden's burned toast. "And she was going a come in like the cavalry and rescue you down yonder."

Afton looked alarmed. "Oh no, Miss Eden, you must never go into the deep Thicket. It's much too dangerous."

"So everyone keeps telling me."

"But it's true! Please, don't ever go down there. You just don't know!"

"You are talking about where you live, Afton. Your home. The place where your family lives."

"Yes 'um."

"If it's so horrible, how can you live there?"

"It's different for me. They're my people. I'm not in harm's way."

"But I don't understand why I would be in harm's way if I simply came to see about you?"

"Little girl, you beat ev'rthing. Afton and I say, just don't go down there. So, just don't!"

Eden knew Miss Alma had ended it.

⊱⊰⊹⊱⊰

By mid-afternoon, Eden felt like a nap. She had spent the morning helping Miss Alma with the laundry, and now she felt like pampering herself. She gathered sweet-scented wildflowers as she returned to the house and laid them on her bed. The warm morning and the scalding laundry tubs had wilted her like collards in a steam pot, so she took a quick bath to relax, sank onto the overstuffed bed and closed her eyes, breathing in the sweet fragrance of the flowers.

But just as she was dozing off, she heard the murmuring of hushed voices. They drifted up to her from outside. She moved to the window to listen to the disembodied whispers below.

"But I'm alright. They didn't hurt me. You didn't need to worry so."

It was Afton.

"I can't help but worry. I love you so much." It was a hushed male voice.

"You must never go down there. They'd kill you for sure."

"I don't care. I'd rather take my chances than see you harmed in any way."

"But it didn't come to that. And I'm sure it won't."

"Sweet Afton," the man said. Then there was silence.

Eden smiled at the romantic interlude. Soon the man was hurrying across the yard and away from the house. Eden suspected he had left his car on the main road and walked in through the woods. When he reached the spot where the drive was swallowed up by the forest, he turned to wave to Afton.

Eden gasped, "Boone!"

She fell away from the window so he wouldn't see her, and when she looked again, he was gone.

Eden's smile broadened and crinkled the corners of her eyes, as she lay back down on the feather bed, her arms behind her head. She tried to nap, but it was no use. Her thoughts were electrified—the notions were so delicious. *Romeo and Juliet* right here in Two Rivers. Hadn't Ryder said that Boone was taken? Boone had denied it, but he hadn't been truthful. The truth was what she had just heard, Boone declaring his love for Afton. It was too, too delicious!

⊱═◈═⊰

Sleep was hard to find that night, and Eden found herself staring at the dark ceiling as the moon was covered by heavy, gray clouds. She breathed in deeply, and in the releasing of it, she heard muffled voices. They were just mumbles, two people talking, but there was a distinctive soft wailing in the background. Who would be here at that time of night and were they in distress? Perhaps someone was on the porch, someone in trouble and needing help.

She sat up and tried harder to hear. It seemed to be a man and woman quarreling. She tip-toed to her door and put her head into the hallway to listen better, but to her dismay, they seemed more muted than before. But it was the soft wailing that concerned her most.

She stepped into the hall and walked slowly to the top of the stairs. Nothing seemed amiss below, so she took courage and began to descend toward the voices. It was when her foot touched the last of the stairs that the voices suddenly quietened, and she paused. Only the cricket's chirps could be heard then. But the whole house seemed to be asleep.

Just then the moon escaped the clouds and filled the rooms with mellow light. All seemed as it should be. She moved slightly toward the rear of the house, her ears straining for any sound, but there was none.

She took two more steps when there came a slow grinding sound behind her. She turned slowly and in the muted light, she could see that the front door knob was moving ever so slowly. She stared at it as if hypnotized. Then her feet walked toward it with the thought that it might not be locked, and she needed to lock it quickly. But reason intervened, and she stopped and stayed back.

Just at that moment, the heavy oak door burst open to reveal the black silhouette of a dark, giant of a man, hair flying in the wind, with one arm raised menacingly as if wielding a weapon. A guttural moan escaped his mouth, and Eden screamed even louder.

She fled to Miss Alma's room off the kitchen, slammed and locked the bedroom door behind her, and flung herself across the bed onto the old woman.

"Miss Alma, Miss Alma! Wake up!"

She was sobbing with fear, as she felt the old woman's large arms wrap around her.

"A man! A huge man just broke into the front door."

She felt the old woman's arms tighten around her, but she quickly stood as best she could on her trembling legs and shouted, "Where is the gun? Don't you have a gun?"

But there was no sound.

"Miss Alma, please. Where is your gun?"

She rushed toward the dresser, hopeful that she would find the only hope they had. She felt for a gun, causing items to fall heavily to the floor, some shattering.

Just then the bedroom door flew open, and the lights flickered on. Eden was blinded for a moment, and all reason left her as she screamed, turning to face whatever enemy was at the door. To her shock, it was Miss Alma standing in the doorway.

"What is it, honey?" What you so upset 'bout?"

Eden half screamed, half gagged, as she turned back to stare at the old woman's rumpled bed.

"But you were in bed. I was hugging you." She began to cry, "I felt your arms around me."

"Not me, little girl. I heard some talking out on the back porch and went out to check on it. Then I heard you yellin'. Had trouble opening that old back door again. It seemed to be stuck for a little while. Then, funniest thing, that old door just opened by itself. Ain't that a funny thing? Then I come in here to hear you yellin' for my gun."

Eden stared back at the rumpled bed, and she could still feel the weight of the heavy arms that had embraced her. She rushed to Miss Alma, pushed her aside, and stared down the dark center hall. The front door was tightly closed, and there was no giant of a man standing there. None of it was real. None of it made sense to her. Eden couldn't stop trembling. Miss Alma could see how pale she was, so she set her down at the table and poured her some iced tea.

"I know it's late, but let's sit a spell and talk. I don't think you're wanting to go back up them stairs right now."

Eden made no objection and accepted the tea.

"There's something wrong with this house, Miss Alma."

"Little girl, you don't have to tell me that. I been in this house a long time. Nothin' goes on here surprises me."

"So, I'm not crazy?"

Miss Alma chuckled, "I 'spect we're all a little crazy down here in the Thicket, 'specially us folks on the river."

"I talk to it," Eden said slowly, dropping her head to stare at her iced tea.

"I know," Miss Alma said matter-of-factly.

"You do?"

"I hear you up there, havin' your little talks. I 'spect Afton has too."

"Oh no, I hope not."

Miss Alma smiled, "You don't understand. The house ain't a bad thing. We feel like it has taken care of us over the years. That's why me and Miss Annaliese loves it so. After all my days here, I'd be sad if it turned back to just a stack of wood and bricks. It's a comfort to me, 'specially now that the old age is on me."

"But what I saw in the front doorway wasn't anything you could call friendly. It was pure evil. I could feel it."

"Well now, there's lots in the Thicket that ain't friendly, and sometimes things come up to the house from that ol' muddy. But the house protects us."

"Not this time. This time it let something in, something awful."

"Sometimes we see things that ain't really there. I don't know why it let that nonsense happen to you. I do believe, though, that there was a purpose to it. Or the house would never have let it happen."

"Who do you think it could be?"

"The only man that comes to mind would be old Camden Gentry. There could be reasons he doesn't want you in the river house. He was a tall man, angry and mean in the end. And the house never liked him."

"You're talking about this house like it's just as much a person as you and I."

"This is the Big Thicket, little girl. We live in a different physical realm than elsewhere in Texas, full of all sorts of demons and devils. But lots of God-fearin' folks callin' down God's angels. Not those sweet, purty angels on Christmas cards. Angels that God sends are huge and powerful and in full armor. And ain't no force on this earth can claim victory over 'em. I just put my faith in God to keep us safe from what's lurkin' in the Thicket." She patted Eden's hand, "You should too. Those angels are here, watchin' everything this ol' house says and does, 'cause I call 'em down to help us every night."

Miss Alma's words were soothing, and Eden felt better hearing them. But still, she was glad when Miss Alma said, "Come on, little girl, and I'll walk you to the stairs and make sure the front door is locked. We need to get some sleep."

Miss Alma held onto Eden's arm as they walked to the front door and made sure the bolt was set correctly. It was. It had been locked the whole time. But that was not a comfort to Eden now. Locks didn't seem to matter. Miss Alma stood at the bottom of the stairs and watched as Eden ascended them.

When she reached the top step, Miss Alma said, "Remember, some things we think are there, ain't really there at all."

Eden looked up as she heard a soft giggle fade away through the high ceiling. She turned back to Miss Alma, who only smiled and motioned for her to go on to bed, and she did.

October yielded to November, and the air cooled considerably, causing Miss Alma to search for her wool coat. She had had it forever, a gift from the Ol' Missus when they both were younger. Once warm inside its many folds, Miss Alma constantly lifted the collar to her nose, the smell of it bringing back a flood of memories. Her children sat on her lap while she wore this coat year after year, their little bodies snuggling close. But they were all gone now. Just like her Thaddeus.

Eden thought the coat looked exhausted, like Miss Alma, but she knew Miss Alma would never give it up. Frayed threads soared loose from their once perfect seams, leaving gaps that let in the chill. But no matter, for porch sittin', the coat still served Miss Alma well.

Miss Alma was in a talkative mood that late afternoon. Eden knew it had been brought on by the stories that the old coat was telling her. Eden relaxed and listened as Miss Alma talked about her children.

"My, my, little girl. I can still see my Aubrey comin' up that drive, herdin' my whole parcel of younguns' before her. Every day 'bout this time they'd be comin' in from that ol' school down on the main road. It was a school for little colored children. They couldn't go to white folk's school back in them days, you know. The Ol' Missus had 'em put up that ol' one room down on the highway just 'cause of my babies. But once it was there, little colored babies began to pour out of these ol' woods and get some learnin'. Ol' Missus say they wouldn't be doin' nothin' in this world without gettin' some learnin'. She wanted to see all the little babies readin' before they went out into the world, so she paid for a teacher herself. A good thing she done, don't ya' think?"

"An excellent thing, Miss Alma."

"Aubrey, she helped her mama so. It all fell to her while I was up at the main house workin' for the family. But that little girl, she never complained. She was so glad to have a safe place to live. She just counted her blessin's and tended to her baby brother and sisters right well."

Eden wondered about Aubrey. *Had the Ol'Missus' investment in her paid off?*

Miss Alma continued, "That sweet girl, she done good for herself. The Ol' Missus, she help her pay to go to teachers' college over in Nacogdoches, and after a while, she was teachin' little babies herself, and sendin' money home to help her brothers and sisters go to school too. Done that all her life. Never even got hitched. Just helpin' them little babies to learn so they could be somebodies."

"Aubrey sounds like a wonderful person, Miss Alma. I know you must be so proud of her. Where is she now?" Eden asked.

"She's there," Miss Alma said, pointing across the field.

Eden half expected to see Aubrey walking up the drive. But following Miss Alma's pointed finger, she saw the tops of the gravestones over past the tree line. In that moment, she regretfully remembered that Miss Alma had said she had outlived all her children.

She had noticed the gravestones that first day when she wound her way up the dirt drive, but had not thought of them since. They seemed out of place, floating arched tops peeking nervously above the tall, wind-battered Johnson grass.

"The cemetery?"

"Yes, ma'am."

"Um, perhaps that will give me a clue as to who lived on this property before me."

Miss Alma smiled, "Just won't let it go, huh? You go look, little girl. But all you'll find down yonder is my babies. Ol' Missus put 'em there. She loved my babies like I did. Back then her man was buried there too. But the Ol' Missus' daughter, she dug her daddy up and moved him up to the big house. She said her daddy ain't sleepin' through eternity with a bunch of colored children. Ain't that a silly thing to do, little girl?"

"Seems silly to me," Eden agreed, "Silly or just plumb mean."

Miss Alma nodded, "Ain't nothin' but dust there now. All of 'em gone to be with Jesus. It just wasn't fittin' to disturb the Ol' Missus' man like that. Might near kilt the old Missus, it did."

"Does it still bother her?" Eden asked.

"You're a crafty ol' fox, little girl. Yes, the Ol' Missus is still alive. But not much bothers her these days. They say her mind is near gone now. I used to sit with her ever'day, but when her mind went bad, her daughter told me not to be botherin' her mama no more. They took her from me, me what's loved her, and put her in the care of strangers at some place I ain't never heard of before. They don't let me see her. Maybe she's dead by now. No, no she's not. I'll know in my spirit when she leaves this ol' world."

"She's still alive, Miss Alma."

Miss Alma's brow furrowed, and she slowly turned toward Eden.

"How do you know?"

"I just do."

Miss Alma took a deep breath. "It might near kilt me when they took her away. I was to take care of her forever. I just hope she ain't thinkin' I abandoned her. That plays heavy on my ol' mind. Life is hard, ain't it?"

Eden didn't answer. She didn't need to. A breeze clipped her face in a puff of piney woods scent, and her hair tapped her cheeks. Luther lifted his hind leg and began to scratch the back of his ear, as his metal tag jingled on his collar. *Perhaps it's time to shake things up*, Eden thought.

"She's in Rose Haven over in Coldspring."

Miss Alma's eyes grew huge.

"What you know 'bout that, little girl?" Miss Alma asked, her sadness turning to incredulity.

"More than you think." Eden couldn't help smiling a mischievous smile, knowing she'd piqued Miss Alma's curiosity.

But Miss Alma still frowned, "Who you been jawin' with?"

"Oh, different ones."

That began a season of Miss Alma fretting, pouting and muttering "Humph!" whenever Eden entered the room. After all, these were supposed to be Alma's secrets, not Eden's.

Zandy, no longer the runt of the litter, had grown strong over the last few weeks. On a lazy Saturday afternoon, Nub showed up at the back door to take the little piglet back to her mama. At first, Miss Alma looked stricken. Eden thought she was going to chase Nub off with the broomstick she was holding. But to Eden's surprise, she began to sweep away at the old, plank floor.

"Take her," Miss Alma said without looking up from her unnecessary chore.

"Now Alma, you knew it weren't forever," he muttered through those stained teeth.

"I know. Just take her. Go on. This time next fall she'll be on someone's breakfast plate."

Nub didn't move. A huge frown line joined the other deep ruts and crevices that crisscrossed his leathered face.

"Come on now, Alma."

"Ain't no never mind to me," she spit out. "Take her!"

Eden put an end to it by picking up the little piglet and handing her to Nub, who accepted her help gratefully. He'd never done anything against this old woman, and he didn't want to cause Miss Alma any more pain than she'd already known in her forsaken life. All he could do was nod in appreciation to the outsider, turn and disappear into the forests.

"Think I'll just lay down a spell," Miss Alma said.

Eden pondered how slowly she walked. Her feet seemed to drag with each step as if weighed down with lead sinkers.

"Tired, so tired," she mumbled as she closed the door.

Eden thought on how many times Miss Alma had lost her own little babies, and because life continues in a consistent pattern, she was still losing her babies. The thought of it left Eden feeling worn-out too. She washed Zandy's bottle and hid it in the back of the cabinet under the sink so Miss Alma wouldn't see it again. Then she carried the wooden box bed down to the barn and hung it on a nail in the back. Miss Alma didn't need to be reminded of the little piglet again.

That night as they sat on the porch, Lizzie and Luther came up and pressed their cold noses against Miss Alma's hands, then rested their heads on her knees. She rubbed the tops of those brindled heads and smiled again. Life went on.

⊱⋆⟡⋆⊰

"Aunt Mim, you ol' sea monkey! Been forever since I set eyes on ya'," Miss Alma said early the next morning to the giant standing on their back porch.

Aunt Mim was over six feet tall, broad, impressive and white as goat's milk, with freckles across her nose like a school-girl. Her salt and pepper hair was crimped and held with Miss Breck permanent clips in a knot on the top of her head. She wore coveralls and worn-out, muddy work boots. Eden wanted to grab her camera, but she only smiled. *Is there no end to the absurdity of Two Rivers?*

"This here must be the little gal I been hearin' so much about," Aunt Mim said, as she eyed Eden through wire-rimmed glasses that sat on the end of her small, but bulbous nose.

"Yes 'um. This little girl is Eden Devereaux. Little girl, this here is Aunt Mim."

"Miss Mim?" Eden mumbled, intimidated by the imposing size of the woman.

"Aunt Mim, honey. Everybody calls me Aunt Mim. I'm Mimosa Callahan."

"Callahan?"

"Yes 'um. I'm Clarice's sister-in-law. She's done a whole lot of talkin' about you. She thinks of you affectionately."

Miss Alma rummaged through the boxes Aunt Mim had brought and dumped some of it onto the countertops.

"Hot dog, Mim. Look at all that pork!"

"Cletus butchered early this year. Your freezer workin' good?"

"Absolutely!" Miss Alma said, looking further. "Sugar, salt, flour, meal, all there."

"I've got more."

Eden and Miss Alma followed her out and brought in boxes of laundry soap, a thick blanket, more cornmeal, sugar, and some large cans of lard.

"Aunt Mim takes care of all us country folk who ain't got ways to get into town. Been helpin' me out since Ol' Missus left."

"That's nice. But I can take care of things for Miss Alma now."

"Oh?" Aunt Mim said, eyeing the girl with raised eyebrows, "You stayin' here then?"

"I mean, as long as I'm here, I can help."

"How long will that be?" Aunt Mim asked.

"I don't know," Eden answered honestly.

"She has a feller over in West Texas," Miss Alma volunteered. "I heard him say he wanted her home by Christmas."

"A feller, you say?"

"Yes 'um, a nice lookin' feller," Miss Alma said.

"His name is Wynn Beckett, and I did tell him I'd *try* to be home for Christmas," Eden acknowledged.

"Home!" Aunt Mim clucked. "You silly child. This here's your real home, and you need to be takin' care of ol' Alma now."

"Aunt Mim, hush," Miss Alma cautioned.

Eden seized upon her words, "Why do you say this is my home, Aunt Mim?"

"Just is. That's all. You belong here."

"But why, Aunt Mim? Why do I *belong* here?"

Aunt Mim got right in her face, looking down nose to nose, and sputtered, "Cause I'm Aunt Mim and I say so! Besides, Alma wants you here, and that's good enough for me."

Miss Alma chuckled, "You don't be agitatin' Aunt Mim, little girl. We all tip-toe 'round her ever since she kilt her husband down on the river bottom. No siree, we keep our thoughts to ourselves, she's such a gruff ol' billy."

There was a moment when Miss Alma's words hung in the air like a feather floating in slow motion, no sound, no movement, no breath. It was the word 'kilt.' Then both women laughed out loud.

"You ol' toad," Aunt Mim bellowed, "You'll have this child believin' you!"

"Why not? Can't say it ain't sort'a true, now can ya'?"

"No, not exactly, but you don't need to be scarin' this child. Eden, I'm not as scary as folks 'round here say I am."

To Eden's disappointment, the conversation turned to what Mimosa Callahan was growing in her fall garden this year.

Later, they watched as Aunt Mim bumped her station wagon across the grassy yard and headed on her way.

"Where's she going now?" Eden asked.

"Down to the bottom landers, I 'spect. They love to see her ol' station wagon comin'."

"But I thought you said they don't let townies go down there?"

"Did you get a good look at Mim, little girl? Aunt Mim goes anywhere she pleases. Ain't nobody 'bout to mess with her. Them people down there respect her good and proper. She takes 'em food, clothes, and medicine. She's an old bobcat, but she's a good-hearted old bobcat. She'd give you the shirt off her back if you needed it."

"But we don't. Haven't I been bringing groceries home for us? My mother left me plenty of money. We don't need Aunt Mim's charity."

"Ain't charity—just kindness. Ol' Missus gave Aunt Mim a large sum of money to do this for me. I reckon I'll be with my Thaddeus long before that money is gone. She gives Mim money to help out the bottom landers too. My Ol' Missus' is a sweet thing, a tired, sad, old sweet thing."

"I'd like to meet her."

"Over my dead and bleached out bones. You'll not be pesterin' her at this stage of her life."

Eden backed down quickly. She understood that Annaliese Gentry was beyond talk and reason anyway. Clarice had assured her that the head of the Gentry clan didn't have enough reason left in her aged head to give Eden any answers. But the thought of meeting the Gentry matriarch still intrigued her, and she knew in her heart-of-hearts that one day soon, she surely would.

# Ten

Miss Alma and Eden finished with supper and saw Afton off to her home downriver. They settled on the front porch, watching and listening. The fireflies were so numerous that the Big Thicket seemed lit up like a Christmas tree. Lizzie and Luther began to cry deep in their throats. Not a menacing growl or a whimpering fear, just guttural noises that came across as resigned and forlorn.

"Yep. They'll be here soon. Lizzie girl, she knew it first. Hear them ol' hounds whinin'?"

"Yes, ma'am."

Miss Alma seemed to be expecting someone. Eden was indeed curious, but she had learned Miss Alma liked secrets and surprises. She reckoned the old woman wanted her to ask who was coming. But she felt mischievous and said nothing.

"Yep, they'll be here soon."

Miss Alma cocked her head to see Eden out of the corner of her dark, brown eyes.

"I guess so," Eden shrugged. She could feel Miss Alma's agitation, and the corners of her mouth curled, but she said nothing more.

Miss Alma frowned, "Jehoshaphat, little girl! Ain't you at all curious!"

"No, not particularly."

"You best be, 'cause they is here," she said, pointing behind Eden.

*Oh sure,* Eden thought, and she turned to look behind her. As she suspected, no one was there. She felt Miss Alma had to be proud of her deception, and of Eden's gullibility. She turned back to Miss Alma, an unamused smirk on her face, when she felt a slight pressure on her knee. Eden looked down at a tiny hand, five little fingers with long nails, quite human looking except for the grayish-brown fur. Slowly lifting her gaze, she was looking at two black, shoe-button eyes. She hurled herself from the chair, upsetting a bowl of field peas Miss Alma had been snapping earlier and leapt behind the old woman, who was laughing so hard she tilted her chair backward.

"Whoa, chair!" Miss Alma laughed. "Little girl's got company alright."

"Miss Alma, what in the Sam Hill?"

"Stay yourself, silly girl. Their just my ol' friends."

Drawing in a calming breath, Eden could see that it was two raccoons. The raccoons moved to her feet and sniffed them. They stood up on their hind legs, clinging to her jeans, and tried to peer up at her.

"Are they safe?"

"Now that's a matter of opinion. Took down old Lizzie once, and she ain't never been the same. She and Luther, they stay clear of these two. They know me, and they ain't never hurt me. Now you ..." Miss Alma smiled, "I don't know 'bout you."

"What do they want?"

"Somethin' to eat, I reckon."

"You stay here and entertain your guests," Eden said, sliding down the porch wall toward the door. "I'll get them something to eat."

She hurried into the house and let the screen door slam, as she heard Miss Alma say, "Bring 'em the left-over cornbread. They like that."

Eden did as she was told. Standing just inside the screen door, she shoved the screen open and tossed the cornbread over the edge of the porch into the yard. The two coons leapt from the porch and fell on the bread like starving children. Lizzie and Luther bounced to their feet when the cornbread hit the ground, not ten feet from them. But the masked coons were on it before the hounds could even move toward it. The old dogs, resigned, settled back onto their pine needle nests in the yard.

"Where did they come from?" Eden asked, sitting down and leaning forward to watch the pair.

"The little one there, that's Queen Esther. Nub found her as a sucklin'. Her mama was kilt by a car up on the highway. I nursed her with a baby bottle just like I did my little Zandy. She was as tame as a kitten till she got it into her head she wanted a husband. Then there was no more messin' with her scratchin' and clawin'. We finally just let her go. A short time later she come scratchin' at the back door, and she had that old male with her. We call him Sampson. We give 'em food when they come callin'. They know this here's a safe place."

"They really are cute."

"Yep. One spring they come marchin' up with three little young'uns in tow. Cutest little things, all marchin' in a straight line. First Old Sam, then Queenie, and last the babies. I sure wish I had me a picture of that now." She sighed, "Their visits'll get fewer and fewer, and someday we'll realize the time's been too long, and they'll either be dead or turned back into the wild. I'll miss 'em then."

Miss Alma laid her head back and hummed some lullaby Eden didn't recognize.

"Yes, 'em. Time will come when they won't come back. Just like all the babies."

❧━❊━❧

When Eden entered the kitchen the following morning, Afton met her with such innocence that it melted Eden's heart. *How young she is,* Eden thought. *No wonder she and Boone had to keep their relationship a secret.*

"Oh, Miss Eden, have you seen what a beautiful mornin' it is? Just look at all that sunshine out there." Afton was smiling from ear to ear.

"You're happy this morning," Eden said. "A body would think it was more than just the sunshine."

"A body would be right," she said softly, while setting Eden's scrambled eggs on the table.

"Where's Miss Alma?" Eden asked.

"She's doing laundry down in the shed. I tried to stop her, told her to let me do it, but she just said she needed some mind clearin' and to let her be. So, I did just that. Is that okay, Miss Eden?"

"Of course, it is."

Afton suddenly stood totally erect and put her hand over her mouth.

"Oh dear ... going to be ... sick ..."

Afton flung herself out onto the back porch and emptied her stomach of her breakfast over the porch's edge. Eden came out with a cup of cool water and a wet cloth, but Afton shooed her away.

"Don't look, Miss Eden. It'll shame me sure."

"Then let me leave these here," Eden said, setting them down on an upturned washtub and returning inside the house. Through the open door, she could see Miss

Alma coming across the yard. The old woman was frowning at Afton, but Afton motioned her into the house before collapsing on the porch steps and wiping her face with the wet cloth.

"Humph!" Miss Alma said.

"What?" Eden asked.

"Just ain't fittin' for that young girl. Devil is an evil ol' thing. He always muddies up the waters."

"What?"

"I may have to take a razor strap to that bottom land girl."

Eden was surprised at Miss Alma's lack of sympathy.

"But the poor girl is sick. I hope she doesn't have the flu. It's too early in the season for the flu, don't you think?"

"Ain't got nothin' to do with the flu," the old woman spat.

Eden watched as Miss Alma washed a clump of radishes she'd pulled from the garden earlier that morning, and began to cut off the green, leafy tops with their red and white color silhouetted against the cocoa brown of her hands.

"Too late in the season to be growin' up radishes too. But here they is."

Eden said nothing.

"I tell you, it ain't fittin'!"

"Okay Miss Alma, what is not fitting?"

"That child gets sick ever' mornin' 'bout this time."

It suddenly dawned on Eden what Miss Alma was inferring.

"Pregnant? You think she's pregnant?"

"I sure do. It's them bottom landers down there. Don't got a lick of sense in any of 'em. Won't let no preacher go down there to teach 'em right from wrong, so the babies just grow up heathen' like. I was hopin' better for Afton. But she's just like the rest of them old hound dogs. Oh, she's prettier. But she's just like 'em, pretty and stupid and now she's in a family way. Got no chance now to make it out of them dark woods."

There was a gasp, and the two women turned to see Afton standing in the doorway with a stricken look on her face. She covered her face with her hands and began to whimper.

"Lord preserve me," she sobbed. "Oh, Miss Eden, what you must think of me."

Eden helped the girl to a chair at the table and sat down opposite her. "Is it true? Are you going to have a baby?"

"I don't know," she sobbed, then softer, "Maybe." She hadn't really allowed herself to think about it.

"Are you or ain't you?" Miss Alma demanded.

"Miss Alma, please," Eden said as the girl buried her face in her arms as they rested on the table, unable to look at the others.

Miss Alma frowned at Afton and wiped her hands on her apron, "Girl, when was your last time?"

"Last time? Too long ago, I 'spect."

"Then you is!"

"Oh, merciful Father God!" Afton said and began to sob louder.

Miss Alma stood over her, "Who's the pa?"

Afton only shook her head.

"You got to tell us, girl. He has to own up to his part and take responsibility."

Still no answer.

"Girl! He's got to marry you. Do you hear me! Your papa'll beat it out of you. He'll see to it that the snake who's done this marries you."

Eden gently took Afton's hand.

"Don't you want to marry this man?"

"Oh yes, ma'am, more than anything, I do." Afton's eyes lit up.

"Then you love him?"

"With all my heart, Miss Eden. How could I be in this way if I didn't? But I'm so ashamed."

How innocent she seemed at that moment.

"Then we'll just be about planning a wedding."

But that only made Afton start to cry again.

"Lordy," Miss Alma exclaimed, "Must be somethin' wrong with the feller. You been foolin' 'round with an already married man, girl?"

"No, ma'am. Oh, no ma'am."

"I'm plumb perplexed," Miss Alma said, throwing her hands up in the air.

There was a moment of silence. Eden said softly, "Do you think your folks know?"

"No ma'am, no one could."

"Does the ol' snake who's done this know?" Miss Alma asked.

"No, ma'am." Afton stared at her hands on the table. She couldn't look either woman in the eye.

Eden broached things slowly, "Afton, I know the whole of it."

Afton's eyes, filled with pain, finally stared back at Eden.

"Oh no, Miss Eden, you couldn't."

"But I do."

"You mean he told you 'bout us?"

"No, but I know anyway."

Miss Alma looked confounded.

"Then you tell me, little girl. Who is he?" Miss Alma demanded.

"It's not my place to tell anyone. That has to come from Afton."

"Then start the tellin' of it, Afton, before I strangle you."

"Afton, excuse Miss Alma's manners. You know she would never hurt you."

The old woman croaked her familiar "Humph!"

"But think, Afton. We are your friends. You're going to need friends now. You're going to need our help."

"But what can you do?"

"We won't know until you open up to us. Trust us and let us help you. Surely you can see the sense in that."

There was a long silence, then Miss Alma settled down and said, "Girl, you are in one big mess. Guess we might as well embrace it. We'll look for the hidden joy and focus on that."

Her words melted Afton's heart. She realized Miss Alma didn't hate her after all.

Afton sat still, staring at the milk jug on the table, and when she finally spoke, her words seemed tired and resigned. She looked at Miss Alma, "My baby's father is … Boone Bohannon."

Now it was Miss Alma's turn to gasp, "Oh, my lawdy have mercy. A townie!"

⊰⸎⊱

It was a simple thing really. They told Afton's family that Miss Alma had become seriously ill and Afton needed to move into the river house to take care of her twenty-four hours a day. When Eden offered to double the girl's wages, which usually went directly to Afton's father, Carl T., they readily agreed. Two days later, Nub brought the girl upriver with almost everything she owned in the world packed in two brown grocery boxes. Eden put her in the bedroom across the hall from her own room.

Afton felt strange being in the family's quarters, but she couldn't stand up to Eden, and she knew it. Her Miss Eden had become special to her. She would never go against anything Miss Eden told her to do.

"But Miss Eden, I shouldn't be up here at all," she said, as a last protest.

"Nonsense, Afton. The only reason Miss Alma is not up here is that she has such trouble climbing the stairs. A time may come when you do too. If that happens, we'll put a bed in the back parlor for you."

"Nobody's ever been as nice to me as you, Miss Eden," the girl said, throwing her arms around Eden. Then, as if mortified by what she had done, she pulled away and blushed.

Eden put her hand on the girl's shoulder and said, "Oh, I suspect one other person has been nicer. Boone is such a nice young man. You're lucky he loves you and chose you over all those other girls in town he could have had. Y'all made a mistake. God forgives us when we make mistakes if we're truly sorry and ask Him to forgive. Do you know what the Bible says about that forgiveness?"

Afton shook her head no.

"It says he throws it in the deepest part of the sea and remembers it no more. Think about that. As far as God is concerned, it never happened. And he is not happy with the folks that go fishing in those waters to bring it up again."

Afton's childlike grin spread across her face, "Miss Eden, what should I do now?"

"I think it's time to give Boone Bohannon a call."

# Eleven

It was nearly six-o-clock when the black Ford pickup came bumping down the drive. Ryder applied the brakes too quickly, and the tires slid across the pallet of pine needles, causing Lizzie and Luther to skitter away.

"Hello, Ryder," Eden called from the porch.

"Hello yourself, Miss Eden," he replied.

"And Boone."

"Hello, Miss Eden."

"Just Eden, guys."

"Okay 'just Eden,'" Ryder grinned.

"You two are just in time. We've laid out a nice supper table for you. Would you like to wash up?"

"What? No finger bowls on the table?" Ryder asked. "Why, I heard you West Texas gals are all curtsy and bob, but not much substance."

"Did you now? I'll have you know when I invite guests, I expect them to behave."

"Wrong guests then, ma'am," Ryder said, winking at Boone.

"My lady," Ryder said, bowing in a courtly gesture, and offering Eden his arm. She led them to the dining room where the table gleamed beneath an ivory Battenberg lace cloth. The old china was Flow Blue, and the Ol' Missus' silver glistened in the soft glow of the candles.

Ryder pulled out the chair at the head of the table and Eden took her place as the men sat to either side of her. The kitchen door swung open and Afton tip-toed in, carrying a tray on which rested three small plates of salad. Boone placed his hands on the table's edge as if to rise, while he kept his eyes on the girl, but she didn't look at him. She placed a plate in front of each of them, and retreated to the doorway, pausing as she heard Eden say, "Could you bring another salad, please."

Afton looked confused. "Yes, ma'am."

There was a moment's silence as Ryder and Boone shared curious looks across the table.

"I thought Afton left here before dark came. The river ain't safe after dark," Boone said.

"Sometimes things change. Sometimes for the better, sometimes for the worst. Only time will tell," Eden said, slowly for effect.

"Uhm, how mysterious," Ryder grinned.

"Afton will be staying here all the time, at least for a while."

"How'd you get her old man to agree to that?" Boone asked.

"I believe it's what we call money."

"Ooooh."

Afton returned with the extra salad.

"Where shall I put this, Miss Eden?"

"Here," Eden said, removing her own salad.

Afton looked confused. Eden caught the girl's wrist as she stood. Both men rose simultaneously.

"Sit here in my place, Afton," Eden said.

"Oh, no ma'am. I couldn't."

"You can, and you will," Eden said, catching her by the shoulders and forcing her into the chair. "Ryder, pick up your salad. We'll take supper in the kitchen. These two have some talking to do."

Ryder was curious, but he did as he was told without comment and followed Eden from the room.

Boone could only stare after them as they left. Once the door closed behind them, he looked down at Afton who hadn't raised her face from the salad. When she finally looked up at him, he loved the way the candlelight made her green eyes sparkle. To Boone, she looked small and fragile, sitting there stock still, not allowing herself to breathe deeply. He slowly returned to his chair, placed his hand below her chin and lifted her face toward him.

"Afton, what's going on?"

"Miss Eden, she's been so good to me, Boone."

"That's good. I'm glad you'll be staying here around the clock, even for a little while. I don't feel like you're safe down on the river bottom."

With huge, green eyes shining, she said, "I love you, Boone. I always will, no matter what you do. I don't ever want to do anything to hurt you. I'd rather die first."

Boone took her hand. "Afton, what's wrong?"

She couldn't look at him, and she felt tears forming as she continued, "I won't tie you down. I mean, you have such a good life layin' out in front of you. You should be free to do what you want. And I—"

"Afton, are you breaking up with me?"

"Oh no, Boone. It's not that."

"Then what is it?"

She bit her lip hard so he wouldn't notice it's trembling. She drew in a deep breath and in the releasing of it, she formed the words, "I'm going to have a baby."

Boone couldn't hide the shock in his eyes, and she recoiled from it. But immediately the jolt of her words subsided, and he sat back with a smile.

"A baby? You're going to have my child?"

She wondered if he was questioning that he was the father. Words flashed in bright bursts in her head. *See*, her head said, *he accuses you. He doesn't really love you. You'll be alone now. You will be cursed. God won't accept you.* Tears began to run down her cheeks as she began to imagine what it would be like to be an unwed mother. Her life was already hard. How much more could she bear?

"You're angry," she said.

"Oh no, sweetheart," he said, leaning in and taking her face in his hands. "Afton, I do love you. And I want to marry you. You can't possibly doubt that. I didn't know how I could make that happen. But this will help speed things up. It'll give your daddy a reason to let us be married. Don't you see? We'll be alright."

Tears still flowed, but now they were borne out of relief rather than fear. Her arms wrapped around him in pure joy. But truth intervened.

"But Boone," she whimpered, "Papa will never agree with us gettin' married. If he finds out, he'll kill you."

"We'll figure out a way," Boone said.

"No, Papa's too dangerous. He must never know it was you. I can't marry you, Boone. It would be a death sentence for you. Don't you see?"

Her voice became frantic, and he tried to calm her by speaking softly and slowly, "We will find a way. I promise you."

But even as he spoke the words, her head shook a resigned no against his cheek. Dread settled over her.

〜❖〜

The middle of November brought days of heavy rain, and the earth swelled along with Afton's belly. It was becoming noticeable now, and Eden feared that someone would see, releasing all the fury of the world on them. It seemed a strange thing for a body to be so afraid of her own father. Yet Eden knew Afton was terrified of the man, and what Carl T. Donner would do if he knew. Boone wanted to marry her, but her fear for Boone held her back. As long as they didn't know about Boone, he would be safe.

Eden knew Afton would never tell who the father was. But Afton's brother had seen them together once early on, and when he told his papa, Old Carl T. had taken his strap to her. He was so angry and brutal. He might have beaten her to death if her mother had not intervened. Afton never told Boone, never let him see the bruises, never confessed that *that*, is why she missed those days working for Miss Eden.

Boone came every evening after work, and Eden allowed them to sit in the front parlor together. Eden liked Boone, and she trusted him.

Sometimes Ryder came with Boone and Eden would sit with him on the front porch. He made her laugh, and she needed that. Ryder looked so much like a little boy, with his baby blue eyes and mischievous, dimpled grin. Eden could tell he was expecting more from her than she was willing to give, but these restless autumn nights worked wicked magic on a heart, creating a light-headed flurry of sparks that were, at the least, disconcerting.

On one of those hypnotic nights, she let Ryder sit close and hold her hand. But it was Wynn she thought of when she crawled into bed that night, and she felt wicked to have led Ryder on.

Clarice invited Eden to have Thanksgiving dinner with the Callahans, but Eden regretfully declined. She couldn't leave Miss Alma and Afton alone on Thanksgiving. They were her family now. Besides, she had finally gotten them to agree to sit down to a Thanksgiving meal in the formal dining room.

Boone and Ryder were coming too since Eden planned the meal for noon and the men would have the time to be with their own families later in the day.

"This ol' dining room's so glad to be used again," Miss Alma said, as she laid out the table. "It'll be like ol' Thanksgivin's past. Only no babies. Holidays needs babies, now don't they!" Then she remembered Afton, and shut her mouth, worried that she had been insensitive.

Ryder and Boone came early, at eleven. Boone sought out Afton, who was in the kitchen basting the turkey. Her eyes lit up as she watched him pass through the kitchen door. Her hands were in heavy oven mitts, and she didn't know what to do with them as he lifted her up to swing her around the room before planting a kiss squarely on her lips.

"Happy Thanksgiving, little sweetheart!" he said before turning to the stove. "Smells great in here."

"I love cookin' for you, Boone. I hope you like everything. I know how much you love pumpkin pie, so I made two."

Miss Alma came bustling into the warmth.

"Shoo, shoo now, the two of you. It's all done now. Just needin' a little more time in the oven. Now shoo out of my kitchen."

Boone walked Afton out onto the coolness of the back porch and moved to the far end where Miss Alma was out of earshot. He sat down on the steps and pulled Afton down beside him. They hadn't been out there long when those inside the house heard a loud whoop and holler.

"Yeee haw! Yeee haw! Hey, everyone!"

Boone was pulling Afton through the back door.

"Gosh a' Mighty, everyone! We're off the carpet for good!" He pulled Afton along the center hall toward the front door.

Eden and Ryder stood in the parlor doorway. "What in the Sam Hill is it, Boone?" Ryder demanded.

"She'll marry me! The little girl'll marry me! Whenever I say. And the sooner, the better!"

Miss Alma was standing in the kitchen doorway clapping her hands together as Boone scooped Afton up in his arms and swung her in a wide circle, her feet kicking in the air. Eden was caught up in it too and cheered for them. Ryder lifted Eden and began to swing her around too, even though she protested and pushed against him. In a gale of bubbling giggles and whoops, the men jostled through the front door and swung the girls out onto the porch.

"Whoa there," someone said, and the twirling motion stopped abruptly, as all four looked down at J. D. and Paige at the foot of the porch steps. Ryder and Boone dropped the girls, feet first, and righted them as they, simultaneously, stepped away from them, as if they'd been caught doing something childishly wrong. Eden felt light headed and wondered about Afton. She glanced at the girl and was immediately drawn to her melon shaped belly. Eden felt the taste of fear scorch the back of her throat. She flashed on Paige, who was staring at Afton and watched, mesmerized, as an evil smile began to spread across Paige's lips. Certainly, no one else was smiling then.

J. D. spoke first, "My mother sent this over for your Thanksgiving dinner," he said to Eden, holding out a stack of three covered Pyrex bowls. Ryder stepped in front of Eden and took them.

"That's so nice of her," Eden said. "Please thank her for me, until I can thank her myself."

There was another awkward silence. Quickly Eden asked if they'd like to come in and have some raspberry tea. They were all relieved when J. D. declined.

He whisked Paige back into his car, and wishing all a happy Thanksgiving, hurried away from the strange encounter.

⊱━━⊰

As he turned onto Camp Ruby Road, J. D. tried to figure out what had just happened. There had never been awkwardness between him, Ryder and Boone before, but that had definitely been awkward. He was unnerved that their close friendship could fray so suddenly. They, Ryder and Boone, were still tightly bonded, one for all and all for one. He was the one feeling like an outsider, and he didn't like the feel of it.

"What was that all about?" he finally asked, noticing how still and quiet Paige was.

"Wasn't it obvious?"

"What?"

"Didn't you see?"

J. D. was baffled.

"That servant girl!" She turned slowly and deliciously made her point. "She's obviously pregnant."

His mind hadn't acknowledged what his eyes had seen until Paige spoke it out loud. But, as if a light flickered on, he suddenly knew.

"Afton Donner?"

"Obviously!"

"Oh, brother! There's trouble!"

"Trouble for Boone!" she said.

"Boone?"

"Didn't you see how intimate he was with her. It's his, alright."

"But Paige, she's from the river bottom."

"I know. That must be why they've kept her hidden out here. I bet no one knows. Especially that old daddy of hers. And did you see that West Texas strumpet?"

J. D. cringed at the slur.

"Why, she's out there carrying on with Ryder as well."

"Now wait. You don't know any of that."

"You saw them. That was more than just a Baptist picnic going on!"

"Paige," he said, wanting to change the course of the conversation, "we can't tell anyone about this. Do you hear me? Not even my mom or your dad. Absolutely no one. It's none of our business."

But Paige had turned from him and was staring out the window as the pines sped by in shades of pastoral greens and deep emeralds. It was then that the malice she had against Eden began to germinate into an achievable plot of revenge. And Afton would pay the price.

# Twelve

The weeks that followed Thanksgiving saw a dark pall over Two Rivers, and it unnerved the three women living in the old house on Camp Ruby Road. The sky looked like a Texas Blue Norther, but without the intense chill. Indian summer was hanging on too long. The sun became a stranger, retreating behind overcast skies day after day, and the house had begun to speak to Eden again.

Mid-morning found her sitting cross-legged on her bed, thumbing through a copy of *Seventeen*. Eden heard the house breathe deeply, and she looked up to see her bedroom door slowly inch open. She waited, but no one entered.

"Afton?" But there was no answer.

She walked to the door, her bare feet tip-toeing as if she might disturb the house. But no one was there. The hallway was empty and darker than usual. Eden realized she had been holding her breath, and she let it out as she tip-toed back to the bed, leaving the door ajar.

There was a groan. Or was it a cough from the lungs of the house as it sucked in air from the slightly cracked window and set the curtains to fluttering. The white lace danced away from the skin of the walls. Slowly, purposefully, the door closed itself, the sound of the latch clicking bounced off the bedroom walls.

*That had been no trick of the wind,* she thought. *The closing of it was too slow.* This time she leapt from the bed and threw the door open. As she expected, there was no one in the hallway. She closed the door again, turned as she put her hands on her hips and said, "I am not afraid of you! Now go away and leave me alone!"

A quietness received her words as she stood still, listening, drawing in strength from her boldness. The sound of a little girl's laughter came softly into the room and encircled her. She turned in a circle as she slowly followed the giggles around her until it finally faded away. But she had seen no one, not Miss Alma, not Afton, and especially not the little girl who had chosen to team up with the house in attempting to scare her away. *Or is she there to warn me?*

It was the closet door that chose to slam just then. At that sound, her courage failed her, and she abandoned the room for now.

"Come on, Miss Alma," she said, sailing into the kitchen, her keys already in her hands. "You and I are going for a drive."

The old woman looked at her suspiciously.

"Why don't you come too, Afton?"

"I think I need to lie down awhile, Miss Eden, if that's okay with you."

"Of course, it is. I don't think we'll be gone long."

Eden drove Miss Alma away from the town and alongside the river. It was the first-time Miss Alma had been in a convertible.

"Lawdy, lawdy, I feel like a movie star."

The wind whipped her hair in all directions until Eden handed her a scarf and laughed as Miss Alma tried to stabilize the damage. The trees were still slightly speckled in their fall colors, displayed like breathtaking tapestries.

Even as the two women enjoyed them, the wind was shaking the colored leaves from their trees, sending them swirling to the ground in red and gold flames. As the car sped over them, they were whipped up into the air again for one last dance, before they drifted back to the roadway to languish and decay. *All living things must die.*

At noon, Eden pulled into the Feedlot Café. Miss Alma grabbed Eden's arm and said, "I can't go in there. It's a white folk's place."

"Don't be silly. I hear they have the best barbeque in town."

"Maybe so, but won't be given me none of it."

"I'm not going in without you!"

"Then none of us be goin' in."

"Oh yes, we are," Eden insisted.

With that, Eden dislodged Miss Alma from the car and pulled her through the café door. At first, the café grew silent. Then a low murmur began to spread from table to table, as the waitress approached them in the doorway.

"Can I help you, ladies?"

"We'd like a table, please," Eden said.

The waitress, chewing gum, stared at them nervously before shooting a look over her shoulder at the others who watched them as if they were specimens under a microscope.

"We don't serve coloreds in here."

"That's ridiculous," Eden said. "All we want is a little barbeque. We heard yours was the best in town."

"That's true. But, like I said, we don't serve coloreds. Now if your friend would like to go around to the back door, we'll give her a plate to go."

Eden's shock turned to anger, and she wasn't about to let Miss Alma be treated like this. She dug her heels in stubbornly and prepared herself to go head to head, knowing the waitress would have to back down eventually if she saw how resolute Eden was.

"You can't be serious! You have plenty of empty tables. We'll take one now, thank you," Eden insisted. Her loyalty caused her to make an Alamo-style stand for what she felt was Miss Alma's honor, and she drew a line in the sand with her imaginary saber.

Eden took one step forward when a heavy hand grabbed her arm and squeezed it painfully, causing her to wince. She turned and stared into the angry eyes of Jake Gresham. He looked different from the morning he stood on her porch in his crisp, linen suit. Now he wore jeans and a western shirt, and his boots were caked with mud, evidence that, like most men in Two Rivers, he ran cattle on the side.

He spoke slowly, "We don't want her kind in here, girl. And we don't need any outsider telling us different."

But even as Eden's eyes flashed anger, someone else gently pulled her away from Jake Gresham's grip.

"Now Jake, calm down. There's no need for this," J. D. Callahan said, placing his hand on both women's backs and guiding them toward a table in a far corner. Over his shoulder, he said, "I'll share my table with the ladies. No harm was done here. We'll just have three lunch specials and be on our way."

One couple, disgusted, gathered their things up and huffed out of the café. A few more stared angrily at the back of Miss Alma's head. But there were the others, and there were more of them, who wondered why Miss Alma should be treated so impolitely. Miss Alma was silent, carefully studying her hands folded in her lap. Those kind souls who were sympathetic tried to catch her eye with a kind smile of encouragement. It was all they dared do in a public place, under public scrutiny. After all, they had to live with these people, and people could be cruel. Though they tried to express their sympathy with their eyes, Miss Alma would not look up at anyone out of fear for what she'd see there.

"Blast it, Eden! What are you thinking?" J. D. growled, once they were all seated and people went on with their meals.

"Don't jump on her, Mr. J. D. She just don't know. She's just a baby girl. Ain't walked in the real world much."

"Putting you both through this isn't the best way to learn!"

Eden felt his anger. He was harsh, and she wasn't sure why. Hadn't he been on her side?

"I'm sorry. I didn't know things were still like this."

J. D. softened, "That place you're from, Rising Star, they don't have many colored folks, do they?"

"No. I don't know of any. It's a small place."

"So, you've never seen the reality of prejudice, have you?"

"I guess not," she said softly.

Miss Alma reached out and patted Eden's hand. J. D. could see the affection she had for the girl.

"Eden," he said, "things will change. I'm sure of that. But it'll take time. And for some, it'll be a painful evolution. But Eden, Miss Alma's too old to fight that battle. It's best left to others."

"I didn't know this was going to happen. Otherwise, I never would have insisted she come in here. She tried to tell me so, but I'm just so headstrong. I'm sorry, Miss Alma."

"Baby girl, don't fret none. I don't. I just move along like the flow of that ol' muddy. I don't pay no never mind to folks like in here."

They heard Jake Gresham's voice vibrate across the room. "Nora, don't you dare serve that old colored. If she wants barbeque, she can dang well come over here and get it herself," he said, holding his language in check in deference to the ladies in the room. Jake Gresham was angry, and Eden thought there was more to his anger than just this. She was also sure Jake would tell Paige about this and J. D. would have to deal with Paige's anger too.

She told Miss Alma to remain seated as she rose to get their plates. But J. D. caught her shoulder and pushed her back into her chair.

"I'll get them," he said.

Eden started to open her mouth, but the look in J. D.'s eyes brought her into instant submission. She allowed herself the peace of his handling of it.

J. D. crossed the room and retrieved two plates of barbeque. He placed Miss Alma's down first, then Eden's. Then he brought the iced tea that Nora had put on the bar. Nora followed him back with his plate and tea and served him. As she leaned over them, she said under her breath, "Sorry y'all. It ain't me, but y'all know how Jake gets."

"Don't worry about it, Nora," J. D. said.

When she walked away, Eden said, "But J. D., I hope we haven't gotten you in trouble with your fiancée's father."

Fiancée? That sounded strange to J. D. and wasn't exactly true.

"Jake Gresham thinks too highly of himself," he said.

"So, does that li'l gal of his," Miss Alma added.

Her remark shocked Eden, but J. D. only laughed and said, "Paige is a handful. Just like old Jake."

"Two peas in a pod," Miss Alma grinned. "That man could use killin'."

"What?" Eden said surprised.

J. D. grinned, "You know, Eden, in Texas ''cause he needed killin' is a valid legal defense."

That made them laugh, and Eden hoped folks were still watching to see how unaffected they were by their cruelty.

"Tell me, Eden, what have you found out about your mysterious benefactor?" J. D. asked.

"Not too much. I've mostly found out that people around here keep their secrets to themselves."

"Sounds like a good virtue to me," J. D. said.

"Only if you're the one holding the secrets."

Eden looked at J. D., and her eyes pleasured him. She was speaking to him, but he was lost in the look of her. She saw him tilt his head to study her face and she could tell he wasn't really listening.

"... do know that much ... Gentry land ... Annaliese Gentry ... but don't know why."

He willed himself back to her words.

"I just don't know why the Gentry family hasn't approached me to get their land back. Your mom told me they've never let an inch of that land leave the family. From what I hear, with Annaliese Gentry's mind gone, they could have her declared incompetent and would have grounds for suing to get it back."

"You're making a good case for them. Tired of Two Rivers already?" J. D. smiled.

"No, of course not. I like Two Rivers."

Eden suddenly remembered that she hadn't told Miss Alma all she knew. When she looked at the old woman, she saw dark, saucer-shaped eyes staring at her.

"You knowed all that?" Miss Alma said.

"Yes ma'am, but I don't know it all, not the important things. J. D., Miss Alma knows everything, I suspect, but she refuses to tell me anything," she sounded playfully irate. "Do you think you could get her to talk?"

"Let me see, how did they use to torture people to make them talk?" he said, grinning at the old woman. "They used to shove bamboo shoots under their finger-nails till they talked. I wonder if she is ticklish? That might work."

"You ol' silly," Miss Alma chuckled, "I don't break that easy. Why I've had lots worse done to me in my time."

"Worse than torture?" Eden asked.

Miss Alma grew pensive, "There are things worse than torture."

J. D. grew still, "Whatever would that be?" he asked.

There was a moment of silence as some people walked into the café and spotted Miss Alma.

"My Gawd," a fat-bellied man in suspenders bellowed. He grabbed his wife's arm and pulled her back out the door. "What's the world comin' to, Thelma?" he said as they left.

Miss Alma noticed Eden picking at her food and volunteered, "This barbeque ain't so good. Why don't we leave it for now?"

"Yes," Eden replied, looking around the room, "Let's go. It's hard to breathe in here."

"I must really be awful company," J. D. teased.

"Oh no," Eden said, placing her hand on his arm. "It's just not comfortable for Miss Alma."

Jake Gresham saw Eden's hand on J. D.'s arm, and it made him seethe.

"I 'spect it'll cause you more concern than me, little girl," Miss Alma replied. "You and Mr. J. D."

"I understand completely," J. D. said.

"Where do we pay?"

"Don't worry about it, ladies. I'll take care of it."

"I'd argue, but I'd really like to go now. Thank you so much for all your help and for lunch."

J. D. walked them to the door.

"Hey, you dang thieves!" Jake bellowed.

J. D. didn't turn around as he opened the screen door for the ladies. He just lifted a hand in the air to silence Jake and said, "I'm paying for them, Jake, so cool your tar heels."

As Eden stepped through the door, she turned and glared defiantly at the people who stared at them, finally coming to rest on the kindness in J. D.'s own eyes. She smiled a silent thank you.

"I'm glad we took a stand today. It's a little chink in their wall," she whispered to Miss Alma. Still, she was glad to be outside where the air seemed fresher, unaware of Jake Gresham's hard eyes that followed her car as it sped down the highway.

Eden couldn't get away quickly enough. Nor could she apologize enough to Miss Alma. It was all her fault that they had been in that awful situation. This old woman, who had become dear to her, had done nothing to the people in the café. Their reaction to Miss Alma was a complete mystery to Eden. As hard as she tried, she could not find the why of it. She felt guilty that she had forced the old woman into a potentially dangerous situation, unaware of the real danger that would explode around them just a few miles down the highway.

# Thirteen

Halfway home it began to sprinkle and Eden had to pull over to put the canvas top up on the car. But not before she and Miss Alma sustained a sheen of light mist. The mid-afternoon darkened quickly, as heavier rains broke loose from the charcoal clouds. Her windshield wipers swooshed back and forth rhythmically, as Eden strained forward to see the line dividing the farm-to-market's narrow lanes. She turned her headlights on and squinted.

"I can't see nothin'," Miss Alma said, as Eden pressed forward against her seatbelt. A blaze of lightning cracked open the sky, and they braced for the inevitable boom.

"One, two," but before Miss Alma reached three, a huge clap of thunder exploded above them and jarred the car. Or had she briefly left the edge of the pavement and gone onto the gravel? Hard to tell.

"That strike was too close. We needs to be home, safe and sound," Miss Alma said.

"I know. We'll be there soon."

Heavy sheets of rain bombarded the wipers, and they groaned to maintain their rhythm. There was a sudden crash, and Eden felt her head snap back against her seat. At first, Eden thought they'd been struck by lightning, and she struggled to maintain control of the car. A second crash caused her to slightly fishtail, and she looked in the rearview mirror to see a large pickup truck bearing down on them. Its headlights flashed in the mirror and burned Eden's eyes. Miss Alma yelled as she turned to see the huge truck assault them a third time. This time it pushed them to the edge of the road and into the ditch. The car rocked a moment, then rested in the mud.

Eden could barely make out the truck that had stopped above them on the highway. *Did a door open?* In her fear, it didn't occur to her to lock their doors. She just sat terrified in the heavy rain.

Eden thought she heard a horn and saw more lights. *Is the truck still there?* It was hard to tell. She was breathing heavily when her door was jerked open. Both women screamed at the dark figure that leaned into the door opening and grabbed Eden by the shoulder.

"Eden! Eden! Are you okay?" But they just sat there blankly.

"Eden, It's me, J. D."

"J. D.?" Her arm grabbed his and almost caused him to topple forward.

Miss Alma cried out, "Thank you, Jesus!"

"Are you okay? Are you stuck?" he yelled.

"Yes," she answered, as raindrops splashed off him and bounced onto her face.

"Come on. I'll take you home in my car. Miss Alma, you stay put. I'll come back for you once I get Eden settled."

"Stay put yourself!" She yelled, throwing open her door and following them up the embankment.

Eden was drenched as J. D. pushed her into the front seat. Miss Alma slid in behind them. He turned on the inside lights to see Eden's face. She was pale. Her eyes stared straight ahead.

"Miss Alma, you okay?" J. D. asked, turning toward her.

"I'm doin' my best to be. Are them headlights up there?"

J. D. realized that it was indeed headlights, and that was what had captured Eden's attention. They seemed far up the road, and at the moment, to be standing perfectly still.

"What happened?" he asked, but Eden remained quiet.

"Eden!"

Miss Alma spoke up, "A truck, a big ol' truck, run us off the road. Hit us three times and pushed us into the ditch."

Looking up, J. D. noticed that the headlights in front of them seemed closer.

"Lock your door, Miss Alma," he said, as he reached across Eden to lock hers. Miss Alma did as she was told, then she reached over the seat and began to rub Eden's arms.

"Little baby's cold," she said. "It's okay, little girl. Mr. J. D.'s here. We'll be just fine now that Mr. J. D.'s here."

J. D. started his car, and his lights flashed on. Like magic, the mysterious headlights in front of them disappeared, as if they turned off onto some phantom side road.

"You ladies are coming to my house for the night," declared J. D.

"No, sir, we can't," Miss Alma insisted.

They were relieved when Eden finally spoke, "We have to go home. Afton is there alone. We can't leave her alone in this storm."

He couldn't argue with that, and he knew it. All he could do was move slowly onto the highway and head toward Camp Ruby Road, keeping an eye out for any sign of the menacing truck and its tell-tale headlights. The brunt of the storm had passed by the time they made their way up the winding drive to the house. The sky had lightened, and Eden breathed easier.

"Somethin's wrong here," Miss Alma said.

"What?" J. D. asked.

"Look at ol' Lizzie and Luther there. They don't ever stand out in the rain like ducks. They go under the house or up on the porch. Why you think them ol' hounds are standin' out there, all drenched and such?"

"J. D.?" Eden said. "Miss Alma's rocker is turned over. It wasn't like that when we left."

J. D. leaned across Eden, opened the glove compartment, retrieved a 38 revolver and checked the cylinder.

"If I ask you ladies to stay locked in the car, will you?"

They both shook their heads no, and he was not surprised.

"Alright then, stay behind me and go slowly."

He stepped from the car and Eden crept out behind him. Miss Alma fell into step behind them. When they entered the house, nothing seemed amiss. Eden called out, "Afton? Afton, where are you?"

But there was no answer.

"J. D.?" her hand clutched the back of his shirt.

"Don't jump to conclusions," he said, and he yelled too, "Afton? Afton!"

"Afton!" Eden called louder.

"Girl, you here?" Miss Alma yelled, "You answer me right now!"

But she didn't answer.

"Where was she when you left?" J. D. asked.

"She was going upstairs to take a nap."

J. D. glanced up the stairs, "You two stay right here and don't move!"

Miss Alma couldn't easily climb the stairs, and he was sure Eden wouldn't leave her. He hurried up the stairs, and while he disappeared, they held their breaths and listened. Eden wrapped her arm around Miss Alma's shoulders and wondered which of them she felt shaking.

She heard him before she saw him emerge at the top of the stairs, "All's well up here," he yelled coming down, taking the stairs at a run.

They moved throughout the house searching each room.

"Maybe she's down at the wash house. Maybe she had some washing to do," Eden said.

J. D. asked, "In that storm? Not likely."

Eden entered the kitchen to find a warm kettle on the stove where Afton must have been making tea. She stepped out onto the back porch and called out, "Afton! Afton!" J. D. followed her and stood behind her in the doorway scanning the hay meadow.

Eden heard a gasp and turned to see Miss Alma staring at the cupboard. She followed her stare and saw a large knife stuck in the side of the cabinet. Moving closer, she could see what Miss Alma saw. Written in red were the words, BLOOD FOR BLOOD.

"Wipe it off," she heard Miss Alma say. "Wipe it off before little girl sees."

But Eden was already staring at the knife that seemed to be holding the words up. Each individual letter, smeared across the wood, dripped to the floor.

Eden felt a dreadful fear, as J. D. pulled the two out onto the front porch and sat them in the porch rockers. He then went about the business of removing the knife and scrubbing all signs of the red away. It was actually paint, he could smell it, but it was intended to be perceived as blood, and J. D. didn't want them to have to look at it again. He knew the sheriff would be angry. He could well be tampering with evidence. But at that moment, Eden and Miss Alma were more important to him than Sheriff Delaney.

Eden didn't speak. Nor did Miss Alma, who rocked vigorously while her mind refused to settle down. She finally said, "They got her."

"Who?" Eden asked.

"The bottom landers. They know, and they come and took her. Dear Lord, dear Lord! What are we to do now?"

"I'm calling Boone," J. D. said as he stepped out the door.

"You know about Afton and Boone?" Eden asked.

"It was rather obvious at Thanksgiving," he said over his shoulder as he went back inside to make the call.

❧━━❀━━☙

Boone arrived within ten minutes with Ryder in tow.

"What do you mean she's gone?" he yelled while tumbling from his truck.

"Gone where?" Ryder asked.

"Calm down guys," J. D. said. "Here's the fact of it. Someone ran Eden and Miss Alma off the road up by Gum Gully."

"We saw her car," Boone said.

"I came upon them and brought them home. When we got here, there was no sign of Afton."

"But there was a sign," Miss Alma moaned.

"A sign? What?" Boone persisted.

"A blood feud, Boone," J. D. said.

It was the first-time Eden heard those words spoken, but it wouldn't be the last.

"What's a blood feud?" she asked.

Ryder moved to stand by Eden and said, "It's a bottom lander thing, an eye for an eye, a tooth for a tooth. If they think they've been wronged in any way, they're quick to call a blood feud … and it's usually to the death."

Eden heard J. D. tell his friends about searching the house, finding it empty, and coming across the gruesome message smeared across the cupboard.

"It looks bad, Boone," he concluded.

"We should call Sheriff Delany," Eden said.

"No!" they all yelled at once.

J. D. knelt in front of her and said, "That won't do any good. They don't adhere to our laws. If Sheriff Delany went in there after a blood feud is declared, he'd disappear too, and then what? We have to figure this out ourselves, without starting a war between them and us. This could get really bloody otherwise."

"I'm not waiting! I'm dang well going in after her now," Boone bellowed, "I can't stand to think what they might be doing to her while we just stand around and discuss it!"

"She's one of them, Boone. She'll be safe," Ryder encouraged. But even as he said the words, anxiety sank its teeth into Boone's heart.

"I'm goin'. And I'm goin' now!"

Boone threw himself from the porch. Ryder and J. D. jumped after him, but he flung them off in a rush of adrenalin. His truck door was still open, and he reached under the seat and stood, waving a pistol as J. D. and Ryder righted themselves.

"Whoa, Boone," Ryder said, throwing his arms up.

"Oh Lawdy, Oh Lawdy," Miss Alma cried.

"You ain't stoppin' me!" Boone snarled.

They stood perfectly still as he slid behind the wheel. Hanging out the window, he yelled, "I'll find her and bring her home," as he screeched away, leaving his friends staring in disbelief.

# Fourteen

Mimosa Callahan bumped her worn out station wagon over Miss Alma's backyard and skidded to a stop on the wet grass. J. D. had called his aunt, believing she was their best hope. If not to get Afton back, at least to find out what had happened to her and if she was alright. Aunt Mim had agreed. She was a part of Old Texas, a descendant of Stephen F. Austin's *Old Three Hundred*, and there wasn't much that scared her, not even the people on the river bottom. Within the hour, Aunt Mim found herself deep in the Big Thicket, approaching their beat-up shanty town. Three armed men, in dirty overalls, stepped from the Thicket and blocked her way.

"Go home, Mimosa Callahan," one of them yelled.

"No sir, Duhon. You get out of my way right now. I'm coming through," she yelled back.

"We know why you is here. Now you just turn 'round and scat!" one man said.

"Move, you ol' hard-headed mule," another spat out.

She inched her station wagon forward.

The men stood their ground and leveled their rifles at her. As she inched right up to their knees, one of them let go a round, and it shattered the passenger side of the windshield and pierced the seat.

"Dang it, Harley," she yelled, jumping from the wagon, "Ain't you got a lick of sense in your head!"

She stomped right up to the gaping men. It was not the reaction they expected, and now they were being stared down by this giant bear of a woman looking down at them.

"I got more sense than you, old woman, if you think you're comin' in here," he yelled back with less conviction. "Now turn 'round and git!"

Aunt Mim grasped Harley's rifle barrel and pushed it up toward the sky, spitting out obscenities that would have made Miss Alma blush. The third man raised the butt of his rifle to strike her in the head, but to his surprise, someone behind him grabbed the barrel.

"You ain't hurtin' Aunt Mim," Nub Henry said. Nub slugged the man in the jaw and sent him tumbling to the ground. The other men took a step back.

"What you want, Aunt Mim?" But Nub knew. Everyone on the river already knew.

"I've come for Afton."

"They ain't goin' let you have her."

"Maybe, maybe not. But I ain't leavin' here without at least seein' her. You got that, Nub."

"I got it. Go on up there. Go see the girl. You won't like it!"

"They better not have hurt her," Aunt Mim said, marching past the four men and up the road, kicking up leaves and debris with each giant step.

Mimosa Callahan was formidable. Her six-foot-plus height and considerable girth set her apart, even from the bottom landers. Her wild, unkempt hair was flying in all directions in the wind. Fear pushed on before her, and those that saw her coming gave no more thought of trying to stop her. Instead, they pulled back in nervous apprehension about what this woman was about to do.

After all, they had only seen her on holidays or when she brought them food and medicines. But the huge smile that accompanied that Mim was gone, and the scowl on her face was unnerving, even to them.

She soon found herself pounding on the pine plank door of Jewel and Carl T. Donner, almost hard enough to burst the palm of her hand wide open.

"Jewel! Jewel Donner, you open this door!"

When the door swung open, Aunt Mim stared into the bushy-browed eyes of Carl T. Donner, arguably, the evilest man in the Big Thicket.

"Dang your meddlin' hide, Aunt Mim. What you doin' here?"

"I've come here for Afton, old man."

"Gawd, if you ain't the most brazen hussy!" he bellowed, his breath hot and sour.

"Brazen or not, I mean to take her back with me."

Jewel Donner appeared behind her husband, her eyes red-rimmed and swollen. Just past her, clinging to her mama's skirts was a little girl, with the most enormous eyes Aunt Mim had ever seen. Afton's little sister, she supposed. How had this forsaken place become the horrific home for such a sweet looking child? The girl seemed to be silently pleading with her. Whether out of fear or respect for her mama, she did not speak. But there was something in the child's eyes, something important, something urgent.

"Let Aunt Mim take her, Carl T.," Jewel Donner pleaded, "She ain't no good to us no more. No man'll have her now. She'll only be a dead weight 'round our necks all her life. Just let her go."

"Ain't given her to no townies!"

"Ain't townies," Jewel pleaded. "That ol' colored woman and that foreign gal. They ain't neither of 'em townies, and you know it."

"'spect that's true 'nough," Carl T. contemplated.

"Carl T.," Aunt Mim said, "Eden Devereaux has grown fond of your girl. I'm sure she'd pay a good sum of money to have the girl back. How does a hundred dollars sound?"

"A hundred!" Jewel cried in amazement. "That would set us right for nigh a few years, Carl T. Get us a new plow. Please, let Aunt Mim take her."

"How'd I get the money?" he asked.

"Nub could bring it to you."

"You swear, old woman?"

"I do. And you know I stand by my word."

After a brief pause, he said, "Go drive your wagon up here. I'll have her brother, Jeb, put her in it."

Relief washed over Mimosa Callahan like the rain that had just washed over The Big Thicket. Within minutes, she had pulled her wagon up to their porch, where Carl T. sat in an old rocker that was missing most of its slats. Afton's brother came out carrying his sister, wrapped tightly in a rag quilt. The younger child followed behind her brother and again, her eyes seemed to be pleading. But Aunt Mim didn't know what to do for the child.

"Hello, honey girl. What's your name?" Aunt Mim finally thought to ask.

She opened her mouth to speak, but Carl T. stopped her with a heavy hand on the child's shoulder.

"You keep away from me and mine, old woman. I may be givin' you one of my gals, but you ain't getting' no more from me."

"I wasn't going to take her," Aunt Mim scowled.

As Carl T. walked back into the house, a bird-like voice whispered behind her, "Calico. My name is Calico."

"Girl!" Carl T. bellowed from inside, "Get in this house!"

As she turned, it pulled at Aunt Mim's heart to leave the child behind. She could see the little girl's face, pressed against the screen door, watching the station wagon pulling away, taking her sister away forever. For this child, the world was still dirty, bleak, and painful.

Aunt Mim could tell something was wrong with Afton when her brother appeared with her. They must have beaten her severely. The girl moaned, and her eyes rolled up into her head, but at least she was alive. At least they'd let Aunt Mim have her.

"Put her in back, Jeb," Carl T. had said. "And get that quilt back. She ain't leaving' here with nothin' but the clothes she come in. You hear, boy?"

"Yeah, Pa," Jeb said, and he did as he was told.

Aunt Mim could hear Afton moan with each bump as they lumbered along the bottom lander's only in-and-out road. She talked to Afton, but the girl didn't answer. Once Aunt Mim hit the highway and felt safe, she pulled her car off the road. She took her coat around to the back of the wagon to wrap around the girl. But when she opened the rear door, she wretched. There was blood all over the girl. Afton lay on her back and Aunt Mim became painfully aware that her belly lay flat against her pelvic bones. The baby had been cut out. Her thin dress stuck to her body, where the stickiness of the blood clung to it, and Mim was surprised that it smelled just like the hogs at butchering time. As she stared at the mess, she was aware that she was also smelling some sort of honey-suckle plant that must be growing nearby, and its scent would forever be intertwined in her mind with this scene that was making her ill. She forced herself to move, wrapped her coat over Afton and sped down the highway, heading toward the hospital.

Eden entered the emergency room first, followed by J. D., Ryder, and Miss Alma. The shock of lights above her head stung her eyes. The odors were pungent and medicinal, and she crinkled her nose.

"We're here for Afton Donner," Eden told the receptionist, who glanced up at her while chewing a huge wad of what Eden could smell was caramel candy.

"Have a seat in the waiting room, and we'll send the doctor out to talk with you when he is available."

She felt summarily dismissed and did as she was told. But it was Aunt Mim who stumbled into them first, crossing the room in two of her giant steps.

"She'll be alright. She'll live. But, oh, that poor little thing!" Aunt Mim said, breathlessly.

"What do you mean, 'she'll live?'" Eden asked. But before Mimosa Callahan could answer, Doc Tobias came and cordially asked them to sit down.

"I understand the girl is living with you, Miss Devereaux?"

"Yes, sir," Eden replied, and Ryder took her hand.

"Aunt Mim has explained the situation to me, that you were hiding Miss Donner from her family because of the pregnancy. You felt it necessary for her safety, right?"

Eden felt her cheeks burn. There would be no hiding the baby now. It would be all over town by midnight. Boone would feel the hateful sting of the Two River's elite.

"Yes, sir, that's true. Is she alright, Doctor?"

"It's still touch and go, but I think she'll be alright. Still in shock at this point, and just wanting to sleep. But that is a good thing right now. I've sedated her."

"And the baby?" Eden asked.

He glanced at Aunt Mim first.

"Miss Devereaux, the baby is gone."

Eden didn't understand. "She had a miscarriage?"

"No, ma'am. They cut her open and took the baby."

Eden fell back in her chair. Her mind didn't want to understand what she had just heard. It was unthinkable.

"Did a doctor?"

"No, ma'am. A crude gash, almost as if it were meant to cause pain, sewn back together with unsterilized, dressmaking thread. I had to reopen it and clean it out. I needed to remove the afterbirth which they left behind, almost as if they wanted her to become infected ... as if they wanted her to die slowly, but not technically by their hands." He looked down and slowly shook his head, "Or maybe it was just ignorance. I've never seen anything like it in all my born days. Something really needs to be done about those bottom landers! The sad thing about it is, probably no one will ever be held accountable for what they did to that girl."

"But Afton will make it, won't she, Doc?" J. D. asked, mostly to relieve Eden.

"I think so. Our biggest problem now is infection. I'm giving her blood and heavy doses of antibiotics, and she'll need to stay here for a while to be monitored. The nurse will tell you if you need to bring her anything from home. In the meantime, it's just waiting and watching."

Eden spoke softly, "Can I stay with her tonight?"

Doc Tobias had already noticed Eden's paleness. He himself, in the profession for nearly forty years, had been sickened by it too.

"I think you all need some rest. I've given her something to help her sleep. She'll be out all night. Maybe for several days. She'll have a nurse with her at all times since she's in ICU. She'll be safe from those people. Go home. Get some rest. You may be able to talk with her in the morning."

As they all rose to leave, Doc Tobias took J. D. aside and asked, "How do I report this?"

"We don't need vigilantes going off into those woods half-cocked. I mean, with Boone still out there and all. And now there is this sorry business. We certainly don't need a war with the bottom landers. I'd hate to think about what would happen to Sheriff Delaney if he goes down there, even with a large group of men."

"How about if I call it a spontaneous abortion? That will be understood as a simple miscarriage on the records."

"I think that would be for the best, Doc. Thanks."

The others had already left the room, save for Eden and Ryder, who then walked Eden to his car and drove her back to her house. He stayed the night, stretched out on the sofa in the parlor, keeping watch all night long. At one point, while deep in sleep, one of the blue ticks barked, and he opened his eyes to catch a glimpse of what looked like a little girl, in the glow of the candle she carried, moving up the staircase. But when he rushed to the doors of the parlor, there was no one on the stairs. He frowned and pondered, then decided that it must have been a dream. But he had trouble getting back to sleep just the same, and he startled with every creak of ancient wood the rest of the night.

# Fifteen

Eden woke early the next day and saw Ryder off. J. D. had her car pulled from the ditch, and Johnny and Slats had washed the mud from it and returned it. She was grateful. As she pulled into the deserted parking area of the hospital, she saw a tarnished looking, little girl rushing toward her.

"Please, ma'am. Can you help me to see my kin?"

"Your kin? Who would that be?"

It was hard to hear the girl. Her voice was soft, and her head hung forward, causing her stringy hair to cover her face.

"Afton Donner, ma'am."

Eden lifted her chin and brushed the child's hair back behind her ears.

"Who are you?"

"Calico Donner," the girl said, not looking at her.

Eden looked around, but at this early hour, there were few cars on the lot.

"Are you from the river bottom?"

"Yes, ma'am."

"How did you get here?"

The child grew uncomfortable and shuffled from one foot to the other.

"I walked here, ma'am."

"From the bottom?"

The girl nodded.

"But, it's so far," Eden said, realizing she must have walked during much of the night.

There was a strained silence, before the girl said, "But I had to come. I know what they did. I saw it."

Eden put her arm around the girl's shoulder and felt her shallow breathing. The girl stiffened at the intimacy, but she asked, "You're Miss Eden, ain't you?"

"Yes, I am."

The child's dress was worn, and she was barefooted. She needed a good bathing to remove the smell of the bottomlands.

"Please, ma'am. Them folks inside, they told me to go away. They said I had no business in their hospital. But I do. I do have business. I have to know. I mean, I was sure she would die if Aunt Mim hadn't come. Did she, Miss Eden? Did she die?"

"No, she is alive, and they are taking extremely good care of her. The problem is that they think it's probably too early for her to have visitors."

"They said 'cause I'm dirty and barefooted."

"That's something we can easily take care of. Come on, Calico Donner, let's go get you some shoes."

"Oh, no, ma'am. I ain't got no money."

"Well, I do."

"But I can't let you spend it on me, ma'am."

"That's my decision and not yours," Eden said, taking the child's hand, and seating her inside the car.

The stores were not quite ready to open, so Eden took Calico to a donut shop for cinnamon rolls and milk. The child was hungry and grateful. She hadn't eaten since the last noontime.

Calico Donner had stepped into another world. Even though Eden wanted to help this child, perhaps she was doing her an injustice, dangling charms in front of her that Calico Donner may never be able to have again.

The sales clerk at J.C. Penny's was kind as she fitted a dress to the little girl and found her a pair of matching shoes. Eden placed undergarments on the counter when she checked out. "Nice ... what you are doing for this child," the cashier said.

*There are still kind people in the world,* Eden thought.

Once back in the car, Calico said, "Ma'am, I never seen a place like that before. You mean you can go in and just pick out a dress—and so many to choose from. There ain't that many dresses in all the chifforobes down on the river bottom."

"Do you like the dress we bought?"

"Oh, ma'am, I love it! But I can't keep it," she whispered as if it were a secret. "My papa must never know 'bout this, that I came to town to see my sister, or that I met you and let you do all these nice things for me. He'd beat me good and hard. But maybe if I could just wear it to get into the hospital, then I'd give it right back. I promise."

"Won't your family be missing you this morning?"

"No, ma'am," she said softly.

There was an uncomfortable silence again, but Eden didn't push.

Calico turned away from Eden, so she barely heard the child say, "I run away from the house a lot. When my papa gets angry and mean, he hurts me. He slaps me or hits me with things. I've slept down by the river just to be away from that house. All the people down there is poor, but they ain't mean to their kin like he is. He was mad last night, just 'cause my mama was sad 'bout Afton. He hit her, and I knew he'd hit me, too. I was sad, too. My brothers, they run out of the house and just left us.

They're scared of him too. But I stayed for my mama. But when he picked up that old whippin' stick, my mama yelled at me to run. And I did."

This was no life for a child, and Eden realized that that had been Afton's life too. How had she not understood the other world in which Afton lived? Both Afton and Miss Alma had tried to tell her, but she just wouldn't listen. She felt angry with herself.

Calico continued, "I've run away before, staying gone sometimes for days if I could find some food. Ashamed to see any of our neighbor folks. I tell you it's dark and fearsome, bein' all alone at night in the Thicket."

"I don't think I can even imagine it."

Eden was relieved when they reached her house.

"I'd like you to get cleaned up before you change clothes. How about a bubble bath?"

"A what?"

"You've never heard of a bubble bath?"

"No, ma'am."

"You're going to love this."

Eden prepared a warm bath in the claw-footed tub, and Calico giggled as the pink bubbles began to form.

"It smells so sweet."

"That's the scent of lily of the valley. Are you familiar with those flowers?"

"No, ma'am. But I do love how they smell. I wish my mama was here to see this, the bubbles and all, to smell this—what did you call it?"

"Lily of the valley."

"It's my most favorite smell ever. I hope I can always remember it."

The problem was that she *would* remember it, and sooner than she thought.

"Here are your new clothes. There is shampoo so you can wash your hair too. Take as long as you wish, and when you're finished, we'll go back into town and see Afton. Okay?"

"Yes, ma'am," Calico said, and as Eden closed the door, she heard the child say, "God bless you for all of this, ma'am." Eden wondered what this child knew about God and who had told her, living in such an unholy place.

Once downstairs, Eden heard the back screen-door slam, as Miss Alma came into the kitchen. She found her with a basket of clothes she had retrieved from the clothesline.

"Guess who is upstairs," Eden beamed.

"Now, how's I goin' to know that?"

"Come on, just guess."

"Better not be a man up them stairs! The way you is actin', it must be the Queen of Sheba."

"Oh, come on. You can do better than that."

Miss Alma did her famous 'Humph!' and began to fold the clothes. "You tell me right now, little girl."

"It's Calico Donner."

"Who?"

"Calico Donner. Afton's sister. Hasn't Afton ever mentioned her?"

"No, she don't talk much about family."

"She's just a little girl, but she walked all the way into town because she thought Afton was going to die. She saw what they did to Afton, Miss Alma."

"Oh, my lawdy. That's horrible. That child will be scared forever. Where is she then?"

"Upstairs, having her first bubble bath."

"If you ain't an ol' crazy, bringing her here for a bubble bath," Miss Alma chuckled.

"No, Miss Alma, the fact of it is that they wouldn't let her into the hospital. They told the poor thing she was too dirty to see her sister."

"Ain't that a mean thing to do. Next, they'll be tellin' me I can't see her either cause of my color!"

"I'd never let that happen."

"I know you wouldn't, honey. I know you wouldn't," and Miss Alma smiled at her.

"Anyway, you should have seen her light up like a rocket over her new dress and shoes."

"New dress and shoes?"

"And the scent of the bubble bath! She loved the smell of lily of the valley."

"Why you doin' all this, little girl?"

Eden suddenly sobered, "I'm doing it because I love Afton. I feel so helpless while she is in the hospital, and I want to do something special for her. I'm sure this would make her happy."

"I'm sure it will, little girl."

Calico Donner spent a half hour soaking until the bubbles were all popped away. She scrubbed herself and washed her sticky hair. At home, they never lingered in a bath. They either took a quick one in the creek in the dead of night or if they filled a washtub in the house during the winter, they all took turns, one after the other. The scent of their multi-bath water was never what you could call sweet.

Her mama had once gotten a small bottle of cologne in one of those charity boxes that were sent to the bottom landers at Christmas. She held it up to the light to see the sparkles in the cut glass bottle. But her papa had jerked it out of her mama's hands and yelled, "We don't have to smell like 'em, too!"

He had thrown it across the creek. But late that night, her mama sneaked out and found it. She dug a hole with her bare hands, buried it, and mumbled to herself, "It still belongs to me and always will. I may not be able to wear it or hold it, but it's mine." She made a vow to herself. "Someday I'll have pretty things."

But she knew better.

"Someday my life will be different. Someday he'll be dead." That thought and that pretty bottle were a long time ago, and Jewel Donner still waited.

"Ma'am?"

The voice came from the staircase.

"Yes, honey, we're back here in the kitchen," Eden called out.

She came to the sound of Eden's voice and paused in the kitchen doorway.

"Oh, Calico, you look lovely," Eden said. Her words had the power to make the child smile.

"Calico, I'd like you to meet Miss Alma."

"I'm honored, ma'am," the girl shyly stammered.

"Well now, little Donner, you come here and let Ol' Alma see you."

Calico came into the room and took a few steps toward the table.

"Yep, I see it. She does have her sister's eyes. Yep, I see Afton in her. How old you be, little Donner?"

"Seven, ma'am. Or maybe eight."

Miss Alma laughed, "As old as all that, huh? And I'm sure you'd like to be a lot older. Right?"

"Yes, ma'am."

"Now, how come, little one? What's so important you got to hurry up and get on with?"

"If I was older, I could leave the bottom land for good," she said.

Calico Donner was different. Like Afton, she had not only survived, but had held onto her innocence. No, Calico Donner had none of the rough edges you would expect to see in children raised in such poverty, by adults who don't care enough to help their own children overcome the hard life on the river.

"Are you ready to see Afton now?" Eden asked.

"Yes, ma'am."

"Miss Alma, would you like to come?"

"I'll wait here. Feelin' a might poorly today. Don't know if I could take seein' …" her voice trailed off.

"I know," Eden said, understanding the emotion in Miss Alma's voice. "We'll give her your love."

"Thank you, little girl. You come back real soon, little Donner. Ya' hear?"

"Yes, ma'am." But even as she said it, she doubted it would ever happen, and that was okay. Today would be enough.

⊱━━♦━━⊰

The parking area was almost full when they arrived at the hospital. The entrance doors glided open effortlessly and made Calico laugh. She liked the sound of her little shoes clicking on the gray tile floor. Eden held her hand as they stepped up to an older lady sitting behind a desk. Calico recognized her from earlier that morning, and she lowered her head, to not be recognized. But to her surprise, the woman smiled at her and said, "Hello, honey."

"What room is Afton Donner's?" Eden asked.

"Afton Donner?" the woman suddenly frowned and looked at them from above her glasses.

Eden felt the disapproval, the prejudice the townies had for the river bottom people. She wasn't a part of either side, but she knew this woman thought they were less than … *less than what?* All because they were here to visit a bottom lander.

Even the tone of the woman's voice had changed. "Room 201," she said curtly.

"Which way would that be?" Eden asked.

The older woman sighed condescendingly, "Take the elevator there to the second floor, and turn left when you get off."

Eden pulled Calico along and pushed the elevator button. The child turned to glance behind, only to see the older woman frowning after them, with her nose wrinkled. The elevator doors slid open, and they stepped inside.

"What a tiny room, Miss Eden," she said as the doors closed, and she felt the room rise. She squeezed Eden's hand.

"It's moving!"

"It's taking us up to the second floor," Eden smiled.

"How?"

"You know, I'm not sure. I've never thought about it before. I know there's a cable that it's attached to."

Eden was beginning to see things from a different perspective.

When they reached the room, Afton looked as if she had merely fallen asleep. A nurse was in the room, changing her IV bag.

"How is she?" Eden asked the nurse.

"She seems a little better this morning, but she hasn't gained consciousness yet. The doctor thinks that's probably a good thing, and we shouldn't worry about it, at least until the fever breaks. We had trouble getting it down in the night."

"Is it alright for us to be here?"

"Certainly. But there's no point in staying long. Are you Eden Devereaux?

"Yes."

"The doctor left orders to let you know when she wakes up. But I doubt that it'll be anytime soon."

"Thank you," Eden said, as the nurse left the room.

Calico smiled, "She does look like she's doin' okay, Miss Eden, not like she was at home. Ever'thing here is so bright and clean. Just look how white the sheets are. I don't think I've ever seen sheets this white." Calico looked up at Eden and continued, "Oh, I'm sure your sheets are this white and just as fresh smellin' as this room. This is one the finest rooms I've ever been in, 'cept yours of course."

"See, I told you they were taking good care of her. We shouldn't stay long though. Is there something you would like to say to her before we go? I'm not so sure she can't hear us or doesn't know that we're here."

"But she's asleep. She can't hear me."

"I think some patients who can't wake up right away, can still hear us sometimes. Go ahead and speak to her as if she was awake."

Calico took her sister's hand and leaned in close, so close Eden could barely make out the words.

"Sister, I hope you can hear me … and I hope you know how much I love you. I don't know if I ever told you before, but I do. I'm sorry I couldn't help you. I wanted to. I really did. I heard you hollerin', and I prayed for God to save you. How could I live down yonder without you there? You was the only one kind to me. I'd be so alone if you was to die, so Afton, please don't die. Please."

Eden walked around the bed and put her arm around the little girl's small shoulders.

"Do you think she heard me, Miss Eden?"

"I know she heard you. God heard too, and the Bible says *'the prayers of a child availeth much.'* You don't have to worry anymore." And they both believed it.

Eden heard Calico sigh, "We can go now. It'll be alright." They needlessly tip-toed out of the room, quietly closing the door behind them.

Once Eden left the hospital and hit the farm-to-market, she turned her car toward the river bottom.

"Where we goin', ma'am?" Calico asked.

"I'm taking you home."

"Oh no, ma'am. You can't. Papa can't never know I was with you today."

"But that's silly. He'll be glad I brought you back home."

"Please!" It was like a shriek that tore from the girl's throat, and Eden pulled the car over.

"What is it, Calico? Why are you afraid?"

"You don't understand yet. If my papa knows where I been, and who I been with, he'll purt' near kill me."

"Alright then, I'll drop you off at the turn to the river."

"No, ma'am. Take me back to your place to get my ol' clothes. I can't go home in these."

"You don't want them?"

Eden recognized her mistake the moment she said it.

"Of course, I do. But I can't have 'em."

"I wasn't thinking. I'm so sorry."

"Miss Eden, you been better to me than anyone ever was, 'cept maybe Afton. You keep these clothes for me, and maybe one day, I'll get to come back and wear 'em."

But Eden knew she never would. It was not in Calico's power to go where she wanted to go or do what she wanted to do. She was a Donner, a spawn of ol' Carl

T., and a bottom lander. What right did she have to walk among the townies? Eden was finally learning their rules.

"I'll keep them for when you come back," Eden said, just the same. "You are always welcome in my home." *My home.* That sounded nice. "Yes, you come back, and I'll give you all of my lily of the valley. You can wear these clothes, and we'll eat Miss Alma's homemade cinnamon rolls and milk and sit out on the porch. Miss Alma's rolls are better than those in town anyway."

*Such small talk!* Eden knew that it was unlikely that Calico Donner would ever come back. She hoped for the best for the child as she drove her to her house, where the child changed into her old clothes. Afterward, she drove her to the farm-to-market, pulling into a grove of low hanging tallow trees where they wouldn't be seen, and the two hugged goodbye.

As soon as she entered the woods, she rubbed dirt onto her skin and to her hair, then hurried through the deep woods to her house, where she found her mother rocking on the porch.

"Where you been, girl?" Jewel Donner asked, without looking directly at her daughter.

"Just around."

"Just around? That mean in the Thicket?"

Her mother saw her looking up at the rusty, screen door.

"He ain't here. But he'll be back come night," her mama said. The child felt relieved, at least for the time being.

Calico had gone to bed early, hoping not to see her father that night. But she was still awake when she heard the screen door slam shut, and her father bellow for his supper. She could hear her mother drop the plate on the table, and there was silence for a time. Brusquely, her father's gritty voice said, "She here?"

There was another silence, and Calico hoped she wouldn't be betrayed, but she was.

"Where?" she heard him ask, then he was in her doorway staring at her.

"Where you been, girl?"

"Walkin' in the woods," she said.

He half turned to go, and she took a deep breath. He slowly turned back and walked over to her bed.

"You look different."

She didn't say anything.

"You wash your hair or somethin'?"

"Yes, sir. Down in the creek."

Then it hit him. He picked up the sweet scent of lily of the valley on her, much the same way that animals pick up the scent of humans in the Big Thicket, but this was the scent of townies.

"What the blue blazes is that sweet smellin' stuff on you?"

She felt fear—so did her mother in the other room, because Jewel Donner had smelled it too.

Carl T. grabbed her arm, flung her from the bed and onto the floor. The impact caused her to bite her tongue and draw first blood.

"Townies! You smell like townies!"

A groan escaped her, and her eyes filled with terror, as she saw him remove his worn, cracked belt.

"Soap. I found some of Aunt Mim's Christmas soap."

Amidst a string of profanity, he beat her with all the strength he had. She cried out at first, then fell ominously quiet. In the other room, Jewel Donner heard the hollow thuds of leather on flesh. She put her hands over her ears and began to hum, *It is Well with My Soul.*

# Sixteen

It was the fourth day after Afton's ordeal that Eden became concerned that she still hadn't awakened from the strange sleep where her time in the Thicket had sent her. Doctor Tobias told Eden there was nothing to worry about, Afton's mind needed to heal as much as her body did.

Afton had been feverish for the first two days. Eden watched as they pumped antibiotics into her system, and as of the third day, her fever had broken. Eden sponge bathed the girl as she had each day and brushed her hair away from her face.

Clarice and J. D. came just as Eden had finished slipping Afton into a fresh hospital gown.

"How is she this morning?" Clarice asked, giving Eden a brief hug.

"About the same. At least the fever has subsided."

Eden took the small tub of sudsy bath water to the bathroom and emptied it into the sink.

"You're taking such good care of her, hon," Clarice called out after her.

When Eden returned, she asked, "Any news of Boone?"

"I'm afraid not, but we're still hopeful," J. D. said.

It was a painful thing, this waiting. Eden was told Sheriff Delaney had taken a few men down to the bottom lands, where they were nervously greeted by angry looking men who looked like they should have lived a century earlier. But no one gave them any information. They'd also sent Aunt Mim. But everyone along the bottom said they hadn't seen him, that he wouldn't have gotten in, in the first place, so they should look elsewhere. That fooled no one. She knew Boone was there somewhere, and that it was paramount that he be found before the Thicket could exact its worst possible toll.

A large group of town people had fanned out and walked the woods that bulged around the river bottom, careful to stay outside of the deepest parts of the Thicket. But still, there was no sign of Boone. J. D. and Ryder, along with Johnny and his buddies, cruised up and down the backroads country, searching for a glimpse of Boone's pick up, but to no avail. It was as if the Big Thicket had become a black hole and swallowed him up. As each day passed, Eden grew increasingly fearful that there wouldn't be a good outcome.

"How are you holding up, dear?" Clarice asked.

"I'm fine," Eden said softly.

"Southern people are a strange lot," J. D. declared. "If we were standing in the middle of a burning building and someone asked us how we're doing, we'll always say, 'just fine.' You look like you could use some sleep."

"It's hard to sleep. Every creak of the house makes me jump."

She didn't tell him how she and the house had entered into an uneasy truce. But the peace she had made with the old house had shattered the day the house had let them kidnap Afton. Now she imagined bottom landers hiding around every corner. She no longer thought she had imagined the long shadows that walk across the yard and she found herself drawn to the windows at night looking for them.

"Oh, my dear, I do wish you'd come stay with us for a while," Clarice smiled. "We just rattle around that big old house of mine. Why, I'd love to have the company."

"Believe me. I'd love to stay with you. I really would. But Miss Alma won't leave the Camp Ruby Road house, and I won't leave Miss Alma."

"You are both welcome at any time."

Eden could see J. D. smiling at her from across the room. He knew how loyal she was to the old woman. She would never replace Bett in Eden's heart, but she was coming close.

"I guess I could sneak up behind Miss Alma and throw a tow sack over her and drag her kickin' and screamin' to Mom's," he teased.

"I wouldn't want to be you when that tow sack came off!" Clarice laughed.

Laughter was a good thing just then.

A moan brought the attention of each of them. Then there was a movement of one hand. Afton Donner was trying to return to them.

Eden rang for the nurse and placed her hand on Afton's forehead. There was movement, as Afton's eyes were waking up. They slowly fluttered opened, but swirls of light were clouding her vision.

Her eyes were open. She knew that. As she pondered the partial blindness, she began to see rays of light flashing. Slowly, ever so slowly, her sight returned, and her mind functioned again. At first, she was only aware of a bright fluorescent light on the ceiling. *Not my father's house,* she thought. Someone took her arm and felt for a pulse. She turned toward the touch. A lovely lady in white was there. Afton smiled faintly, and she wondered if the lady was an angel, but immediately she understood she was a nurse.

"Pulse is normal," the nurse said. "The doctor has been called. But she appears to be doing just fine."

"There's that 'just fine' again," J. D. said.

"Thank the Lord for healing mercies," Clarice said.

Afton tried to speak, but could not. The nurse raised the head of her bed and helped her swallow some water. She felt Eden take her hand and sit on the edge of the bed.

"Afton, how do you feel?"

She still had trouble speaking. "I don't know," came out hoarsely.

It was honest. Her hands rested on the sheet beside her, where they had lain the last four days. But now she placed them on her stomach, and she suddenly realized the baby was not there. She pressed inward as if searching for it, and the pressure brought pain.

"Miss Eden?" She looked up into Eden's eyes, childlike and scared.

"I'm sorry, Afton. The baby's gone."

Afton only looked confused. She felt a light touch on her shoulder and turned to find Clarice.

"Afton dear, I'm Clarice Callahan, J. D.'s mom. We stopped by to see how you were doing. We'll leave you alone to talk with Eden. If we can do anything for you, please let us know."

Afton only blinked, as J. D. nodded to her before escorting his mother from the room. Once the door closed behind them, Afton turned back to Eden.

"Please tell me, Miss Eden. Where is my baby?"

"You don't remember anything?"

"No, ma'am."

"That is probably a good thing, Afton."

Eden and the nurse looked at each other, and the nurse moved to the door.

"Call me if you need me," she said as she left them alone.

"But my baby, where is my baby?" She pressed again on her stomach and grimaced from the pain. "Miss Eden?"

"Afton, do you remember being taken from the house?"

"I was at the stove and ..." She tried hard to remember. "I think I heard a noise."

"Was the house locked?"

"No, ma'am. I don't ever think to lock it. Miss Alma always locks it, usually at night. I don't ever remember finding the house locked up when I've come upriver from the bottom. Besides that, the house looks out for Miss Alma and me. It would never let anything happen to us."

Eden found those words to be strange. It registered that she may not be the only one who communicated with the old house on Camp Ruby Road. She laid that aside for the moment and continued with the matter at hand.

"And you saw no one?"

Afton's face scrunched up, "There was something."

"What?"

"I'm trying to remember. A cup fell off the table and shattered. It was loud."

"What else do you remember?"

"It's so fuzzy. They came into the house. It wasn't locked like it should've been. I was making tea, I think ... yes, the kettle was whistlin'. These men, they were big, and they grabbed me. I fought 'em as hard as I could, but I couldn't stop 'em. I was real scared."

She paused and took a deep breath.

"At first, I thought they were townies, out to teach me a lesson like they taught poor old Nub's wife. But I noticed we were headed toward the river. My papa met 'em in the woods, and I calmed down, thinkin' I was safe, at least from those men. He took me back home to mama.

He was yellin' and she was screamin' and cryin', trying to get between us. Then I saw his arm go up in the air. He was holding something—like a board or a tree branch. It cracked down on my head and—I don't know nothin' else."

The room was quiet for a moment.

"Miss Eden?" she asked.

"We sent Aunt Mim to your daddy's house, and she brought you back, brought you here because there was blood."

"Blood? My blood?"

"Yes. Afton, you have to be strong. But that won't be hard. I know you're a strong girl."

Afton didn't understand. All she wanted right then was Boone and the baby.

"The baby is dead."

Afton didn't move or speak.

"Do you understand what I said?"

"But ..."

"Your daddy knocked you out, and he took the baby from your body."

She began to understand and started to rock back and forth slowly.

"There's no baby?"

"No."

"There's no baby!" she said louder, as the rocking grew more exaggerated. "*Nooo,* Miss Eden! *Nooo!*"

Eden took the girl by her arms and tried to stop the rocking, but she could not. Afton's body was stiff and unyielding, and Eden released her.

"No, no, no!" Afton continued to say, and a small light flickered in her eyes. "Boone! I want Boone! Please, Miss Eden, get me Boone. Boone will make things alright again."

Eden's heart sank. It was a thing she couldn't do for the girl, and as she explained why, a wail tore from the girl's throat that could be heard all the way to the nurse's station.

# Seventeen

The first Sunday after Afton came home, Miss Alma felt a deep need to be with people of faith. Where once she had never missed a Sunday-go-to-Meetin', now, with her body deteriorating, she remained in the warmth of her old house, and read her scriptures in the comfort of her bed.

But with all that had happened, she felt compelled to surround herself with folks who would speak peace into her life and quote verses over her like, *"No weapon formed against you shall prosper."* She woke Eden early, knowing the girl would be tired after her ordeal with Afton.

"Little girl. Little girl!" Miss Alma called from downstairs, "I need you to take me to church, little girl, and I ain't whistlin' Dixie. You get up right now and take me!"

"Okay, okay. Give me a few minutes to get ready!"

When Eden came down the stairs, she was dressed in a blue Jackie Kennedy style, nubby, tweed suit with a matching pillbox hat.

"What you thinkin', little girl?"

"I'm thinking we're going to church."

"It's a colored church, crazy girl. I just need you to give me a ride."

"I'm a color too. Kind of a beige-pink, wouldn't you say," she said, as she held her arm out and examined it.

Miss Alma laughed, "You're a silly thing!"

But she made no further objections to Eden tagging along. Though many at the church stared warily, they were all polite, shaking her hand, and welcoming her to their gathering.

The church was in a large, two-story building with a square corner steeple that soared above the foyer. It was splashed with fresh, white paint, that brightened it up in the green grove of white oaks that had sprung up around it. There was a stone walkway from the parking area, which separated at a point to circle around to the cluttered cemetery in the rear. There were picnic tables off to the side that reminded Eden of the Sunday 'dinner-on-the-grounds' from her childhood.

Eden looked for differences, the things that separated these folks from herself, but she could find none. They were friendly, well dressed for the most part, and respectful in their behavior. They were nice to her. She didn't understand this chasm that separated people by skin color. At any rate, she had missed Sunday morning church, and so, she prepared to enjoy the service.

Eden could tell they took enormous pride in their building. It smelled of ancient, worn wood, furniture wax, and lemon verbena scented polish.

"This is a beautiful church, Miss Alma."

"Sure is, little girl. Used to be the town folks' church. We met in a one-room lean-to down by the river back then. That old thing had wing-windows."

"Wing-windows?"

"You know, windows covered by a board hinged on top, and you pulled 'em out and propped 'em open with an old board or a tree limb. A row of 'em down both sides to get a breeze goin' through. Got hot in the summertime down by that ol' muddy. But we got the cool air machines now in the windows."

"How long have you had this building?"

"Oh, I don't know. Guess 'bout forty years, more or less. The Gentry's, they built their big ol' church uptown when Two Rivers began to spread away from the ol' muddy. Miss Annaliese, she said she'd give the new downtown church to the Baptist for free if they give this here ol' church to us. So here we is, in this fine old buildin', with these nice ol' oak pews. Ain't they purty?"

"Yes, ma'am, they are."

"But Miss Annaliese, she say it has to stay Baptist. She wouldn't have no Methodists or Presbyterians meetin' in here. Ain't that a silly thing? We don't exactly know what we is, 'cept Christians. We just all meet here. But we call it The Call to Glory Baptist Church just for her sake."

Eden liked the name.

"When we moved out of the ol' river place, the bottom landers moved in. But they don't meet much, and they're lettin' it fall down. I swan, they're a bunch of godless heathens. They'll have a weddin' or a funeral there once in a great while and maybe meet on Christmas or Easter. But, glory be, how they don't give no place to the Lord on his day!"

The music started as an elderly lady pounded the keys of an antique organ with a strength that defied her spindly arms. A younger man stood and began to sing, *I'll Fly Away*. Pretty soon, everyone was on their feet, clapping and hollering out the verses in a manner that was strange to Eden.

At first, she was almost offended. Church was supposed to be a place of reverence and quiet dignity, wasn't it? But she found herself clapping along with the fast-paced rhythms and singing out the revved-up verses to the second song, *When the Roll Is Called Up Yonder, I'll Be There*.

Somewhere to her left someone had moved into the aisle and was doing a little jig while shouting, "Glory! Glory!"

She wanted to giggle, and she covered her mouth with a gloved hand. Joy flooded into that room, and Eden could feel its anointing. It brought peace with it, a thing she could actually feel. *This,* Eden thought, *is what sustains these people through the indignities they have been forced to endure. How incredibly much the Comforter had to offer these world-weary people!* She was glad she had come.

The following day, Eden drove to the Woolworth Five-&-Dime for tinsel and blinking, colored lights. In the afternoon, Miss Alma went with Eden into the north woods where Eden cut down a lovely little pine tree and dragged it back to the house. It wasn't especially big, barely four feet high, but once covered with blinking lights, glass balls, and tinsel, it made the parlor sparkle. Miss Alma added ornaments from years passed that brought smiles to her face, ornaments that had graced former Christmas trees and knew the secrets Eden longed to know. On the following morning, Miss Alma and Afton awoke to find wrapped gifts from Eden under their little tree. Christmas was coming at last.

But try as Eden might to brighten their world as Bett always had, a deep sadness still lay upon them. Indeed, the days following Afton's return to the house on Camp Ruby Road were pitiful things. A gray haze fell over the lowlands and spread across the river and sent foggy fingers up into the hay meadow behind the house on Camp Ruby Road. Eden could only watch Miss Alma feeling like a pitiful thing herself, as she moved her porch sitting from the front to the back, just to be close to Afton as she worked in the kitchen.

Afton had trouble focusing on the simplest of tasks. Eden told her to stay in bed and rest. But Afton needed to be up and about, to feel the familiarity of her usual chores, to smell the scent of the old kitchen, to work with her hands, and to set her thoughts aside for another day, when she could better cope with her new reality, and Boone. *Where was Boone?*

After the noon meal, Miss Alma lay down for a spell, so Afton came out and sat on the back steps. The fog was slowly creeping up, swallowing up the meadow. It breathed upward from the ground and shrouded the tall pines as it moved forward. Afton measured the pine straw covered ground from the foot of the stoop to where it vanished in the fog. To her amazement, she was captivated by a weighty snort as Ol' Twelve Point stepped out of the fog. He pranced, lifting his legs as he approached. Catching Afton's scent, he planted his feet firmly and tilted his rack downward.

Her eyes met the old buck's in an almost human connection and seconds passed. They simply looked at each other, uninhibited, unafraid. For the first time since her ordeal, a smile overtook her. Ol' Twelve Point politely nodded to her, as any gentleman would, before he stepped back into the recesses of the ghostly curtain. Afton thought of Alice stepping through her looking glass, and she felt compelled to follow, but knew she would not. Being lost in the dense fog was too much akin to her nightmares, where she searches and searches through the darkness for Boone and the baby. Afton knew that Ol' Twelve Point knew exactly where Boone was, but he couldn't help her any more than all the others. She lay her forehead on her knees and fought back the tears, weary of the burden she carried.

Nub Henry was an enigma, even to the river bottom people. Sometimes he stayed in Miss Alma's smokehouse. She kept a cot down there for him. However, since Eden had arrived, he was seldom seen around the old homestead. He had only been there in the first place to watch out for Miss Alma, and now he figured that West Texas gal was doing that for him. He had a fondness for Miss Alma that went beyond what folks thought. Not a romantic fondness, but one borne of common sorrow. Nub was the only one, besides the Ol' Missus, who knew all of Miss Alma's story. He knew what she was hiding, and his heart was tender toward the old woman because he was hiding from demons too.

Nub could step in and out of people's lives totally unnoticed. When he was around, they hardly knew it. He moved soundlessly from one point to another. When he disappeared into the pine thickets, Eden assumed he was returning to the river bottom society. But Miss Alma told her that no one, not even the bottom landers, knew where he lived when he wasn't staying in their smokehouse. There was never a clue left behind to confess of his whereabouts, and not a man alive could track the old-timer. Nub Henry, perhaps more than anyone alive, knew every inch of the Big Thicket, its brightest clearings, and its darkest recesses. It was in one of those dark recesses that Nub Henry came upon the pitiful thing, all dead leaves and mud, blood, and torn flesh. Nub had found Boone Bohannon.

It was an unusually warm day in the middle of December. Eden sat at the kitchen table writing a letter to Wynn, trying to explain everything, hoping he'd hear her heart and understand why she wouldn't be home for Christmas. She had to be careful, couldn't tell all. The truth would bring Wynn to her doorstep, and he would insist she return to Rising Star. Once Eden saw him again, she knew her resolve would wash away. In a moment, she'd leave this all behind—maddeningly unknown, maddeningly unsolved. No, Miss Alma needed her, and now Afton was her responsibility. She and Miss Alma were all the young girl had. Perhaps there was still Boone. She said it out loud as if to reassure herself, "There's still Boone."

Eden stretched her legs out under the table and sat back in the rabbit ear chair. When she lifted her face toward the open door, she jumped to see someone standing in the backyard, not thirty feet from the porch.

"Nub!" It escaped her lips as a breath. She glanced over at Miss Alma's door, but it was carefully shut while the old woman napped. When she looked back, her eyes locked with Nub's and were held as in a vise. Nub nodded. It was an unspoken command. Eden left the table, the comfort of the kitchen, the familiarity of the porch, and found herself firmly planted eight feet before this primitive creature-man. It occurred to her that Nub had only spoken to her on that first day when she, a menacing stranger, had approached Miss Alma's world uninvited.

His gaze was set on her like flint, as if sizing her up, appraising her Texas mettle. When he spoke, his voice was deep and rusty.

"Boone is dead."

It was as simple as that. He paused, and she knew all depended on her at that moment. She fought looking shocked. She fought bringing her hand to her mouth to muffle a sob. She willed herself to be still and quiet and spoke soundly.

"Where?'

"Found him in deep woods. Brought him up river. He's on the pier. Don't know nothin'. You tell 'em, I don't know nothin'."

Eden nodded.

He continued, "Call Jefferson Dixon Callahan. He's the boy's friend. You let him tend to this sorry business."

Again, she nodded, and as her heart pounded violently against her chest, Nub turned and disappeared back into the woods.

Eden made a frantic call to J. D., but there was no answer, so she called Ryder.

"Hey, you cute girl—"

"Ryder, I need you out here right now. Will you come?"

"In two shakes of a lamb's tail," he declared.

He was true to his word, careening his truck up the drive, scattering pine cones and leaves into the air. Eden sat on the front steps, carefully holding herself in check, but the minute he stepped from his pickup, she flung herself at him.

Ryder stood speechless, then he grinned his enormous grin, wrapped his huge arms around her and said, "Well, I'll be Sam Hill!"

"Ryder, Boone is dead," she finally managed, and Ryder's grin faded fast.

Ryder took her by the shoulders and held her away from him.

"What are you talkin' about, Eden?"

"Nub was here. He found Boone and brought him up and put him on the pier."

"Oh, my Lord! Oh, my Lord!"

Ryder turned her around and moved with her in tow into the house where he called Sheriff Delany. Before he had completely hung the phone up, Ryder was already making his way out the back door. He sidestepped the porch steps and leaped from the porch, yelling for Eden to stay inside. She watched as Ryder cleared the hay meadow and at that moment, Miss Alma stepped from her room, still groggy from her nap.

"What is it, little girl?"

Eden told her.

"Where's Afton?" Miss Alma asked.

"Taking a nap upstairs."

"Lordy, Lordy, that's a good thing. Lord, please keep that child asleep!"

But Eden knew only the Lord could do that because Sheriff Delany came flying up the drive with his cherry-tops flashing and his siren blaring. Eden met him at the front door as he rushed through the house and out the back, crossed the hay meadow in no time, and vanished into the woods. Then their world exploded.

Two deputies arrived, followed by an ambulance, some men who heard the police dispatch, and finally, Bick Bohannon, who had been called by one of the men. The deputies stopped Bick and told him to wait at the house. He stood stiff and noble on Eden's back porch. Miss Alma offered him some coffee, but he declined, and Eden noticed that his hands were shaking. Another car pulled up. The Reverend Voshawn helped his wife and Bick's wife from the vehicle. They all waited on the back porch, no one talking, no one making eye contact, no one daring to believe what they were about to see.

It seemed like a blue moon before Eden saw the men coming up from the woods. The ambulance attendants carefully carried their stretcher and the body bag that weighed it down. Bea Bohannon began to sob loudly, and Bick's hands trembled more violently. Bick placed them beside his face and fell to his knees. The men surrounded him and helped him to a chair beside his wife. Eden kept thinking how grateful she was that Afton remained asleep, unaware that the girl stood frozen behind the hazy glass of an upstairs window, watching the scene below, and fully well understanding all things.

Before the procession reached the porch, a man and two women Eden didn't know, came around the end of the house, went right to the Bohannons and began to offer comfort. More came. Eden felt a hand touch the back of her neck, and she jumped. She turned to look up into J. D.'s eyes. He had come with Clarice, Johnny, and Slats. Eden turned and buried her face in his shirt as he ran his hand up and down her arm.

"Hang on, Eden. Just hang on."

"It's Boone, J. D. That's Boone on that stretcher."

"I know it is." Then he said more slowly, "I know it is."

The rest of the day seemed to move in slow motion. Eden felt as if she was trapped in a snow globe with bits of fluff floating all around her. She tried to find a way out, but there was none.

The ambulance left, the Bohannon's left, their friends and comforters left, Clarice among them. Ryder followed his friend into town. Even Johnny and Slats had to go, to run away from the river and what it had regurgitated up this time.

Only J. D. remained to sit with Miss Alma and Eden in the kitchen as Sheriff Delany questioned her about Boone, knowing she could shed little light on it. Everyone knew the story by now, how Boone and Afton had loved each other, though it was doomed from the start, how she had gotten in a family way and been hidden away with Miss Alma until her daddy stole her back and took the baby. Lastly, how Boone had disappeared looking for her in the Thicket. Eden told him about Nub coming up river with the body and telling her to say to the sheriff that he didn't know anything. He had only found the body and returned it to the place it belonged, to those who claimed it as their own.

Sheriff Delany wanted to speak with Afton, but Eden assured him the girl knew nothing of any of this. She asked him to please wait, at least until tomorrow, after they had a chance to tell her about Boone and let her get over the shock that would surely follow. But Afton knew the whole of it already.

꧁꧂

Christmas arrived a week after Boone Bohannon was put in the ground. And with it came a renewal of peace and hope, and the first real cold spell of the season. *It's as it should be*, Eden thought, *a warm Christmas would be absurd.*

Miss Alma took Eden and Afton to her church on Christmas Eve, where they felt welcomed, and they ushered in Christmas with familiar carols of peace, good-will, and joy. But Afton couldn't feel the joy. Not yet.

The following morning, they slept late. Following a breakfast of hot, buttered fruit-cake, they opened their gifts to each other. Eden was surprised to find a sterling charm bracelet from Wynn. He had sent it to Miss Alma and asked her to slip it under the tree. With it was a letter of disappointment that they wouldn't be together this Christmas, but that he hoped she'd find her answers and be home soon. In truth, after the last few weeks, Eden longed for those carefree days in Rising Star.

Afton was also surprised with another secret gift Miss Alma had hidden under the tree, a lovely cameo broach from Beatrice and Bick Bohannon. A card in it read,

*Since you were special to our son, you will always be special to us as well.*

*We hope to get to know you better.*

*Bea and Bick.*

It made Afton cry again, but these were less painful tears.

There was yet another gift under the tree, up past the long branches, clinging to the trunk, and Eden couldn't understand why Miss Alma ignored it.

"What about that gift?" Eden asked after all the gifts had been opened.

"Little girl, that gift, it be there ever' Christmas. Kinda like the old decorations."

Eden looked confused.

"I put that gift there back when the Ol' Missus was here. It was my gift to her, a scarf I knitted before my ol' fingers got so gnarled with this ol' arthritis. But they come before that Christmas and took her away. It was weeks before I got to see her again and, not long after that, they told me not to come back. So, I kept it, and every Christmas I put it back under the tree to remind me of happier Christmas'."

"Okay, Miss Alma, that's the proverbial last straw. You get your coat. We're delivering that present."

"Oh no, we ain't!"

"Oh yes, we are!"

"Oh no, we ain't!"

"Oh yes, we are!"

On they sparred, as Eden forced the old woman into her heavy coat and put her felt lined hat on her head. Eden stuffed her in the car, and they were still saying, "Oh no we ain't," and "Oh yes we are!" But Eden was reassured by the easy way in which Miss Alma let herself be pulled along. She knew the old woman really wanted this.

"You coming, Afton?" Eden asked.

"No, ma'am. I'll wait here."

"Then you lock all the doors while we're gone."

"Yes, ma'am."

With that and Miss Alma's famous "Humph!", Eden headed to Coldspring.

# Eighteen

Rose Haven Nursing Facility was aglow with the excessive glare of Christmas lights. They draped over the doors, wrapped around the porch posts and encircled potted topiaries. But once inside, Eden was overwhelmed by the reality of this final part of life. The stomach-turning scent of decay and dying clutched her by the throat, and she had trouble swallowing. As she moved through the lobby, she blinked at the stark white walls and the brightness of the overhead lights that sterilized the ghostly people who were wrapped in pretty, pastel blankets. Many were dead already, but their bodies continued to go on while they continued to hope for that last heartbeat. She watched as they tilted to the sides of their wheelchairs, mouths gaping, trying to regain the unconsciousness of sleep, hoping it would be their last.

As she made her way to the nurse's station, she had to dodge shriveled hands that grabbed at her. She could hear mumbled words.

"Honey, I'm so cold."

"Who are you?"

"Where is my husband?"

"Can you help me?"

"Are you my daughter?"

One wilted lady blocked their way, and she snagged Miss Alma's coat. Miss Alma extricated herself as the lady sang *Jingle Bells* to no one in particular. She wore a red bow that attached a sprig of mistletoe to her white hair, and she asked Eden if she was Santa. Eden assured her that, though she was not, he would be there soon, and she smiled.

Eden and Miss Alma hurried through the maze until Eden inquired of the duty nurse. "Can you give me the room number of Annaliese Gentry?"

"That's room 204 in B Hall."

"Thank you."

As they headed down B Hall, they ran a maze of wheelchair-bound people, who mindlessly moved along without thought or destination. *Just something to do*, Eden supposed. It broke her heart to see these people.

Annaliese Gentry was old. Older even than Miss Alma. Age draped across her like a worn-out veil of thinly drawn-up flesh. But as old and spent as she was, she still held onto a hint of graceful charm that reminded Eden of a dying rose, a white one that had lost all but its last petal which would soon flutter slowly to the ground. Eden stood over her, looking down at her as she slept, and was struck by her lingering beauty. How lovely Annaliese Gentry's hair was, curled about her face, her nose straight, her high cheekbones sunken, yet well defined.

She looked like *Sleeping Beauty*, awaiting the kiss of her handsome prince to bring her back to life. But the prince had stayed away too long. Time had drawn lines across her features. Her hands, resting on her chest, were fine boned. The flesh sunk in around those bones and blue veins lay across them like roads upon a map. Her nails were well manicured and painted pink. Her fingers bore rings that spoke of a background of wealth.

Miss Alma placed the old gift on the nightstand to be opened later. It looked out of place among the gauze, the medicine containers, and the plastic juice cups.

"Should we wake her?" Eden asked.

"You sit over there, little girl. We'll wait for a spell till she wakes up."

Eden did as she was told, sitting in a chair across the room, observing the tender expression on Miss Alma's face as she looked down at her old friend. Miss Alma reached out and stroked Annaliese's hand.

There was a soft moan, "Cam? Cam is that you?"

"No, ma'am. Your Mr. Cam ain't here. It's only me."

Annaliese Gentry opened her eyes and looked confused.

"Don't worry, Miss Anna. Ol' Alma's just come to call."

The emotion that overtook Annaliese Gentry was swift. Her eyes filled with tears that made trails down the wrinkled ravines of her face.

She took a deep breath, and in the letting go of it, she whispered, "Alma."

The two women smiled at each other, and for a time they just let silence speak for them. Eden felt like a voyeur, watching something she should not. The bond of love that passed between the two women was remarkable, and such a private thing that Eden felt compelled to excuse herself. Yet she was unable to move. She sat in silence and looked down at the dull, linoleum floor.

Annaliese finally spoke, "Where have you been, my old friend?"

"I been home, at the river house."

"But they told me you were dead."

"Who told you that?"

"Martin and Edith. You didn't come anymore, and I kept asking for you. And one day they said you had died."

"*Nooo!* They told me I couldn't come to see you no more. Said I was to stay away from you."

"Dear God in heaven! Why would they do such a thing?"

"You know why," Miss Alma said, looking briefly at Eden.

There was silence again after a slow, labored breath escape Annaliese's lips. A nurse came in, and Annaliese stilled herself and stared unseeing at the ceiling. The nurse lifted Annaliese's limp hand and took her pulse.

"Time for your medicine, Mrs. Gentry." Then louder, "Mrs. Gentry!" But there was no response. Annaliese lay there like a thing already dead.

"Keep talking to her. Maybe she'll hear you," the nurse said.

Miss Alma nodded, and the nurse left them.

"Miss Anna, they think you ain't there in your mind no more."

"I know," Annaliese answered, coming back to life. "It's so much easier. Otherwise, they want you to sit out there with the others, or make you do crafts or sing-a-longs or such."

Annaliese took Miss Alma's hand, "It's Christmas, Alma. Remember the fine Christmas' we had when the children were little?"

"Oh, yes ma'am. You always loved Christmas. Like you was little yourself."

"I loved all the children, Alma. Mine and yours."

"I know you did."

"They were like hope to me."

"Yes, ma'am, they was. And they loved you, too."

"They were all we had back then. But it was enough, wasn't it?"

"Yes, ma'am."

"I never see them anymore. Do you, Alma?"

"No, ma'am. Mine's all gone now, and yours ... well, maybe things is for the best."

"Maybe."

"Miss Anna, I done brung you someone to see. I hope I done right."

"Who is it, Alma?"

Miss Alma turned to Eden, but Eden still felt like she was standing outside watching intimacies through a glass picture window. She had to will herself to stand and walk across the room to become a part of this intimate scene.

"Miss Anna, this here's Miss Eden Devereaux."

The name brought instant recognition, and Annaliese Gentry put her hands over her heart that was beating harder than it had in years.

"My baby. Oh, my baby," she whispered.

Now it was Eden's turn to be confused. Annaliese Gentry had recognized her name. She knew who she was. Maybe she would tell her why she owned the old house on Camp Ruby Road, and why this lovely lady had once made the decision to give it to her.

Miss Alma patted Annaliese's shoulder to calm her.

"She don't know nothin', Miss Anna. She showed up 'cause her mama died, and she came into her inheritance."

"The river house? My river house?"

"Yes, ma'am."

"So ... do you like her, Alma? Is she fine?"

"Oh, yes ma'am. She's a fine lady."

Annaliese Gentry sighed as she stared at Eden so steadfastly that Eden became self-conscious and felt herself blush.

"Ma'am. I need to know why you deeded this property to me. I was told it was Gentry property and that it came from you. But I don't understand why. Why did you deed this to me and stipulate that it be sealed until my mother's death?

"My little sweetheart, how could I do any less?"

Something flashed in Eden's mind, a bit of recognition. Was it being called 'my little sweetheart?'

"Child," she continued, "you are beautiful. I knew you would be. Just look at you, such a fine, young lady."

"Ma'am, who do you think I am?" Eden said the words slowly, forcefully.

"Oh Alma, I'm so tired. I can't do this now. Alma, dear, dear old friend." Annaliese took Miss Alma's hand and pressed it to her cheek. "Don't forsake me again. Come whenever you can."

"I will, Miss Anna. I promise."

"Now go away and leave me to my thoughts."

Eden was being dismissed, and yet she had gotten no answers for her effort.

"But ma'am …"

"You leave Miss Annaliese alone, little girl. Can't you see she's plumb worn out?"

"Yes, but—"

"No buts," Miss Alma said, taking control of the situation, and pulling Eden from the room.

⊱⋇⊰

They arrived home to find Aunt Mim's station wagon sitting in front of the house. She and Afton met Eden at the door.

"Merry Christmas, y'all!" Mimosa Callahan boomed loudly. Her huge smile spread across her face like a garish caricature and accentuated her rosy cheeks.

"Merry Christmas back at you," Miss Alma said.

"Ladies, I'm headin' down to the river bottom. Got lots of food and clothes and toys for the kiddies. Things are always peaceful down there at Christmas time. It's a good time to heal. I thought Afton might like to go see her mama and sister for Christmas."

"Absolutely not!" Eden said.

"Now Aunt Mim," Miss Alma said, "You know that ain't a good idea!"

"But I think it is, Alma. Let's all declare some *peace on earth,* at least today."

"The question is, do you think it's safe?" Eden asked.

"She'll be safe with me. I know for a fact her mama's sorry 'bout everything that happened. Her mama and that little Calico, they cry for her all the time, and her old daddy has had time to spell on it, and I think he might regret what he done in the heat of anger, though I don't think he'll ever admit it."

"That weren't just anger, Mim," Miss Alma said, "that was pure evil!"

"Afton," Eden said, "What do you want to do?"

"I want to see my sister. I worry about Callie. I want to go, Miss Eden. I don't know why, but I'm powerful homesick some days. And it *is* Christmas."

"No child! You can't," Miss Alma insisted.

"Please, Miss Alma, I miss my little sister so much."

"Then I'm going along, just to see that Afton and everything is done safely," Eden said.

"Oh, no you ain't," Miss Alma growled.

Eden hugged the old woman and said, "Let's not do *that* dance again!"

"Little girl, who'd there be to keep *you* safe?"

"What am *I,* Alma? Chicken feed?" Aunt Mim frowned.

"You just too big for your britches, little girl. And Mim, you just plain ornery!"

"You're probably right. But I'm still going," Eden smiled.

"Humph!"

The station wagon bucked and jolted down the wash-board of the red clay road, clanking their teeth together and snapping their necks.

"You'd think the county'd take better care of these roads," Aunt Mim said. "Guess they're afraid of the bottom landers like everyone else."

Eden became aware of grinning, toothless men along the roadway who carried shotguns and jugs. She noticed the wagon slowing down as a few of the men waved them along. They knew Aunt Mim, and they knew that on Christmas she would have a load of food for their bellies along with clothes and toys for their children.

At first, the woods gave way to a house or two, shabby as they were. Soon, it opened up to reveal a little village—ancient buildings grouped around a central store, all in need of a fresh coat of paint. *Mercy, it's a dirty looking place*, Eden thought.

Aunt Mim pulled up to the boardwalk in front of the store and stepped out into the gumbo mud they called a street. Eden got out too, but Afton sat still inside the vehicle. People came out of the store and greeted Aunt Mim.

"Hey, you old cuss, Merry Christmas," the man who owned the store called out.

"Merry Christmas back at ya'," Aunt Mim smiled.

"Boys, come help here," the man called. Men spilled from the store and began unloading Aunt Mim's treasures onto the boardwalk. To them, Aunt Mim was Santa Claus. They gave no mind to the kindness of the church folk who provided these treasures.

Someone was clanging a bell, and people began to spill from the houses and the forests to congregate around them. Aunt Mim told Eden that each ribboned box pretty much held the same food and each family was to get one. However, Eden would have to go through the other boxes to find toys and clothing that would fit the size and ages of the children who were circling them excitedly. A little girl was  sucking her thumb and staring at Eden with curious, blue eyes. Eden pulled out a large Tiny Tears baby doll, still in its box, not the usual hand-me-down. Eden watched as the little girl's whole face changed, first to surprise, then to delight. She looked from Eden to the doll and back again.

"Yes," Eden smiled, "It's for you. You can take it."

Still, the little girl held back. Gently, Eden pressed it into her arms and heard the most musical giggles.

Afton had joined Eden and was fitting the clothing to the children. It was like an opiate, the feeling that came with the expression on the faces of the children. Eden understood why Aunt Mim did this each year.

The people gathered their treasures, and family by family, washed away from them into their houses to examine their fine new things. No one let himself think about the fact that their Christmas came from the townies whom they despised, those people who made them feel low and common and wanting in their ways. But it was those that obeyed the scriptures to help the poor, the orphans and the widows that provided too. They never wanted to admit that there were some townies who were kind at heart. Who, then, would they have to expend their white-hot, inbred hatred toward? Perhaps they were afraid they'd turn on each other.

The few people who remained were eyeing Eden suspiciously. She was sorting through the remainder of the things they'd brought, wondering what to do with the last of it. Her back was tired, and as she stood, she put her hands on her hips and stretched backward.

An old International farm pickup, rusted and mucked up with mud, was slowly moving past them. The man who drove it turned briefly, and their eyes met. There was no reaction, no look of acknowledgment, no expression at all on his face. He turned his eyes back to the road. It was then that Eden saw the woman who sat beside him, still as a statue, staring straight ahead.

Eden's breath burst from her lungs, and she screamed, "Bett!"

No one moved. No one spoke. They all looked at her as if she had lost her mind. The truck continued its slow motion along the road and away from them.

"Bett!" she screamed again. "My mother!" Her eyes saw yellow explosions and the whole world turned black and vanished.

The next thing she knew was the chill of a wet cloth touching her face, and off in the distance, she heard her name called.

"Eden, Eden. Wake up, honey!"

It was Aunt Mim's voice. She forced her eyes open and looked up at a half dozen faces staring down at her.

"Kiddo, what do you mean goin' out like that?" Aunt Mim was chiding, "You scared the wits out of me."

Eden sat up slowly. The few old men who looked down at her stepped back.

"I'm sorry. I don't know what happened," she said. But she did know. She had seen Bett. Bett had passed right there, in front of her. *But, how could that be?*

Aunt Mim cautiously helped her to her feet. But all she could think about was what had brought her to Two Rivers. A disembodied voice, Bett's voice, had called her to come and find her, and now she had. She had found

Bett. She knew how crazy she would sound if Eden told them that she had just seen her dead mother drive by. She needed to continue carefully, without raising suspicions.

"Aunt Mim, did you see that truck that went by?"

"Truck?"

"Old farm truck. Had two people in it."

"No, honey, I didn't."

"But you must have! Afton?"

"No, ma'am. I was busy with the boxes."

She looked around as the old men moved back into the store, save for one.

"That were old Boggs Dupree," the man said.

Eden jumped at his words, "And the woman with him?"

"That were his daughter, Angie."

Eden was on the verge of telling Aunt Mim that it was not someone named Angie Dupree at all. It was her mother, Bett. But she held back, knowing how insane that sounded. Her mind was still reeling from it when she noticed how stock-still Afton had become. She followed Afton's stare across the street to where Afton's mother stood.

"Mama?" Afton called out, but neither of them moved.

Carl T. had appeared on the porch behind the woman, and his stare was not at all friendly.

It was Aunt Mim who yelled out, "Jewel Donner, you come here and wish your baby girl a Merry Christmas!"

Jewel took three steps forward when Carl T. yelled out, "Jewel!", and she froze in place.

"Mama?" Afton pleaded, her voice shaking.

Carl T. shouted at his daughter, "Thought I sold you to them rotten rich townies. What you doin' back down here? I got my money for ya'. No different from sellin' any old, worn out cow. Thought we was rid of the sight of you!"

Afton gasped.

Eden took Afton's hand and drew her into the street to her mother. Aunt Mim followed and went on across to Carl. T. Their conversation was not pleasant. Voices were loud in the crisp Christmas air.

Jewel Donner and her daughter only stared at each other. Then Afton moved into the circle of her mother's arms, and they both hugged as if they never intended to let go. No one except Afton saw the little girl, Calico, trapped behind Carl T. in the prison of a house. No one except Afton saw the familiar bruises on the little girl's neck and arms or her discolored cheek, as she watched her mama and her sister embracing in the street. None of them saw the dull darkness in her eyes where once there had been fire. None of them saw Calico fall to her knees feeling utterly hopeless. Only Afton saw and knew, and it cut her to the quick. Afton had come home, but only for a moment in time. Within minutes, she would be gone again, and he would still be there.

# Nineteen

The next morning Eden doubted her own sanity. Either that or believe in ghosts. It must have been some trick of lighting, shades, or shadows, that made this Angie Dupree look like her mother. *But still ...*

At noon, a young man in a neatly pressed suit appeared at the door with an envelope for Eden. It had the feel of crisp, linen stationery. Miss Alma recognized the raised-lettered crest as she handed it to Eden and said, "From the Gentry's."

Eden ripped the envelope at the end and pulled out a stiff card.

"Well?" Miss Alma asked, trying not to appear too curious.

"I'm cordially invited to a New Year's Eve Ball," Eden said, with haughty flair.

"At the Gentry's?" Miss Alma asked, unimpressed by Eden's dramatics.

"Yes."

Nothing more was said, but Eden could feel Miss Alma's disapproval. She was going into the lion's den where she could get all her questions answered. Either that or be torn asunder by their sharp claws. Either way, the invitation was welcomed.

On the night of the New Year's Eve Ball, there was static electricity in the air. It crackled in Eden's ears and sent tension down her spine. She had waited as eagerly as she had for the Harvest Ball. She had taken just as much care in her decisions about what she would wear.

Eden drove two hours to Foley's in Houston to find the perfect evening gown to meet the Gentrys. It was wine velvet, off the shoulders with a slightly flowing, floor-length skirt. A wide, pink satin belting draped around her waist, and she wore Bett's pink pearls. She pulled her hair back with a pink satin band and let it fall, long and straight, down her back. She felt quite sophisticated and extremely nervous.

As she stood at the enormous entry door of what could only be called the Gentry Mansion, she felt insignificant and out of place. If only she had Ryder to escort her, or J. D. But she was sure J. D. would be accompanying Paige. At any rate, she felt awkward arriving alone. The door swung open with a swoosh that sucked her forward, and a liveried butler stood before her.

"Miss," he said, stepping aside and bidding her enter. He led her to a large room where people were mingling, dancing and enjoying plates of festive looking foods.

A woman came to her with her hand extended, and as Eden took it, she announced, "I'm Raina Gentry. You must be Miss Devereaux."

"Yes ma'am, but please, call me Eden."

"You must call me Raina."

She took Eden's hand and folded it under her arm, pulling her into the magnificent room and began to introduce Eden to the other guests, many of whom she'd already met at the Harvest Ball.

"Martin! Edith! Look who I have here!"

Those names were familiar to Eden. They were the ones who had told Annaliese Gentry that Miss Alma was dead. They were the ones who told Miss Alma never to see the ol' Missus again. The two extended their hands to Eden while issuing plastic smiles, as Raina Gentry introduced them.

"Miss Devereaux," the man called Martin said, "How nice to meet you at last."

"It's entirely my pleasure. Please, call me Eden."

"Why, the whole town is abuzz over you, my dear," Edith said.

"I can't imagine why," Eden smiled.

"Such a mystery about you. Showing up as you did from nowhere, and moving into Grandmother's old river house," Edith Gentry said.

"Grandmother's?"

"Yes," Edith continued, "Annaliese Gentry is my husband's grandmother." She looked at her husband who was frowning at her.

"I'm sorry, dear," Raina Gentry said. "We've lived here so long, and we forget our manners sometimes. Martin is my son, and Edith is my daughter-in-law. Annaliese Gentry is my mother."

Finally understanding the genealogy, Eden was about to ask if they knew why the Gentry matriarch would deed the river house to her, when something stopped her, just a feeling, but compelling just the same. She was relieved when Ryder stepped in front of her, took both of her hands, and stared at her new gown.

"Well, well, now. Miss Eden Devereaux, as I live and breathe. Are you sure you aren't some Hollywood starlet? You look too gorgeous for the likes of all of us. How 'bout a turn around the dance floor?"

Eden, smiling at Ryder, glanced at Raina.

"Go ahead, dear. We can talk later," Raina said, "Enjoy yourself while you're in my home."

Ryder led her to the dance area, and they began to sway to *Begin the Beguine*.

"Thanks, Ryder," she said, as they moved to the music.

"For what, darlin'?"

"Rescuing me yet again."

"I thought that was J. D. 's job." He grinned down at her. *Dang, she's cute*, he thought.

"Between the two of you boys, I seem to keep getting rescued a lot! Now normally, I'm pretty self-sufficient, but around these people, I do get a little uncomfortable. And you, Ryder Lee, are a welcome sight tonight."

Ryder smiled at that, and he made it a point to stay beside her throughout the evening. He liked the way she clung to his arm when Jake Gresham was around. Jake's only acknowledgment of her though, was one obligatory nod.

Jake spent the evening dancing with Raina Gentry, who laughed too loudly at his jokes. Was it Eden's imagination or was there something going on between Raina Gentry and Jake Gresham? Did anyone else notice? But everyone else was caught up in their own intrigues. It was a time for coquettish flirtations, and even Eden was not immune to the nighttime spell that was being weaved around her. She laid her head against Ryder and allowed herself to enjoy the feel of his arms around her as they danced. But in her heart, she was dancing with Wynn.

J. D. and Paige brought Clarice and Aunt Mim, who cleaned up surprisingly well. Eden wouldn't have recognized Aunt Mim if she hadn't bellowed, "Hey there, little girl," across the room. Clarice looked embarrassed and waved to her too. J. D. gave her a huge smile, admiring her new gown. Paige glanced her way once but was totally uninterested.

Paige wore a stunning dress covered in silver sequins, low cut and tight, and trailing a short train. At her throat was a diamond necklace and in the pile of curls on her head, she wore a small silver tiara. J. D. was as grand as Paige, in his black tux, his hair slicked back with pomade. His shoes were patent leather and nicely polished. The couple sparkled, and as he and Paige danced, all eyes were drawn to them.

Eden was lost in her own thoughts when Ryder stopped dancing. A quiet fell over the crowd at first. The orchestra stopped in mid-song. She looked up into Ryder's face, but he was staring across the room. She looked where his attention had been drawn, and there stood Nora Dancy, in the doorway, with a revolver in her hand.

Nora didn't speak a word. She didn't have to. Eden instinctively knew why she was there. It had been obvious even to her, an outsider. Nora Dancy had become Jake Gresham's cast off, replaced by the more socially suitable Raina Gentry. Perhaps no one had been surprised since Raina was acceptable in the eyes of the town's elite and Nora was not, nor ever could be. It was as simple as that. A liaison between Raina and Jake would not leave a stench in the nostrils of those folk who kept careful score of these things. There was no sympathy for Nora, no one to mourn the years she gave to Jake.

In a split second, everything turned the color of insanity. Nora raised the gun and fired. A bright yellow flash flared and turned to oozing red, as Jake was hit and fell. Raina screamed and ran, as Nora fired off another shot. But it was Clarice who grabbed her chest, who became the wide-eyed sacrificial lamb, who fell backward into the crowd. Men surged forward, subdued Nora Dancy and took the gun from her trembling hand. But it was much too late.

Jake Gresham sustained a superficial wound, a bullet to his shoulder that tore through his expensive tux and left smoke in its wake. He would spend New Year's Eve in the hospital and go home the next morning.

*But Clarice!*

Eden would never forget the look on J. D.'s face as he cradled his mother's head and watched frantically as her life's blood spread out into the patterns of the plush Persian rug. The bullet had collapsed a lung. She stopped breathing on the way to the hospital, but they resuscitated her and quickly put her on life support. She had lost too much blood though, had stopped breathing much too long. There had been a lack of oxygen to her brain, a thing of horror to doctors. She lay limp, gray, and lifeless, save for the machines that breathed for her, causing her chest to rise and fall unnaturally. She languished for three days, but it was a thing already done when Doc Tobias asked J. D. to make a decision no son should ever have to make.

Eden was there with Ryder, lost in the group of friends, and she heard Doc Tobias's words, "It's time to let her go." She remembered her own time of letting go, and she was on the verge of tears. Slowly, she slipped out the doorway. All she could think of was J. D. and Johnny and the pain they were going through. She had gone through it herself, and it had undone her. All she could utter was a prayer of mercy for the brothers, and the ghosts left behind.

At first, Paige had been horrified that another scandal had been laid at her doorstep. Just when J. D. needed her most, she had locked herself away in her house and refused to see anyone, feeling completely humiliated. It was her father's indiscretion that had caused all of it. She knew the shame her mother had known. Paige finally emerged to take her place by J. D. and receive all the well wishes that were extended in his direction. No one mentioned her father or his role in it. Not to her, anyway.

Doc Tobias took Paige aside and told her that he was going to ask the family to remove the life support. His purpose was to prepare Paige to help J. D. through this difficulty, but it had the opposite effect. She couldn't cope with J. D.'s pain, so on that day, she was conveniently indisposed. She went to Lufkin to visit her cousins, and they took her to lunch and to a movie. She stayed the night, and when she returned the following day, she figured it was a thing already done.

Eden sat at the kitchen table feeling weary. Her arms rested on the oilcloth that covered the table, and her head lay on them. The cloth smelled like the kitchen, a scent of years of coffee and bacon and turnip greens. She was not destroyed by the idea of stopping the life support but felt she should be. J. D.'s heart would be ripped open, and she could not stop it.

Is today the day that they would let her go? They would speak dark molasses words that were more to comfort themselves because the doctor had said she was gone already. How is this life bearable at times? Could a body's heart actually break itself open, torn apart, flesh from flesh? She was suddenly aware that she couldn't feel her own heart beating.

J. D. had fled the hospital. He had approved this unspeakable thing, and now he needed an escape. Once behind the wheel of his car, he laid rubber and headed blindly down any road that appeared before him.

*I'm the strong one, the oldest, the man of the family now. Got to be strong for Johnny, for Aunt Mim, for everyone. Paige doesn't like to see men cry. Can't show weakness now,* he thought. He gritted his teeth together.

He turned right at the river and watched it flow past him. Its calmness comforted him, and he felt he could breathe again for the first time since signing his name to a paper that would bring an end to his mother.

The river moved away from the road and J. D. panicked as he found himself losing the calm he felt in the flow of that old muddy. He pulled his car over into a clump of low-branched pin oaks and remembered. He could see his father as a young man teaching him to pull fish out of that river. When they were young, Johnny almost drowned once, but J. D. had saved him. They weren't supposed to be swimming alone, and they never told their mother about it. His high school crowd loved camping out on sandbars on areas of the river only accessible by boat. Clarice never knew about that either. She thought they were camping on their friend's farms.

His mother would soon be gone, and he would be an orphan. The word caused the panic to explode again. No mother to call when he needed her, no father to take him on hunting trips into the Thicket. Who would spoil his children? Who would take care of Johnny? Who would see to Aunt Mim in the future? Who would their friends come to for advice or help? He would have to be strong for everyone, and he didn't know if he could do it.

Memories spilled out, exposing his life and his mother's role in it. He knew that he couldn't be for Johnny what she had been. He picked a wildflower and laid it in the palm of his hand, gritted his teeth and crushed it. He would try. Yes, he would try his best to replace his mother for everyone's sake.

He needed the river. He felt like he was caught in an undercurrent that was pulling him toward it. Someone was coming. He blinked back tears as a car approached. But it was insignificant, a stranger who sped by without even noticing how bravely erect he sat.

Leaving his car behind, he sought out the smell of damp earth and found himself fighting his way through dense brush, muscadine vines, and cattail reeds. He came upon a small clearing, some thirty feet from the water's edge and it was enough. He sat there like a man-child, drawing up his knees under his chin and wrapping his arms around them, thinking this is how he formed in her womb.

*Strong! Be strong for them!* He had to be their rock.

He put his forehead on his knees and shut his mind down completely. Though he was awake, he knew nothing that went on around him.

The afternoon flowed by as smoothly as the old muddy. J. D. knew he'd been there a long time, and his eyes scrunched closed to fight this thing his mind willed away. He refused to let himself think about it. But there was no comfort in that either.

He hadn't seen Eden at first, the bright purple slacks with a warm purple and yellow sweater, walking down the path that ran along the water's edge. She had gathered a bunch of late blooming wildflowers and held them loosely in one hand. She too had sought the comfort of the river. She was not aware that J. D. sat, statue-still, in the small open patch, only moving his eyes to watch her as she ambled, stopping here and there to pick a flower. She would lift it to her nose, breathe deeply, then press it into the multi-colored regime of other petaled captives. Her search led her directly between J. D. and the river. There, as if she was a deer sensing the bead of a rifle barrel, she turned her head and looked into J. D.'s eyes.

The sounds of the Thicket were quiet now. Or were they just unheard by the two? His first thought was how awkward this should be, but it was not. Her eyes were like a balm that even now was soothing his failing heart. His body softened as he stood and willed her to move toward him and she did. His mind bid her come, and she came, slowly, willing, one step, then the other, until she stood before him. They were inches apart, perfectly still, almost not breathing, not a word spoken between them.

Eden lifted a hand and ran her fingertips along J. D.'s jawline, and he closed his eyes. Her hands cupped his face, and when he opened his eyes, she was staring at him as if to etch his face into her mind. J. D. buried his frown in her hair. Now he could cry for his mother. Cry for what he'd lost. Cry, and know that life would go on.

They sat down on the moist grass and Eden put her arm around his shoulder to let him cry against her. His pain became her pain.

After a while, his tears depleted, he lay back on the ground with his arms behind his head. Eden didn't look at him. It was then that J. D. realized that this thing of such pain had happened to Eden not so long ago. She, too, had buried her mother. She had felt this horrible thing.

All around them life went on. The river sloshed against its banks, the birds flew above, and somewhere far off, a crow cawed three times. Bugs buzzed around them, and J. D., finding some peace, drifted off to sleep in the afternoon sun.

"J. D.? J. D., where are you?"

J. D.'s eyes slowly opened as if they didn't want to open at all. Where was he? His heart thought of his mother then and tore again. But he remembered Eden, and the edges of his pain softened. He sat up and reached for her, but found only the dry grass where she had sat. The bouquet of flowers she had gathered lay strewn beside him, and he lifted one to his nose and breathed in. He wondered if anyone else could comfort him as she had, and he was grateful she had become a part of his life.

"Eden?"

He spoke her name in a reverent whisper. But there was no answer.

"J. D.? Are you there? J.D?"

It was Paige, who had seen his car, and was coming through the undergrowth, stumbling into the clearing. She caught the toe of her sling back pumps on a sapling root and literally fell into J. D. 's arms. Purring like a cat, she turned to face him with a coquettish smile and looked into his eyes.

"Why J. D.! You've been crying!"

It was almost an accusation, an ugly thing that stole his peace again. *How could he love this woman and not the other? Oh, yes, because the other loved someone else.*

Johnny Callahan had stayed with his mother, but for a brief time. He, too, left the pain and ran to the peace of the river. There was a secluded place beneath the tallest of the palmettos where he left his daddy's old pole and tackle box hidden away. Johnny sat down beside them and unconsciously placed a hand on the cold metal box.

It was a reminder of the father he had loved and lost, just as he was losing his mother. Sitting there, crossed legged, he felt the familiar sting in his eyes, and he closed them hard to stop the inevitable.

"Here son, use this."

The rusty voice was beside him, not close, but close enough to toss the gyrating minnow onto the ground beside him. Someone was handing him the pole. His eyes traveled the length of it, to the leathery hand with the dirty nails, up the worn cuff of a sleeve, to the gray, wiry beard.

It was Nub.

Johnny tensed, his body poised to run.

Nub, the phantom menace for every scary campfire story. Nub, the backwoodsman with the glass eye, who could put spells on you. Nub, who they all were sure, was responsible for the howling deep in the dark woods of their nightmares. Johnny did look into those fearsome eyes, but there was no menace in the raggedy backwoodsman. Nub said nothing else, but sat down on a grassy patch and stared across the river to the far bank.

Johnny slowly stabbed the hook through the minnow and lowered it into the water. A cold wind was blowing against his face, and the river smelled clean. Johnny began to relax and allow himself to be soothed by the slapping of the water against the dirt bank. It was a time of peaceful quiet.

When Nub finally spoke, Johnny jumped, surprised by the gravelly words, "Your mama was nice to me once. Brought me chicken soup and a pecan pie out at Alma's when I was bad sick one winter. Told Alma it was just for me, and the lady didn't even know me. But Alma said she was 'bout the nicest lady in town. I believed that then and I still do."

Nub paused, then Johnny said, "Thank you, sir."

Sir? When had Nub Henry ever been called 'sir'? Years of tension melted from the old man's guts, and he felt right proud to know this Callahan family, even this youngster. It was important to know who the good folks were, and who the bad ones were.

Time passed. Johnny Callahan didn't know how much time exactly, but he felt he'd been there almost an hour. For the first time, he turned to say something more to the old man. His words would be surer now, less emotional. But to his astonishment, Nub was gone. It was that way with Nub, moving in and out of the Thicket, specter-like. That's why the legends about him had grown. This would not be the last time Nub Henry would be a comfort to a Callahan and those they loved.

The sun was setting when J. D. managed to get away by himself. Almost as an unconscious thought, he found himself heading down Camp Ruby Road. His mind was full of Eden. He wanted to … no, he needed to thank her, and let her know how helpful she had been to him. And he kept reminding himself of Wynn Beckett's claim to her. He had never plowed in another man's field before. So why was he feeling so drawn to Eden's house? He could smell heavy pine as he made his way to Eden's door. He remembered this smell when he'd found Eden unconscious on the river's banks. This scent was all over Boone when he finally came home from the bottom lands.

He knocked, and Miss Alma was standing in front of him, encased in the house, restrained by the rusted screen door that she made no effort to open.

"Oh, little boy, little boy."

"I'm no little boy, Miss Alma," he said, thinking she was sad about Clarice.

But she repeated it again, "Oh little boy, little boy."

In truth, it was endearing. She was so fond of Eden, whom she addressed as 'little girl.' Maybe she had formed a fondness for him too.

"Would you please tell Miss Eden I'd like to see her?"

"She's gone, little boy. She's done gone."

"Gone! Gone where?"

"She come flyin' in here a few hours back, and she says she had to go. She says to me how sorry she was, but she just had to go away. Oh, Mr. J. D., what'll me and Afton do without her?"

"Where did she go?"

"Back to where she come from, I 'spect. She packed up and went flyin' out of here like she was on fire."

"She went back to Rising Star?"

"Yes, sir. Back to Risin' Star and to that Mr. Wynn Beckett. Said she needed him right now."

Miss Alma didn't like Wynn. Wynn would mean that she would lose Eden to that other place. No, Miss Alma realized it was J. D. she wanted for her Eden, not Wynn Beckett, silly as it was. Mr. J. D. was going to marry Miss Paige, and Eden was gone. Things would never be the same for any of them now.

J. D. opened the screen door, took Miss Alma's arm, pulled her onto the porch and sat her in her rocker. "Now tell me exactly what happened."

"Well, when she come home, she was so sad, so heartwrenchin' sad. I don't know why. She'd only been for a walk. But it was like her heart was breakin' and her life's blood pourin' onto the ground."

J. D. sat down beside Miss Alma and laid his head back on the old porch chair. It was him. He had given her too much of his pain. He had drowned her in it.

"She mustn't be gone. You and Afton really do need her. We all need her, even me."

His voice was soft, and Miss Alma almost didn't hear the end of his sentence. It wasn't news to her. Perhaps she was the only one who knew that J. D. needed Eden too, just as much as she did, especially now.

"Well, Mr. J. D., the minute she come in the door, the phone was ringin', and that Mr. Wynn Beckett was yellin' so loud I could hear him. You see, someone told him 'bout Boone and all that sorry business, so he told her to get in that little car and get herself home right then and there. She was too sad and tired to argue with him. She just did what he said to do. Who you think is mean enough to go callin' that Mr. Wynn Beckett and tellin' him all those sorry tales?"

J. D. could only think of one person—Paige. He knew she wanted Eden gone. Now she had gotten her wish. She always got what she wanted. Always.

"And now she's gone away from us," Miss Alma said. "And the hurt of it is, I don't think she'll be comin' back."

As if by divine command, the moment those words tumbled out, the sun dropped behind the tops of the pines and the dark of night covered them.

⊱⊰✥⊱⊰

It was late when Eden reached the Austin city limits and pulled into the Weary Wanderer Motel. She called Wynn to tell him she wouldn't reach Rising Star until the next day. He was disappointed, anticipating her return later that night, but he told her he would be waiting at her mother's house the following day.

Just as she drifted off to sleep, the old dream came once more, and she woke up in a panic.

"Why? Why won't it stop?" She pulled the sheets up tight beneath her chin and shivered. Not even the thought of Wynn comforted her. She had never felt this forsaken.

When she was able to sleep again, her dreams brought new images of a familiar, dear, old worn-out black woman sitting in her rocking chair in the middle of a high corn field. Eden found herself lost in that corn-field, frantically searching for the old woman. She could hear her singing a hymn, one of Bett's favorites.

*"Come home. Come ho-o-ome. Ye who are weary come home.*

*Softly and tenderly, Jesus is calling, calling, oh sinner, come home."*

*But I Have Promises*

*To Keep ...*

# Twenty

There are lots of religions in the Bible Belt—Southern Baptists, Presbyterians, Catholics, Pentecostals, and the like. There are those exclusively southern religions that guide them as surely as the stars and the moon guide their crop planting and animal husbandry. Texans call holy such things as home and family, love of country, and devotion to granddaddy's farm. They love their dogs, their old pickups, the Farmer's Almanac, granddaddy's Smith and Wesson, porch sittin' and Bible readin'. Let it suffice to say that football is in a league all its own. Why, Granddaddy would forget all about his pneumonia, tank up on aspirin, and head to the local high school to see his grandson in a 3A playoff. His doctor, sitting at the other end of the bleachers, having refused even emergency calls for the next three hours, would not find Grandpa's presence there unusual.

But a Texan's highest calling, after his call to his God, is to family. In the South, family is everything. The first thing they say when meeting a stranger is, "So tell me, who are your people?"

That question might seem strange to a Northerner. But in the South, it's a request for your entire genealogy. Chances are that generations back, your great-great-great Uncle Buford had married their great-great-great Aunt Maudie, and once you were established as family, nothing would be denied to you. There were no secret hand-shakes, but a nod and a wink were just as good.

Eden had never had a sense of family. Never had known her father or his people, or her mother's as well. When she was little, she made up a family. All her friends knew that her daddy was a highly-decorated Air Force pilot, who was overseas defending their freedoms. Her grandfather was the mayor of a little town in the Panhandle, where he also owned a vast cattle ranch and several oil wells. Of course, those oil wells were the reason she and Bett had lived so comfortably over the years, even though Bett had only held a part-time job at the county library. At least that was the family history she had made up.

The day after her return, winter roared into town as loud as an Aggie war chant, leaving a layer of frost and ice to cover all of Rising Star. A few days later, a rare sifting of snow settled across West Texas and trapped her in the house. Wynn was with her much of the time, but she knew he had to return to Princeton in a few days to begin the next semester.

The morning he left, the temperature dropped even further, and a heavier snow fell. Eden sat in her mother's kitchen, sipping hot cocoa, and watching white flakes float past the kitchen window. The radio was playing Elvis Presley's, *Are You Lonesome Tonight?* Her lips sound-lessly formed "yes." The weatherman reported that they hadn't seen this much snow since the thirties. Eden believed it, and she worried about Miss Alma and her frayed winter coat, not realizing that the Thicket had a way of holding weather like this at bay.

A day came when Wynn was gone, and she could stand the imprisonment no longer, so she wrapped herself in layers of clothes and pulled her car out of the garage. She was heading in no particular direction. Pasture upon pasture passed by her until she topped a hill and came upon a wooded area full of mesquite and scrub brush, all covered with mounds of glistening white.

She stopped the car on the road since there were no other cars out and about, and she let herself enjoy the shapes and designs the crystalline powder made. Immediately she thought of Robert Frost's poem, *Stopping by the Woods on a Snowy Evening*, and she recited it out loud.

"Whose woods these are I think I know.
His house is in the village, though;
He will not see me stopping here
To watch his woods fill up with snow.

My little horse must think it queer
To stop without a farmhouse near
Between the woods and frozen lake
The darkest evening of the year.

He gives his harness bells a shake
To ask if there is some mistake.
The only other sound's the sweep
Of easy wind and downy flake.

The woods are lovely, dark and deep.
But I have promises to keep,
And miles to go before I sleep,
And miles to go before I sleep."

But Eden didn't know whose woods these were any more than she had known whose woods those were on Camp Ruby Road.

Her stopping here served no higher purpose than did the old farmer's in the poem, but the surreal beauty held her as surely as it had the old farmer that dark evening. As with the farmer, the physical world pulled her back, as she realized she was getting low on gas and needed to return to town. There were miles to go before she could sleep, but she wouldn't rush. Sleep was not kind to her.

When Eden returned to Bett's house, she paused out front and stared at the frosted windows. With the snow on the roof and the icicles hanging from the eves, it reminded her of gingerbread houses she and Bett had made. It seemed empty, with vacant rooms where lost spirits lingered, and she didn't want to go inside.

All her Rising Star friends had long since gone off to school or jobs in Dallas or Houston or Austin. Even Bett's old friends seemed to be dying off one after another.

It suddenly came to her that Rising Star was *not* her home anymore, and probably never would be again. One week after Wynn left for college, Eden packed her things and headed back to Howard Payne College to finish her degree. From there, she didn't know. What she did know, was that it would not be Rising Star.

She easily fell into her old life on campus, hooking up with former friends and throwing herself into her studies. After a week of painstakingly catching up on her classes, Eden was grateful for Saturday so she could sleep late and lounge around the dorm. When night fell, she found herself drawn to the sound of chordant male voices singing, *Let Me Call You Sweetheart, I'm In Love With You.* She went to her window and curled up on the sill like a cat. Below her in the gardened quadrangle, there was a celebration going on, a traditional pinning ceremony.

Young, black-suited men from one of the fraternities, were standing in three rows singing, as young ladies from their sister sorority came out single-file, dressed in matching white formals, and formed three rows opposite the men. A young man stepped forward and took the hand of a young lady across from him. Eden sighed as she noticed the sweet smiles on their faces. He attached something to the girl's dress, and Eden knew it was his fraternity pin, a serious token of love only one step short of an engagement ring. As the song ended, the young man kissed the young lady, and everyone cheered. The men broke into their fraternity song as each young lady took the arm of one of the men and the couples marched single file, back into the sorority house where the ladies, no doubt, had refreshments waiting. Eden placed the palm of her hand against the glass and smiled, as the last of them disappeared behind the closed door, shutting her out of their world.

She remembered that night, two months later when Wynn arrived for the weekend and gave her his Princeton pin. There would be no ceremony for her since she didn't attend his school. Nor did she belong to a sorority. But it had been romantic all the same. They had gone to Lake Brownwood State Park, where he had spread a blanket and produced two stemmed goblets and a bottle of ginger ale, which he called the poor man's champagne. She was sad when he had to fly back to his other life at Princeton. But she put her social life aside and concentrated on her studies.

April arrived, warm and sweet-scented. On the ninth of the month, Eden found herself stepping from a college bus that had ushered a group from HPC to the new *Eighth Wonder of the World,* a global event attended by many prominent people, including the president of the United States. They were at an exhibition baseball game between the New York Yankees and the Houston Astros, the first game ever to be played in the enormous spaceship façade of the newly completed Houston Astrodome. It was the largest air-conditioned ballpark in the world, the glassy ceiling soaring over two hundred feet above the field.

Crowding into their seats, the college kids were quieter than usual, their eyes taking in the huge expanse of the architecture. As the opening ceremonies began, the commentator excitedly called everyone's attention to a spotlight, and Eden saw President Lyndon B. Johnson standing in an elegantly proportioned sky box across from them. Eden's friend handed her tiny opera glasses that magnified President Johnson, and she watched as he smiled and waved at the crowd.

"Is it really the president?" someone to her left asked. She nodded, but she was no longer looking at the president. Somewhere to his left, immersed in a sea of faces, was a familiar smile. Someone moved, blocking her view, and her smile disappeared.

"Move! Move! Move!" she whispered to herself.

There it was again. Focusing, she saw the face of Jefferson Dixon Callahan.

Her heart began to pound, and for some reason she didn't understand, tears began to sting her eyes. She blinked until they were gone and wondered if she could make her way past the Secret Service men to talk with him. She had so many questions to ask.

*Is Johnny coping? How is Miss Alma doing? Does the old woman miss me as much as I miss her? Does he miss me?*

Of course, she couldn't ask him that.

She brought the glasses back to her eyes and searched again. She felt like a voyeur, watching his face as his eyes swept the Astrodome. He put his head down, and she blinked as she watched him briefly kiss Paige Gresham, sitting beside him.

*Oh yes,* she thought. There was Jake Gresham too, only six rows up from President Johnson, schmoozing those around him with his Gresham money and prestige. Eden dismissed the idea of trying to make her way over to speak with J. D. After all, who was she, that the Secret Service would let her get that close to the president? She returned the opera glasses to her friend and tried to concentrate on the game for the next two hours. But from time to time, her eyes strayed to the skyboxes and strained to make out familiar faces.

By the end of the game her stomach was aching, and she was glad when it was over, and the final score was announced. She began to fight her way through the crowd to get to her bus. Once on board, Eden was unusually quiet during the ride back to Brownwood. She was able to lose herself in sleep. But from time to time, the bus hit a bump, and her eyes opened as ribbons of random yellow streetlights streaked across her face. Later, when they reached the college, Eden remembered thinking how grateful she was that she didn't have any dreams as she slept.

—⊰❈⊱—

It was spring in East Texas, and the woods were bursting with azaleas, dogwood and redbud blossoms, plus those magnificent magnolias. The Big Thicket was coming back to life. All across the region, small hometowns celebrated nature's rebirth with all sorts of festivals. There was a Black-Eyed Pea Festival in Athens and a Watermelon Festival in Beaumont. There were Dogwood, Redbud, and Azalea festivals. Closer to the Gulf were Crawdad, Shrimp, and Alligator festivals.

Eden had gone to the Anahuac Alligator Festival with a group of her friends and had tasted gator tail for the first time, after having been told it was only chicken. She rode the Ferris wheel and ate cotton candy. She watched a man wrestle a live gator and voted on the best boat in a regalia of decorated shrimp boats that paraded past them in the bay. Her choice had not won but had come in second and received a trophy.

The young man who accepted it, held it high in the air as the crowd applauded. Eden found him staring at her, and he winked. She quickly looked away. When he leapt from the platform and headed in her direction, she purposely lost herself in the crowd.

On the late-night ride back to school, her girlfriends carried on a discussion about her as if she wasn't there.

"She is such a lost cause! I can't believe her. He was a dreamboat."

"Boy, would I have liked to go sailing on that boat!"

"Forget the boat. I was trippin' on the boy."

"And he picked the only one of us who didn't give a flip!"

"Yeah, but Eden's got a boyfriend."

On and on they went, and Eden was glad when the conversation turned to the boys back at their school. She became sleepy, turned her face toward the window and let her forehead rest against the coolness of the glass. The moon was not bright, and the field of stars gave it a dark, foreboding backdrop. When she closed her eyes, she thought about Wynn and saw his face in the glass. But when she fell asleep, she dreamed of Two Rivers, Miss Alma, young Afton, and J. D.

Then there came the other dream, the dream from her childhood, the dream that had taken her to Deep East Texas where she had lived as a child, the place where she had now fled from the people who had become so precious to her.

⤝⟞✠⟝⤞

Eden had signed up for archery classes at Howard Payne, and by April she was on the women's archery team. Her schedule had been hectic, especially during finals week, which coincided with two competitions.

Her coach called the group of lady archers together on the last day of finals and said, "We have been invited to participate in a series of exhibitions the first week of June, and I need to know who will be available to participate."

A few of the girls had commitments. But eight, including Eden, were free to go on the tour. The coach announced that they were to leave in three days as he passed out their itinerary.

When Eden was back in her dorm room, she leafed through the itinerary material. The tour began in LaPorte, stopped in Baytown, Anahuac, and High Island before they moved inland to Livingston, Woodville, Lufkin, and Two Rivers.

Eden's heart skipped a beat.

‹———◈———›

The tour had seemed longer than it actually was—eight towns in five days. After the Lufkin exhibition, the ladies boarded the HBC bus and headed to Two Rivers, arriving after nightfall. The darkness hid the town from Eden, and she was glad. But even as tired as she was from the last leg of the tour, she found it hard to fall asleep in her neon-lit, roadside motel room.

The last exhibition was at ten the following morning, followed by archery lessons for any children who were interested. A group of little girls from a Brownie troop had gathered around Eden, and she was showing them how to hold the bow when she heard a familiar voice.

"Humph! What in the world they wann'a learn that for?"

"Miss Alma!" Eden said, handing her bow off to one of the little girls, and turning to hug the old woman.

"Little girl, little girl! You a sight for these tired ol' eyes, you sure are."

Another voice said, "How 'bout some lunch with a couple of ol' country crows?"

"Aunt Mim!"

"Hello, honey. You're lookin' real good."

Eden turned back to the brownie troop and was grateful that another archer had taken her place and was showing the children how to shoot an arrow.

"What are y'all doing here?" Eden joyfully questioned.

"Come to see you," Aunt Mim said.

"But how did you know I was on the team?"

"The newspaper ran a photo of the team. Imagine, us openin' up the paper and seein' you standin' there. Our little girl, playin' Robin Hood! Humph!"

Eden hugged her again. "Oh, how I've missed you!"

"That's good to hear. I mean, after not a word, a card, a letter! I bet you'd of blown in here and out without even a phone call if we hadn't showed up here today."

"I didn't know what to do, Miss Alma. I mean, I've been so busy, really distracted over the last few months. But I did want to see you. Honest, I did."

"Humph!"

"Honey girl, you're seein' us now. How about comin' home with Alma and me and havin' some sandwiches for lunch?" Aunt Mim asked.

"I'll just let the coach know."

⊱⟞✻⟝⊰

Once they were settled around the table in Aunt Mim's breakfast room, Eden allowed herself to relax and be a part of their lives again.

*Family!* It felt like she had family.

"So," Aunt Mim started, "When you comin' back?"

Eden was honest. "I really don't know if I am."

"So, you been in school all this time?"

"Yes, ma'am, most of it."

Miss Alma frowned, "You got to come back here, little girl. You belong here now. What is there left for you in that little place you come from?"

"Nothing really." Eden realized it was true.

"Well then," Aunt Mim chimed in, "You can come now that the semester is over and at least spend the summer with us. How about it?"

"Maybe I could, just for a summer visit. But Wynn won't be pleased about it."

"You let a man run your life when you ain't even hitched to him?" Aunt Mim asked, rolling her eyes toward the ceiling.

"I know we aren't married yet. But I do listen to Wynn. He has a good head on his shoulders, and I value his opinion. He cares a lot about me."

"That his pin?" Miss Alma asked.

Eden had forgotten about the pin. She ran her finger over its smooth surface.

"Yes."

"That mean you're engaged?" Aunt Mim asked.

"Not exactly."

"But it means you're about to be, right?"

"I suppose so."

"Humph!" Miss Alma frowned. "You marry that Mr. Wynn Beckett and you ain't never comin' home."

"Wynn's home is in Rising Star. And he does love West Texas."

"I know that chil'," Miss Alma said, "But that ain't your home no more. I 'pec you know it by now as well."

Eden only smiled.

When she rode out of Two Rivers that afternoon on the college bus, it was with a promise to return to them for an extended summertime visit within the next week.

# Twenty-One

It was already past midnight when Eden drove up to the house on Camp Ruby Road. Her car lights splashed across the porch and lit up the rooms behind the windows. She stopped the car and turned off the headlights, draping the house in black again. She knew Miss Alma was probably asleep in her room in the back of the house. She stepped from her car, paused to stare at the old home, and a smile crept across her face. The thicket smelled fragrant, just as she remembered, and Eden realized how glad she was to be there in what was feeling more and more like her home.

She reached into the back seat to grab her suitcase when she was startled to feel Lizzie, or was it Luther, press a warm nose against her hand.

"Hello there," she said. "Miss me?"

The hounds only stared up at her.

"Let's be quiet so we don't wake Miss Alma, okay?"

One of the hounds grabbed her pant leg and tugged her toward the house. Halfway across the yard, she looked up to see a flicker of light in her bedroom window. She paused, wondering who would be upstairs in her room. Lizzie whined, and Eden bent to pat her head.

"What is it, Lizzie?"

The hound whimpered and followed Luther under the porch. Eden shrugged and looked up at her bedroom window. The tiny light was white-silver, and as she watched it flare up more brightly, she saw a little girl's face as it moved into the window frame to look down at her. Eden noticed how dark her hair was, and how she had the most beautiful eyes she had ever seen. Neither she nor the little girl could look away. Soon Eden began to feel uncomfortable under the eerie gaze.

The porch light switched on, and Eden blinked as she heard Miss Alma call out, "Little girl, that you out there?"

"Yes, ma'am," Eden called back, happy to see the old woman in the doorway. When she glanced up again, the light and the girl were gone, and only darkness was framed in the window.

Eden rushed up the steps as Miss Alma threw the screen door open. She dropped her suitcase and gave Miss Alma a huge hug.

"You sure are a welcome sight, little girl," Miss Alma chuckled.

"And I've missed you and this old place so much!"

"Now that's mighty fine to hear, but not at one in the mornin'. You get on in here and get to bed. We can talk in the mornin', and you can tell me all you been doing these last months."

"It's so good to be home, Miss Alma," Eden said, at the foot of the stairs.

"I'm real glad your home too, honey. Now scoot off to bed."

"Alright," Eden said, but halfway up the stairs she stopped and added, as an afterthought, "Miss Alma, who is the little dark-haired girl in my room?"

"What little girl?"

"The one upstairs."

"There ain't no little girl upstairs."

"I just saw her standing in the window."

"Little girl, you must be full of moonshine and turnips. I tell you, ain't no one in the house but Afton and me. And Afton's sound asleep like you should be."

Miss Alma was right. There was no one in Eden's room. Still, she searched upstairs, trying not to disturb Afton, until she felt comfortable enough to crawl into her bed.

As she lay there, she spoke softly, "Hello, you wonderful old house. Are you happy to see me?" But there was no answer, and she wondered if she really expected one.

It felt good to be tucked into the Ol' Missus' feather bed under the eaves of Miss Alma's house. Of *my* house. Wynn had been furious with her, of course, for returning to Two Rivers for the summer. Yet, he conceded that she should have her way in this. Wynn did, however, plan to come stay a while as soon as he tied up loose ends and moved his dorm things back to Rising Star. He would help her then to make a decision about what she would do about the house and the land. He was hoping she would sell it.

She lay in the dark, willing her mind to think about Wynn. The creaking of the old house kept pulling her back to the little girl in her window. It had been so real. She simply couldn't have imagined it. A floorboard groaned, and a tingle crept up her neck and into her scalp. Sitting up and looking around, the whole house sighed violently. She had returned, and she fancied that her returning had brought the house back to life. A swaying of moonlight on the far wall caught her eye, and her mind conjured up the form of a child in the shadows. She gasped, then chided herself for her flights of fancy, as she lay back onto the soft pillows. In the quiet, she heard the soft, childish giggles coming from somewhere in the house. She pulled her sheets taut under her chin, and told herself again, it was all her imagination.

Sleep was slow to retreat that first morning back. Her eyes refused to obey, and she had trouble opening them. When she finally did, her room overwhelmed her with sweet emotions. This wonderful, old room, this glorious, old house, this was home to her. Even the smell evoked strong emotions, that musty scent of ancient wood and old things. The Ol' Missus lingered in the scents as well as the sights.

Sunshine streaked the room through the windows, and the smell of bacon drifted up from the kitchen. Afton was up!

She wrapped herself in her silk kimono and literally bounced down the stairs two at a time. She flung the kitchen door open, and there was Afton, standing at the stove as always. The sight of her brought a soft, surprising giggle from Eden's throat.

"Miss Eden!" The girl lit up like Christmas morning, and the two hugged. Afton's hair smelled river scented, and Eden found herself laughing like a schoolgirl. She'd missed these people and being home felt good.

"Eden, as long as you're giving out hugs ..."

"J. D.!" she shouted, spinning around.

He had only been teasing yet she threw her arms around him, and he took full advantage of the situation and hugged her back. He could have taken more pleasure in it, except for the fact that they had such an amused audience. When she pulled away from him, she kept her eyes on his face, as if searching for something.

"J. D., I'm so sorry I left the way I did. I mean, just running out on everyone. I should have been here for you. I should have stayed for ... for ..."

"For my funeral?"

It was then that Eden saw Clarice Callahan sitting in Miss Alma's rocker and the blood drained from her face.

"I'm so sorry, honey. I didn't mean to startle you like that," Clarice said.

"But ... they ... s-s-s-said ..."

"They were wrong," J. D. smiled. "They forgot who they were dealing with."

"And the power of prayer," Miss Alma added, chuckling.

"But they were going to pull the plug on the life support machines."

"They did, hon. But I decided not to go. Why ... I don't even have any grandchildren yet. And Johnny is too young to be without a mother. Of course, there's probably no hope for this one," she said as she winked at J. D., "but what can I do?"

"We heard you were coming back," J. D. began, "But we weren't expecting you here this soon. Otherwise, we would have prepared you ahead of time."

J. D. stood behind his mother and placed his hands on her shoulders affectionately. "She's still not up to par yet. But she's made great progress."

"I can see that," Eden smiled, giving Clarice a hug too.

"Actually, we came to see Miss Alma. But she's as ornery as ever and as tight-lipped."

"Tight-lipped about this house?"

"Yes, dear," Clarice said.

J. D. sat down at the table with Miss Alma and said, "We found out some information, and we wanted to ask Miss Alma about it."

"What kind of information?" Eden asked.

"It seems my son has taken up your cause and has spent some weeks trying to find some answers for you."

Eden smiled at him. *He's a good friend,* she thought.

"Have a look at this, dear," Clarice said, as she slid a piece of paper across the table. It was copies of newspaper articles from the forties.

"J. D. found these clippings in the records at the library."

Clarice gave Eden a moment to glance over them before she continued, "After I read them, I sort of remembered something about it. I was a young girl with a child of my own back then. But I remember my mama talking about it."

Eden looked down at the clippings.

### GENTRY HEIR MISSING

Reminiscent of the earlier kidnapping of the Lindberg baby, Sheriff Joe Sherman Nettles, of Two Rivers, confirmed that the granddaughter of one of the founders of Two Rivers, and bank president of Lone Pine State Bank, Camden Gentry, has reported the disappearance of his only grandchild, Carrie Elizabeth Gentry. The child, aged four, was put to bed on Thursday night. Her disappearance wasn't discovered until the following morning when her nanny went to wake her and found her missing. A search of the property revealed a broken basement window and a rear door slightly ajar, but no sign of the young heiress.

Another clipping read:

### THE SEARCH CONTINUES

It's been one month since young Carrie Elizabeth Gentry disappeared from her grandfather's estate in Two Rivers, and there are still no concrete leads in the case. The family, distraught over the disappearance, has hired the renowned private detective, Dan Matthews of Galveston, to aid in the search, but to no avail to date. The child's parents have had to flee to Europe to escape the constant attention of the press during last month's ordeal. The child's grandmother, Annaliese Gentry, has reportedly taken to her bed and will see no one. It is rumored that her health is not good due to the situation. Anyone with any information on this case should call Sheriff Joe Sherman Nettles, as quickly as possible. There is a $10,000 reward for the safe return of the child.

The last clipping read:

## ANNIVERSARY OF THE GENTRY KIDNAPPING

One year ago, today, Camden Gentry reported the kidnapping of his grand-daughter, Carrie Elizabeth Gentry, and one of the heirs to the formidable Gentry Estate. A statewide man-hunt turned up no leads, and today the case remains unsolved. There was never a ransom note sent to the Gentry family, which led many to speculate that, as in the Lindberg case, some-thing went horribly wrong and the child may not have survived. Annaliese Gentry, the child's grandmother, remains a recluse to this day, still dis-traught over the loss of the child. Camden Gentry tells this reporter that the family has never given up hope that the child will be found and returned to them and that the $10,000 reward is still intact.

Eden looked up, and all eyes were on her.

"You think I'm this Carrie Elizabeth Gentry? You all think that, don't you?"

"It makes sense, Eden," Clarice said.

"But it's ridiculous!"

"Is it?" J. D. said. "Eden, you sensed that you lived here until about that age. And the way Annaliese Gentry treated you at Rose Haven was like a long-lost grandchild, don't you think? Even Miss Alma said your name was the wrong name, remember?"

"Humph!" Miss Alma said, as she stood and poured herself another cup of coffee, "You folk leave me out of this."

"But we're on the right trail, aren't we?" J. D. pushed.

"Humph, little boy!"

"But that would mean that Bett Devereaux wasn't my real mother! That would devastate me. I know her better than anyone. She could never steal a child away from their real mother. I promise you; she would never have kidnapped me from another family, or been crazy enough to take me from such a prominent, high profile family. Tell me this then, how would Annaliese Gentry know that I was her granddaughter, even if it was true?"

They had no answer for that.

Eden said, "Maybe we could talk to this Sheriff Nettles. Maybe he'd have more clues that the paper didn't print."

"I tried that, Eden," J. D. said, "But he died back in '59. An automobile accident out on the Keechi Fork Bridge."

"How about this detective?" She searched the article for his name. "Here it is, Dan Matthews of Galveston."

"That's another strange thing, Eden," Clarice said. "J. D. tracked him down. He's retired and living in Austin now. Seems he never heard of the Gentry kidnapping. He even checked his old files for us. But there was nothing on this case."

"But that doesn't make any sense," Eden said.

"We know," Clarice answered.

Eden spent a perfect evening sitting on the front porch with Miss Alma, watching the familiar fireflies again. In her mind, she fancied that they had hidden themselves away until she came back to them. Tonight, they had come out to celebrate with her. Miss Alma would have called her fantasy plumb silly. But she didn't care. She loved her house, her yard, and even her fireflies.

"These quiet country evenings are what I missed the most, Miss Alma."

The old woman smiled as she shelled her bowl of field peas.

"Tell me all the news," Eden said, "What all did I miss?"

"Let's see now. You know 'bout Miss Clarice. She done a miraculous God-thing. Nothin' but a God-thing. You know she decided to not press charges against that poor thing, Nora Dancy. I 'spect she felt ol' Jake Gresham had it comin'."

"So, they let Nora go free?"

"They did at first. But ol' Jake found out about it, and he filed charges against Nora for wingin' him. After all the years that poor woman gave him, and he saw to it she went to jail. Got four years for it, too. That whole jury thought ol' Jake had it comin', but if they was to let her go, it'd put 'em all in jeopardy when half of 'em is doin' the same thing! Now he's taken up with that Raina Gentry. What a pair they make! Both of 'em meaner than spit. Why, if they died, everyone else in town would be restin' in peace!"

"Raina Gentry! That was little Carrie Elizabeth Gentry's mother, right?"

"That's right."

"Now I know y'all are wrong! There's no way *that* woman could be my mother. No way in … well, you know."

"Little girl, it's a sad thing in life that we don't get to pick the families we get borned into. We take what the good Lord gives us and hope for the best."

"What happened to Raina's husband?"

"He never come back with that woman when she returned from Europe. They say he was too destroyed by it all. But not nobody ever heard from that man again. Some rumors had it that he was dead soon after by his own hand. But no one knows for sure. No one really tried to find out."

A gust of wind caught the tail of Eden's dress and rustled it around her.

"Know what else, little girl. You done lost one of your beaus, runnin' off like that. Mr. Ryder, he might be near off the carpet."

"He is? With whom?" Eden smiled.

"It's sort of a new thing, but he and Afton are purty much sweet on each other."

"Afton! Why, Miss Alma, that's wonderful. They make a perfect match."

"Now, I think so too. But I know her ol' daddy ain't goin' to like it at all. But he's done give up on keepin' her down on the river bottom. The Bohannons, they sort of took her to heart. They treat her like she's their own daughter."

"I'm so glad for her. Afton is too fine to spend her life down on the river."

"Then there's Mr. J. D."

"J. D.?"

"Yes'em. He and that Paige Gresham, well, they be marryin' the end of the month."

Miss Alma paused for Eden's reaction, but there was none, and the old woman frowned in disappointment.

"I 'spect you and that Mr. Wynn Beckett be tyin' the knot soon, too. Right, little girl?"

"Oh, I don't know. Maybe, maybe not. Anyway, he hasn't exactly asked me."

Old Luther lifted his hind leg and scratched behind his ear. Lizzie rolled over on her side and stretched out beside him.

"Them dogs sure are getting on up in years. Why, they're most near as old for dogs, and I am for people."

They sat silently for a time, while Eden pondered unanswered questions.

"Tell me about your Thaddeus. Why didn't he come here with you and your children all those years ago?"

Miss Alma's hands stopped their shelling and lay limp across the pile of pea hulls. She put her head back on the rocker and took a deep breath, letting it out slowly.

"Thaddeus, he loved us so. He worked hard to put food on our table, helpin' out at the sawmill when they needed him, huntin' and farmin' when they didn't. God blessed us back then, and my children never knew hunger when their daddy was with us. We had a small little house back then. Weren't nothin' much, but it kept us warm in the winter and kept the rain out."

"Where was that?"

"Utopia, Mississippi. Do you know what utopia means, little girl?"

"Yes, ma'am, I do."

"I can say it was our utopia, sure 'nough. We was so happy back then, a fine family, blessed and full of love and hope."

Eden listened to Miss Alma's labored breathing and felt it sounded unnatural. At another time, she decided, she would talk to her about seeing a doctor. Instead, she said, "But he didn't come here with you. How come?"

"He would have if he could."

"Why couldn't he?"

"You ain't nothin' but persistent, ain't you, little girl?"

Miss Alma tried to feign anger, but all she could do was smile at Eden. She was just too happy having her little girl sitting back on her porch with her.

"I just love you, you old thing." Eden said, "I want to know all about you. Nothing wrong with that, now is there?"

"No, I 'spect not."

Eden must have hit a nerve because Miss Alma began to open up about the dark recesses of her past.

"We all went down to town on that dark day. Oh, it was a bright and sunny Saturday, but oh, such darkness lurkin' there in that mean ol' town. My Thad had the money he'd made that week at the sawmill. He gived it to me to buy flour and cornmeal cause our bins was empty. And he said to get the kids some penny candy. Oh my, my babies was excited 'bout that. They seldom got to go to town, and only had that penny candy once before at Christmas time. We walked the four miles from our little house, but it weren't bad. People was used to walkin' back then. We sang and laughed all the way to town.

"When we got there, them town folk, they just stared and stared like we was a bunch of scarecrows come to life. You see, colored folk didn't come much into Utopia. And them white folks, they liked it that way. But all we wanted was a little flour and cornmeal and them penny candies. My babies could feel it too. They got real quiet when we got around them white folk, and they kept they's little eyes down to the ground.

"When we got to the store, my Thad, he turned to tell me and the babies to be respectful of them what's inside and not to speak till we was spoke at. While he's tellin' us that, he reached for the door behind him, not realizin' it had already opened and a white gal, a Miss Dorothy Ketchum, was comin' out. His hand accidentally touched her shoulder, and she began screamin' real loud. He didn't mean to, little girl, he didn't even know she was there. But she kept screamin' that he'd touched her. Her daddy and uncles, they come runnin'. She got plumb hysterical, and my Thad, he kept tryin' to explain. But no one would listen. They began to beat my Thad, all of 'em. I was screamin' for them to stop and my babies was all cryin' and clingin' to me. They was saying awful things to my Thad, callin' him awful names. Then I saw my Thad fall to the ground. They was stompin' him hard with their dirty ol' boots. He called out to me. He say, *'Run! Run!'* So, I grabbed my babies and run as hard as I could. When we was a good ways down the road, I looked back. I saw that gal's daddy pull a pistol from his belt and take aim. I told my babies to keep runnin' and not look back. But I did, and I saw the flash and heard the pistol fire. Then they cheered. They actually cheered! Like they done a great thing. They committed murder in God's sight, and they cheered about it.

"Me and my babies, we was too scared to go back home. We was afraid they'd come for us too. I couldn't go to my papa, or he'd become a target for their hate. We huddled together in the woods that night, and the next mornin' we began to walk west. After three days of walkin', eatin' some berries and raw greens we found in the woods, we was worn out. We come to a train water tower. My babies climbed up the tower and got some water to drink, but I was too tired to do it. They splashed some down on me. After a while, a train come along, and it stopped to water up.

"I asked the man on the train if we could ride, and he said it would cost us some money. He asked me where I wanted to go. I held out my poor ol' Thad's money and told him just as far as this money would take us. He took the money and said to go get in the red car. It was a cattle car, but it was empty. Hadn't been cleaned out though and it smelled real bad. We sat in the doorway trying to breathe the air outside. It was a whole day on that train before I began to feel safe from them awful people in Utopia. I don't think my babies ever felt safe after that day. They thought them folks would come and get 'em and stomp 'em to death, too. They had nightmares, all of 'em, all their lives. But you know about nightmares don't you, little girl."

Eden didn't answer. The story Miss Alma had just shared with her made her feel sick inside. She absolutely felt paralyzed by the horror Miss Alma and her children had been forced to watch.

"You hear me, little girl? You still have your nightmares?"

Eden reached out and took Miss Alma's hand. "Miss Alma, I'm so sorry for what you went through. How were you able to stand it?"

"My strength's always come from the Lord, little girl. There ain't no other way to bear such things in this world. At one point, three days after we hitched on the train when it stopped at another water tower, the man told us to get off, he'd taken us far 'nough, and he'd be loadin' some cattle at the next town. Me and my babies didn't say a word. We jumped out of that smelly ol' cattle car and began to walk down the tracks. We come to a river and walked along its banks till we found a clearin' where we could rest without bein' seen. There was muscadines and poke greens along the fence lines, and we ate all we wanted. But it was hard on our stomachs, and we was sick a lot. Aubrey and my little River Lee walked on down the river the next day, and they found a pier and a boat. There was a fishin' pole in that boat. My babies left the pole, but they took some line and a hook. They made a fishin' pole from some cane growin' on down the river, and by nightfall, we had some fish to eat. River Lee still had his flint rock, and so we was able to build a fire to cook 'em. We were able to get warm again for the first time since we run.

"Days ran into more days, and I didn't know what to do, little girl. We couldn't stay there, but we didn't have no place to go. We didn't even know where we was. I couldn't have told you what state we was in. Our whole lives was comin' from that old muddy then. We drank from it, we bathed in it, we took our meals from it. Can you see why I love that ol' river so?"

"Just like the bottom landers."

"Yes. We was seen by some fisherman on the river. They told Camden Gentry 'bout us campin' out there on that muddy ol' river and he was bound and determined to chase us off. He come a-ridin' up on that big, white horse he had back then. But he had Miss Annaliese ridin' with him. I thought she was the most beautiful lady I'd ever seen. She told him we wasn't doin' him no harm. I 'spect he still wanted to look big in her eyes back then, so he said we could stay as long as we needed to. I still remember him liftin' her up onto her horse, and she leaned down and kissed him right there in front of us. I ain't never seen a woman kiss a man outdoors like that.

Then she looked at me with that beautiful smile of hers, and she winked like we had a secret 'tween us. Anyway, by nightfall, she had sent us some blankets and a big pot of stew. In a few days, she moved us up to a little outbuildin' behind the big house, and she fed and clothed my babies. I never forgot all she done for 'em. From that day on, I purposed to be all she needed me to be. So, you see, little girl, we didn't choose anything. But that great lady, she chose us. She been takin' care of us, ever since. And I set out to bless her as best I could for what she did for my babies and me."

Eden became aware of the clack of her rocker moving back and forth over the old porch boards as she went on.

"She told me I had a right to be crazy. Once she said she'd like to be crazy too. That way she could do what she liked. She had trouble keepin' her reins drawn in. I used to think she'd been happier down on the river bottom, where they wasn't so many rules to abide by. I sure do love my Miss Annaliese. She didn't never treat me like a hired girl. I always felt like her friend. 'Course, that didn't sit well with her family."

Eden was staring straight ahead. Her mind was playing out the scene Miss Alma had just described to her, the horror of her Thaddeus' death, their frightened odyssey to Texas, and finally, their protection under Annaliese Gentry. But, according to Miss Alma, what men meant for evil, God used for good. Miss Alma was convinced the hand of God was in it all, as she was somehow guided to the Ol' Missus' and a life that was probably better than they would have had in Utopia, Mississippi.

"But Thad," Miss Alma continued, "Oh, how I've missed my Thad. As I grew old and wrinkled, in my mind, he remained young and handsome. But I ain't never wavered in my devotion to him. Never looked at another man. Certainly, never gave no one else Thaddeus Mayhew's place in my heart."

# Twenty-Two

Just before dawn, Eden began to dream again, but not the dream of her childhood. In this dream, she is dressed in a white, gauzy gown, barefooted and running through the Thicket in the semi-dark of dusk. Suddenly the woods open to reveal the river bottom village. She watches as people mill around an old barn, unaware that she is there. They are laughing and dancing to fiddles and harmonicas.

There is a loud laugh that is familiar to her. She sees the wiry red hair being flung about in the same breeze that is causing her hair to slap against her face.

"Mama? Mama!"

The woman turns and looks Eden square into the eyes. But there is no recognition. The woman turns away and continues to laugh with the others who are gathered around her.

"Mama! Mama, please!"

But the woman goes inside the barn with the other revelers, and their laughter dies away as the doors close behind them. The whole area is still and empty, and she is alone as the sun quickly falls behind the pine tops. The dark of night swallows up the barn, the mud road, the village, and everything around her. Suddenly, Eden jerks awake.

Early afternoon found J. D. on the farm-to-market road that led back into Two Rivers. Paige had kidnapped him from his office and spirited him away to the river park for a picnic luncheon. He complained that he didn't have the time, but Paige looked so pretty, and she had prepared the picnic basket herself. How could he say no? But J. D. had to cut the picnic short because of an early afternoon board meeting. Paige had pouted, but complied, happy for the brief time he had allotted her.

"That was a good lunch, hon," J. D. said on the ride back to town.

"I just wish we could've stayed out at the park longer. You've been so busy lately. You never seem to have time for me anymore."

He put his hand on her knee, "I'll always make time for you. I canceled the Kirby's appointment at one, didn't I?"

"Yes, but I wish you could've skipped the board meeting too."

Paige slid across the seat and wrapped her arm around his neck. She kissed his cheek, then nibbled his ear lobe. When he didn't respond, she became more persistent. But he had been distracted by the sight of a red sports car, that had turned onto the road that led to the river bottom.

"Blast it!" he said.

"What?" Paige shrunk back, wondering what she had done wrong.

"Eden!"

"Eden Devereaux?"

"Yes. She just headed down to the river bottom."

"That's silly, Jeff. She went back to West Texas months ago."

"Actually, she came back the day before yesterday."

"Day before yesterday? How do you know that?"

"I saw her yesterday."

"For heaven's sake, where?"

"Out at Miss Alma's."

Paige flounced over to her side of the car. "What were you doing out at that forsaken, old place?"

"Mom and I went to see Miss Alma. We didn't know Eden had come back."

"Oh, sure!"

"No, really. I'd found some old newspaper clippings, and I wanted to ask Miss Alma about them. But you know Miss Alma. She's not going to give out any information about her Miss Annaliese, even if it might help Eden. I don't understand any of that."

"How long have you been gathering information for Eden Devereaux?"

"I spent a few afternoons at the courthouse, looking through some old record books, that's all."

"You can't have a long lunch with me, but you can take afternoons off for that! Jeff, I'm not going to put up with that girl disrupting our lives again. Do you hear me?"

"We'll have to talk about it later. Right now, I'm sorry to say, we're going to have to follow her. It's not safe for her to go down there alone. I don't know what she's thinking!"

"Jefferson Dixon Callahan, don't you dare take me down to that horrible place!"

"I don't have any choice, Paige."

"Like heck, you don't! Jeff, don't you dare turn that wheel!"

Paige shrieked as his car turned and began to bounce along the pitted road.

Eden caught the bottom landers off guard. No one had been standing down the road stopping the interlopers. She pulled up to the store, where she had passed out Christmas gifts the previous winter, but she didn't get out of her car. The man who owned the store recognized her and walked to the edge of the boardwalk curiously.

"Can I help you?"

"Yes, thank you. Can you tell me where I can find Angie Dupree?"

"Angie? She lives down yonder," he said, pointing down a dirt lane, "At the very end."

J. D. pulled in beside her and, as a group of river bottom men began to mill around them, J. D. went to Eden's window.

"Eden, what in the world are you doing?"

Two men moved toward J. D. but the man on the boardwalk raised his hand slightly, and they stopped.

"What are you doing here, J. D.?" Eden asked.

"I saw you turn off the highway. Eden, you know better than to come down here, and especially by yourself!"

"There's someone I have to see."

"Who?" J. D. was losing his temper, and he was keenly aware of the men who were gathering about.

"That's none of your business," Eden said defiantly.

"I'm making it my business. You start your car and come back to town with Paige and me right now."

A dirty, gapped-toothed bottom lander walked up to J. D.'s car and stared at Paige. As her eyes registered disgust, he smiled and spit his chaw out where the tooth gaped.

"J. D.! Take me home now!" she yelled.

The men that had gathered only laughed at her shrill voice.

"J. D., if you don't come on, I swear I'll go without you!"

"Just a minute, Paige."

"No J. D.! I mean now! Come now!"

"He ain't no dog, lady," someone yelled at Paige.

"J. D., you have that board meeting to get to, remember!" Paige yelled.

Eden was getting alarmed, as more people began to gather around them.

"Please, J. D., just go. Take Paige back to town," Eden said.

"Not without you."

"But you're ruining everything."

"What, Eden? What am I ruining?"

They heard J. D.'s car start and saw Paige behind the wheel. She backed up slightly and called to J. D.

"Are you getting in?"

J. D. turned to Eden, "Will you come with us?"

"I can't. Please believe me. I really can't."

He turned back to Paige, "Go on back to town, hon, and tell Sid that I won't be back for the board meeting this afternoon. I'll call you later when I get home."

He heard an oath he had never heard Paige use before as she gunned the engine and fled down the road in a swirl of angry dust.

The locals guffawed at Paige's retreat, chunking pine cones, and waving mock good-byes. A rock hit the back window and left a crack. She floored the gas and bounced around from one pothole to another, cursing all the way to the highway. J. D. felt sorry for putting her through that, but at least she was safe now, which is more than he could say about Eden or himself.

"Now what?" J. D. asked.

"Get in," Eden said, resigned.

She slowly pulled down the narrow dirt trail toward the Dupree place, as the men gathered on the boardwalk behind them. The store owner explained that she was a friend of Aunt Mim's and had helped with their Christmas gifts. Though she didn't know it, she had nothing to fear from them.

"What's going on?" J. D. asked. "What is so important that it's going to get me skinned alive by Paige?"

"I'm sorry about that, J. D. But I didn't ask you to tag along. It's just that I have to see someone."

"Who?"

"Angie Dupree."

"Who's Angie Dupree?"

"Someone I saw when I came down here with Aunt Mim last Christmas."

"You've been out here before?"

"Just that once," she admitted.

"I didn't know that."

"You don't know everything about me, J. D. Callahan," she said, and her defiance made him smile. "I helped Aunt Mim give out food and Christmas gifts if you must know!"

"Actually admirable, but a little crazy."

"It wasn't to the children down here."

He felt ashamed for having said it.

The Dupree house stood square at the end of the muddy trail, and the ruts led their car right into its front yard and up to its porch. Like all the houses on the river bottom, it looked as if it had seen better days. However, it was large and solidly built—not a tarpaper lean-to, like many of the houses on the river.

J. D. saw a woman sitting on the porch, a red-haired woman in a floral sundress. She was staring at them suspiciously.

"Is that Angie Dupree?" he asked. Eden didn't answer.

He noticed how still she had become and her face had paled.

"Eden, what is it?"

She didn't take her eyes from the woman, but her hand moved to his, and she placed a photo there.

J. D. looked at it, then up at the woman on the porch.

"Where did you get a picture of that woman?"

"That's a picture of my mother."

"What?"

He looked more closely at the photo, then squinted at the woman.

"But I thought your mother was dead."

"She is."

"I don't get it."

"I don't either. But that's why I'm here."

The woman left the porch and moved toward their car. She put her hand on the hood and leaned forward to see Eden more clearly.

"Can I do somethin' for you folk? You know this here's private property."

Eden couldn't speak, her lips just wouldn't work for her, and she was having trouble controlling her emotions. It was as if Bett was standing there, and she desperately wanted it to be true.

There was an awkward silence, while J. D. got out of the car.

"I'm J. D. Callahan, ma'am. I was wondering if you could tell us if you know this person."

He held the photo out and watched as the woman blanched. Now she was the one unable to speak.

"Do you need to sit down?" J. D. asked.

"I think you'd better leave."

"Not until we get some answers, ma'am."

"Where did you get that photo?" the woman asked.

"That's a photo of this lady's mother."

It was Angie Dupree's turn to stare. "That right? This here a picture of your maw?"

Eden nodded.

"It's obvious you and she are twins," J. D. said.

"Where is the woman in the picture?" Angie Dupree asked.

J. D. paused and looked at Eden, who looked down at her hands.

"I'm sorry to have to tell you, ma'am, but she died about eight or so months back."

Angie Dupree looked like someone had punched her in the stomach. Her brow furrowed and for a moment, she had to look away to hide her emotions. She finally said, "I can't tell you folks nothin'. I don't know who that woman is. Now, if ya'll will just be goin'."

She turned and headed back to the porch.

"But ma'am."

"You better go, or I'll call my daddy on you. Go on! Get off our land! He won't be as understandin' as me. He'll get his rifle out. Do you understand me? Just go!"

J. D. paused for a moment before he opened Eden's door.

"Slide over and let me drive you home." For once, she did as she was told.

Her car slowly moved back down the trail and away from the shantytown under the careful scrutiny of men, many of whom did not wish them well. When they reached the highway, J. D. patted her hand. But she did not respond, and he didn't speak again until they entered her house.

Eden was glad that Ryder was at the river house visiting Afton when they arrived. They would have to entertain J. D. She excused herself and went to her room with a feigned headache.

Ryder took his cue, kissed Afton goodbye, and drove J. D. back into town.

Eden knew J. D. would call Paige as soon as he got home. She hoped he wasn't in too much trouble.

It would not be Paige he thought about as he drifted off to sleep that night, but the other girl, her mother, and the look-a-like down on the river bottom. For the life of him, he couldn't make any sense of it.

# Twenty-Three

Miss Alma slept through the breakfast hour and didn't emerge from her room until midmorning. Afton had left grits for her on the stove, but she couldn't eat them. By nightfall, Miss Alma was running a fever. The following morning, she was lethargic, and Eden took her to see Dr. Tobias. He gave her a shot and asked Eden to fill a prescription for antibiotics. After taking Miss Alma home, Eden dropped the order off at the pharmacy and walked to Clarice's bookstore to visit while the pharmacist filled it.

"Eden!" Clarice called out as she entered and the bell jingled. "Good to see you, dear."

Clarice was not alone. She and Aunt Mim were having coffee, and they offered her some.

"Ryder came by this morning. He said Miss Alma's feeling poorly," Clarice said.

"Yes, ma'am. I just dropped off a prescription at the drug store, so I can't stay long."

"Eden, J. D. told me about your trip to the river bottom," Clarice said.

Aunt Mim's eyebrows raised. "What you go down there for, girl?"

"I wanted to meet Angie Dupree."

"Whatever for?" Aunt Mim asked.

"Because she looks exactly like my mother," she said, rummaging through her handbag, and handing them her mother's photograph.

Recognizing the face of the woman who looked like Angie Dupree, Aunt Mim exclaimed, "My stars and garters, she sure does."

"I'll have to take your word for it. But that really is an odd thing," Clarice added.

Aunt Mim looked up at Eden, "Say now. I seem to remember something that might help you. Angie Dupree did have a sister, an identical twin sister. I remember now, the two of them, years and years back. Two little red headed girls, like two peas in a pod. Couldn't tell 'em apart. Let's see. Their names were Angelina and Bettina. So, if the woman on the river is Angelina or Angie ..."

"And my mother's name was Bett, short for Bettina! It fits!"

"What did this Angie Dupree have to say?" Clarice asked.

"J. D. showed her the picture. But she said she didn't know who it was. Isn't that silly? It must have been like looking into a mirror."

"Your mama must have been Bettina Dupree. But I wonder why she called herself Bett Devereaux? There were a bunch of Devereauxs in Two Rivers a good spell back. Who was your daddy, dear?" Clarice asked.

"She would never talk to me about my daddy. She even got angry if I brought it up. I learned to leave it be. Aunt Mim, the next time you go down to the river bottom, could you ask some of the folks about this Bettina Dupree? Maybe find out when she left Two Rivers and why?"

"I'll do what I can. But they're a tight-lipped bunch."

Wynn came at the end of the week and moved into the back room at the end of the upstairs hall. Eden was glad. Miss Alma wasn't getting better, and on his second day there, he helped Eden get her into his car to take her to the hospital for tests. For half a day, she was poked and prodded, bled and x-rayed. Finally, Doctor Tobias called Eden into Miss Alma's room to explain that Alma's kidneys were shutting down, and things were not looking good.

"What does that mean?" Eden asked.

"Her kidneys are failing. Barely functioning. They'll gradually get worse and worse."

Eden patted Miss Alma's hand.

"So, what do we do?" Eden asked.

"I'm sorry, ladies."

Eden frowned. "Do you mean to say there's nothing we *can* do?"

"I *am* truly sorry. The only thing that would help would be a transplant. It's done some in the city, but at your age, Alma, no one would perform that kind of surgery on you."

Eden was shocked. She found herself unable to speak.

"How long, Doctor?" Alma asked, matter-of-factly.

"Alma, some ordinary lady might have a month or so. But you've always been a tough old bird. I 'spect you'll go a-ways further than that."

"Do I stay here, or can I go home?"

"You can go on home this afternoon. No restrictions. You can do anything you feel like doing. Call me when you can't get around much anymore, or if you experience any unusual discomfort or pain. I can help you with that."

Wynn picked them up and drove them home. He helped Miss Alma into the house and placed her on the sofa. Around four, J. D. brought Clarice and Aunt Mim by, and Eden asked them to stay for dinner. Ryder came too, carrying a fist full of his mother's pink daylilies, and Afton placed them in a tall vase on the table. The meal was subdued and uncomfortable. Miss Alma never felt at ease at the dining room table, especially now while everyone spoke softly and tiptoed around as if she was already an invalid. Eden was grateful when they left, and she could finally slip away to her room to be alone. She allowed herself to be sad then and spent out her emotions with her tears into her pillow. Eden hadn't been there for her mother when she went through this. But she would be there for Miss Alma.

The following morning, Eden found Miss Alma sitting in her rocker on the front porch. Eden sat down on the steps and wrapped her arms around her knees. For a while, there was a comfortable silence. The only sound was the chirping of summer sparrows. An acorn fell at the foot of the steps, and Eden looked up to see two squirrels playing chase across the tree-tops.

"I don't want you to be burdened by this, little girl, cause I ain't."

Eden couldn't think of anything to say to her.

"It's like steppin' through a doorway, and one I've wanted to pass through lots of times before."

Again, Eden was silent.

Nub Henry came around the end of the house and walked up to the porch.

"Alma, you okay?"

"I'm fine, Nub. My, how news travels fast 'round here!"

"I just need to know how you're doin'."

"I'm doing okay. When the time comes, I'll be okay then, too. I'll be seein' my Thaddeus again, and my babies."

She was able to smile.

"I envy you that, old woman."

"I know you do, Nub."

Nub looked at Eden and nodded. Eden nodded back. Then he was gone, and there was quiet again.

"Little girl, there's things you want to know, things I can tell you, but I have promises to keep. *I have promises to keep.*"

Eden felt her body stiffen, but she continued to look straight ahead.

"Even if I think you have a right to know them things, I did make a promise, a blood promise. But it was a long time ago. Things was different back then."

Eden turned to her. "Miss Alma, you've kept your blood promise all these years. Do you think that it makes any difference now?"

"I don't know. I just don't know. There could still be trouble."

"What kind of trouble?"

Miss Alma didn't answer. She weighed things in her mind, then took a deep breath.

"I'll cut you a deal, little girl. I'll tell you what you want to know, but you have to do somethin' for me first."

"I'd do anything for you, Miss Alma. You know that. Just name it."

"I want Mr. J. D. to take me back to Utopia, and I'll need you to go help me get around. I mean, he can drive us, and look out for us and all such. But I may need help with dressin' and bathin' and such."

"Utopia?"

"It was my home, little girl, mine and Thad's. I'd like to go home and pay my respects at his graveside. I never got a chance to before. I wonder if our house is still standin'. I'd like to go back there where my babies was born and remember good times we had before."

"But the bad memories ... are you okay with them?"

"It was a long time ago. And with God's grace, I've forgiven them men. The hate I had for them, in the beginning, was only hurting me, not them. If I could put my hands on my Thad's grave and let him know to be watchin' for me, that'd give me a lot of peace."

Eden finally turned to her, "When do you want to leave?"

As expected, Wynn was not happy about it. He wanted to go with them, but Eden said Miss Alma might need to lie down in the back seat, so there just wouldn't be enough room for him to tag along. J. D. was the only young man Miss Eden trusted.

"Eden, you can't be serious! Dragging that old woman out of state to see someplace where she used to live some forty years ago, and when she's about to die anyway!"

"Wynn, I've got to do this. You don't understand how important this is to Miss Alma."

"Then tell me why it's so all-fired important!"

"I can't. It's her story to tell, not mine. You just have to trust me."

"I'm tired of always having to trust you, Eden. Of always being kept in the dark about the things in your life."

"It'll only be for three or four days. Surely you won't begrudge me a few days."

"What am I supposed to do while you're off sight-seeing? Just sit around this dump and wait?"

Eden cringed again. The river house had become precious to her. It felt more like home at that moment than the house she grew up in. It was unkind of him to call it a dump. She understood that he was angry and unsure about their relationship, but he didn't have to be mean.

"That's a decision only you can make."

"Stop all this nonsense and come back to Rising Star with me."

"So that in a couple of weeks I can see you off to Princeton again, then sit around all day, totally alone, in my mother's old house? Even all our high school friends have gone off to school or jobs."

Wynn gritted his teeth. He recognized it as truth, as well as another losing battle.

"When do you go?"

"Day after tomorrow."

"Then I'm leaving tomorrow."

"I hate to hear that, but that's your choice to make."

⊱━━━❀━━━⊰

Across town, J. D. was having the same battle with Paige.

"Jefferson Dixon Callahan, I won't have it. I just won't have it! Why we're in the middle of planning a wedding. I need you here to help with the decision making."

"Hon, you're capable of taking care of that all by yourself. After all, you haven't liked any of my ideas to date. So, go ahead and plan it the way you want. You will anyway," he teased. He kissed her on the tip of her nose playfully. To him, she was like an untamed colt, and he just needed to give her lots of rein.

"What will my friends think, my betrothed going off for a week with an old colored woman and *that* girl!"

"Don't be disrespectful."

"Jeff, if you go, I swear I won't marry you when you come back!"

Paige recognized it as a tactical blunder the moment the words passed her lips. She wished she could take them back. She knew J. D. didn't respond to threats, and she certainly didn't want to hand him over to Eden on a silver platter. He was still the best catch in Two Rivers, and she always got the best. She was so close to closing the deal, yet she knew she had to walk carefully. She was glad when he didn't respond to her threat.

"We're leaving the day after tomorrow. I thought we could spend tomorrow together. Maybe drive over to Houston and see a movie at the River Oaks. Would that make you happy?" But he knew nothing would make her happy now. He also knew that when he got back, she would pout, ignore him for a while, then all things would be as before.

❦

The following morning, Eden was sitting at the kitchen table when Wynn came down the stairs, suitcases in hand. She could see him as he went outside to load them into his car, letting the screen door slam. When he came back inside, he came straight to her.

"Won't you reconsider? Please come home with me."

It was a bad choice of words because Eden felt like she was home. *Why can't he understand that?*

"Let's not do this. You know I can't."

"I know you *won't*, and that's the truth of it. I mean, you could if you cared enough about me."

"I love you, Wynn. Seems like I always have."

"Just not as much as you love that old woman!"

"Shush, she'll hear you!"

"Walk me out then."

A morning breeze wrapped around the house and whipped her hair out of place. She pushed it back with her arm, revealing her remarkable eyes. He took her face in his hands, stared into the blue tinting of those irises, and frowned.

"This has the feel of finality to it."

"Don't be silly," she said, putting her arms around his waist.

He kissed her for a brief few seconds then he got into his car and drove off. Eden felt sad that he didn't even look back.

Paige hadn't been able to sleep the night before. Today, her Jeff was leaving her behind to take a trip with *that* girl. She couldn't even bring herself to think about it. Desperation is a powerfully motivating force, and it propelled Paige from her bed before daylight. She thoughtfully considered her wardrobe before choosing an outfit that she felt would keep her in his mind the whole time he would be gone. It was a pink cashmere sweater vest that she usually wore over a blouse. But without one, she felt confident in her allure. Her cream skirt was shorter than usual, revealing her tan legs. She fixed her hair to perfection, swept up with pearl clips, and she doused herself with the heavy scent of *Shalimar*. This was the image she would send him off with, and maybe he wouldn't be able to go at all. She could imagine, couldn't she?

J. D. saw Paige's car as he turned off the highway onto Camp Ruby Road. She was sitting on the hood, waving at him as he pulled in beside her, surprised to find her there.

"Paige," he said, getting out, "what are you doing out here this early?"

"I just had to see you once more before you left," she said, jumping down and putting her arms around his waist. Her carefully choreographed veneer didn't go unnoticed as she smiled at him.

"Hon, that's great, but I'm running late."

She put her arms around his neck and pulled his face close to hers until they were nose to nose. "I love you sooo much it hurts sometimes. I can't wait until we're married."

She started kissing him, but he pulled back too soon, and she took it as a rebuff.

"What's wrong?"

"I know what you're up to, Paige. Some sort of seduction scene to make me stay. But it won't work. Now, go back home, and I'll see you in a few days."

She cursed at him, stomped back into her car, hit the gas pedal, fishtailed, and sped back toward town, kicking up dust and debris into his slightly amused face.

# Twenty-Four

By noon, the trio had passed over the border into Louisiana and eaten burgers at The Happy Cajun Café outside of Alexandria. Eden looked sweet in her plaid seersucker blouse and blue pedal pushers, affixed with a navy belt. She wore no jewelry, minimal makeup, and the sweet smell of honeysuckle.

"Children, how about singin' ol' Alma a song?" the old woman asked.

"Sure," J. D. smiled, "what would you like to hear? We take requests."

"They was a song my Thad used to sing to my babies. I think it was called, *Hush-A-Bye*. You know it?"

Eden looked at J. D. and began to sing.

"Hush-a-bye, don't you cry, go to sleep, my little baby.

When you wake, you shall have, all the pretty little horses."

J. D. added his voice.

"Dapples and grays, pintos and bays, all the pretty little horses."

That began a game of trying to see how many different songs they could come up with before nightfall. They took turns naming songs and had to sing at least the first verse or the chorus. The first one to get stuck would lose and would have to tote the winner's luggage into the motel that night.

By dusk they'd totaled up an amazing number of songs from Perry Como's, *Catch a Falling Star*, to Johnny Cash's, *I Walk the Line*, from Bobby Vinton's, *Blue Velvet*, to Gene Pitney's, *Only Love Can Break a Heart*, from hymns like *The Old Rugged Cross*, to silly children's songs like *I'm a Little Tea Pot*. That one had left them both laughing like school children. They'd gone through all the Christmas songs they knew, and musical vignettes from *Oklahoma* to *South Pacific*. They knew they were winding down when J. D. began *The Star-Spangled Banner*.

Suddenly Eden was blank, and J. D. shouted out in victory, "The master! You may address me as *Your Majesty* the rest of the trip!"

Eden mumbled that now he would be insufferably arrogant for the remainder of the trip.

Miss Alma, smiling in the back seat, spoke up, "We in Mississippi yet?"

"Yes, ma'am, just over the line," J. D. answered.

"Say, children, it's gettin' mighty late. We best be findin' a place to lay down these ol' bones."

J. D. stopped in the next town and got rooms. He helped Miss Alma from the car. She was stiff from the long ride, and he had to steady her while toting her suitcase. Eden brought her own bag in and helped Miss Alma to one of the beds, where the old woman stretched out comfortably.

"My, they stuck us in the back of this place, didn't they?" Eden said.

J. D. pulled her aside and said, "When they saw Miss Alma, they said they didn't rent rooms to coloreds."

"You're not serious!"

J. D. nodded, "But when I threatened to make trouble for them, they decided discretion is the better part of valor, and they gave us these rooms in the back. But of course, there won't be any other guests placed close to us until we leave."

"That's just fine with me."

J. D. walked to the motel diner and bought them roast beef sandwiches for supper. When he got back, Eden had Miss Alma in her nightgown and tucked into one of the beds. They spread the food out on the other bed and ate it picnic style while sitting cross-legged. Now the challenge was to see who could flip a chip highest into the air and catch it in their mouth. J. D. leaned back too far to catch his chip and fell from the bed, crashing into the wall making a loud thud. The two broke into laughter, but Miss Alma scolded them like little children.

"Stop that now, young'uns. You two are actin' like a couple of bottom boys. If you ain't careful, you're goin' to get us thrown out of this here place!"

That only made them laugh louder as Miss Alma said, "Humph!"

After a while, Eden took a shower, and J. D. turned to *Alfred Hitchcock Presents* on the black and white television. When Eden came out in her pink terrycloth robe and fuzzy slippers, she found J. D. and Miss Alma staring attentively at the screen.

"Say, people," she started.

"Shush," they both said, neither of them looking at her.

J. D. was propped up on a pillow, and Eden sat down beside him.

"You need anything, Miss Alma?" she asked.

"Shooo honey. I sure do like this here TV thing. Just looky."

Eden thought, *when we return home, Miss Alma will have a television set of her own. I'll see to it.*

Eden curled up on her side, and soon she had fallen asleep.

When the program ended, Miss Alma said, "Weren't that somethin'. I got to get me one of them things. Weren't that show the scariest thing you ever seen in all your born days?"

J. D. turned the set off and stretched out across the bottom of the bed, propping himself up on one elbow.

"Tell me why it's so important for you to go back to Mississippi. You have family there?"

She poured out the whole sordid tale about Thaddeus and his murderers. Halfway through her story, Eden sighed heavily and turning slightly, pushed against J. D. with her foot. He wondered if she was doing it on purpose to knock him off the bed.

"So why in Sam Hill do you want to go back to a place like that?"

"To be there at my Thad's grave. I'll never again get to see the place where we was in love, and where my babies was borned. I need to pay my respects."

She yawned then, and J. D. sat up and smacked Eden hard on her backside. She shrieked and sat up as Miss Alma shushed them again.

"Dadburn it, J. D.! I was asleep!"

"No welching, if you please."

"What are you talking about?"

"I won. Now get out there and carry my suitcase into my room."

"You've got to be kidding!"

"No, I'm not."

"I'm not about to go out there dressed like this, just because ..."

But before she could finish, he stood up, grabbed her arm, and hoisted her over his shoulder. He marched right out to the car and unlocked the trunk before putting her feet back on the ground, as she tried hard to stifle her scorn.

"There it is."

He motioned to the black suitcase.

Eden stomped her feet in fury and yanked it hard from the trunk. It was heavy, but she was not about to let him see she was having any difficulty. She marched from his car to the next door down and waited for him to open it, which he did ever so slowly. When the door swung open, J. D. took the suitcase and set it inside.

"Why, Miss Devereaux, I don't think it's at all proper for a young lady to come into a single gentleman's room," he teased. "Now you be on your way, and though I had a nice time today, there'll be no goodnight kiss for you."

"Kiss, indeed! What you need is a good slap!" she said, stomping back to her room.

J. D. stood in the doorway of his room until she was safely inside and he heard her click the lock. He showered and crawled into bed, still smiling as he thought of yet another song they had missed, and he began to hum, *It Had to Be You.*

><><><

The desk clerk gave J. D. a wake-up call at seven the next morning and connected him to Eden's room.

"Hello?" she barely mumbled.

"Hey, I thought of another song. 'Good Mornin', good mornin', we've slept the whole night through. Good mornin', good mornin' to you'."

"Good grief, J. D. What time is it?"

"It's seven, and time for us to be on the road."

"Just one more hour please," she begged.

"Sorry. I've mapped out the route to Utopia, and we need to get started."

"Ugh!" she groaned. "Okay, we'll be ready in about forty-five minutes."

"Thirty!"

"Okay! Okay!"

By twelve noon, they had reached the outskirts of Utopia. They stopped for an early lunch and asked the waitress if she could give them directions to New Hope Baptist Church, Miss Alma's daddy's church, and the place they'd have buried Thaddeus Mayhew.

"No sir, I can't. But I'll look it up for you in the phone directory."

"Thanks."

When she returned with their check, she had the address and the directions written down for them.

As they passed through the center of Utopia, Eden asked Miss Alma if she recognized anything. But nothing was as the old woman remembered. That was to be expected in the span of sixty years. After a few miles, Miss Alma gripped the seat and leaned forward with excitement.

"Yonder it is. Look-a' yonder. That's New Hope. Lord have mercy. It's still there and it ain't changed none at all."

The church was small with a high steeple that almost disappeared into the clouds. It was freshly painted a bright milk-white. Off to the side was a parking area and beyond that was a cemetery nestled into the edge of the woods. The graves were ringed by an ornate iron fence. J. D. was able to drive all the way up to the iron gate, where they stepped out of the car and into the bright sunlight.

No one spoke as J. D. swung the gate open and the rusted hinges screeched. At first, Miss Alma hung onto Eden's arm. But once inside, she moved from grave to grave, recognizing names and remembering. There was the resting place of her own mama and papa, her sister Juno, and Juno's husband and children. She found her grandma on her father's side, and her best friend when she was a young girl. She had died at only twenty-nine which made Miss Alma sad. Then she stumbled upon Thad's mother, Lois Mayhew, and his father, Sam. Around them were their children, Thad's brothers and sisters, and their families.

J. D. saw the stones labeled Mayhew and he moved close to Miss Alma. She reached out and took his arm the moment her eyes fell on what she had been searching for—Thaddeus Samuel Mayhew. J. D. walked her to the stone, and she ran her fingers across it. It was cold to her touch, hand-hewn, and not smooth. She bent down and placed both hands palm down on the earth that covered her Thad and breathed the scent of it.

"Could I be alone, children? I want to talk to my Thad. Tell him all about his babies, all about those things he never got the chance to know. Go wait for me in the car. Now scoot."

"Sure," J. D. said, taking Eden's arm, and guiding her back toward the gate.

They had taken only a few steps when Eden gasped. At first, she stood still, planted like one of the gravestones. Then she spun around with such determination, that J. D. was momentarily thrown off balance.

"Eden!" he said, as she hurried back to Miss Alma.

"Oh, my Lord in heaven!" Eden cried out, as she took Miss Alma's arm.

"What is it, little girl? Why's you so riled?"

"Eden, for heaven's sake," J. D. said, catching up to her.

"Look! Just look!" she said, pointing at the grave-stone.

"What?" Miss Alma cried, but J. D. saw it already. It was right there, staring back at them, Thaddeus Mayhew's death date.

"The date, Miss Alma! Look at the date!"

She did. For a moment, it didn't register. Then her hands flew to her mouth.

"But ... but that say he didn't die back in the twenties. That say he died only four years ago!"

A wicked wind hit them square in the face, hard and summer hot. The clearing grew still and silent until somewhere, far off, a covey of quail took flight, and their eyes followed them upward, to look away for just a moment, to think about what was exploding in their minds. Standing in the hot sunshine, Miss Alma grew cold and began to shake.

# Twenty-Five

Eden put Miss Alma into the car and worried that she was hyperventilating. Her breaths were quick and labored. She hurriedly wet her handkerchief at the faucet against the church building, crawled into the back seat, and bathed Miss Alma's face with the wet cloth, as J. D. swiftly drove them back into town. He stopped at the first roadside motel they came across. Once Eden had Miss Alma comfortably stretched out on her bed, she asked if she needed to see a doctor.

"No, no. Just let me rest a while and think."

"What can we do for you?" J. D. asked.

"Help me understand it, little boy."

"I wish I could. But I don't understand it myself."

"J. D., do you think we could go to the courthouse and see if there are any records on Thaddeus? Surely, we can find some information about him," Eden said.

"Let's check the archives of the local newspaper first."

"Miss Alma, will you be alright if we leave you alone for a few hours?"

"Go, children. Find out what you can. I need to know the truth of it."

The old woman closed her eyes and didn't speak to them again.

An elderly woman with a graying French twist guided them to the basement of the newspaper building and showed them large binders of old newspapers.

"What do you need?"

"We aren't exactly sure," Eden said, "We need to look at summer issues from the mid-twenties."

"These are all labeled on the spines," the woman said, pulling one out and placing it on a long table. "This is May through September of 1923. Be careful with the pages. These newspapers are quite fragile."

"Thank you," J. D. said, as the woman left them.

"It's so dusty down here," Eden said, waving her hand in front of her face, as she opened the huge binder.

J. D. pulled another from the shelves, placed it on the table beside hers and began to leaf through the large pages. She didn't know how long they had been there. She only knew it had been quite a while, and she'd lost track of time when J. D. said, "Don't you think we'd better go back to the motel and check on Miss Alma?"

"Just a minute," she said absentmindedly, as J. D. began to shove the binders back into their dusty places on the shelves.

"J. D., come here. Take a look at this."

J. D. read the headline over her shoulder: Colored Man Molests Young White Girl.

"Is it?" she asked.

"I think so. Yes, look here."

He read out loud, "'A local colored man, T. S. Mayhew, went before judge M. L. Mayo this morning to be indicted on charges of molesting a white child yesterday morning, in plain view of local citizens at O'Dell's Grocery and Feed. He was badly beaten by a crowd of men who were outraged by the incident and even shot in the shoulder by the girl's father. Judge Mayo held Mayhew over for trial.'"

"He didn't die! He wasn't killed by that mob! Keep looking!"

J. D. continued through the papers until they came upon another article, *Molestation Trial Begins Today.* Only two days later, a final article, *Mayhew gets Ten Years for Improper Conduct with a Child.*

"Remarkable," Eden said as J. D. slowly closed the binder and placed it back on the shelf. "Alive all those years and Miss Alma never knew. Why didn't he find her? Why didn't he try to get in touch with her in all those years?"

"Maybe he didn't love her as much as she loved him," J. D. said.

"I don't believe that."

"We've got to tell her the whole of it."

"I know. But I sure wish we could spare her this final pain. She's been through so much already."

⊱━❦━⊰

Sitting in the motel room, Eden took Miss Alma's hand and leaned close.

"Miss Alma, your husband didn't die the day you and your children fled Utopia."

Miss Alma didn't respond to Eden in any way.

J. D. sat down beside her and said, "He was badly beaten and shot in the shoulder, but he didn't die. He went to trial for molestation and was found guilty."

"Molestation? You mean that white girl? Why ... it was an accident! I tell you he didn't even see her there! He was just trying to open the door for us."

"We know. But they found him guilty and sentenced him to ten years in prison."

"I can't believe it! My Thad lived! He lived!"

"Yes ma'am, he sure did."

"He was in prison all those years?"

"The first ten anyway."

There was a long silence while they let Miss Alma digest it.

"Little girl, little boy, I think I'd like to be alone a spell. Why don't y'all go someplace and leave me be a while."

"I don't think that's a good idea. Why don't you let me stay with you?" Eden said.

"No, child. I need to think on this a spell. And I need to pray."

"But," Eden began, but J. D. silenced her by putting his hand on her shoulder.

"Eden and I will be right next door. If you need us, just knock on the wall, and we'll come."

Miss Alma smiled up at J. D., "You're a good man, Mr. J. D. Callahan."

J. D. left Eden in his room while he went for takeout at the motel diner. When he returned, she was leafing through the phone directory from the bedside table.

"Look at this. There's a listing in the phone book for a T. S. Mayhew!"

J. D. took the book and laid it down on the nightstand.

"Enough of that for today," he said. "We'll check it out tomorrow. But for now, you need to relax for the rest of the evening. We've had a hard two days."

She didn't object when he put his hand on the back of her neck and began to squeeze the tight muscles at the base of her neck. She rolled her head from side to side and uttered a soft sigh. She thought it should have felt too intimate, but it did not.

"That was nice," she said when he stopped.

"How about dinner and a movie?" he asked.

"Sounds like a date to me," she smiled.

"It is what it is," he said, handing her a plate of chow mein and egg rolls. He pulled sodas out of a sack and popped their caps off before giving her one, and lifting the other into the air.

"A toast to the greatest detectives since Sam Spade," he said, clanking his bottle against hers.

"We are pretty good, aren't we?" Eden smiled.

"An amazing investigative team."

After eating, Eden asked, "What now? The movie?"

J. D. turned the television on, but there was nothin' that seemed interesting to either of them.

"I have an idea. We can't leave," J. D. said, "But wait here a minute."

He went out to his car and pulled a box out from under the rear seat. He placed it on the nightstand beside Eden.

"Chess! How did you know I played?"

"Just a guess."

"You carry a chess set around in your car?"

"Leftover from college days. I'd forgotten it was there until now."

"You and Paige don't play?"

"Paige is more of a checkers kind of gal."

"That's funny. I'd have thought bingo. You get to win prizes."

They laughed as they set up the board.

The game went slowly, lasting most of an hour, when Eden declared, "Checkmate!"

"I demand another game. That was a fluke!" J. D. said.

"Don't be such a sore loser. Just face it, I'm smarter than you," she said, grinning.

He threw his pillow at her.

"Hey!" she said, throwing it back.

"Hey, yourself," he said, whopping her with it, and pinning her down.

They were breathless when they stopped laughing, and Eden looked up into J. D.'s dark eyes.

"J. D.," she said, righting herself, "it's really wonderful of you to do this for Miss Alma. I know she appreciates it, and so do I." He smiled as she went on, "I think I'd better go check on her, don't you?"

"Let me go," J. D. said, going to the door. "She likes me best anyway," he teased, then ducked as she threw the pillow at him again.

Eden heard him tap on Miss Alma's door, but there was no answer, so he used the passkey. Miss Alma was sleeping peacefully, so he quietly closed and locked her door, and returned to his own room.

"She's fine. Sleeping," Eden heard him say. She had turned on the television and was watching the beginning of a movie.

"What's this?"

"*Kings Row,* starring Ronald Reagan. He is sooo dreamy. Don't you think?"

"Oh, sure ... I do!" he exaggerated. "So, what else is on?" he said, turning the channel.

"Hey! I was watching that!"

"But it's a girl's movie!"

"So? I'm a girl, in case you hadn't noticed."

"Oh, I've noticed. Believe me, I've noticed," he grinned. "How about this?"

"What is it?" she asked.

"You haven't seen this? *Pork Chop Hill?* It's a great war movie!"

"War movie? No way!"

She got up to change the channel, but J. D. grabbed her wrist.

"So why do you get to make the decision?" he asked.

"Because, as we determined earlier, I'm smart and you're not. Remember?"

"However, I'm stronger," he said, holding her by her wrist.

"No fair! You aren't playing fair!"

"Okay, we'll settle this in a fair and adult manner. Rock, paper, scissors."

Eden laughed, but agreed it was the only *adult* thing to do.

"One, two, three!"

Eden's rock beat J. D.'s scissors, and he pouted as she turned back to *King's Row*.

Eden didn't know what happened next. One minute she was watching *King's Row* and trying to come to grips with Cassandra's mental illness, and the next minute she was opening her eyes to the faint glint of early morning light scraping passed the gap in the motel drapes. Eden didn't move. She had been there all night. The thought of it made her blush. J. D. lay against her back. She could feel his chest rise and fall, and the puff of his breath behind her ear.

J. D. didn't move as she reached across him, took her motel key from the nightstand and quietly slipped from the room. The minute she closed the door behind her, J. D. opened his eyes and smiled. He could still smell the scent of her on the pillow, as he pulled it to his chest and buried his face in it.

❧⊱✦⊰❧

By nine o'clock the trio was heading to the address Eden found in the phone book for T.S. Mayhew. J. D.

didn't mention the night before, and Eden wondered if he realized she had stayed there the entire night. She felt shy around him now and had trouble looking him squarely in the eyes. But J. D. did know, and he found her sudden shyness amusing.

"I know this road," Miss Alma said, "This is the road to my house. Mine and Thad's."

Eden was looking at house numbers going by.

"There!" Miss Alma cried out, "That was our home!"

It was an old place that looked like a farmhouse that a neighborhood had grown up around over time. It needed painting, and the bases of the porch posts were almost rotted away. J. D. asked the ladies to wait in the car, and Eden noticed how carefully he walked up the steps that looked none too stable. A handsome older man, slightly graying at the temples, came to the door.

"Sorry to be bothering you, but I have a lady in the car who used to live here. She was wondering if she could look around, just for memory's sake."

The man looked over J. D.'s shoulder to stare at Eden and Miss Alma.

"Ain't no one lived here but me and my mama for years upon years," he said, pushing open the screen door, and stepping out onto the porch.

J. D. extended his hand and said, "I'm J. D. Callahan."

"I'm Sam Mayhew," he said shaking hands. Who is the lady who wants to see our house?"

"Miss Alma Mayhew."

"Miss ..." he stuttered, and his craggy face grimaced. "Miss Alma Mayhew, you say?"

"Yes, sir."

"My mama ain't going to like this. Not at all. But tell her to come on ahead."

Eden helped Miss Alma from the car and up to the house.

"Miss Alma, this is Sam Mayhew. Sam, this is Miss Alma Mayhew and Miss Eden Devereaux."

"Sam, you say?" Miss Alma asked.

The man nodded at the ladies and motioned for them to come inside.

"Mama! Mama, we got company!" he called out.

A small woman with snowy, white hair scrunched up into a knot at the top of her head, came into the room. Her expression was hard, her dress was shabby, and she didn't seem pleased to see them standing in her parlor.

"This is my mama, Tandy Mayhew. Mama, this here is a Mr. ..." he stumbled.

"I'm J. D. Callahan, ma'am, and this is Miss Eden Devereaux." He crossed the room to Miss Alma and placed his hand on her shoulder. "And this is Miss Alma Mayhew."

The woman looked as if she'd been slapped. She steadied herself with the lamp table, and her expression changed to anger, as her old eyes flashed pure hatred.

"Thad's Alma, standin' right here in my living room!" she spat out. "I'm glad he's dead!"

"Now, Mama, calm down," her son said.

"I think we'd better all take a deep breath and calm down," J. D. said. "May we sit down?"

Tandy only shrugged, but Sam motioned toward the sofa and nodded.

Tandy was the first to speak. "What you people want?"

"I just found out my Thaddeus didn't die in a mob attack, way back in the twenties," Miss Alma said.

"He weren't *your* Thaddeus! He was *my* husband, and I know all about that sorry business," Tandy growled.

Now Miss Alma was the one to cringe, and tightly clutch the arms of her chair.

"Maybe we should go," Miss Alma said, trying to maintain her pride.

"No, ma'am!" Tandy said, "You stay, and I'll tell you what you done to me!"

"Now Mama," Sam said, "this woman ain't done nothin' to you. You know that."

"Blast!" Tandy spat, "Blast you, woman! I never wanted to think on you again, Alma Mayhew."

"But what I ever done to you?"

"Ain't that a stupid question? What's you ever done to me!" Tandy said, but she allowed herself to relax and sit back in her chair.

"Thad was out of prison four years when I met him. He was almost twice my age, but oh, he was a fine-lookin' man. I decided to marry that man early on, and he even knowed it. But all he did back then was look for you and his children. Had all his family searchin' while he was in prison. Then the minute he gets out, he just work at the mill and earns gas money to take off on weekends and search town after town in all directions. Took me a long time to get him to marry me. And swellin' with Sam here's the only reason he finally did."

Sam looked down at his mother's frayed rug and felt shame.

"I thought I could change him, make him love me the way he loved you. But it never happened. His whole life, wherever we'd go, he was always a-lookin', hopin' to find you or one of his other babies. I's scared to death back then. I's scared of what would happen if he found you. What would he do with Sam and me? The ghost of you hung over this house as surely as if you was here in body.

That man never could love nobody else. Never gave me a chance. And I hated you because of it."

"I'm sorry, Miss Tandy. That must have been awful for you," Miss Alma said softly.

"Don't feel sorry for me. He's the one died a broken man, sad and wasted and callin' out to you on his death-bed. You! A woman he ain't seen in near fifty-five years. I was here cleanin' and cookin' and tendin' to him right up to the end. I remember lookin' at him when he was a-dyin', and he looked me square in the eyes, but he didn't see me. He couldn't see nobody but you. And I wished him dead."

"Mama!" Sam gasped.

"I did! God help me! I just wanted it to stop, this hurtin' over a man I gave my life to, who never loved me back."

There was an awkward silence. Finally, J. D. stood up and said, "We'd better go. Sorry to have bothered you, ma'am."

Shocked by the answers they received, they knew it to be true, but it didn't make anything better. As they moved to the door, Miss Alma turned and looked at Tandy with tired eyes. Tandy, feeling the old wounds opening again, felt tears coming and turned away.

Sam caught J. D. as he stepped out the door.

"Mr. Callahan, that weren't the whole truth of it. My mama is a hard woman to live with. He might have loved her if ..."

He looked back toward his mama, but she had already left the room.

"Could you wait one minute?"

"Of course," J. D. said.

He paused on the porch as Eden put Miss Alma back in the car. Shortly, Sam was handing him a wooden box.

"This was my daddy's. I kept it hidden from my mama all these years. She'd have thrown it out. Give it to the lady. It rightfully belongs to her."

# Twenty-Six

Eden was glad when J. D. drove off. She could feel a malevolent spirit in Tandy Mayhew's house. She wanted to be safely away from the overwhelming anger. What kind of evil plot had kept Miss Alma and her Thaddeus apart all these years? It must have never occurred to him that his Alma would have the strength and determination to run so far. But fear does strange things to a body. Sixty unbelievable years of him searching for her and her believing him dead. How different their lives could have been.

Once Eden got Miss Alma back to the motel, J. D. handed her the box.

"I know this box. This here was my mama's jewelry box. Course we's too poor to have jewelry, so my mama called it her treasure box. She kept all sorts of trinkets in it. Where'd you get this, Mr. J. D.?"

"Sam gave it to me while y'all were getting into the car. He thought you should have it."

"Oh, Miss Alma," Eden said, plopping down beside her, "do open it. It could be a treasure chest for real!"

"Full of diamonds and pearls and such, hum?" Miss Alma teased.

"No, ma'am. Full of memories and remembrances and such."

"Yes, that it could be, I guess."

"So, open it! Let's open it!" Eden said, as excited as a kid on Christmas morning.

Miss Alma lifted the lid and dumped the contents onto the bed.

"Looky here, my daddy's shavin' mug. And Juno's baby cup."

They were the most obvious items. Her hand paused a moment over the smaller things.

"Little girl, little girl, look at that!"

"What is it?"

Miss Alma lifted a small bit of ribbon.

"This here's a lock of my hair and a lock of Thad's hair. Look how my mama braided them together into this ribbon. Ain't that somethin'?"

Miss Alma laid it in the palm of her hand and closed her fingers around it.

"My mama pressed this into my hand on my weddin' day and said this means my Thad and me always be twined together our whole lives. If we'd knowed the future then, we'd have knowed how true that'd be. My mama, she thought a lot of my Thad."

"What's this?"

"Oh my, that was a brass button come off of Thad's old coat. I set that out with some thread to sew back on when I got home from town that day. But I never got back home. Weren't that a strange thing to keep? Look here, my mama's sparkly."

"Her what?"

"Her sparkly. That's what we called it. It was the only necklace she ever owned. Ain't it purty?" Miss Alma held up a discolored chain with a piece of amber colored glass hanging from it. "And it still sparkles after all these years."

"Oh look. Who is that?" Eden said holding up an old cabinet card photo.

"That was me and my first baby, Aubrey. She ain't but a few months old there."

"Why, Miss Alma, you were a real looker!" Eden teased.

"Sure was back then, sure was," she chuckled.

Miss Alma showed Eden and J. D. each piece of her past, that lay like faded petals strewn along a garden path, each one holding a special memory. Last was what appeared to be another cabinet card that had fallen face down, and Miss Alma turned it over.

"Oh my!" she sighed, and she pulled it to her chest.

"Miss Eden, Mr. J. D., I'd like you both to meet my husband, Thaddeus Samuel Mayhew." She turned the picture so they could see it.

"He's so handsome!" Eden said, taking the card and examining it.

"Had to be to catch me," she said proudly. "That was a regretful part of my life, that I didn't have no picture of my Thad. You know, no matter how much I loved that man, the memory of what he looked like seemed to fade over the years. I could hardly remember." Gently, she took the photo back. "But just look at him. Look how handsome and fine he was."

She frowned suddenly, "Still, I'm sorry he lived such a bad life. I wouldn't have wished that on him, no matter what."

"He loved you so much," Eden said.

"But he should have forgot me and made a new life for hisself."

"You didn't forget about him, either."

"No, I guess my mama braided us into that ribbon too tightly."

Eden was glad when they began the trip back to Texas. The little treasure box had been worth all the hardship of the trip. They had seen the face of Thaddeus Mayhew and knew why they were braided together all their lives.

Miss Alma seemed weaker than when they left, so Eden suggested they drive straight through, sleeping in the car. She and J. D. took turns at the wheel, and by the following nightfall, they rode into Two Rivers on old Highway 6. They were all, what Miss Alma called, bone tired.

"I envy you your Thad," Eden said as she tucked Miss Alma into her own bed that night. When she curled up in her bed upstairs, she smiled, thinking of Miss Alma's Thaddeus and the beribboned cord that knit the two together forever. That was the kind of love Eden wanted. She wondered if J. D. was thinking about that too.

Miss Alma slept late the following morning. The trip had depleted her strength, and Eden knew she needed the extra rest. Eden told Afton about the trip over a cup of homemade sassafras tea, while morning shadows were still filtrating into the kitchen.

"How tragic! How romantically tragic!" Afton said.

"I think Ryder is capable of such strong emotions."

"Do you?" Afton smiled.

Eden looked up through the screen door and saw Nub standing at the foot of the back-porch steps. She walked over to the door and smiled at him.

"So, you back?" he asked.

"Yes, Nub."

"She okay?"

"Yes, Nub."

The old backwoodsman nodded and walked off into the Big Thicket. Eden watched until he disappeared into the underbrush.

"How curious Nub Henry is," she mused out loud.

"Yes'um, Miss Eden. But he has a right to be."

"What do you mean?"

"Cause of what happened to him."

"No one has ever told me Nub's story."

"The story goes, that way back before Miss Alma even came, Nub Henry had the most beautiful wife on the river. She was a healer."

"A what?"

"A healer. One of those folks who heals with plants and clay, herbs and such. Her mee-maw taught her about the plants and things. Then one day she was called into town because one of the townies had a sick child, and their own doctor couldn't seem to help. She treated the child, but it died anyway. At the funeral, the child's mama heard the papa say what a fine and comely girl Nub's wife was. That man's wife was a jealous woman, and her grief brought out her meanness. She told everyone that Nub's wife was a witch and that she had cast a spell on the child that caused it to die. She even said Nub's wife had bewitched her own husband when he tried to defend the girl. The town was young back then, wild in those days, crazy insane. It weren't colored against white. It was white against white, evil against good. That poor girl was only trying to help. There wasn't much law around yet either. The night after that child was laid to rest, a gang of men went out and got that poor girl and hung her from that old tree that hangs out over the river at the flatboat crossin'. You know that one?"

"I think so."

"Nub tried to stop 'em, but there was too many of 'em. It took a big bunch of 'em to hold Nub back, but they did. They said he screamed like a banshee when they hoisted her up into the air, her hands tied behind her back and her legs kickin' about. But she just looked at Nub and never said a word, not a sound. They said they was sure she was a witch, 'cause she didn't holler out or nothin'. But my mama said she just knew it wasn't no use, and she gave up and let it happen."

"That's horrible!"

"Nub was never quite right after that. He disappeared for years, livin' way off in the Thicket, all alone like John the Baptist in the wilderness. When he finally came out, he never liked bein' around people much. Never wanted to be touched or nothin'."

"Do you think he knew what happened to Miss Alma?"

"I'm sure of it."

"That explains how tender-hearted he is toward her. They both know what it feels like to see a loved one die at the hands of an angry mob that is so in the wrong, but so sure they are right."

Eden stood at the back door, leaning against the frame, and looked out across the hay meadow.

"There are more prejudices in this world than the obvious ones aren't there? All we hear about is racial injustice. But this dark thing between the bottom landers and the town is just as evil," Eden said. "The gulf between the wealthy and the poor is as wide as the gulf caused by the color of someone's skin. And if you're white and poor, and have the audacity to be beautiful, then prejudice doubles. Has to be born out of jealousy or something just as evil."

Afton sighed, staring into her teacup. Her words were gentle when she finally spoke.

"We always felt that the townies hated us. So, we simply hated them back. I was raised to believe they was all pure evil. Then I met Boone. I was swimming in the river, and there had been heavy rains up north. The rainwater had swelled the river, and I got caught in a current I couldn't handle. I kept goin' under, and I couldn't breathe. I was drowning. Then I felt this strong arm catch me, and Boone's face was against mine, and I relaxed and let him swim for both of us. When we finally made it to shore, I was so relieved to be alive, I just fell down and began to cry. Boone sat down beside me, and put his arm around me, and rocked me until I could settle myself. He was so nice to me. I knew he wasn't some evil thing from town. Boone was just a boy, no different from me and mine. I owed him my life. I saw people differently after that."

Eden listened without turning around. She knew all about torment. It had come to her in the night in her dreams. She felt hypnotized by the sight and scent of the hay meadow, and she didn't even turn when at last she spoke, "Hate is the evil thing. It's a powerful sin. And there is such torment in sin. People are so tormented because they can't let go of their hate."

Miss Alma moved slower when she finally emerged from her room. Eden noticed the swooshing sound of her slippers as she slid them along the floor.

"How do you feel today?" Afton asked.

"I guess you'd be sayin' poorly. But don't y'all never mind me. I've had my trip. I can go now in peace."

Eden and Afton looked at each other and understood.

"You ready for your grits?" Afton asked.

Miss Alma didn't answer. She sat down in her rocker by the back door. Afton scooped up some of the sticky sweet mush and plopped it into a small, crock bowl.

"Here Miss Alma, you eat this now while it's still hot," Afton said.

"Honey chil', I'm not able to right now. You set it on the stove. Maybe later I can have a go at it."

Afton did as she was told.

"I guess today is the day of reckonin'?" Miss Alma said, turning to Eden.

"If you don't feel like doing this now, I can wait."

"Now's good a time as any. I made a deal with ya'. You go fetch me my Bible in my chiffonier, the old Bible with the torn back."

The Bible was indeed torn along the spine, and its pages were yellowed and loose. Eden handed it to Miss Alma, who placed it reverently before them on the table.

"This here was the Ol' Missus' Bible back when she was a child. I've had it for safe keepin' cause of this." She pulled a folded sheet of paper from its pages and let her fingers run across it before offering it to Eden.

"This is what you want, little girl."

Eden touched the paper as reverently as Miss Alma had. She didn't know why, but she felt it had to be of great importance. She unfolded it and spread it out before them on the table.

"This is a birth certificate!"

"I know, little girl. It's what you been lookin' for. It's you, little girl."

"Me?"

"You been wanting to know who you are. Well …"

Eden looked at the name, Carrie Elizabeth Gentry.

"Now wait," Eden said, staring at the document, "I can't be a Gentry. This cannot possibly be me. I tell you it's not. I'm convinced I'm a Dupree."

"You *can,* and you *is,* little girl. And that's all I'm sayin'. I promised to tell you who you are, and I done it. Now leave me be 'bout it all."

"But if this is true, how did I end up in Rising Star? How did I end up with my mother? With Bett Devereaux? I mean Bettina Dupree? Miss Alma, I don't want to be a Gentry!"

Miss Alma took Eden's hand, and Eden leaned forward hoping for more answers. But that wasn't what she got.

"Little girl, I done called Mr. J. D. to come fetch me. It's time for me to be goin' now."

"Going where? What are you talking about?" Eden asked, confused.

"Back before we went to Mississippi, I made arrangements to go live with Miss Annaliese at Rose Haven. I has this need to watch over her till my time comes. Or hers. It's what I done seems most of my life anyway."

Eden was caught off guard. "Miss Alma, no. Stay here with us."

Miss Alma smiled and patted Eden's hand. "It's mighty nice to be wanted, and I'm going to miss both of you baby girls. But it's somethin' I got to do, kind of like the trip home. Just a burnin' inside sayin' do it, do it. Now that you're here to watch out for Afton and Nub, I can go easy."

Eden didn't say anything more.

"I love that ol' Missus. Me and Miss Annaliese, we are special bonded. We been forged by fire you know. She needs me now. My bag is still packed from the trip, and there are three boxes of things I filled before we left. You and Afton go sit them out on the porch for Mr. J. D."

They did as they were told.

Eden didn't see J. D. when he came to get Miss Alma. She had said her goodbyes before he arrived and gone upstairs to her room. But as J. D. drove away from the house, he turned to see Eden watching from the upstairs window. He saw Miss Alma wave and Eden slowly waved back.

Once they disappeared down the drive, Eden lay down on the bed and stared at the papered ceiling. She didn't know how long she lay there when she heard a knock on her door.

"Come in."

Afton entered with a tray, "I brought you some tea."

"Thank you, Afton. Sit it here." She indicated her bedside table.

"Can I pour it for you? I mean, may I?" Afton smiled at her grammatical error.

"That's okay, Afton. I can do that myself."

"Oh please, Miss Eden." Eden saw panic in the girl's eyes. She realized that this was Afton's way of coping. Afton needed to tend to her, as she had tended to Miss Alma, even as Miss Alma would now tend to her Miss Annaliese. It was a southern thing.

"Yes, Afton. That would be nice. Two spoons of sugar, please."

Gingerly, they smiled at each other.

❧⟜✠⟜❧

When night fell, Eden briefly sat on the porch, but it wasn't the same without Miss Alma. She carried the newly discovered document to her room and inspected it. It was official looking with its gold seal. *Carrie Elizabeth*

*Gentry.* She wondered what they had called her. *Carrie? Lizzie? Beth?* The newspaper account had just called her the missing child. *Why don't I have any recollections of any of these names?*

Eden read the legally created words that pointed to the new truth of her life. Mother, Raina Louisa Gentry. Father, Ashley William Devereaux.

Circuits fired in her brain. *Devereaux! But I wasn't christened Carrie Elizabeth Devereaux! Did that mean that Raina Gentry and this Devereaux weren't married? Yet, wasn't Raina married at the time of my birth?* It was like pages of a book being flipped through, offering quick answers. But with each answer came more questions.

# Twenty-Seven

The following weekend, Eden agreed to accompany Afton upriver for a picnic lunch with Ryder. They wore their swimsuits under their sundresses, intending to go for a swim. Afton's small rowboat glided along the surface of the water, and Eden noticed how muddy brown the water appeared, probably from the heavy rains that blew in a few nights earlier. As Eden skimmed along, the water became clearer and more transparent, until it finally appeared blue-white again. Afton stopped rowing as they approached a long pier at a wide bend that sent the river flowing in a slightly different direction. The tree was there, Eden noticed, where they had taken the life of Nub's wife and sealed his fate forever. It was an old tree, gnarled and graying from an icing of moss. It moved in the wind and seemed to come alive as they approached it. Two limbs had broken off side by side, and their whitened bases seemed to form eyes that watched them as they arrived. Multi-armed branches waved at them as a squirrel sat and munched acorns, dropping their caps into the water with one pinging off the rowboat.

"Hey there, ladies," Ryder yelled, as he ran out to the end of the pier. His voice made the tree dead again. Eden admired Afton's skill as she maneuvered the skiff perfectly, edging in close, until Ryder caught its nose, grabbed the rope, and tied it to a pier.

He helped Afton from the boat and gave her a crushing hug that caused her to giggle like a school girl. Truth be told, she wasn't much more than a school girl, but her life experiences had aged her beyond that. Ryder set her away from him, "Goodness, you're a sight for sore eyes!"

Only then did he remember Eden and helped her from the little boat, reaching behind her for the picnic basket.

Ryder took Afton's arm and steered her along the pier, his boots clomping on the weathered wood. Eden followed, amused by the burly cowboy and his little lady.

"Fried chicken for you and chicken salad for Mr. J. D.," Afton said.

"That's my girl," Ryder grinned.

Eden's eyebrows raised. "J. D.?"

"Yes 'em," Ryder beamed. "We're kind of relivin' some good times on the river before the ol' boy gets roped permanent like. Guess you'd call this a bachelor party."

"Eden! Hello!" J. D. got up from a large quilt and walked toward them. "This is a nice surprise. I didn't know we were having ladies. Come say hey to the boys."

Two others were sitting on an old quilt, surrounding a strewn stack of playing cards. Eden recognized them from the Harvest Ball.

"Howdy, ma'am," they each said. The one in the beat-up straw hat tipped the brim.

"Seat yourselves," they said in unison.

"What's going on?" Eden asked, sitting down on the quilt.

J. D. began to explain, "Way back in high school, we used to sneak up here on a Saturday afternoon to play poker and smoke cigars."

"Cigars?" Eden laughed, "Not really!"

"Oh, we thought we were big shots, a bunch of fifteen-year-old kids trying hard to grow up fast."

"That's what fifteen-year-olds do," Eden smiled. "Where'd you get the cigars?"

One of the friends, Billy Mack, spoke up, "Ryder was such a hoot back then. Before we got cigars, he'd cut sections of grape vines, pass 'em out, and we'd smoke 'em."

"You smoked grape vines?" she asked incredulously.

All the boys laughed. "We were only about twelve then. But don't that sound like Ryder? Anyway, after those early times, and a few bad stomach aches, Jody Paul here, got to sneakin' 'em from his granddaddy's house."

"Thank goodness we can just buy 'em now," Jody Paul spoke up, tossing a box of King Edwards onto the pile of cards.

"Let's light up for old time's sake," Billy Mack said, plopping back down on the quilt.

"Food first, cigars later," J. D. said. "Gentlemen, thank Miss Afton Donner for the fine spread." He emptied the basket's contents onto the quilt, while the men clapped and hooted their approval. Ryder leaned over to kiss Afton's cheek, and she blushed again.

"You did real good, little darlin'," he said to her.

"How did you know that I didn't prepare this wonderful meal, J. D. Callahan?" Eden asked, trying to sound offended.

"Oh, I've heard about your cookin'. Been warned to steer clear of it."

"By who?" she asked.

"Miss Alma for one. Remember the burned toast when you were doing the cooking?"

She had to concede that he had heard correctly.

The men fell on the food with the same enthusiasm they had for their sweethearts, running cattle, and hunting for the biggest rack of the season. They weren't sure when they crossed over the line, and were no longer eating out of hunger, or even pleasure, but had actually delved into pure gluttony. Finally, they fell back onto the quilt and patted their bellies.

"Now don't get mad, Ryder, but I full well intend to steal this little gal away from you if I can. She's too mighty fine for the likes of you, Ryder Lee!" Billy Mack grinned.

"Well now, Billy Mack, you go ahead and try. Ain't no shame in the tryin'. But this little sweetheart, she's stuck to me like pine tar!"

"That true, Afton?" Billy Mack asked.

Afton nodded with a huge smile.

J. D. watched Eden smiling at their playful exchange. He found himself remembering when she tried to comfort him by the river those many months back. He tilted his head as his eyes followed the length of her slender arms. J. D. imagined the feel of them again. But he remembered who he was and how inappropriate these thoughts were. Reluctantly, he willed himself back into the game and tried to keep his mind on Paige.

Jody Paul spoke up, "Let the games begin!" He gathered up the cards, shuffled and dealt.

Afton sat close by Ryder, trying to follow the game. Before long Eden lost interest, walked to the head of the pier, and decided to get into the water.

The gathering paid no attention to Eden, save for J. D. Her sundress fell onto the beginning of the pier as she stepped out of it and walked out over the water. Eden's swimsuit was a modest one piece, less revealing than most.

Still, J. D. could admire her soft curves and the graceful way she moved.

"J. D.?" Jody Paul was saying.

"Huh?"

"I said it's your turn."

"Oh, sorry," J. D. said, as his mind returned to the game. Looking up from his cards he saw Ryder grinning at him with an accusing smile.

"'member ol' Paige?"

J. D. cleared his throat, "Of course, I remember Paige."

The others laughed along with Ryder.

"I reckon' that purdy West Texas gal is up for grabs, huh?" Bobby Mac smiled.

Jody Paul threw down a challenge, "Ain't wearin' nobody's brand."

"No local brand," J. D. declared. "But she's wrapped up lock, stock, and barrel. A Mr. Wynn Beckett. He's had that little girl off the carpet for a long time, way back since high school days."

"Don't see him around, so till I see a ring, I'll keep that little doe in my sights," Jody Paul said.

"Deal me in on that," Bobby Mack grinned.

Irritated, J. D. felt the desire to wrestle them to the ground and use pain to make them back off, the way they had settled things when they were boys.

Somewhere a horse whinnied, and the men became alert. They scanned the tree line but saw nothing. A lazy clip-clop drew their eyes to the same spot, and soon they were standing, their feet planted firmly apart. They pulled their hands up into fists as they saw the bottom landers. J. D. glanced toward the pier and saw Eden sitting on the end, dangling her feet in the water, oblivious to the intruders.

The three men on horseback were barefooted and wore threadbare coveralls without the benefit of undershirts.

One of them held a shotgun. No one spoke, and their silence grew louder and louder. Each remained frozen, statue-still, sizing up the others. Eden must have moved, because the three horsemen, as if on cue, turned their eyes toward her. J. D. did too. She had seen the horsemen and stood to face them. J. D. moved onto the pier and picked up her sundress. She met him halfway, and he handed the dress to her. She quickly stepped into it, as he turned his attention back to the horsemen and obstructed their view.

"That there the one been keepin' Afton?" one of the horsemen yelled to J. D.

J. D. didn't answer.

Again, there was an uncomfortable silence, and J. D. felt Eden place her hand flat against his back as they moved back toward the others.

The one who spoke turned his eyes toward Afton and said, "You should be with your own people, girl."

Ryder stepped in front of Afton. "She's where she wants to be," he said.

The horseman started to challenge Ryder's statement until he saw Afton wrap her small hands around Ryder's arm. His expression turned to disgust, and he spit off to the side of his horse.

"Did you know her daddy promised her to Harley Wick before y'all stole her away?" the horseman said to Ryder.

"Doubt he'd have her now, seein' how she smells like you townies," one of the others said, and the three laughed.

J. D. noticed how Ryder's face had flushed an angry crimson. He planted himself firmly beside his friend.

"Leave it be," Jody Paul said under his breath to Ryder.

Ryder knew they could take these bottom landers in a fair fight. However, there were the two girls to think about, and the bottom landers had a shotgun. He wouldn't put them in harm's way.

The one who spoke, turned his eyes toward Eden, "Wouldn't mind a bit of that myself," he said slowly. The other two laughed again, but he didn't. It was obvious they were pushing for a fight.

The first horseman turned his attention back to Ryder. "You best be watchin' your back, Ryder Lee. Don't forget about that Bohannon fella." He reined his horse to the left and moved back into the brush followed by the other two, and they spurred them into a gallop.

Once the horsemen were swallowed up in the Thicket, the men looked at each other and nodded, almost as if to signal that they'd be there for each other if, and when, the time came. They didn't speak, didn't identify what that time would be. But they knew all too well where this was going. For a moment, they thought about their missing comrade. They remembered Boone. J. D., Jody Paul, and Bobby Mack wanted to take up swords, and circle Ryder to keep him safe like they did when they were kids.

"Well, boys," Ryder finally said, "Let's light up some stogies and get back to the game."

They returned to their quilt and felt it was not strange that the young ladies joined their tight circle now. They kept their eyes on the outer edges of the woods.

As the afternoon drifted on, Eden grew sleepy, and J. D. found her tilting against him. Her head fell against his shoulder. When he looked up, the others were grinning, and for a moment he wondered if he was blushing. Vexed, he went on with the game and puffed on his cigar.

The sun was in descent, only about an hour from falling behind the pine tops, when they heard what sounded like the soft lilt of female giggles. A sudden, loud gasp drew their eyes to the path that lead to the farm-to-market.

"Jefferson Dixon Callahan! What are those women doing out here?"

Katie Mae Harris and Lottie Latrelle came stumbling out of the dense brush.

"J. D., if Paige knew you were out here with them," Lottie said, "Why, she'd call off the wedding!"

"Then you won't be tellin' her," Jody Paul said as J. D. spat out, "Dang!"

"You bet your boots I'm tellin'," Lottie said.

Eden, whose eyes opened with the first gasp, slowly sat up. The two town girls stared at her, and she felt her whole body flushed with embarrassment. How had she gotten there, leaning against J. D. like that? She couldn't remember.

Lottie and Katie Mae were Paige's friends, her confidants, and in this case, her infiltrators. They all knew these two had been sent out to spy on J. D. Eden felt as if she had done something despicable, just because she was there.

"Care for a cigar?" Bobby Mack said lazily, grinning at the two girls.

"Bobby Mack Hensley! This isn't a joking matter!" Lottie spat.

"How 'bout you, sweetheart?" he said to Katie Mae.

"Do you mean it?" she answered, smiling, "I've never even had a cigarette."

"Katie Mae!" Lottie said, "This isn't a tea party! Our best friend's betrothed is cheatin' on her."

"J. D. ain't cheatin' on anyone," Ryder said, standing. "He's done nothin' but restrain himself for Paige's sake. And we ain't going to have you tellin' tales that just ain't so. Do you understand me, Lottie Latrelle?"

As Lottie took a step backward, Katie Mae said, "We really didn't see anything, Lottie. Nothing was going on here."

Lottie turned on her friend, "Whose side are you on, anyway?"

"How 'bout bein' on my side, little darlin'?" Bobby Mack said with his most wicked smile, "Come have a seat here by me, Katie girl."

For a moment, it seemed that she might join them before Lottie grabbed her arm and pulled her back along the path to the road. Over her shoulder, she yelled, "We'll just see if Paige thinks this is so innocent!" Katie Mae could only blink at Bobby Mack as she allowed herself to be pulled along by her friend.

"We might as well have sent out engraved invitations for all the traffic that's been through here this afternoon," Ryder said.

J. D. turned to Eden, "I'm really sorry about that. It was wrong for Paige to send them out here to check on me."

"Those girls never actually said that Paige did," Eden said. "Maybe they came out on their own. Maybe Paige didn't know they were even here."

"Come on, Eden," Jody Paul balked, "They're on their way right now, hopin' to stir up trouble."

"Maybe Lottie," Bobby Mack grinned, leaning back onto his elbows, "But not that cute little Katie. I think I won her over."

"You wish, honcho," Ryder laughed, pulling up a handful of grass, and throwing it into Bobby Mack's face. Turning to Afton, he asked, "You okay?"

Afton nodded, and he squeezed her hand.

"Dark's comin' on. You ladies better be headin' back down the river," Jody Paul said.

J. D. and Ryder exchanged glances. J. D. said, "I don't think you ladies should be alone on the river right now, especially since bottom landers are around. It doesn't feel safe."

"Why don't you and Ryder go back with 'em," Bobby Mack said.

"Ryder, you definitely should go back with them. In light of the explaining I already have to do, I'd better go back with the boys," J. D. said.

"I'd be glad to go with Ryder and the ladies," Jody Paul volunteered, stepping directly in front of Eden, and smiling down at her.

Ryder placed his hand on Jody Paul's chest and pushed him back.

"On second thought," Ryder grinned, "I'm not sure Afton's rowboat will hold more than the three of us."

"But, but ..." said Jody Paul, looking disappointed.

Bobby Mack said, "Too bad, ol' fella," as he and J. D. pulled him away.

Ryder put the girls in the rowboat and handed Afton the picnic basket. J. D. watched from the pier as they headed upriver, and he wished he was in the boat with them. He kept telling himself it was because of the encounter with the bottom landers and that he was worried about them.

As he lost sight of Afton's boat, he turned back to his friends who had gathered up everything, and they headed up the path to Bobby Mack's Jeep. But J. D. was too worried to go home once Bobby Mack dropped him off in town. Those horsemen were itching for a fight, and that was downright unnerving!

J. D. found himself headed toward Camp Ruby Road and to Eden's house. Once there, he crossed her hay meadow and walked to the edge of the pier. He only had to wait about fifteen minutes until Afton's boat came into view. J. D. stepped back, not wanting to be seen, and he breathed easy again. Knowing they were back safely was enough. He left before any of them saw him.

Eden caught sight of her landing. Her eyes swept across the river's glassy surface, and the moist breeze flung her hair back. She was home. She lifted her chin into the breeze. What none of them saw were the three horsemen who stood across the river opposite Eden's pier. If they had, they would have been worried. What they also didn't see was Nub Henry, transparent among the heavy brush, watching the three horsemen.

❦

As they suspected, Paige's girlfriends had hurried to her house and reported what they had seen, with feminine embellishments. Lottie told Paige that they had been treated in a lowdown manner by the men.

"Oh, they weren't that bad, Lottie," Katie Mae corrected her.

"What are you talking about? They were awful to us! If their mamas knew how they acted, they'd have their hides!" Lottie said, indignantly.

Annoyed, Katie Mae closed her mouth and didn't agree or disagree with Lottie again. Paige sat as still as a stone monument and listened without comment. When Lottie was through, Paige remained composed and thanked them for the information.

"I think I need to be alone now," Paige said.

"Are you sure?" Lottie asked, disappointed that she wouldn't get to see one of Paige's fits of rage. "Let's go back out there and tell them off! I bet they're still there, even in the dark."

"No!" Paige said icily. "Let him stew awhile, worry about me for a change. I can't jeopardize this now. Otherwise, she wins."

Lottie and Katie Mae exchanged glances. They knew, as everyone did, that Paige Gresham was spoiled and always got her way, no matter what. They wondered if she really did love Jeff Callahan, or if she simply wanted another trophy. They, or at least Katie Mae, felt sorry for the future that J. D. would have with this girl.

"Maybe you'll decide it's innocent if you give yourself time to think about it," Katie Mae said. She shrank back under both of her friend's icy glares.

Once they left her, Paige picked up her crystal powder jar and, without changing the blank expression on her face, hurled it across the room, blinking as it shattered against the opposite wall, sending shards of glass and dusty powder drifting across the room.

When she spoke to J. D. on the phone later that night, she didn't mention the picnic, and neither did he. Though he was thankful to have dodged the bullet, he was both amazed and nervous about her calmness. It wasn't like Paige to hold back, and he was hoping that she had turned over a new leaf and would stop being so volatile. But still, he waited for the volcano that he was felt would eventually erupt.

# Twenty-Eight

Nub Henry was old and feeling his age as he moved silently through the moon-lit river bottom when he came upon the three men sitting around the campfire, drinking moonshine. These were the three he had seen earlier across from Miss Alma's pier. He had waited for a time, then tracked them. Nub was first aware of the acrid scent of smoke, and as he followed it, he became aware of men's voices, slightly hushed, then excited and full of laughter. He stood close, confident in his ability to be invisible among the trees.

"We'll show 'em!"

"You bet we will!"

"How you two 'spectin' to do that?" the third man asked.

"Well …"

There was a brief silence. Then one of the men let out a whoop.

"What is it, Cooter? What you thinkin'?"

*Cooter?* Nub thought. *These must be those Tucker boys.*

"What's that West Texas gal's name again?"

"He called her Edith, I think. Or maybe Evelyn."

"No man, it was Eden, like the Garden of Eden. You know, in the Bible."

"From West Texas no less. Boy, does she need a lesson in East Texas humility!

"And that's where we come into it."

"What, Spud? What we goin' to do?"

"Look, old man Donner, he went in there and took his baby girl back to the river where she belonged. Then they come and tempted him with money. I still can't believe he took their dirty money. Sellin' off your own kin for rich folk's money, that's so low down. I say we go get her and take her back to the bottomlands for good."

"But what if she don't stay again?"

"Oh, she'll stay alright. One way or the other."

That comment made the three laugh.

"Yeow man," Skeets chuckled, "She can stay on the river or in the river. And we'll see that she knows them's her only two choices."

"When we gettin' her?" Cooter asked, excitedly.

"Let's go home, get somethin' to eat. When it gets past midnight, and they's sound asleep, we'll go in, and take her out of that ol' house."

"There's only females in the house. Should be easy enough."

They laughed as they stomped out the fire, mounted their horses, and slowly headed down a dark path away from the river.

When Nub Henry could no longer hear the crackle of dead leaves beneath the horse's hooves, he headed straight to Eden's house.

❦

*What in the world am I doing here?* Eden asked herself, as she crouched behind the large bridal wreath bush, dressed in her pink pajamas and robe. The blossoms on the bush matched the color of her pajamas and gave off a sweet scent that mingled with the earthy, nighttime smells.

Earlier that night she had come downstairs for a snack and to recheck the doors. Miss Alma had seen to it that the doors were locked each night. *Why can't I remember if I'd locked them myself?* It was late, a little past eleven. She was sitting at the kitchen table and listening to the quietness. She pulled her pink robe around her pajamas and wiggled her toes in the fuzzy slippers. Wordlessly, she wished for the morning, when Afton would be up in the kitchen, and this feeling of emptiness would be gone.

She was telling herself to go back to bed when there was a tap on the back door that made her jump and set her heart racing. It was a soft tapping, and at first, she confused it with the ticking of the clock. When she realized someone was, indeed, on her back porch, she grabbed the fireplace poker. She placed her back against the wall beside the door and called out.

"Who is it?"

"Nub Henry."

*Something's wrong,* she thought. She looked out the glass pane in the door, and it was indeed Nub. Still, her heart beat erratically as she clicked the lock and opened the door.

"What is it, Nub? What's wrong?"

Nub told her about the three men he had heard around the campfire. Eden was sure they must be the three horsemen who interrupted their picnic earlier that day. Remembering them and the greasy hatred in their faces gave her chills.

"Should I call J. D.?" Eden asked Nub.

"No, ma'am. I'll take care of it. Where's Miss Afton?"

Funny, that was the first time he had called Afton "Miss," a new sign of respect for the girl.

"She's in bed asleep."

"That's a good thing. Let her sleep, and you go on to sleep too. Lock up good and let me handle things. Don't worry none 'bout it."

Eden was uneasy, but she agreed, and she tried. She really did. For about an hour she attempted to sleep. Disquieted, the house pressed in on her thoughts and pushed her out of bed. It breathed and creaked, and she didn't know what it wanted her to do. Eventually, she threw caution to the wind and donned her robe, tip-toed out of the house, took up her position behind the bridal wreath bush and waited. She had left the door cracked open in case she had to make a run for the safety of the old house. But as she knelt there, nervous and restless, she turned to the sound of a slow grating, almost like nails across a chalkboard. She watched mesmerized as the kitchen door slowly closed shut. She knew if she rushed at the door, no one would be there. She was exactly where the house wanted her to be, and she wondered why.

*How long have I been here,* she wondered? The moon was huge, obscuring the stars and lighting up the night in a hazy veil. Night things buzzed around her and the sound of them lulled her, calling her to an uneasy sleep, but she fought it.

Eden sat with her knees pulled up under her chin, and her arms wrapped around them. Her head bobbed forward twice, then rested on her knees. Her eyes closed, and though she fought against it, she felt herself drifting into unconsciousness. All was going dark when a burst of distant laughter brought her back to life.

"Shush, you dang fool!" she heard from far off.

Eden's eyes searched the back and side yards, the hay meadow, and the forests beyond. *Where is Nub?*

There was silence for a time, then a cough, followed by hushed laughter. They were closer, perhaps just across the hay meadow.

She was glad for the full moon, and the light it afforded. They would have to leave the protection of the forest and come out into the open to reach the house. Just as that thought came, so did the three men, and Eden's heart began to pound wildly.

They were crouched low, bent over, and moving quickly. Again, she scanned as far as she could see, but there was no sign of Nub anywhere.

Eden panicked. She was poised to sprint back to the porch, for it occurred to her that the door was unlocked and Afton, whom these men had come for, was asleep and unaware of the danger in the middle of the hay meadow.

*Now,* she thought, *I must get back inside and lock the door.*

Eden stood and braced to run, aware that she would probably be spotted by the bottom landers. But all she could think of was Afton asleep and unprotected in her bed under the roofline. *Why, oh why, has Nub let me down? Why did I trust him in the first place? I should have called J. D. or Ryder. This is serious business, and now, because of me, Afton and I are both in danger.*

Just as her mind told her feet to run, she heard a swishing pop, and her eyes were drawn to the side yard.

"What the heck?" escaped from her lips, before she covered her mouth with her hand.

A column of fire flared up over one of the tombstones in the center of the little cemetery. From it, tendrils of fire trailed in all directions, and more columns of fire popped up above each of the tombstones.

"Oh, my Gawd!" one of the men in the field yelled, "What's that, Spud?"

The three men stopped and stood tall, their eyes as round and wide as that ancient moon that was spotlighting them. They could each feel a shiver covering their skin, and the hair on the back of their dirty, red necks began to rise.

"Ain't that the old boneyard?"

No one answered him.

As still as statues, in the center of the hay meadow, all eyes were drawn to the center tombstone where the fireballs originated. Something began to rise above the stone, something white, ethereal and frightening.

"A haint! Oh Gawd, it's a haint!"

Cooter screamed like a little girl, turned, and ran at breakneck speed toward the river.

"Spud? Do you see it too?"

"But it can't be. Ghosts ain't real!"

"Oh, man, that is a real ghost. We're starin' right at it," he said, as he took a step backward.

Spud's voice rose and cracked, "And it's starin' at us! We better get out of here! I ain't messin' with no haint! Ever!"

The two men turned and ran as fast as they could until they disappeared into the darkness of the forest.

It all happened so fast, Eden didn't have time to move. She watched the apparition as it briefly started after the men fleeing for their lives. But her heart pounded with fear when it turned. Eden realized it was staring directly at her, and she cowered behind her bush with her pulse throbbing. She feared her legs would buckle and send her tumbling to the ground.

The ghost was moving now and heading toward her, but she couldn't find the strength to run. As it moved closer, the white, ethereal covering began sliding forward and slipped to the ground.

"Nub!" Eden cried.

Nub was smiling at her. *Have I ever seen him smile before?* It seemed as strange as the role he had just played in the old cemetery.

"I knew you was behind that bush all along," he said, stomping out the fire on his ghostly sheet. "You infernal females don't never do what you're told to do."

His words were harsh, but his voice was soft.

"Nub, I'm still shaking."

"They ain't comin' back, girl. No, they'll never be back!"

"But I'm still shaking."

"It serves you right for not stayin' inside the house where you'd have been safe. No matter now, them three'll tell all the bottom landers 'bout this here haint. Nobody'll be comin' round here to bother you or Miss Afton when this tale gets out and runnin'. Bottom landers is a superstitious bunch. If they think these dead folks want Afton to stay here, they won't be botherin' her or you no more."

"You're a clever man, Nub Henry."

"Well, you ain't clever, standin' out here in the chill air in them sleep clothes. Now go on inside and lock up. I got fires to put out."

He watched as she took a few steps toward the house. Then she turned and said, "Thank you, Nub. You're a good friend." She didn't wait for a response. Not from Nub.

He stood watching until she disappeared into the house, then used the old sheet to beat out the small flames that still burned. Dang, she was a sweet gal after all. For the first time, Nub was glad that she had come, that she had been there for Miss Alma. He hoped that she was going to stay in Two Rivers this time.

So did the house.

# Twenty-Nine

Eden awoke the following morning hoping J. D. hadn't had to endure Paige's wrath. Maybe her friends had managed to keep silent. After all, the picnic had been innocent. She didn't even know J. D. or the others would be out there. Despite all that, heavier on her heart was the thought that Raina Gentry was her mother. She was still wondering how she could possibly accept that fact. The only notion that made any sense to her was—*Not Possible!* Bett was, and would always be, her mother, no matter who birthed her. When she came downstairs, she found Ryder sitting in her kitchen having coffee with Afton.

"Just thought I'd check on you ladies," he said, with his strong Texas drawl. "I know y'all must be missin' Miss Alma. You doin' alright, Eden?"

"It'll take some getting used to, not having her around. I feel like a mama cat whose kittens have been given away. I wander through the house looking for her, even though I know she's not here."

"You let Afton be a comfort to you," he said.

"She is, Ryder," Eden said, smiling at the girl. Eden knew it was more than Miss Alma's leaving that had brought Ryder out their way. He was still worried about the three horsemen from the day before. Eden started to tell him about what had transpired in the night, but she felt it a private thing between herself and Nub. Maybe another time she could share what had happened. They needed to know because once this place was known as a haunt, none of them would dare come around again. Yes, she would eventually tell them, but not now. Now it felt good to share a secret, just between herself and Nub. It made her feel more a part of this new life and the people who shared it with her. Deep inside, she began to feel safe again.

To be honest, Eden wondered if the house was indeed haunted. More than just alive—actually haunted. Exactly who was the little girl in her window on the night she returned? She couldn't have conjured up such a beautiful child.

"Miss Clarice wants you and Afton to come have some lunch with her at the bookstore at noon," Ryder said.

"That would be nice. It'll get our minds off all these other things."

Afton felt uncomfortable. She was not used to being a part of the townie's social set. Nonetheless, they talked her into it, and by noon, they were munching tuna salad sandwiches at Clarice's table in the back of the bookstore. J. D. was there when they arrived, and Clarice had insisted he stay. In truth, he was glad to join their circle. It felt comfortable to him. Easy, like home.

They heard the shop bell jingle, and were aware of someone milling around the store, but continued with their luncheon.

"Clarice?"

The voice was velvety and thick as honey.

"Clarice Callahan, are you in here?"

"Yes, ma'am, right here," Clarice said as she rose and moved toward the voice. "Hello, Raina. What can I do for you?"

"I'm looking for a book called *Peyton Place*. I heard it was really good and that I would enjoy reading it."

"I don't think I ordered it. Heard it was a bit racy. But I can have one shipped to me. It'll be here in three to four days. Would you like me to do that?"

"Alright. But for heaven's sake, why don't you keep a better selection of books?"

"That's not the sort of book I get a lot of requests for. How about a sandwich? Have you had lunch yet, Raina?"

"I've already eaten, but I'll have a cup of tea if you have any."

"Sure. Come on back."

J. D. looked at Eden and crinkled his nose as Raina followed Clarice to their table. Raina seemed shocked to see J. D., Eden, and Afton there.

"I didn't know you were lunching with these people," Raina said. "Perhaps I shouldn't stay."

"Don't be silly, Raina. Sit down and visit a spell. You know J. D., and you've met Eden, haven't you?"

"Of course."

"This is Afton Donner."

"Hello, ma'am," Afton said shyly.

"Hello," Raina said, hardly glancing at the girl. She knew where that girl was from, and she'd heard all the tales going around town. How had this happened, sitting down to tea with a bottom lander? It turned Raina's stomach, but she couldn't figure out a graceful way to excuse herself.

Clarice handed Raina a cup of tea, and Eden's eyes locked on Raina's fingers as they wrapped around the cup. *There* was the ring from her dreams! The black stone with the "R" in the center, circled by diamonds. But in the dream, when the child's eyes followed up the arm to the head, there was no face to be seen in the darkness. Now there was the face and not the face she'd have wished for at all. It was a confirmation, and Eden suddenly felt sick.

Raina was saying something to J. D. and Clarice. Eden could see her mouth moving, but her words were like far-off mumblings. Surprising even herself, she blurted out over their conversation, "You're my mother!"

The two women and J. D. fell silent as they turned toward her and stared.

"Eden, honey," Clarice said, "What are you talking about?"

"Don't be silly," Raina said, smiling a cool, plastic grin. "I don't have any idea what you are talking about. But I do know that's not possible."

"It is possible. And it's also true. Bett Devereaux wasn't my birth mother, you were."

"That's absolutely preposterous!"

"It's not! Miss Alma showed me my birth certificate. Apparently, I was christened Carrie Elizabeth Gentry. You were listed as my mother, and Ashley William Devereaux was my father."

"Eden, what are you saying?" Clarice questioned.

J. D. only watched Eden's face, but said nothing.

"It's true, Miss Clarice," Afton said softly, "I've seen the birth certificate, too. Miss Alma showed it to us yesterday. It was in an old Bible of Miss Annaliese's."

"Oh, that old colored woman! She was always stirring up trouble. But this is laughable," Raina said.

"I know it's true now. I remember that ring you're wearing from the night you sent me away."

"What? This old thing? Why I've had this forever."

"I know, I've remembered it forever, and I've dreamed about it forever."

"I won't listen to any more of this absurdity," she said, rising from the chair. "If you'll excuse me, Clarice, I think

I'd better leave before I'm accused of being a spy for the CIA!"

"Sit down, Raina Gentry!" a voice boomed.

It was Aunt Mim coming from the back hallway. She had let herself in the back door, and she wasn't alone. She moved to the back of Raina's chair and smiled as Raina slowly returned to her seat. "What a strange twist of fate to find Raina here," Mim mumbled.

Aunt Mim smiled down at them all. "It's true, Clarice. Raina is Eden's mother, and here is further proof."

It was Angelina Dupree who was standing just past Aunt Mim in the back hall. When Raina saw her, she lost her breath, as if she'd been punched in the stomach.

"Folks," Aunt Mim continued, "this is Angelina Dupree. Angie, I believe you've met Eden and J. D. Of course, you know Afton. This is my sister-in-law, Clarice. And I guess you can say you know *about* Raina Gentry."

"Yes, ma'am. I surely do know about Raina Gentry. I know how a body can commit a murder and can pay off the law, and go free. But not totally free. Right, Raina Gentry?"

"I don't know what you're talking about!"

"Yes, you do!" Angie continued. "You know how that man of yours wanted my sister and would've left you in a minute for her if you'd have let him. It galled you to know that they had a child together, a child conceived 'bout the same time your own child was. You didn't want him. But you couldn't stand lettin' her have him."

Angie paused to shake her head, and the ladies looked at Raina as the blood drained from her face. J. D. stood and placed his hand on Eden's shoulder as Angie went on.

"Ash Devereaux tried to stay away from Bettina. But he couldn't. She and her little girl were like a boil on you, that wouldn't go away, right Mizz Gentry?"

There was no answer.

"Go on, Miss Dupree. Eden needs to hear this," J. D. said.

"She was a wicked woman, an evil tramp," Raina lashed out, "For heaven's sake, she was a bottom lander!"

"No, she wasn't evil. She was a good girl, like Afton here," Angie said. "She was a deceived woman. You were the wicked woman, Raina Gentry. You saw her walkin' along the road the day Ash Devereaux told you he was leavin' you for her. In your anger, you ran her down like a dog in the road. Only she didn't die that day. It was my little niece, Annie, you killed."

"It was an accident!" Raina cried. "Everyone knew that at the time. I was acquitted in a court of law. You remember that Mim, don't you?"

Angie countered, "Woman, there were witnesses, and you know it. But they was from the river bottom, so their word was of no account. Your daddy paid that judge to rule it an accident. But my people saw you turn that wheel, and hit the gas, and head straight for 'em. That's why my papa called for a blood feud. Blood for blood. Your life for Annie's life."

"But, how come I was raised by your sister?" Eden asked.

"When this Jezebel heard about the blood feud, all she could think of was savin' her own life. She made an offer, her daughter to replace Bettina's dead daughter if we'd call off the blood feud."

Eden gasped. *Could a mother really do such a thing? Give her own child away?* In disbelief and anger, she slowly asked, "So Raina gave me to Bett to call off the blood feud against her?"

"Yes 'um, that's what she done. But I thought we should've killed her anyway. Bettina wanted you 'cause you were Ash Devereaux's daughter, and she knew after all that sorry business that their time together was over. They reported you missing and sailed off to Europe, and as soon as they arrived there, Ash disappeared, and never made contact with this woman again."

"And Bett?" Eden asked.

"Ash called her from Europe and begged her to join him. But she said Annie's death would always be between 'em and he had to let go. Bettina couldn't want a man who could give his baby away. She never heard from him again after that. Now her job would be to save this here child from the Gentrys. Bettina could never come back here 'cause everyone knew her little girl died. How could she explain you? They all knew the Gentry girl disappeared, and she feared that they'd think she kidnapped you, and they'd put her in prison for life, and give you back to this awful woman. And she loved you too much to let that happen."

Raina looked small. Her shoulders drooped, and she hung her head as the truth was painfully regurgitated.

Angelina continued, "Your mama, Bettina, changed her name, and started a new life for the two of you over in West Texas. She took his name because you were a Devereaux, and that galled Raina. She had her lawyers purge every mention of Ash's name from all legal papers, 'cept that birth certificate old Miz Gentry hid away. But that snake sent your mama money ever' year, bein' scared to death she might come back and expose it all."

"How could she do that?" Eden asked softly.

"Money could do anything in Two Rivers back then. Her daddy was rich, and he ran this town."

"And Annaliese Gentry? What was her role in all of this?" J. D. asked, mostly for Eden.

"Her role? She had no role. She did what ol' Camden Gentry told her to do. Mostly that was to keep quiet. But it crushed her. She really did love you, and my sister always knew it. Over the years, Bettina sent her pictures, and let her know how you was gettin' on. Then one day, Bettina's letters started to be returned. I guess that's when they put the lady in that home over in Coldspring. It was Annaliese Gentry who gave your mama the greater money, so you two could live high off the hog. Raina here, didn't know about that. Every Christmas ol' Miz Gentry sent Bettina a huge check so that you could have a proper life for a blood Gentry, as she saw it. No, Annaliese Gentry didn't have no role in the evil of all this. But her man did. And it was a crushing thing to that marriage, too."

There was silence. Raina slowly stood and smoothed the front of her dress. "I won't be needing that book, Clarice." Stoically, she turned and left the shop without looking back.

"I'd like to think of you as my aunt," Eden said to Angie Dupree.

"I'd like that too. I loved my sister. Raina Gentry may have taken Bettina and Carrie away from us. But I know she loved you as much as she loved Annie. Otherwise, she'd have never stayed away from her family. She loved you that much."

"I'd loved to have known Annie," Eden mused.

Angie Dupree reached into her shirt pocket and dropped a photo onto the table.

"That was my little niece, Annie. I thought you might like to see it."

Eden was unable to look away from the little girl in the photo.

"Oh my, what a beautiful child," Aunt Mim said.

"Where did she get all those dark curls?" Clarice asked.

"Ash, I guess. He had that coal black hair."

"And her eyes!" Clarice said, "Why they look like … like—"

"Like Elizabeth Taylor eyes," Eden said softly.

"Yes, that's it exactly," Aunt Mim said.

J. D. remained quiet and watched Eden's face. He had learned her nuances by now and knew there was something else about that photo.

"What is it, Eden?" he asked.

Eden was silent as she looked up, and her eyes moved from person to person gathered around the table. Puzzled, she could only shake her head.

"What is it, dear? What's bothering you?" Clarice prompted.

"I saw this little girl. She was standing by my bedroom window staring at me the night I came back to Two Rivers. But Miss Alma said there was no one else in the house. I thought I imagined it. But I couldn't have made up someone who looked so much like this photo of Annie."

They were all quiet, considering what Eden said. She knew they must be thinking she was losing her mind when Angie Dupree spoke.

"I've seen her too. Always at night. Once by the river, close to my house. And another time, along the road where she died."

"Ain't that the oddest thing?" Aunt Mim said, "I wonder what she wants?"

"Maybe it'll be better if we don't know that, Mim," Clarice said.

They all knew the Big Thicket was haunted. How could it not be with all the violent and senseless deaths over the years? Now there was another legend to add to those other tales told on cold winter nights, to the wide-eyed children in the Big Thicket of Deep East Texas.

That night Eden dreamed the dream again, but this time all the pieces of the puzzle fit. In it, it was Raina who handed her up into that car. It was Annaliese Gentry who cried out and ran after the car in the fog. The dark, foreboding figures suddenly had faces and names and the dream at last made sense. The fear of it was gone now. She was certain that her life was much better because Bett had been her mother. She could be grateful for all the years she had with Bett.

# Thirty

Eden drove to Coldspring the following Saturday to spend time with Miss Alma. She told her what happened at the bookstore, and Miss Alma was glad that someone had finally forced Raina Gentry to examine the harm she had done to so many. Eden's only disappointment was that the ol' Missus slept through her entire visit.

When she returned home, she called to Afton as she entered the front door.

"Out back, Miss Eden."

Eden passed through the house's center hall that seemed unnaturally darkened. Before she made it to the kitchen, she heard the house take a deep breath, and from every room, she heard the house whisper, *Eden.* She stopped for just a moment to recreate Miss Alma's famous "Humph!" as she put her hands on her hips and said, quite forcefully, "Stop that," and continued out the back door.

She found Afton with Ryder and J. D., cleaning catfish.

"What is all this?" she said, glancing back into the house briefly, where everything was quiet and still again. She felt like she had won that encounter, but she didn't speak of it.

"Don't tell me you've never cleaned fish before!" Ryder said.

Eden shook her head. "I grew up in an all-female home in a town, remember?"

"But you're a Texas girl. Come here, kiddo," J. D. teased, "and I'll let you gut this one."

"Not on your life, J. D. Callahan!"

He jumped onto the porch and waved the dead fish in her face.

"Ooooh, they smell!" she yelled, shrinking back. "Get it away!"

Smirking, he returned to his task.

Eden sat on the edge of the porch and let her sandaled feet swing over the side.

"Those sure are tiny things you boys caught. Kind of pitiful, really," Eden teased.

"Oh yeah!" Ryder smiled. "Think you and Afton could do better?"

"Better than those? Piece of cake." Eden taunted.

"I smell a challenge, brother man," Ryder said to J. D. "But we wouldn't want to take advantage of anyone who grew up in an all-female townie's home, now would we, Brother Jeff?"

"You girls up for a friendly fishin' competition?" J. D. asked.

"How hard can it be? We'll take on the challenge, won't we, Afton?"

"If you say so," Afton smiled timidly.

By noon, they were back on the river in Ryder's bass boat, poles in hand, and drinking colas. Every time Eden would start to speak, they'd shush her.

"Fish can sense sound and vibration," Ryder criticized. The rules of the competition were that the first girl to pull in a fish would measure that fish up against the first fish pulled in by one of the boys. It wasn't long before Ryder had tied up a substantial big mouth bass.

"Hot dang," he cried, as he clipped the hook from its huge gaping mouth and examined his prize. "Ain't that a real kicker?"

J. D. looked at the girls and said, "Let's see you top that, ladies."

Only ten minutes later Eden yelled as she began to struggle with her pole. It bent into a high arch and fought under some kind of massive weight.

"That must be a whopper!" Ryder shouted.

Eden continued to struggle with the fish, rocking the boat from side to side. Afton placed her hands on each side of the boat and hung on, and Ryder put his hand on her arm to steady her. Finally, J. D. placed his hands over Eden's and began to help her reel in her fish.

"Hey, J. D., no fair helpin'," Ryder whooped.

When J. D. tugged on the pole, and when the fish surfaced, Eden saw a long, narrow snout filled with huge pointed teeth. Screaming, she released the pole from under J. D.'s grasp. The creature dove deep, dragging the pole and line over the side and into the water with it.

"What was that?" Eden yelled.

But the boys were hooting and laughing. "A gar! An alligator gar! You girls up for a gar fry tonight?"

Eden sat back down as J. D. smiled. "Don't be too upset. You know you have to clean what you catch. And those critters have lots that need guttin'."

"Yuck!"

"Oh, stop teasin' her," Afton said. "At least we brought in the biggest weight."

"Brought in nothin'," Ryder chimed in. "I don't see no fish in this boat, but mine!"

The ladies had to concede the competition to the gentlemen.

As the boys continued to boast of their fishing prowess, Eden said, "So what! We weren't playing for stakes!"

"On the contrary," J. D. said, "Losers fix the winners a big ol' fish dinner for supper."

"That's doable."

When they returned to the house, Eden called Clarice and told her to come out for a fish fry, and to bring Aunt Mim and Johnny. Slats could tag along, too.

By dusk, Afton had fish frying on an open firepit in the backyard the way her mother fixed them. Eden found herself in the kitchen, up to her elbows in shredded cabbage that she was trying to transform into coleslaw when she heard a car horn. She went to the front door and found Wynn bounding up the steps, with a bouquet of flowers and a huge grin.

"Wynn!" she yelled, throwing the screen door open and giving him a huge hug. "You're just in time. We're having a fish fry."

"That explains all the cars," he smiled.

He kissed her hard, and it took her breath away.

"Oh lady, how I've missed you this last week!" he said.

Eden pulled him into the kitchen and finished making her coleslaw as they chatted. She told him about their trip, and how her mystery had at last been solved, though not to her satisfaction, and about Miss Alma and her Thaddeus and how Miss Alma was now with the ol' Missus.

Wynn wanted to shout, but he held himself in check. He was excited that there was no further reason for her to stay in Two Rivers. He began to mentally plan their return to Rising Star and that long overdue proposal.

Eden backed her way through the kitchen's screen door cradling the huge crock of slaw in her arms. Wynn followed with a pan of baked beans.

"Afton, look who's here," she announced, as they all turned toward the pair.

"Hello, Mr. Wynn," Afton responded.

Eden introduced Wynn to everyone gathered around the fire-pit.

J. D. spent the evening sizing Wynn's mettle. In fact, he could find no fault in the fellow. He was personable and polite, and it was obvious he cared a great deal for Eden. But for some reason, all his first-rate attributes irritated J. D. to no end.

Clarice and Aunt Mim understood. They watched their J. D. as he remained quietly in the shadows, listening carefully to Wynn Beckett's every word, every motion, as Wynn talked to Ryder about running cattle in West Texas, and the problems with the water tables and drought. He leaned in to hear little snippets of endearments Wynn would speak to Eden. It was 'my little sweetheart' this, and 'my pretty girl' that. Clarice and Aunt Mim were amused as J. D. absentmindedly walked along an imaginary circle around the group, hands clasped behind his back, watching as Eden attended to Wynn's every need. When she blotted his mouth with her napkin, J. D. winced.

"What man lets a girl do that? The man is not a child," J. D. mumbled. If he dipped tobacco, this is where he'd have spit in disgust. *Get hold of yourself,* he thought. *You're looking for something wrong with the man! Relax, he's a nice guy.*

Eden got up to carry the leftover food inside, and Wynn followed her with dirty plates and silverware. When they returned, the fire had been reduced to glowing embers that crackled and popped, flinging tiny, orange sparks into the air. As its glow softened, the clouds parted, and the moon floated free, lighting their yard and the hay meadow beyond.

"Been a long time since I saw that ol' moon on the river," Ryder said, turning to Afton. "How about a walk down to the pier?"

Afton smiled and nodded.

"Excellent idea. We'll all go!" J. D. said.

That wasn't what Ryder had in mind. He wanted to spend some private time with Afton, yet J. D. wanted to prolong everyone's evening.

"You young folks go ahead," Clarice said, "Mimosa and I will wash up the dishes while you're gone."

"Oh, no ma'am," Afton said, "That's my job."

"Heavens to Betsy! Y'all go and have a good walk," Aunt Mim sputtered.

Johnny spoke up, "As thrilling as that sounds, Slats and I are goin' to head back into town and see what's shakin' at the Bijou. I think they're showing that Paul Newman movie, *Hud.*"

"Okay dear," Clarice said, "You boys be careful now. Take care of the Callahan name, ya' hear?"

"Sure, Mom," Johnny said, giving her a quick hug, before running off after Slats.

"Thanks for the fish fry," he called out as he disappeared around the end of the house.

Clarice shook her head and mocked, "My sons! The embodiment of manners!"

Aunt Mim laughed. "Now Clarice, at least he did remember to say thanks before he got out of sight."

On the back steps, dirty dishes in hand, Clarice turned to see the young folks disappear into the woods. Ryder and Afton arm in arm, Wynn and Eden arm in arm, and finally J. D. Clarice grieved thinking how awkwardly Paige would fit into this little group with J. D. That made her sad for him. Clarice and Aunt Mim never thought her son's wedding would actually take place.

Paige Gresham was not their choice for Clarice's oldest son. They always felt he'd come to his senses eventually, but it hadn't happened. With the wedding only two weeks away, they were steadying themselves to accept the girl into the family.

The patch of forest between the hay meadow and the river remained hidden from the moonlight. It was too dark, and as they stepped carefully over and around roots and brambles, Afton tripped, but Ryder caught her and cautioned the rest about the large tree roots.

When Eden stepped from the leafy canopy, she noticed how the moonlight trickled down the bank, and drifted across the water, causing small diamond splashes to explode in the water. That familiar river breeze slapped her face as she left the windbreak of the forest and walked out onto the pier. She sat down, took off her shoes and dangled her feet in the water. They all did, pushing their pants legs up, and lining up along the pier like seagulls along an ocean jetty.

Afton began to talk about how important this old river had always been to her people. It was the most Eden had ever heard her talk about her life. Eden carefully listened as Afton talked about playing in the river as a child. She said they'd bathed in it, drank from it, caught fish in it when there was nothing else to eat. She even admitted to helping her mother cook a gar once because they hadn't eaten in two days, and it was all they had. Afton tried to explain how hunger is a powerful driving force once you know it. But they didn't know it as they had never gone without food before. It was hard for them to imagine. Still, they loved Afton for it. It made her who she was, and she was different from the bottom landers.

Eden began to see how different, how harsh, Afton's life had been from her own. *What had caused a century of animosity of one group of people against another,* she wondered. *Could anyone even remember? Certainly, no one here knew what had caused it, or where the beginning even was.*

"Look." Wynn pointed. A star fell from the sky and disappeared into the treetops across the river.

"A shooting star!" Eden exclaimed, "We can all make a wish, and it has to come true."

"I sure know what my wish is," Ryder drawled, kissing Afton's forehead.

Eden was quiet, pondering what her wish would be. She closed her eyes and made her wish.

"What did you wish for?" Wynn asked.

"Don't answer," J. D. said quickly. "If you tell, it won't come true."

All was quiet again as each one flung their own dreams and wishes into the air, only to wonder if it had been a mistake and if they should take them back.

J. D. laid back on the pier, his arms behind his head, "Look at how big the sky is," he said.

"Mmm," Eden sighed, "So beautiful."

"You can't always see the stars from town," J. D. said, "All the town lights make them disappear."

"We didn't have much in the bottom land, but we always had the stars," Afton said softly, and Eden envied her that.

Eden knew it was late when they headed back through the woods. Clarice and Aunt Mim were sitting on the back porch and could see them in the middle of the hay meadow, splashed in buttercream moonlight.

Suddenly, Eden caught both Wynn and J. D.'s arms.

"Look!" she whispered.

At the edge of the tree-line, some forty feet to the left of them was a dazzling column of fireflies. It was as if they were captured in a mini tornado, circling round and round into a tall column, some six feet high. These were her fireflies, the ones she had abandoned for Rising Star, and the ones that had welcomed her home with a dazzling display on the night she returned. She was drawn to them, her hand extended.

She whispered, "Don't anyone move."

She walked in slow motion to the tower of blinking lights, and to her delight, the glowing bugs didn't disperse into the forest. Ever so slowly, she stepped into the column and found the fireflies circling her while a few landed on her setting her hair aglow. They received her, celebrated her, and she felt joy in the midst of their dancing together. She lifted her arms and began to turn slowly in the direction the fireflies were swarming. A dark cloud briefly covered the moon, and the darkness only accentuated the tower of light that she had become. She rotated until her back was to the rest of them. When the clouds parted, the moon flooded the meadow with light again. Suddenly Eden realized she was looking into the eyes of someone standing just inside the line of trees.

She screamed and sent the points of lights scattering across the meadow in all directions. Eden ran toward the others, screaming that there was someone in the woods. As she reached the safety of her friends, Wynn stepped toward her. But it was J. D. she ran to, and she threw her arms around his waist. Eden recognized the error the moment she did it, and jerked away, trying to redeem herself. But the harm was already done.

"Eden?" Wynn said, confused.

Eden made a vain attempt to divert attention from what she had done, "Someone in the woods! Someone was watching us!"

J. D. asked Wynn to take the ladies up to the house, while he and Ryder went to investigate.

Clarice and Aunt Mim had been watching from the back porch. "What is it?" they called out.

"Someone was in the woods watching us!" Eden called back. She kept glancing up at Wynn, but his face remained emotionless.

J. D. saw the eyes first, and he reached out to grab Ryder's arm and stopped them both where they stood. The foliage let bits and streaks of moonlight through. One ribbon of light fell across yellowed eyes that were staring back at J. D., and his skin began to tingle.

"Who's there?" he called out.

"Don't be a'feared," a low, disembodied voice said.

"Who are you and what do you want?"

"Nub. I got somethin' here for you, Mr. Ryder Lee."

"For me? What could you possibly have for me?"

Nub Henry stepped forward, exposing himself. He placed a large basket on the ground before him.

"Boone Bohannon's," was all he said, and he was gone.

J. D. and Ryder didn't move for a moment, trying to listen as the old man walked away. There was no sound at all, almost as if he were a disembodied ghost. The unnaturalness of it gave them chills.

Ryder picked up the basket. It was heavy and covered with a cloth. He pulled the fabric back and found a tiny, pink baby sleeping underneath.

"Oh, my Gawd!" Ryder said, "It must be Afton's baby! Afton and Boone's! It didn't die after all!"

# Thirty-One

The sun was well up, and a glance at Eden's clock told her it was already nine-thirty. She dressed quickly and came downstairs to find the front door standing open, with Wynn sitting on the porch steps. She sat down beside him.

"The house isn't much," Wynn said, matter-of-factly. "It'll need a lot of work. But the land here is pretty nice. Seems fertile. Good for crops. Plenty of room for cattle if you clear some woods."

With all the excitement the night before, Wynn and Eden hadn't had a chance to talk. She put her arm through his and laid her head on his shoulder.

"I've really fallen in love with the Thicket, Wynn."

"I know you have. And somewhere along the way, you've fallen out of love with me."

His words surprised her.

"That's not true!"

He patted her hand as it rested on his arm.

"Oh, you love me alright. We've got a long history. But you aren't in love with me anymore. Not like back in high school. It never happened again, like it did for us back then. I miss us, the way we used to be."

"We're not the same people we were then."

"So, you feel it too?"

She sighed but didn't answer. She didn't have to. He knew already.

"It feels like we've lost something really precious. I thought we could get it back. But you belong here now. And I don't. There's no place for me here, Eden. I'm not a part of this world. And I don't think I can ever be."

Again, she remained quiet, and it disappointed him. He had hoped she'd counter his accusations and fight for him, but she didn't.

"So!" he sucked in a big breath, "It's time for me to exit while I still have my dignity."

"Wynn, no. I don't want you to go. Stay for a while longer and let's talk about it. Who knows what to-morrow will bring?"

"Always the optimist," he said, kissing her forehead. "But I didn't unpack last night. It'll be better if it's quick. Speeches and departing loves are alike in that shorter is always better. I don't think I could bear to see you in J. D. Callahan's arms again."

"There's nothing between J. D. and me. He's marrying Paige Gresham in a couple of weeks."

"There's more than you think, sweetheart. Now, send your wounded warrior off with one last kiss."

She did, more a hug than a kiss, then he was gone. She stood alone on the steps.

"I'm sorry, Eden."

It was J. D.'s voice.

With all the commotion and the new baby, she hadn't realized that he had stayed over with Ryder, sacked out on bedrolls on the back porch. Now he was standing just inside the screen door, unable to pull himself away from the scene he had just witnessed.

"You heard?"

"Yes, and I'm sorry."

She turned to look into his eyes. "Of course, he was wrong. He just didn't understand what good friends we've become. But he was right about him and me. We were running on our old relationship. We were bound to come to a stop eventually."

J. D. walked out onto the porch and put his hand on her shoulder.

"Come inside. I've got some biscuits and gravy for you on the stove."

By early afternoon, Bea and Bick Bohannon showed up with baby things from the Emporium. They brought a crib, clothes, toys, diapers, and all sorts of baby paraphernalia.

"Where is she?" Bea called out, rushing into the house, "Where is my grandbaby?"

Afton came down the stairs with the child and placed her in Bea's arms.

"Oh, Bick. She looks like Boone did when he was a baby."

"All grandmothers say that."

"But she does. Just look."

Bea turned to Afton, "Thank you for calling us. That was kind of you."

Afton smiled.

"What is she called?" Bick asked, tickling the baby's cheek.

"Boone told me he was really close to his grandmother that died last year. I thought I'd name her Molly, after his grandmother."

Bea started to cry. "Oh child, we love you and the baby so much!"

"Don't go getting all emotional," Bick said.

"I can't help it."

"You doing alright?" Bick asked Afton.

"Yes, sir. Miss Eden has been kind to me."

Ryder stepped forward then and put his arm around Afton before he spoke.

"Mr. and Mrs. Bohannon, I think it's time you knew about Afton and me. We've been together for a long while now, and we plan to be married. We hope that's a right good thing in your eyes."

"Son," Bick began, "You were our son's best friend, and you loved him like a brother. It's not likely we'd question any such decision coming from you."

"If Boone can't be here, I'm sure there's no one else he'd rather have raising his baby girl," Bea said, giving Ryder a hug.

"Good people," Ryder said, as the Bohannon's drove away after playing with baby Molly all afternoon.

The phone was ringing, so Eden picked up.

"Jeff Callahan, please."

The voice was cold and made Eden cringe. She knew J. D. was going to get into trouble for being out there yet again. She handed him the phone, and he immediately knew who it was by the look on Eden's face.

"Hello?"

Eden moved through the kitchen and onto the back porch, not wanting to hear the one-sided conversation. J. D. turned away and cupped the phone, so she wouldn't hear the yelling. He wasn't on the phone long before he joined them on the porch.

Eden wasn't even surprised to see the two people who cleared the tree line and were approaching the house, across the hay meadow. She turned her head and called out to Afton.

"Afton, come here and bring the baby."

Afton stepped out the door just as Nub Henry and Jewel Donner reached the porch. For a moment, no one spoke, then Jewel asked if she could see the baby.

"I know I don't have the right. I let 'em do it and all. But I'm still the grandma, and she's here 'cause of me."

"How is that?" Ryder asked as he and J. D. came to stand beside Afton.

"When they done it, they was surprised that she lived. They dumped her in a box and set her out on the back porch to die. I went out after dark and put blankets on her. It was cold. But the next mornin' she was still alive. I thought I'd lose my mind. She lay out there cryin' for might near two days until I couldn't take no more. I got that neighbor gal, Mary Genell, to carry her to a family downriver, and they decided to keep her as they's own. I was glad 'cause she'd be safe from Carl T."

"How'd you figure that?" Ryder asked.

"I told Carl T. that she died, and I'd done buried her out in the woods. He believed me."

"So, that makes everything alright?" Ryder spat out.

Jewel Donner stared up at Ryder, shading her eyes from the sun with her arm.

"Who you be, young man?"

"I'm Ryder Lee, and I plan to marry your daughter."

"Oh lawdy! I been so worried 'bout that, the longer my girl stayed with you people."

"It's okay, Jewel. Ryder is a good man," Eden said softly, "Now, come see your granddaughter."

Eden took the child from Afton and handed her into Jewel Donner's arms.

Ryder had a question, something that had been bothering him. "How did Carl T. find out about Afton and the baby?"

Jewel looked up. "A note come one day. Bubba Walters brought it. Said he was to keep quiet 'bout where it come from. But he told us anyway. He said that Gresham gal gave him two dollars to take it to Carl T."

J. D. suddenly felt sick. "Paige Gresham?"

"I reckon so," the old woman said.

J. D. realized that it was Paige who had set this whole sorry business into motion. He felt like someone had punched him in the gut. He turned away and walked to the end of the porch.

Eden followed him. "Maybe it wasn't Paige," Eden said. "Lots of girls in town would look like Paige to a bottom lander."

But she kept seeing the cunning smile on Paige's face that Thanksgiving morning when they discovered Afton and Boone with Eden and Ryder. J. D. hadn't even noticed the girl was expecting, but Paige did. Paige had almost seemed glad as if she had been vindicated in some way. Eden wondered how well J. D. really knew this woman he was about to marry.

As Jewel cooed at the baby girl, Eden turned to Nub, "How'd you come by her?"

"A baby should be with her mama. I went there and told 'em that."

Short and to the point, as always. She knew the river folk feared Nub and wouldn't want to tangle with Carl T. or his woman.

"Nub, I know all about what happened to me as a child."

Nub looked away and spat as she approached him.

"You were the man in the old car who carried me away from Two Rivers that night, weren't you?"

"I done it 'cause ol' Cam Gentry said to."

"You don't strike me as being a man easily pushed around by someone just because they have money and social standing and they tell you to."

"I done it 'cause I had feelin's for Bettina, and she wanted you. I knew I was too ol' for that young girl, but she was mighty special. Nobody thought you should be brung up by Raina Gentry anyway."

Now standing directly in front of him, she said, "You did the right thing. I want you to know that. My life was much better with Bett than it ever would have been with Raina. Thank you, Nub." Gently, she put her arms around the dirty scarecrow of a man and hugged him. He stiffened and didn't move. He hadn't been touched by another human being since they'd murdered his wife. When Eden let go and stepped back, she tried to discern the look in his eyes. She could see that he was fighting emotions.

"Thank you for all you've done for Afton and me and Miss Alma."

Eden couldn't know how remarkable J. D. found her at that moment. He didn't know anyone, man or woman, who'd have gotten close enough to the filthy backwoodsman to actually touch him. Yet Eden had put her arms around him. He thought she was more than completely remarkable.

Nub and Jewel were asked to stay for supper, but they declined. Once they were gone, Ryder and Afton took Molly inside and fed her together.

J. D. joined Eden on the back-porch steps just as the sun was going down.

"This time last night, we were eating fried fish," he said, "completely unaware of the remarkable thing that was about to happen."

"Mmm," Eden mused, as their world was being painted the colors of night.

"How are you feeling?" He asked. "Things are changing quickly for you. Any regrets?"

She smiled, "No, no regrets. It's all as it should be."

"Will you stay here then?"

"I can't even think of going anywhere else."

"I'm glad," he said. "We'd all be lost without you, you know."

Eden felt shy that their faces were so close.

They jumped when they heard the phone ring inside and heard Ryder say, "Hello?"

"J. D.," Ryder called out, "It's Paige."

J. D. frowned.

"It's okay, J. D. Go. I'm fine. Really."

"J. D.!" Ryder yelled out again.

"Just tell her I'm on my way back to town."

"She wants to talk to you."

"Just tell her!"

They could hear Ryder mumbling something into the phone.

"Walk me around to my car," J. D. said.

He rested his hand on the small of her back, guided her around the house and to his car. He placed her against the driver's door, reached up with both hands and pushed her hair back away from her face. He was so close that she could feel his breath on her face.

"J. D.!" Ryder called from far off. Ryder was looking for them out back. "J. D., where the heck are you?"

Eden pushed J. D. back.

"Eden?" J. D. looked confused.

"I think you'd better go," she said softly, as she moved from him and toward the house.

"But Eden ..."

She threw her head back and said, "Paige is waiting. And I have to get on with my life."

She headed toward the front porch, and at that moment it occurred to her that once Afton and Ryder were married, she would be alone in the house on Camp Ruby Road. She loved the place, but she felt intimidated by the night that was coming on and wondered if she could handle the isolation when she had to live here alone. She would have to make peace with the house then. Learn to depend on it as Miss Alma had.

Once inside, she watched from the sidelight as J. D. slid behind the wheel of his truck. For a while, he just sat there, clutching the steering wheel and staring straight ahead. He finally turned his car engine on and looked over at the old house. A soft light drew his eye to an upstairs window where a little girl was looking down at him. His body tensed as their eyes locked. He blinked, and then she was no longer there, but he had seen her. Annie had chosen to reveal herself to him too. He started to run inside and tell Eden, but he held back. What he had just seen didn't seem threatening. J. D. was afraid that he had ruined his friendship with Eden. He had been much too forward. He looked up at the window again, but the child was gone, just as he should be. He gunned the engine and drove away.

Eden ran upstairs, leaving her door ajar, and fell across her bed. She rolled over onto her back and strained in the darkness to see the old Missus' room. The thought that it had been her grandmothers caused her to trace every inch of it with her eyes as she imagined Annaliese Gentry had done, but it was too dark.

She sensed, rather than heard, a soft pop, and from it, a ball of light flared, as if someone had struck a match. The ball of light hovered over her bed, close to the ceiling, and there was nothing near it that could account for it being there. It rolled along the ceiling toward one corner and began to descend. As it slowly fell toward the floor, the first thing that it illuminated was the top of a small, dark head. For a little while, Eden could see the whole of a small child squatting in the corner.

She tried to stay calm, but someone screamed, and she realized it was herself. The scream burst the ball of light, and sparks tumbled onto the child who shielded her head and giggled. Then all was dark again.

Of those who lingered outside, no one heard the scream so, no one came running up the stairs. It was a while before Eden could stop shaking enough to reach out into the darkness and switch on her lamp. As she suspected, there was no child, and nothing seemed out of place.

"Okay," she whispered to the house, "let's come to an agreement. We are about to be alone here, and we need to make peace with each other. I'll take good care of you, but you have to stop scaring me."

After a moment, the lamp flickered off and on. Eden smiled.

"And will you take good care of me, too?"

A breeze caught the curtains, and they fluttered as the hallway door slowly closed, and the lock clicked. The room filled up with what felt like comfort and peace. All she knew was that she felt at ease, and there was no more fear.

# Thirty-Two

The final weeks that preceded J. D. and Paige's wedding found J. D. caught up in the insanity of the over-indulgence. He called to check on Eden a couple of times, but there was always a reason she couldn't come to the phone. He drove out once, only to find that she had gone to Coldspring to spend an afternoon with Miss Alma. Blindly, he allowed all things to move forward and told himself that all was well.

The only chink in Paige's carefully constructed wall around J. D. was Ryder. He was J. D.'s best man, and he insisted on escorting Afton to the wedding. Afton refused to come unless Eden was invited to sit with her. At first, Paige had balked, but later the thought of those two bumpkins sitting there, envying her as she swept down the aisle in her one of a kind, designer wedding gown, delighted her. Let them come and witness her final, unequivocal claim to Jefferson Dixon Callahan. Let all the girls in town come and burn with envy! This would be her day and her day alone.

The night before the wedding, an electrical storm moved through in true Texas style. Flashes of white-charged light lit up the Big Thicket like noontime, and the thunder rattled the windows in their sashes. Eden lay awake listening as waves of torrential rain gusts pounded the old house. In truth, she liked the theatrics of it, and she remembered how Bett used to tell her that thunder was just George and Herman bowling in the skies. That made perfect sense to her, and she never thought to ask who George and Herman were. Eden smiled, thinking how childlike her faith had been then. If Bett said it, she believed it. Even if it was about bowling in the clouds!

In the midst of the storm, Annaliese Gentry had fallen into a deep coma-like sleep, this time for real.

She dreamed she was at home, and from her upstairs bedroom window, she had watched the car pull to a stop down the drive, not too close to the house. Only its headlights were visible in the dense fog. Below her, the porch light flashed on, and she could see Raina pulling little Carrie from the house. The mist wrapped around them as Carrie turned once to look back at the house. Had she seen her grandmother in the window? Annaliese found herself running mindlessly down the winding staircase. Had this house always been this large? She threw the giant mahogany door open and ran into the milky fog. But as she reached the car, it was disappearing into the vapor. She ran after it but was unable to catch it. In despair, she went down, falling hard onto the concrete pavement. Raina only walked away, leaving her alone in the fog. How long she lay there sobbing, she didn't know. But it was Cam, who finally came and lifted her from the pavement and carried her back into the house. Cam, whose many kindnesses had sustained her over the years. Cam, who had given her his strength. Cam, who had loved her. How could he have allowed this to happen? How could he let the child be taken? His own flesh and blood. Was his good name so important that he would stop at nothing to protect it? Was it worth the life of a child?

Old now, she remembered. She sighed in her sleep, and her dreams ran away and her breath left her.

≻──✦──≺

Paige was wide awake, tossing and turning in anticipation of the next morning when she and Jeff Callahan would be married, and she could relax again. Then she planned to give Eden her due. She would banish her from their lives forever and be done with Jeff's knighthood. However, when the storm began, Paige broke out in a cold sweat, worrying that it would continue into the day and ruin her wedding. She lay in bed envisioning her makeup running down her cheeks, her hair wet and matted to her head. She knew she needed a good night's sleep to look her best, but that infernal storm wouldn't let her rest at all. That was one thing her money couldn't help her with, and Paige seethed.

≻──✦──≺

It was getting close to sun-up when, from her room at Rose Haven, Miss Alma was jarred awake by the bright flashes that preceded the explosions of sound outside her fogged-over window. She turned her head to see Annaliese Gentry still folded inside the peace of sleep. Or was it something more? Miss Alma sat up and stared at the faded beauty in the bed next to her's. The light flashed again, and in the brief illumination of the room, Miss Alma saw a dark figure standing quietly in the corner. She reached for the nurse's call button, but something stopped her. Another flash revealed more—a man, a tall man, with knowing eyes, that seemed out of place in the shadows. "Thaddeus?" was all she said.

Afton found herself sitting next to the window, watching the flashes of light as Molly slept quietly in her crib. She knew lightning was dangerous and that she should stay away from the window, but she was drawn to it, as a child is to a garishly lit carnival. She was still at the window as the flashes and explosions tarried off to the northeast, and the morning sun began to send rays of hope over the Big Thicket. The rain performed its last hurrah, before chasing after the light and sound show.

At full light, all that was left to testify of the drama were rivulets of water, trickling from the rooflines and dripping from the tree branches. The air smelled clean. Afton stood at the back door, breathing in the cleansing of it before she began to make breakfast. She glanced over at Miss Alma's door. It felt strange to think that her old friend was not there anymore, waiting to be called to her grits and toast. Afton smiled, remembering how much butter and sugar Miss Alma always put on her grits. When Afton chided her for the unhealthiness of it, she said, "Why I need to be so healthy? The sooner I do this, the sooner I see my Thad." It was as simple as that.

J. D. slept the sleep of those with clear consciences and pure hearts and didn't wake during the night. He came dancing into his mother's kitchen early the next morning, humming *Isn't It Romantic*. He took his mother into his arms and waltzed her around the kitchen until she wiggled free and scolded him for his silliness. He ate her enormous Texas breakfast, perhaps the last of its kind, since Paige was partial to continental breakfasts of pastries and fruit. But this morning, it was eggs and grits, sausage and bacon, thick cream gravy and homemade buttermilk biscuits so light he thought they'd float away before he could finish them off.

&lt;━━◆━━&gt;

By seven that morning, Paige was in a cloud of people who flounced around her, creating what she wished to become that day. There was a man brushing and teasing her hair and another carefully painting special makeup on her face. One girl worked on her long fingernails, while another was giving her a pedicure. Caterers had been there since dawn setting up canopies, tables, chairs, and all the accouterments for the perfect reception. Another crew was placing flowers, bows, ivy, and ribbon all over the sanctuary of the First Baptist Church of Two Rivers. The doves that were to be released as they stepped from the church were cooing in their crates, and the scent from the truckload of flowers filled the air around the church.

As Paige was stepping into her hooped petticoat, across town Ryder was trying to help J. D. with his white bow tie.

"That'll never do," Clarice said. "Here, let me do it. Ryder, hadn't you better go pick up Afton and Eden and deliver them to the church? That should take a while."

"Yes ma'am, you're right. I'll see you at the church no later than nine thirty, J. D."

"Alright, but don't be late. Paige says the wedding starts at ten sharp and they're locking the doors against what she calls *disrupting stragglers*, whatever the heck that means."

That made Ryder laugh.

"I'll be early," Ryder said, rushing out the door.

J. D. threw the window up and yelled, "Do you have the ring?"

"Got it, ol' man," Ryder called back.

❦

Afton looked at herself in the long pier mirror in the center hall. She had never had such a lovely dress. Afton had surely never worn gloves and a hat before. She turned to see Nub through the kitchen door. He had brought her mother upriver to stay with Molly during the wedding. He nodded his approval, as he opened the screen door for Jewel Donner, but he didn't come inside. As much time as he had spent around the old house, he had never come inside, and that was alright with him.

"Oh, my girl! I never seen such fine things before. Just look at you!"

"Miss Eden took me to Lufkin for our dresses. I never saw a store like that. Nothin' but rows and rows of purty, party dresses."

"Can't townies sew?"

"Guess they'd rather not."

Eden was coming down the stairs just as Ryder arrived. Her dress was closed tight at the waist with a double-breasted row of rhinestone buttons. The chiffon skirt flowed out over a pyramid of petticoats. It had a wide shawl collar that wrapped around her shoulders. The colors of the floral print were mimicked in the ribbon on her wide-brimmed straw hat. She was a sophisticated breath of springtime, and not at all the bumpkin Paige was expecting.

Paige had arrived at the church and was spirited away into a secluded side room to await the moment she would stage her entry to the cacophony of ooohs and aaahs. She sat before the gilded framed mirror and kept adjusting a curl above her left eye. Her cousin, Anne Marie Gresham, arrived in her maid-of-honor dress and Paige crinkled her powdered nose.

"For heaven sakes, Anne Marie. Was that dress that tight when we bought it?"

"I guess I put on a few pounds."

"Just suck it in. I don't want anyone focusing on that gut of yours."

"Don't be mean, Paige. It's not that bad."

"Look, this has to be perfect. Everything! Absolutely perfect!"

❦

J. D. and Clarice arrived at the church after picking up Aunt Mim. The bridal consultant rushed him away to a little room at the head of the sanctuary where hundreds of other grooms before him had waited and paced. Clarice and Aunt Mim waited in a vestibule room to be officially seated as the wedding begins.

"So, it's happening. It's actually happening," Aunt Mim said.

"I didn't think it really would."

"Me neither."

"I don't understand it. But I've got to accept it."

"Hate the daughter-in-law, lose the son. That's the way of it, Clarice."

"I know, Mim. Believe me, I know."

Ryder arrived and delivered Afton and Eden to an usher, then excused himself to find J. D. in his seclusion.

"Bride's side or groom's?" the usher asked.

Afton and Eden looked at each other and smiled. "Absolutely the groom's side!" they said to each other, more than to the usher.

As they were seated on the aisle, halfway back, Eden noticed how people stared at them and for a moment she felt shy. Then she lifted her head and remembered that girl whom Bett had raised her to be. Knowing how nervous Afton must be, she put her arm around the girl and gave her a squeeze, while commenting on how lovely the sanctuary was decorated.

The church filled up quickly. The organist began to play *Oh Promise Me.* An usher walked Clarice to her seat in the front row, and Aunt Mim followed. Then Jake Gresham was seated. But just after the pastor, J. D., and Ryder walked to the altar, an older gentleman slipped into the church and whispered something to Eden. It was awkward, but Eden quickly stood and rushed from the sanctuary with Afton in tow. They almost ran into Paige, who was positioning herself in front of the closed double-doors, awaiting her grand entrance.

"What the blasted Hades do you think you're doing!" Paige growled. "You aren't going to ruin my wedding!"

"I'm so sorry, Paige. It's Miss Alma. Something's happened to Miss Alma. I have to go."

"Then get out and stay out, and I mean out of our lives for good!"

Eden paid her no mind, but hurried outside, wondering what to do. She saw Slats leaning over a car, flirting with a cute little blonde.

"Slats!"

"Oh geez, Miss Eden! Am I late?"

"Slats, I have to go to Coldspring fast. It's an emergency. Can you run us home, so I can get my car?"

"Sure. Hop in." He threw open the door of his parent's Impala sedan.

Inside the church, J. D. had seen the confrontation between Paige and Eden before the double doors closed. He turned to Ryder who looked as confused as he did.

Anne Marie Gresham was making her way slowly down the aisle, carefully holding a bouquet of red roses and white carnations. The wedding march began, and the double doors were thrown open to reveal the bride. The congregation stood and turned to perhaps the most beautiful bride they'd ever seen. Paige's hard work and planning had paid off, and the effect was breathtaking. But all J. D. could think about was why Eden had rushed out.

Paige reached the altar and J. D. took her hand, pulling it through his arm, and took his place beside her. As the wedding march finished, J. D. whispered, "What was that all about?"

"Something's wrong with that old colored woman, that's all."

"Miss Alma? Something wrong?"

"If you can believe that!" she spat out under her breath.

"Who gives this woman to be married to this man?" the pastor asked.

Jake Gresham said, "I do," and the congregation was seated.

"Marriage is an institution not to be entered into lightly," the pastor was saying.

J. D. didn't hear anymore. His mind was on Miss Alma. *Something wrong? What the heck does that mean? Why would they have called Eden away from a wedding? It must be really bad.*

Paige noticed him sway forward, and he turned to her.

"I'm sorry, Paige, but if Miss Alma is dying, I need to know," he said, a little too loud.

A ripple of murmurs flowed across the vast room. Aunt Mim stood, quite inappropriately, and said, "J. D., son, did you say Miss Alma is dying?"

Paige was horrified.

J. D. was flushed as he turned and addressed the congregation. "Please, everyone, you're all our friends and family. I know you'll understand. If you'll just give me a moment to make a phone call, I promise I'll be right back."

"NO!" Paige screamed, "You stay right here, Jefferson Dixon Callahan! We're in the middle of our wedding! You are not ruining our wedding over some old, colored woman!"

"Hon, give me a minute, please."

"NO!" she screamed as she stomped her feet. "Blast! Blast! Blast you, J. D. Callahan!"

"I'm sorry Paige," J. D. said softly, trying to calm her. He turned to rush down the aisle, but Jake Gresham grabbed him from behind and flung him back toward the altar as the congregation gasped.

"Good grief, Jake," J. D. said, regaining his equilibrium, "This is a church."

Jake drew his fist back to strike, but J. D. deflected the blow, and Jake, caught off balance, crumpled to the floor pitifully.

"Come on, buddy," Ryder said, pulling J. D. along the velvety carpet, "I'll drive you to Coldspring."

The last thing they heard as they passed through the massive double doors was Paige Gresham pathetically screaming, "I hate you, Jefferson Dixon Callahan! I hate you! *I hate you!* I'm going to scorch the ground you walk on!"

People gasped in horror, but Aunt Mim stood again and applauded, "Good show, honey, good show. Glad to see what could have been J. D.'s future put to an end right here."

People covered their smiles and laughter with gloved hands as Paige continued her tirade against J. D., "I hate you. I *hate* you so much."

But Aunt Mim continued to applaud as a few others joined in with laughter.

"I hate *all* of you," Paige screamed, not knowing what to do. For the first time in her life, she found herself in a situation that she could not control. Her guests had had enough, and they hurried from the church to put an end to her humiliation, but also to let her know that she could no longer treat them as if they were of no importance. They would walk away from *her,* not the other way around. Some pitied her. Some cheered her downfall. But there were none who stayed behind to console her, not one of her closest friends or family stayed, not even old Jake, who exited through a side door.

J. D. had not seen what happened at the church and he simply didn't care anymore. The not caring was refreshing. He knew that when the story turned into legend, and he knew it would, he would not be the villain. Everyone was there, and everyone saw that side that Paige Gresham had carefully hidden from the world. They had had a front-row seat. There was no way she could lie herself out of what they had seen with their own eyes. That thought freed him at last from her long reaching tentacles.

# Thirty-Three

When J. D. and Ryder came running into Rose Haven, they found Eden and Afton seated in the foyer, listening intensely to an older gentleman in a white coat. Ryder rushed over to put his arm around Afton, but J. D. held back.

Eden stood slowly. "J. D., what are you doing here? You should be getting married!"

"I should be here with you," he said softly.

"But ..."

"We'll talk about it later. How is Miss Alma?"

"I was about to tell these ladies," the older man said, "she seemed fine this morning. But about two hours ago, the nurses found her."

"Oh, dear Lord, no," Eden said, sitting back down, and J. D. put his hand on her shoulder.

"I'm sorry, she's passed on," the man said. "Let me take you to her."

When Eden entered the room and saw the peaceful scene there, she wasn't surprised.

"We think Mrs. Gentry died first. It was as if Miss Alma arranged her, hands there on her chest, and hair neatly combed back. Then Miss Alma laid her head down on Mrs. Gentry's shoulder and passed too, just as you see them there. Isn't that remarkable? We can't move them until the coroner comes. This is a bit unusual, you see."

"This is just as it should be," Eden said.

"Be that as it may, the coroner is at a wedding, I believe. But I'm sure he'll be here as soon as it's over," the doctor said.

J. D. and Eden looked at each other and Eden put her hand over her mouth to hide a slight smile.

"He'll be here sooner than you think, Doctor," J. D. said.

Eden crossed the room and sat down in the chair she had sat in that first day she met Annaliese Gentry. The thought of the sweet intimacy these two women had shown her that day touched her again.

The coroner came in, began to examine the bodies and J. D. moved beside Eden.

"What are you thinking?" she heard him ask quietly.

"I was thinking about an old movie, *The Ghost and Mrs. Muir.* Do you know it?"

J. D. nodded.

"The final scene? Do you remember the final scene?"

J. D. smiled slightly, "She died. Then suddenly she was young again, and her captain was there to walk with her, arm in arm, into what comes next."

"Do you think that's what happened? Do you think she's young again, and walking arm in arm with Thaddeus Samuel Mayhew?"

"I do believe they're together now, and that's a fact."

A nurse came in and told the doctor that Mrs. Gentry's daughter was there.

"Shall I bring her down?"

"No, I'll speak with her in the reception room first."

"She doesn't know yet," Eden heard the nurse say. They hurried from the room, not wanting to run into any Gentry.

Behind them, they heard another nurse call out, "Miss Devereaux, Miss Devereaux, a moment please."

They turned as the nurse hurried toward them, pulling something from her pocket.

"Miss Alma said to give this to you if anything was to happen to her." She placed the small cord of braided hair in Eden's hand.

Eden smiled at J. D. Only they knew what it was. Only they knew it was the tiny bits of hair from Alma and Thad that Alma's mother had carefully woven together for their wedding.

The nurse continued, "She said for you to save this envelope and open it when you're alone." Eden was curious. They all were, but Eden slid it into her belt for later.

"We'd better go," J. D. said. "Raina Gentry won't be happy to find us here."

"She won't be happy to find Miss Alma here either," Eden said. "She was never told about this new arrangement."

"Another reason to slip out discreetly. You don't need to deal with her anger right now."

They hurried out a side entrance. Ryder put Afton into his pickup and headed back to Two Rivers. J. D. drove Eden back in her car. She was quiet, and J. D. knew she was hurting. Not for Miss Alma. Miss Alma had what she wanted. But sad for herself, that she'd have to go on without the old woman's familiar smile and endearing *humph*. In truth, J. D. would miss that too. There was so much that passed, along with that old woman, lost forever now.

When they reached the outskirts of town, J. D. turned off the main highway and headed toward the river where he pulled over by the county line bridge and turned to face her.

"J. D., what happened? You were getting married."

"I was getting deeper and deeper into the biggest mistake of my life."

"But the ceremony had started."

"I guess I stopped it," he grinned.

J. D. placed his arm on the back of the seat and pushed her hair back behind her ear.

"What happened to that wonderful hat you were wearing?"

"I left it at the house when Afton and I went home to get my car."

"How'd you get home?"

"Slats."

"So, Slats is good for something?"

"I guess so," she smiled.

J. D. pulled Eden from the car and led her to the bridge. They leaned over the rail and watched the water flow beneath them.

J. D. spoke without looking at her, "I know that envelope was only for you, but I'd sure like to know what's in it. Would you mind opening it? I understand if you don't want to. I just kinda' thought …"

"It's alright, J. D. I don't mind you seeing whatever it is."

Eden pulled it from her pocket and opened it, turning it upside down over the palm of her hand. Out fell a tiny, braided cord, tied to a little note that read,

I thought I'd never get a piece of Mr. J. D.'s hair. Had to ask his Ma, and she thought I was crazy. Yours was easy, little girl. I just borrowed your brush. Anyways, I know you two is to be tied together, just as tightly as me and my Thad. I love you both.

Miss Alma

Eden smiled, and J. D. wrapped his arms around her. Miss Alma's note had emboldened him, and he was able to open up to Eden for the first time.

"The first time I saw you, that day I found you unconscious by this old river, I thought you were the most remarkable girl I'd ever seen. You left me breathless. There just seemed to be some sort of special connection between both of us from that beginning. I found myself falling in love with you, and it scared me."

Eden looked surprised. "But you never said anything!"

"You were spoken for. In Texas, we respect that kind of thing."

"How did you know I was spoken for?"

"I saw you and Wynn Beckett in the hospital lobby, remember? I heard y'all when you thought no one was around. It was obvious you cared deeply for each other."

"You were the stranger in the lobby! I remember now."

J. D. nodded.

"Wynn and I grew up together. Feels like we've been together forever. But that all seems so long ago now. And insignificant."

"I should have cut loose from Paige back then. It wasn't fair to her, the way I felt about you. But I kept telling myself you were a lost cause. You belonged to Wynn Beckett. And I thought I could make Paige and me work."

"I don't want to be the reason you and Paige didn't work, J. D."

"You aren't. Paige is. I thought I could live with her self-centeredness. But I was wrong. It wore far too thin, far too quickly."

They were silent for a time, staring at the river before J. D. spoke. "What about me? How did you feel about me?"

"I was confused by you, intimidated, I guess. You caused emotions that were foreign to me. I didn't know what to do about them. The day you thought your mother would die, the day I was with you by the river, my heart fairly broke. Being beside you in that clearing, feeling so close, and yet knowing you belonged to someone else, made me feel insane. That's why I ran."

"It seems we've been swimmin' upstream for a long time," J. D. said, pulling her closer, and loving the way she laid her head against his chest. "But we don't have to hide our feelings any longer. We're free of your dashing Mr. Beckett and my conniving Miss Gresham. I like this new freedom."

Eden felt herself blush as he brushed her hair away from her face where the wind had blown it, and she felt him kiss her forehead.

"I love you, Eden Devereaux of Rising Star. I have from the beginning."

"I love you too, Jefferson Dixon Callahan of Two Rivers, and also from the beginning."

J. D. placed his hands on both sides of her face and stared deeply into her eyes.

"And now, sweet lady, I'm going to kiss you long and hard. Then we're going to talk about Ryder and Afton and maybe a double wedding. And our wedding is really going to happen."

His kiss made her heady with joy, and she put her arms around him, wanting to stay there, just like that, forever. And she knew, in her heart of hearts, that they would be together for the rest of their lives, tightly woven together just as Miss Alma had woven their hair together, never to be separated again.

As he continued to passionately kiss Eden, the old house on Camp Ruby Road took a deep breath that drew in the curtains and slammed the inside doors. It almost sounded like clapping that echoed throughout the rooms. The house already knew what was happening on the bridge. The house knew everything, and now it felt at peace. It had tried to run this young girl off, but she refused to go. She was strong and faithful to the house.

Miss Anna and Miss Alma were where they should be, with those they loved. Now there was a rightful heir to take care of the house on Camp Ruby Road as the years moved on into the future. Yes, the house was happy for the first time in a long time.

# Epilogue

Deep inside The Big Thicket, Nub Henry felt himself grow tired. The intense, humid heat bore down on him like a weight, and he had trouble catching his breath. He wasn't that far from the shack he'd fashioned deep in the briars and palmettos where no one, not even the river bottom people, ventured. It was his refuge, and he sought it now to comfort his old, worn-out body. It was his home. All he'd known for much of his life.

He came to the creek that carried fresh water from the Lost River to him, so he bent down and scooped some up in his hands to drink. Then he splashed his face with the coolness of it.

A soft giggle brought him to his feet, and he quickly looked around but could see nothing. The giggle drew his attention to the thick trunk of a towering oak. There was never anyone this deep in the Thicket. It had always been his own private world.

As he stared at the sprawling tree, a little girl slowly stepped out from behind it and smiled at him. Her white cotton dress and her dark hair were being flung about wildly by the wind and Nub relaxed under the scrutiny of her beautiful, Elizabeth Taylor eyes. He watched as she waved, then in a hail of bubbly giggles, she ran off into the vines and brambles.

Nub knew she wasn't real, that the Thicket was and would always be a haunted place. Maybe the heat was making him hallucinate. He began to move on, but he realized he was disoriented. He had never lost his way before, but now things seemed unfamiliar. The woods grayed and tilted, as sweat drenched his clothes and breathing became more difficult. To his left, a snake slithered away in the muddy underbrush, but he paid it no mind.

But the heat! He had to stop a minute to catch his breath and realized he needed to sit down for a spell. He rested himself against the broad trunk of an ancient blackhaw tree. A crow cawed in the branches above him, and he looked up, shading his eyes with his gnarled hand. When he looked down again, he was startled to see someone, ethereal, walking toward him.

"My Lord! What you doin' out here?"

A pain hit his chest like a flaming spear and he wretched forward, one hand extended toward the apparition.

"Bett! Bettina!"

His arm fell to his side, and life left him, sitting there all alone as he had lived. The sounds of the Thicket were silent for a moment, quieted by some unknown force.

Ol' Twelve Point appeared from nowhere and stood before him. The buck lowered his rack, almost as a bow, and snorted at his old friend. In that moment, all sounds and movements resumed, and Ol' Twelve Point bounded off into the deep woods.

All around him, the Thicket paid woeful homage to the old backwoodsman, who was no more.

## Twyla Ellis

Twyla Ellis is a descendant of pioneers who came to Texas in the 1840s. She grew up roaming the dense pine forests in The Big Thicket around Livingston, Texas at the homes of her grandmother and great-aunts and uncles. Her family was one of the founding families of Livingston, and her great-great-great grandfather was the first city treasurer in the eighteen-forties. She fell in love with the lush flora and fauna and the haunting feel of The Thicket, its sounds, sights, and smells.

*The House on Camp Ruby Road* is the first of a series of independent novels set in The Big Thicket of deep East Texas, under the banner of "Ghosts of the Big Thicket," which will all have a Southern Gothic bent.

Twyla holds a degree from Howard Payne University and had taught English and Music. She has been a member of NEA, TSTA, and TETA. She was a statewide officer and conference speaker with TETA (Texas English Teachers Association). She has run her own children's party and event planning business, *Parties by Twyla,* as well as *Remembrances Antiques and Gifts* in the Houston area. She is certified in computer graphic design and freelances in her spare time.

Nothing makes her happier than road trips with her family to interesting old Texas towns. She loves church, antiquing, fossil hunting with her husband and sons (they hunt, she watches), Big Bend, old barns, the Alamo (don't all Texans?), exploring deserted buildings, southern revivals, her Pomeranians, Sophie and Missy Rose, and especially, The Big Thicket.

If she had to give you a one-word bio of herself, she would probably say, "that obnoxiously joyful, hug-driven, southern relative that you'd like to hide in the attic, just might be me."

# Reader's Guide

1. Southern Gothic works are dark, edgy and mysterious. They are characterized by "not quite right" towns, with their grotesque and quirky characters, and a façade of crumbling mansions and aristocratic pretense. Two Rivers is such a town. What would you love about living there? What would you hate about living there?

2. Who would you choose to be best friends with if you lived in Two Rivers? Choose either Clarice Callahan or Mimosa Callahan (Aunt Mim) and tell why you would choose her?

3. Do you believe that exposing Raina Gentry in Clarice's bookstore that day, was enough retribution for what she had done? What more would you have wanted to see happen to her?

4. One character most reflects the image of the Southern Gothic grotesque character, and though he was a minor character, he always seemed to rescue the others. Who was he? What did you think of him and why? Did he make you feel disgust, pity, sympathy or sadness?

5. Our society is obsessed with racial prejudice and political correctness. The book does deal with racial prejudice, but can you identify other types of prejudice you see in the people of Two Rivers?

6. If you had to choose one character in the book to rescue, who would it be and why?

7. Can you remember the passage/passages that evoked the most emotion in you? Can you read it and explain why it affected you?

8. Would you have waited thirty-plus years to visit your husband's grave?

9. Was the trade between Bettina and Clarice fair?

10. What do you think happened to Calico after the book ended?

Coming in 2021
from
Twyla Ellis

Twyla Ellis

The Girls of
Cemetery Road

Book Two in The Ghosts of the Big Thicket

## Prologue

## Big Sandy in The Big Thicket
## Deep East Texas
## 1963

There once was a little girl, a beloved girl, who went away. She was there and then she was not. They searched for her for months in the light of day. When darkness fell, they closed their blinds and bolted their locks. During those simmering days of summer, those who slept with their windows thrown open to catch a cool breeze, now lay in pools of perspiration, their windows secured, their curtains tightly drawn against the thoughts of the sinister gaze of whomever or whatever had spirited the little girl away.

Libby was only twelve when she was lost to them. Lost to all of them really. Because in their fear and grief, the whole town cloistered together into one gelatinous mass that swelled the churches on Sunday mornings to pray out their terror. Grief and fear propelled them to their sanctuaries searching for an answer to the mystery and to pray gratefully that it had not been one of their own children. That selfish thought brought many to shame. But they were secretly glad. Oh, how they were glad that their own children still ate at their tables and slept in their beds.

They came to Sunday services to speculate on the fate of the child and what the latest news about her was, hoping that it would cause them and their households to breathe easier when they entered their pristine, little cottages.

"Did they find her today?" they would ask each other.

"Do you think she ran away? Surely not!"

"I heard they saw a girl down by the river with that bright red hair. I wonder ..."

But all they could do was wonder.

Wonder, and wait, and worry.

The child's fate turned into grainy sand that blew away with the autumn winds. The light winter snow, rare in these parts, crushed and smothered all hope deep into the earth, to lay dormant, perhaps forever.

Months rolled by and turned into painful years of not knowing. Until finally Libby's parents were left alone in their sorrow as time gave way to a numbing malaise that allowed the child's memory to fade from their collective consciences. Her soft cheeked face, the bright cinnamon eyes, the special curve of her face had left their remembrances. Even her parents seemed to harden their hearts to thoughts of her, and the pain that trailed heavily after those thoughts. They spoke of Libby no more.

In the end, it was only The Sisterhood who purposely remembered. They had taken a pledge. And so, they met and remembered around the mossy gray memory stone in the woods by Cemetery Road, that marked the place she was last seen, and bore the hand chiseled name of Libby Elizabeth McConnell.

&⊰⊹⊱⊱

# A Note from the Publisher

Dear Reader,

Thank you for reading Twyla Ellis's novel, *The House on Camp Ruby Road*. This is book one in her series, Ghosts of the Big Thicket.

We feel the best way to show appreciation for an author is by leaving a review. You may do so on any of the following sites:

www.ZimbellHousePublishing.com
Goodreads.com
or your favorite retailer

❧·❦·❧

Join our mailing list to receive updates on new releases, discounts, bonus content, and other great books from Twyla Ellis and

Or visit us online to sign up at:
http://www.ZimbellHousePublishing.com

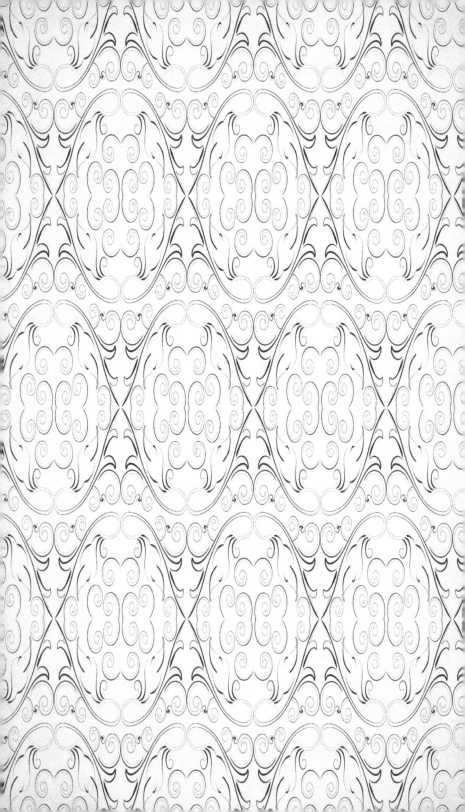